Praise for Peter N. Dudar's
The Goat Parade!

"Definitely a BEST OF 2018!"

—The Haunted Reading Room

"A darkly absorbing journey into evil with a decidedly human heart beating at its core, *The Goat Parade* is a rich and rewarding story that is evocative of the best of Bentley Little. Peter N. Dudar has crafted a gripping supernatural thriller worth every sleepless night it may visit upon its readers."

—Ed Kurtz, author of *The Rib from Which I Remake the World* and *At the Mercy of Beasts*

"*The Goat Parade* is a wild, harrowing rollercoaster ride that takes you from blues clubs to gypsy carnivals to the darkest corners of the human soul. Filled with colorful characters, occult rituals, and more twists than a '50s dance hall, this book will latch onto you and not let go. If Americana horror was a genre of its own, Peter N. Dudar would rule it."

—Morgan Sylvia, author of *Abode*

"Violent and bloody, *The Goat Parade* barrels along like a freight train. Literate, yet raw, I found it to be frightening, and a whole hell of a lot of fun to read. This is horror the way it is supposed to be written."

—Tony Tremblay, author of *The Seeds of Nightmares* and *The Moore House*

The Goat Parade

The Goat Parade

Peter N. Dudar

A
Grinning Skull Press
Publication
PO Box 67, Bridgewater, MA 02324

DEDICATION

For Francine Pavlick, Robert Griffin, and Michael Nardacci.
Three teachers who made a difference

Contents

ACKNOWLEDGMENTS

A brief admission: The drug "Devil's Breath" is not a substance that is found in powdered form. I'm well aware of this fact, and changed it to suit the needs of my story. Please save yourself the trouble of writing to me to point this out. The characters in this story are fictitious or are used fictitiously and should not be construed as factual in any way.

Once again, I owe a debt of gratitude to my friend and mentor, L.L. Soares, who read the original manuscript for this book and took the time to make notes and corrections to steer me in the right direction. I got the idea for this story around a decade ago, when L.L. suggested we collaborate on a Giallo screenplay. Until then, I'd never seen any films by Argento, Fulci, or Bava, so it forced me to examine and practice storytelling from an entirely different perspective. Love and thanks also go to my colleagues in the Tuesday Mayhem Society, who listened to me read parts of this manuscript out loud during our writers' group meetings. Thank you, April Hawks, Morgan Sylvia, and Emma Gibbon. My eternal gratitude to Michael Evans and his staff at Grinning Skull Press, for all their hard work in editing and producing a beautiful book that exceeds my every expectation. I wish continued mutual success for years to come. And finally, to my wife Amy and my beautiful daughters, thank you for the love, support, and encouragement. Thank you for being the candle in my world of darkness.

Prelude to Mayhem

Thursday, June 2nd, on the night of the new moon

The man with the deformed hand placed a tab of acid on his tongue and waited for Lucifer to appear.

He sat at the kitchen table of a bungalow on Ocean Avenue. Red neon light streamed in through the window from the Lau Gardens restaurant across the street, filling the room with unholy shades of euphoria. The house belonged to one of the harpies in his coven, but for the time being, it was *his* base of operations. The house was beyond the usual disarray of broken suburban life. It was in a state of absolute squalor; the sink was filled with dirty dishes, and garbage and empty pizza boxes were scattered across the floor. The air was thick, putrid, and constantly filled with the hum of houseflies and fruit flies and the stench of rot. The odor lingered in the warmth of the late spring evening. Charlene Tibbets, the home's actual occupant, was currently dancing with the other two girls out in the dining room. The sound of "Magic Man" by Heart drifted through the hall between the kitchen and dining room, a strange invocation from the old transistor radio that William Tibbets often took with him on fishing trips before his untimely demise. The radio now sat amid the trash on the dining room table, filling the small house with music. Warren Pembroke glanced down the hallway and watched as they danced. All of them were topless and occasionally fondled each other's breasts as they twirled and spun.

Charlene had been the first of the harpies. She'd been easy to break once he'd gotten her strung out on meth and cocaine. The true test had been when he'd convinced her to murder her husband. She'd smashed him right between the eyes with an iron skillet and then proceeded to bash his brains out until his cranium ruptured like an overripe fruit. She had done it right in their own kitchen where he was now sitting; the blood stains still lingered where they had pooled around the base of the refrigerator. Warren had watched, smiling, as Bill Tibbets gasped and convulsed in the throes of death with that look of surprise and betrayal never leaving his face. When it was over, the two had dragged his corpse down into the basement and dismembered it. Charlene hadn't even bothered to take his pictures off the wall. The bungalow was still a shrine to William and Charlene Tibbets as they had once been. To look at her now was like looking at a zombie; her body was skeletal and had wasted away, her vacant eyes had sunk back into her sallow, leathery skin. Warren watched her dance, swaying like a decayed cattail reed in the breeze. When the other two girls took turns cupping and squeezing her breasts, she moaned aloud and smiled a grin of pitiful ecstasy.

Try, try, try to understand… He's a Magic Man!

The red-haired girl, Caroline Stork, had been a transient. She was young and straight off the bus from somewhere south of Maine, either Boston or Providence. Warren was never sure because her story changed like the seasons. What he *did* know was that she had neither a home nor a family connection that could be traced back to this place. Caroline had been easy to break as well. They all get a taste for the drugs, and then their poor little minds just bend to his suggestion. Caroline also had that sallow, strung-out look about her. Her skin was covered in tattoos; many of them were cheap, hastily drawn sketches that might have been done in prison or by another strung-out junkie friend trading ink for pussy. As she danced and weaved to the music, the light from the dining room chandelier exposed these works of art: a red and gold phoenix, snakes and lizards, a purple and pink pixie under a quarter moon, and a harlequin on his knees weeping into cupped hands. She could have been beautiful, and probably was once upon a time—before the big, bad world got to her.

The redhead was terrible.

Caroline had fucked that last guy as he bled to death. She'd been riding him back in his room at the Downeaster Sunrise Motel, a cheap little tourist hole on Route 1. It was the kind of joint that still used metal keys on plastic, diamond-shaped fobs and allowed people to rent rooms by the hour. Up until that point, she'd been performing just as Warren had instructed her—fuck them, then when they passed out, grab their money and split, but that last time she opted instead to pull a dagger out of her purse and slit his jugular vein. She then rode out his death throes rather than his orgasm like a praying mantis. Within minutes, the cheap motel bed linens squished and dribbled with crimson. The john—some bank executive from downtown—had tried to kiss her lips after she'd instructed him not to and managed to clumsily mash his mouth into her chin. He never even saw the blade until his own blood was dripping off it.

And then there was Abby. As the other two danced to the music, Abby was constantly pawing and fondling their breasts and asses. It was as if she was insatiable and just waiting for the other two to remove their short-shorts so she could have her way with them. As if on cue, Abby began removing her own jeans while her body continued to sway, and then she was stepping out of them and dancing naked, her hands finding their way between her legs to masturbate herself. When she did, the other two women made their way over to her and began taking turns kissing her lips.

Abby Silverstein had told him over and over again that she was a lesbian, that she had no sexual inclination toward him whatsoever. She was more interested in his fascination with the occult and dabbling in dark magic than she was with finding a boyfriend. Abby easily blew off his advances, constantly reminding him that they were kindred spirits and that their relationship would never exceed that bond. Her daddy was one of the richest businessmen in the country. Gerald Silverstein was a global stocks and realties investor. He owned hotels and properties on several continents and was a major player in several international banking institutions. At one point the man had asked Abby what her father's net worth was, but Abby merely laughed and told him that after a certain point, numbers were only a figment of the imagination. Her laughter had been filled with a loathing and sadness that had made him actually feel terrible for asking.

Abby hated her father. Her list of resentments and grievances was at least a mile long, until she'd reached that point of disconnect, that moment where her daddy ceased to be a bonded relation, a moment where, she'd confided to him, he ran his perverted daddy-hands all over her when she was old enough to develop breasts. Now Daddy Silverstein was just a guy who sent her checks to pay the bills while he flew around the world in his private jet and planted his cock in women half his age (*her* age), while her mom stayed home and drank herself into gin-induced catatonia. And that wasn't even mentioning the rumors of his trips to Thailand, where he also targeted young boys in his lascivious pursuit of pleasure.

Abby was dangerous, that much was obvious to Warren, but she somehow played a crucial part in all of this. What that part *was,* he was not sure of just yet. The man recognized the fact that her association with him was, indeed, a way for her to rebel against her asshole father, and that was fine. For the moment, she was budding into a local debutante, with her singing and acting lessons and her public appearances around the city where she helped at charity events and social engagements. Abby was legitimately trying to build a life and reputation of her own, and that had meant keeping her friendship with him in the darkness. The lovely brunette heiress, just as she had dismissed his sexual advances, also dismissed having Warren around for her public appearances. Perhaps the Dark Lord would eventually fill him in on what her association with him really meant. For now, he watched her as she masturbated herself while the other harpies caressed her body and kissed her nipples. He felt the bulge in his jeans begin to throb, and envy overcame him.

Fucking dyke!

The hallucination began.

It started with his right hand—the deformed hand—growing and stretching into a goat's hoof. He watched with terrified fascination as the nubs where his truncated fingers had been hardened into a resin of dead keratin cell tissue. A layer of wooly goat fur sprouted down his forearm, across his wrist, and over the newly formed animal foot. The effect never ceased to amaze and terrify him. Warren knew the metamorphosis was only a hallucination, a temporary alteration that allowed him to commune with the Dark Lord, so he pushed the fear away and searched for the power behind it.

In the dining room, the Harpies were changing as well. All of them were now fully naked and caught in the throes of passion. They were writhing and humping against each other under the light of the chandelier, only now, their hair formed into long, squirming snakes, with their serpentine tongues flicking and probing into the stale air of the bungalow. Occasionally, the snakes would lash out at each other the same way the women were lashing their own tongues out in hot, steamy kisses. The snakes, however, were trying to bite, trying to bury their venomous fangs deep into each other's reptilian scales. The snakes hissed and spat in anger as the women continued to embrace in lust. They looked like Gorgons dancing their wicked mating ritual in some distant circle of hell.

He could feel his mind beginning to open, to unbuckle like a purse flap so that the cosmos could slowly ooze out and flow around him. He felt as if the world was swaying in fluid waves; colors and shapes began to bend and stretch into obscene landscapes. The kitchen filled with the scent of sulfur and brimstone. The flies in the room grew into grotesque gargoyles that chanted in demonic tongues. The man watched all these things with a growing sense of fascination until he could finally hear the approaching lumber of something enormous and terrible. Beastly feet clopped around him, filling his ears and his mind with singular terror.

The Gorgons danced, and from their shadows on the wall, the beast formed itself into an inky puddle of blackness, a wicked monstrosity of burning red eyes and scaly horns and hoofs. The beast seethed and snorted into existence in breaths of smoke and ash.

The man tumbled out of his chair and fell to his knees. "I've been waiting for you, Father Lucifer," he bellowed. "What is thy bidding?"

The Gorgons began to climax in ecstasy, each rearing back her Medusa head and shrieking consent.

"You've done well," the beast hissed. "…and you'll be rewarded for your loyalty. But for now, it is time for you to show yourself to the world so that they will know *who* we are. You must go forth and prepare the world for my arrival."

"And how do I accomplish this?"

"We must gather the sheep," the beast instructed. "We must gather them and turn them into goats and make them do our bidding. I am sending you out to collect the children and corrupt their little minds until they understand my will."

"Yes…yes," Warren whispered. His belly skittered with nervous tingles. The Gorgons in the dining room collapsed into each other's embrace, the snakes in their hair darting and spitting in rage. The redhead looked up at him with a lascivious grin and beckoned him to join them.

"Not yet," the beast admonished. "I have many, many things to tell you. Heed me, and this world shall be yours."

Warren Pembroke listened to every word as the poison in his body melted away the last drops of light. His soul was no longer his own.

Part I

*"Whatever is the lot of humankind
I want to taste within my deepest self.
I want to seize the highest and the lowest,
To load its woe and bliss upon my breast,
And thus expand my single self titanically
And in the end go down with all the rest."*

— *Johann Wolfgang von Goethe, Faust*

Chapter 1

Friday, June 3rd

"Tobacco Joe" Walton was only minutes away from freedom, but instead of feeling enraptured or relieved, the old man was filled with terror. He'd gotten his review from the Mark H. Luttrell Correctional Facility parole board that past January, and after serving forty-three years of a life sentence, them cracker sonsabitches finally saw fit to put him back out onto the streets. Even now, there in his cell in *general populace*, he could picture the warden coming to visit him personally after the results of the review board were certified and submitted to the authorities of Bledsoe County. She was a kind black woman who had known who he was when she arrived at Luttrell back in 2007 and had been advocating for his release ever since. Joe had already defied cosmic odds in bypassing the death penalty, and the fact that he'd managed to not become a target for those bull-queer rapists or the shiv-shanking skinheads, with their Nazi regalia and the rebel flags tattooed on their biceps. Especially since he was somewhat notably famous…at least toward the end of the twentieth century. They had him dead-to-rights when *The Law* showed up at his daddy's farm and found the bodies.

It's because you're marked, he thought, looking down at the fingers of his right hand. Once upon a time, Joe Walton had been right-handed. But after his dealing with Ol' Scratch, things had changed. Now, looking down at his index, middle, and ring fingers, he saw the old, familiar marking; each finger had the number 6 tattooed neatly beneath his fingernails.

Whenever he held his hand up, and especially when his long, black fingers worked their way up and down the fretboard of his guitar, he could see the numbers 666 perfectly etched for all time under the brittle protection of his fingernails. Joe was certain that was all the mark he'd needed to keep out of harm here in Luttrell over the last forty-three years. It was talismanic, whether the other inmates understood it or not.

Forty-three years. Forty-three years of hardened prison life, where daily routines were all he knew and hard labor was the key to his survival. Decades of orange jumpsuits as he and the rest of the stiffs in cellblock B were permitted to leave the grounds to dig flooding ditches along the Tennessee highways and clean up litter and do dirty work for the state while men with shotguns and white, paranoid mistrust watched over them. At one time in his life, Joe Walton had played the blues. In his younger days, he could bend notes on his guitar that would make angels weep. Joe Walton knew a thing or two about suffering, and he had a way about him that could convey that sadness through his music. He was second-generation from the old Delta bluesmen, those old juke joint and street-corner players that had taken gospel hymns and slave songs and mixed them into colored poison for the soul. Those old cats knew what true suffering was all about. Even his daddy, Charles Walton, had been hypnotized by their six-string call. Those songs of lost loves and being cheated and downtrodden, they held magic within them. As a boy, Joe could remember hearing those old songs on the RCA Victor radio in the Walton kitchen, back on their farm in Dyersburg. He could remember his daddy pulling out an old, rusted harmonica and playing along to them after long twelve-hour days in the tobacco fields. Even here, in his cell, he could imagine his Daddy at the kitchen table, blowing away on his harmonica as the sweat dripped off the ebony skin of his face while his mama cleaned the supper dishes. Those were the last happy memories of his life, the ones he clung to when there was no hope left at all.

The clock on the far wall of the corridor read 11:45 in large, red, digital numbers. At 11:55, the warden and two of the prison's armed deputies would be coming to his cell to officially declare his sentence to be "served in full," and then they would be escorting the newly released civilian Joseph Walton, prisoner #197356834, through the corridor of the cell block and out into the main building. His personal belongings, what little he had, would be returned to him, and then he would be escorted to the front doors of the facility and released on his own recognizance. He'd seen the drill performed for hundreds of prisoners over the course of the last forty-three years, but he'd given up hope on that day ever coming for himself.

Not that he really wanted to leave, not at this point in his life.

Daddy was murdered back in 1972. Mama had died in 1988. She'd been diagnosed with cancer the year before, and although she tried to keep her weekly visits to Mark H. Luttrell to see her only son, eventually her weekly attendance turned into random occurrences. And then she was gone. Joe had wept bitterly at the news, had, in fact, started contemplating suicide once his only living family member had departed the earth and caught that sweet, heavenly chariot up to God's Kingdom. There would be no attending her funeral, no paying his final respects. Warden Dietz, the previous head-screw, could not be bothered to make cell visits. Those he left to his underlings, so he received a visit from Pastor Freeman after the fact.

He could remember Mama perfectly: the way she'd wept at Daddy's funeral, and then later had pointed a shaking finger at those two racist motherfuckers, Leon and Rufus Hickey, in the Bledsoe County Court of Law. He remembered how she told the court after placing her hand on the Bible and swearing to tell the truth that she saw those crackers drinking beer in their pickup truck out on Mason Road and how they'd marched right up to their front door with pistols in their hands just after sundown…

Freedom scared him now. Here, behind the walls of Mark H. Luttrell, he knew his place. He knew when to cop a squat and when to be dressed in his county orange jumpsuit and wait for his cell door to open. Hell, he even knew when them young, ass-raping queers were going to be in the showers, looking for their next easy target. The prison had eventually implemented an anti-rape program, which had been launched statewide in Tennessee, but even then its success rate was highly questionable. They were easy to spot, with their state-issued blue dungarees dragging half-way down their asses and their tube of hair gel, the only lubricant afforded in prison, and even then you could only buy it through the black market, in their shirt pockets. Once you knew who they were and how they operated, you could take evasive measures. The outside world had already passed him by, with the best years of his life spent behind bars and only singing the blues in his mind.

It had been decades since he actually played a guitar.

With both his parents gone and the family farm confiscated by the state of Tennessee, everything Joe Walton had on earth was here in his cell: a few books, some old black-and-white photos of his family, a notebook with some old song lyrics he'd written, and a bunch of old newspaper clippings concerning Daddy's murder and his own crimes, which he'd committed back in the summer of 1973, just before the Law got him and put him away.

The digital clock flicked over to 11:54.

Joe had the nightmare again just last night. A cold, malicious voice he knew only too well from his youth and the tall, crooked shadow of a gaunt white man whose eyes burned fire and whose feet looked more like goat hooves than actual human appendages. It was the same figure who had visited him in his youth. Not at a clandestine meeting at the Crossroads like some of the older bluesmen before him, but while he was working the tobacco fields. The man moved with an unearthly gait, long, angry strides that made him look more like a beast than a man. Young Joe Walton had already owned his first guitar when Ol' Scratch appeared, had bought it with money he'd saved from different odd jobs on nearby farms after the chores on his daddy's farm were done for the day. Joe had been cutting down the huge tobacco leaves and bundling them up into long stalks to be dried back up in the barn. Now, in his dream, Joe was back out in the tobacco fields, once again cutting and rolling the leaves into bundles and tying them with twine, his fingers wet and sticky from the plant's oils. The sun overhead beat down hard, like a burning slap from God's own hand. He dreamed he was singing while he worked, just as he had done as a boy, when Ol' Scratch lumbered toward him through the tobacco fields.

"You sure can sing, boy," the smiling face of the Devil himself told him in the dream. It was the same way he'd greeted him in real life back in 1963, back when he'd just turned thirteen. "But I wonder, can you play that ol' guitar you bought like that? Can you really make it sing as if it had a soul of its own?"

Only, in his dream, Joe was the sixty-seven-year-old convict who was about to be released from prison. That young black boy was long gone, having been suckered into the Devil's snare once already. Back then, Joe Walton was a Negro farmer's son, still working the family tobacco farm, wondering if he was going to be drafted into the Army to fight in Vietnam once he turned eighteen or if he was ever going to escape the farm and find a life of his own. Those days of his youth were peppered with news reports of John F. Kennedy, Bobby Kennedy, Dr. Martin Luther King, and images of American soldiers coming home with limbs missing and their minds damaged from a war that had nothing to do with them. White, Black, Hispanic—there was no escaping the cruelty of war. Those who entered came home different. Joe could remember his daddy in the living room after dinner in front of the old black-and-white RCA television with the set of rabbit-ears antennae that only worked when mama put a patch of tin foil over the revolving hemispheres between them. He was shaking his head and praying for all the poor soldiers that had lost their lives in combat.

"You just better pray to God that he spares you from going to war, boy," Charles Walton had told his only son. "You better get down on your knees every night and ask the good Lord to spare you from all that evil and sufferin'."

"I kept you away from all that suffering," Ol' Scratch had told him in the dream. "Remember, Joseph? Remember that deal we made way back when? I kept my end of the bargain. I gave you talents you never dreamed of and gave you a life that kept you away from going to war. Isn't that what you wanted?"

"You lyin' old bastard," Joe replied. "You kept me from going into the Army, but you took away everything I had for it. As far as I'm concerned, we're square. So you just drag your evil ass back to Hell where you belong!"

The tall, crooked figure laughed. It was an evil laugh that raised goose pimples all over Joe's skin. Even at sixty-seven, he was susceptible to that nails-on-chalkboard laugh. There was no escaping that deep-throated guffaw that drove priests insane and roused the damned to attention. How many souls had been claimed by its sweet sirens' call? How many sinners discovered too late that they'd been tricked?

"You have nothing, Joseph. We both know it. No homestead to return to, nor family to greet you when you get back here. These fields of tobacco—" The Devil raised his hand and swished it over the crop, and under its evil power, the plants immediately wilted and died. "—they're long gone and forgotten. The Walton farm was bought out ages ago, sold to developers who turned it into a hotel parking lot. Kill yourself now and let me take you home."

"The hell, I will!" Joe Walton told him.

The Devil laughed again, and Joe's ears filled with the piercing screams of the damned.

"How will you get by, I wonder?"

"I'll find a way. Even if it kills me. My business with you is all through."

"Is it?" the Devil replied. "Do you think you can pick up where your life left off before you murdered those men? Do you think you can still make a living singing the blues?"

"Damn right, I could." Joe looked down at his hands. His palms were stained with tobacco oil from picking the leaves. There was a gunnysack of tied tobacco stalks at his feet, and he could smell the sweet aroma of the newly picked and bundled stalks. The scent kept tugging his mind toward his childhood, but he was damned if he was going to let down his guard. Ol' Scratch new what buttons to push and which strings to pull. This was the worst kind of battle; it was a tug-of-war for his soul.

The white man with burning eyes and goat-hooved feet stood up tall and smiled. All of this was just a game to him, a chess match where the moves were already calculated and the game all but won. His eyes glowed with fire, and the smile never left his face.

"Well, then, 'Smokehouse Joe,' if you really mean that, then I'd like to help you. I'd hate to see you fail all over again. How many years have you spent in prison? Four decades? That's nothing to an eternity in Hell. A drop in the bucket, really." The evil one glanced up at the sky, and even with the heat of the summer Tennessee sun, he looked cool and composed. This world's cruelties meant nothing to him. "I want to tell you a secret."

"I don't want to hear it," Joe interrupted.

"You don't have a choice," Ol' Scratch answered. "Your soul is already mine. Don't you know that?"

"You forfeited on our agreement," Joe answered, feeling the icy chill of nerve deep within. "You promised me fame and fortune, and you fucked me over."

The Devil laughed. "No, you fucked yourself over. I never commanded you to murder those two boys. You did that all by yourself. All you had to do was leave things alone. I would have dealt with those two thugs who killed your daddy. They're both in Hell right now, thanks to you. No, I never tricked you at all. I gave you exactly what I promised— I gave you talent. And I never took that away from you. You still have it within you, Joe. You could pick up your guitar tomorrow, and nothing would be different. That is, if you knew where to find it…"

"You know where my guitar is?" Joe Walton asked the Devil in his dream.

"Of course I do. If you were to go looking for it, you'd find it in a second-hand guitar shop, somewhere up in Maine. In Portland, I believe."

The fields of tobacco began to smolder and catch on fire. The scent was intoxicating, like a young woman's kiss. The smoke filled his lungs, and Joe found himself gasping for breath. The summer sun wavered in billowing clouds of smoke and darkness. The image pulled one last memory out of his weary, sleep-filled brain.

The smokehouse.

The night Joe Walton killed the Hickey brothers. The night he stabbed them both to death, and then…

Joe had awakened on the morning he was to be released from prison feeling absolutely terrified. His soul was already damned, and only God knew how much longer he had on the planet before Ol' Scratch claimed it. He almost wished his parole meeting could have gone the other way, could have kept him here behind bars where he belonged. But one thing was certain—unless he were to commit another crime and come back here to prison, there was no changing the fate he'd sentenced himself to.

The clock's digital counter flickered to 11:55. Down the corridor, Joe could hear the warden and her armed guards enter the cellblock and make their way down toward the place he called home for the last forty-three years. He could hear the warden speaking to the guards as they drew near, reminding them to keep their weapons lowered, as prisoner #197396834 was now a free man, and no longer a threat to society. They reached his cell, and then the automatic door was rolling open, as if on cue.

"Your guitar is up in Maine," Ol' Scratch had told him. "In Portland."

Joe Walton looked at the space of concrete just above his cell door. At some point, another inmate had etched the words "I did my time in Hell, here in Mark H. Lutrell," long before he became the cell's lone occupant. He'd seen the phrase over and over again during his years of incarceration, but only now did he understand the absolute folly behind them. Whoever occupied his cell before he did obviously didn't know shit about Hell. In reality, prison life actually seemed like a blessing. That was the thought he was pondering when the warden and her guards appeared outside the iron bars, and the door that kept him hostage for all those years finally swung open.

As he was led away to freedom, Joe Walton wondered how many guitar shops Portland, Maine actually had.

❦ ❦ ❦

"Rise and shine, sleepy-head."

Abby gazed down at the man sleeping on the frazzled blue sofa.

Warren's deformed arm jutted out from under the dark curls of his hair. Part of her felt repulsed by its grotesquery, with the missing pinky and the remaining bulbous, crooked digits. He was lying with those digits dangling off the couch in the living room as he slept, an alien colony forever connected to the useless appendage. It had been no wonder that Warren Pembroke insisted that his women did all the killing. He was too instantly recognizable.

He'd stand out like a sore thumb.

Still, there was also something almost irresistibly attractive about those fingers. They looked like exotic sex toys. Abby looked over at Charlene and Caroline still passed out on the floor, their naked bodies intertwined comfortably where sleep finally conquered lust. They looked like discarded ragdolls. Caroline, with all her colorful tattoos and Charlene, with her loose, saggy flesh and sun-aged complexion. Abby found neither of them attractive, nor integral to any of Warren's big plans, but they were both so willing to please sexually and kept her satiated whenever her own urges came on. And they made her feel that much more alluring, if she were to be honest. She wondered if he'd penetrated either of them with those bizarre fingers and if he'd brought them to climax.

She put her hand on Warren's shoulder and shook him. "Warren, can you get up and talk to me for a few minutes before I get going? This is going to be a busy week for me, so we need to hash things out while I'm still here."

His eyes opened, and he force-inhaled an enormous breath of air as if he'd been drowning in his sleep. The depth of blueness in his irises held a cosmos of insanity within them. "I'm up. I'm awake. What do you want?"

Why does he always sound so fucking paranoid?

"I have to leave pretty soon. I was just wondering what you saw while you were tripping." She smiled politely; one of her ways of keeping the snake charmed into serenity. "You know I just love when you tell me your visions."

Warren was still naked as well, and when he yawned, stretched, and sat upright, she noticed the dried patch of blood droplets and semen crusted around his thighs. One of the other women had begun menstruation. Abby turned and looked at the two passed-out women again and noticed that Caroline was, indeed, flowing between her legs. The blood formed rivulets down her skin and onto Charlene's.

It's ME he wants. He's had both of these two already, but he wants me, and I don't know how long I can keep putting him off. And once he's had me, I'll be no different than the other girls.

He reached over to the coffee table with his deformed hand and snatched up a crumpled pack of Camels and a cigarette lighter. He fished one out with his good hand, pushed it between his lips, and lit it. "Did today's newspaper get here yet?" Warren blew the smoke up toward the ceiling, and then his eyes met hers, making Abby nearly take a step backward. Warren's gaze was piercing, intrusive, and she found herself desperately wanting to look away. "Did that clown at *The Beacon* write up anything about the dude Caroline iced back at the hotel?"

Abby broke his gaze long enough to drift into the dining room and fetch the newspaper. When she returned to the room, Warren had already slipped into his underwear and jeans. His black Polo t-shirt was still on the floor, but Warren made no indication that he was going to put it on.

"I went through the paper this morning but didn't see anything. You're welcome to check again for yourself." She dropped the folded paper down on the couch next to where he was sitting. The front page unfurled into a headline concerning an auto fatality up in Bangor.

"What the fuck is wrong with this guy?"

"Who are you talking about?"

Warren sighed and took another drag off his cigarette. "The crime beat reporter. Something Marsh. I can't remember, but it'll come to me. He hasn't reported on *any* of our murders yet. It's getting to the point where I'm going to have to send him a personal invitation. Kick him in the ass and point him in the right direction. Right now, everybody in Maine should be talking about me."

Abby could feel her heart rate racing in her chest. "You're joking, right? You can't seriously want to get us caught."

Warren smiled. "They ain't gonna catch us. Not if we're clever. Not if we do as the Dark Lord has instructed me. We'll always be one step ahead. We've got a lot of work ahead of us." He inhaled again and released the smoke. It issued through his lips and nostrils in serpentine tendrils. "There's an old verse in the Bible—the one about sheep and goats. Sheep go to heaven and goats go to hell. Isn't that what the New Testament says? Right in between 'I am The Way' and 'It's MY way or the highway'?" Warren leaned over and stubbed his butt out in the ashtray on the side table, and then gazed up at Abby. It was a lunatic's gaze, with his pupils hovering like desecrated moons in his irises. "Sheep go to heaven and goats go to hell. Suffer the little children unto me, and let them be like sheep. In my vision, I was standing on a hillside looking down at all the snips and snails and puppy-dog tails, all the pretty little maidens in a row. They were no longer sheep. We changed them."

Abby's eyes grew wide. "What, exactly, does that mean?"

Warren's grin widened. "It means we have to turn them. As many as we can. We have to go out and collect all the sheep and turn them into goats. We need to poison their little minds and bend their will to do as we instruct them. The Dark Lord told me that he's going to be opening the Gates of Hell here on earth very soon, and we are to draw forth *His* army and be ready."

For the first time since she met him, Abby was no longer sure that the man with the deformed right hand could be trusted. People could "disappear," but children… That was a whole different story. Missing children meant grand-scale investigations, high-profile media coverage, and public interaction. There had already been warning flags waving around Warren Pembroke, signaling just how dangerous he could really be. This was the final banner, with his insanity waving for the world to see. "That sounds like a really dangerous task," Abby said. "It sounds like it's damn near impossible."

Warren nodded to the two women lying unconscious on the floor. "Oh, my dear. You have no idea just how easy it can be." His smile was sinister and more grotesque than his hand. "Don't you even think about flaking out on me," he continued, the smile whipping into a snarl. "Not now, Abby. We've gone too far to stop now. You're the one who wanted to dabble in the occult. You knew what you were getting into with me. This isn't about *my* will. This is about *His* will. And if you just try to abandon me or turn against me, *He'll* warn me in advance. I will see you coming a mile away, and I will murder your little-rich-girl ass and send you to hell to meet Him in person. Are we crystal fucking clear, Abby Silverstein?"

Abby nodded, feeling the explosion of dread butterflies taking wing in her belly.

"Say it! Tell me we're crystal fucking clear."

"We're crystal fucking clear."

"Good." Warren closed his eyes and stretched his arms out in a massive yawn. "The new lunar cycle has already begun. This is the first time this century that the full moon occurs on the solstice. We have to make a sacrifice. You need to be here tonight to help with the blood ritual. Got it?"

"I'll be here."

He smiled again, this time much more pleasantly. He looked handsome again, with the cleft in his chin and his square jaw rising up to meet the curly dark hair of his scalp. Rugged and dashing like those old-time Hollywood actors, only with the deformed hand keeping the total package from being perfect. "Now get outta here. You've got places to be today, and I need to get these two useless pieces of shit to wake up and get to work."

Abby hurried out of the room. She snatched her keys and pocketbook off the dining room table and made her way toward the door. *This is the beginning of the end,* she thought. *Sheep go to heaven and goats go to hell. Did he turn me into one of his goats, or have I done this all by myself?*

Chapter 2

"I can't do this job anymore."

Erik Marsh sat back in his chair and placed his palms against his temples, trying to will away the booze headache he'd woken up with but just couldn't shake. He'd been in Editor-in-Chief R.H. Cummings's private office at least a hundred times since the industry legend had signed him on as an intern, but this time things felt different. Erik was still a college pup back then, cutting his teeth on a student rag called the *South Portland Sentinel*, covering throwaway stories like dormitory vandalism and on-campus traffic violations. Here, in the personal safe-room of "Newsroom Ron" Cummings, he was surrounded by framed headline pages screaming historical facts like the Apollo moon landing and the Kennedy Assassination and September 11th. With a simple pan across the room, one could see dozens of Associated Press Awards housed neatly along conspicuous shelves, as well as autographed photos of Cummings posing with some of the greatest political figures and celebrities of the latter 20th century. Everything about the room screamed power and success. Which was why Erik felt more diminished every time he set foot inside it. In his own life, there would never be an office like this.

R.H. Cummings sat behind his desk, his forehead wrinkled in disapproval.

"Seriously, Mister Cummings, I feel like this job is going to kill me. I feel like I'm on the verge of a nervous breakdown all the time. All I see anymore is the worst of humanity. You've had me covering the city crime beat column pretty much since you hired me on fulltime, and for the past eleven years I've done nothing but cover stories of murder and violence and atrocity." Erik stopped massaging his temples and looked up at his boss. "I don't trust people anymore. I can't even look at them without wondering what terrible secrets they're hiding. I feel like a fucking ghoul or something. This job has already cost me my marriage. Kelly couldn't take it anymore, said I was scaring her and my son. Now I'm lucky if I see him once or twice a month."

Cummings leaned back in his own chair and folded his arms across his chest. The man constantly wore white Oxford shirts with a solid blue tie, a garb that could have passed as an ersatz sundial. By 9:00 a.m., the sleeves would be unbuttoned and rolled up. By half-past ten, it would reek of coffee and cigarette smoke. In spite of the ban on tobacco use in public buildings, his office was always a smoking-zone. By noon, the Windsor knot would be loosened and the collar undone. By 2:00 p.m., the telltale perspiration stains would circle under the armpits. Now, at 4:43 p.m., Cummings's tie was off and the top three buttons were undone, exposing a patch of iron-gray chest hair. The old man remained quiet. He picked up a remote control off his desk and aimed it at a television dangling from a gantry in the far corner of the room. He pressed a button and the television popped on, broadcasting a cable news network where another older gentleman was anchoring a news report.

"…word on another homicide in Cumberland County, Maine, which sources are saying looks to be similar in detail to previous mysterious deaths in the area over the past several weeks."

"Erik, do you know who this asshole is?" Cummings nodded toward the anchor on the television.

"Yes, sir. That's Truth Carson. He's the lead for Cable World Media."

Cummings chuckled dryly. "Horse shit! That guy's name is Harold Kirsch. I studied journalism with him back at Harvard. The only reason I jockey a desk job rather than sit in front of the camera is because my dear old mama fell out of the Ugly Tree while she was carrying me. Trust me, that guy's as phony as a three-dollar bill with Obama's picture on it. I'd kill to have his job. It just ain't in the cards for me. Do you see what I'm saying?"

"No, sir." Erik could feel his headache growing worse. And from somewhere below, his gorge was beginning to rise in a volcanic mix of tequila, bile, and stale pizza. Cummings's safe-room was beginning to make him feel claustrophobic; the panorama of grizzly headlines and photographs of tragedies both natural and manufactured, the pictures of crooked politicians, rapists, and murderers had him feeling entombed in a world of the damned. It made his heart pound and his skin go cold and clammy.

"Son, when you took this job, you reminded me a hell of a lot of myself back when I was a lad. I saw the same piss and vinegar in you that still flows in my own blood. Hell, I even remember your interview, back when you wanted the internship. Do you remember that day?"

Erik sighed. "Of course I do. I was sitting in this very seat, practically begging you for a chance to prove myself."

"Exactly!" Cummings nodded emphatically. "And you have. Over and over again. You even told me you wanted to work the crime beat because you felt like you could use it as research for when you wrote your Great American Novel." Cummings chuckled again. "Hell, you were dead-set on being the next Stephen King. Son, you asked me for this job, and I gave it to you. Is this really how you want to repay me?"

"Mister Cummings, I'm not trying to tender my resignation or anything like that. I just need a change of pace. Could you please assign me to something different for a while? That's all I'm really asking. I love my job, and I love working here. I just can't take another day of hovering over a police scanner, waiting for the next big story. It's gotten to the point that when I hear about a crime or an accident, I'm actually *hoping* people die, and in terrible ways, just so I can deliver you a big, juicy column. Both of us know that's what still sells newspapers. The world has become ghoulish, and right now I feel like I'm leading the parade. Do you know what nickname the State Police have given me?"

"Yellow Belly?" the older man offered sarcastically.

"They call me 'Erik the Black.' Anytime I show up to a homicide scene, their running joke is to make the sign of the cross as if I'm a fucking vampire or something. Do you even know how that feels?"

Cummings sighed. He picked up the remote control and turned the volume up on the television. Truth Carson was still speaking about the homicide in Cumberland County, but now the screen was filled with police officers removing a covered body on a stretcher. The crime scene in the background looked eerily like some kind of Devil worship ceremony. Candles and skulls and what looked like animal parts were strewn across what looked like a normal suburban kitchen floor. "Take a good look at this, Erik. This is right in our backyard. Reporters from Cable World Media, Fox, Reuters, Huff-Post, and CNN are all covering this. And here's the part that I need to make crystal-fucking-clear to you: newspapers are on the verge of extinction. If it ain't cable news, it's all online nowadays. In two shakes of a prick, some kid younger than you is typing something up to post online as fast as he can—and doing it badly, I might add. These kids nowadays are so fucking hasty that their spelling and grammar takes a backseat to getting the news out first. I'm fighting with all I've got to keep the *Portland Beacon* afloat and keeping it from strictly being all about local charity bean suppers and high school basketball games. When this shit happens here in Maine, *we* need to report it first. Not that phony, Truth Carson. Not some pimple-faced college grad on the other side of the country. It's up to *us*. Do you understand?"

Erik could feel the room spinning. Jesus, how much tequila *had* he drank back at lunchtime? Half a pint? More than that? He'd spent the evening writing up a column about a mugging down in the Old Port that had gone sour when the perp stabbed the victim with a four-inch lock blade knife *after* the vic handed over his wallet and pocket cash. The victim had survived, but the perp was still at large and, even with a composite sketch by the local police artist, it wasn't likely they were going to find the guy. Not likely at all, even with the local eleven o'clock news crews flashing the perp's composite on the air and asking for anybody with information to please come forward. That's how it is with crime: nobody on the side of innocence ever wants to get involved. "Yes, sir."

"Good. Because *you* should have been all over this story before it broke nationally. Even now, your ass is parked in front of my desk and nowhere near the front line." Cummings was now barking in an irate tone. The wrinkles in his forehead were growing deeper, still, now that his eyebrows were pointing downward in a glare of anger. The perspiration patches under his armpits were grossly noticeable, growing in the lingering afternoon heat. Cummings was still holding the remote control, and in a motion of body language that confirmed complete dismissal, he raised the remote up and turned off the television.

Erik's head was spinning. If he didn't make his escape soon, he risked vomiting in his employer's office. As it was, he was already risking too much. Primarily, his job at the *Portland Beacon*, but R.H. Cummings held more power than that. If he wanted to, Cummings could make sure Erik Marsh never worked again in the industry. A simple reference check would be all it took to make sure Erik's name never appeared in another single byline for the rest of his working days. The fact that Cummings was already insinuating that Erik had somehow let the paper down by not being the first on the crime scene stung like a cold slap in the face.

All the more reason to feel like he needed a change.

Erik thought of his son, Owen, and all the changes the boy was going through without his father around to watch. Kelly was already dating again, already forging ahead and looking for a substitute daddy in Owen's life, one that remembered birthdays and school functions and the other milestones so many other fathers live for. He thought of the night of Owen's fifth birthday; he was supposed to meet Kelly and Owen at Jokers Pizzeria and Arcade to celebrate. Instead, he found himself over on Pearl Street where some drugged-up African-American woman had thrown her infant in an oven and cooked the poor kid until its body turned to cinder. He remembered how Kelly had pulled her passive-aggressive bullshit on him until he started bawling uncontrollably at the things he'd seen that night. God, what the fuck was wrong with people? Why couldn't Kelly be there for him? Why didn't she understand all this darkness in his life? Why had she abandoned him?

Why did you put all this before them? You could have made a living doing other things. Why couldn't you just let this go?

The image of the night that Kelly finally walked out crept into his memory. He'd fallen asleep in front of the computer once again. Truthfully, he passed out after managing to down nearly an entire bottle of Canadian Mist as if it were nothing more than a cup of tea. It had been another late night of trying to bang out his Great American Novel on the ancient Hewlett Packard computer, the empty whiskey tumbler by the keypad and a jumbled paragraph of incoherent words typed out on the computer screen. The story had been cribbed from a series of different crimes he'd reported on in his columns, but the story itself was nothing more than a jumbled mess of one-dimensional characters and questionable plot points. The kicker had been that just before he'd fallen asleep at the desk, he'd managed to type out a single line of poetry, and that poem had been better than any of the fiction he'd ever strung together as an author:

The moon, in its languid stroll across the sky,
Tore a hole in the earth, and watched it die.

When Kelly found him and tried to wake him up to bring him to bed, Erik screamed at her to "leave him the fuck alone and stop trying to poison his career."

The night afterward, Kelly and Owen were staying at her mother's house in Damariscotta, and Erik found himself staring at his poem on the computer screen, trying to remember typing it and shamefully realizing he couldn't.

"Mister Cummings… Ron," Erik stood up and faced his employer. "I need to let this go. If you can't find something else for me, then I need to resign. From the bottom of my heart, I'm sorry, but I can't keep writing columns about murder and violence and suicide and hatred. It's killing me physically and emotionally. I need something else. I hope you can understand."

"Newsroom Ron" Cummings stared at him thoughtfully for a long, awkward moment. His eyes appraised the young man that had worked for the *Portland Beacon* for well over a decade, and Erik could tell that Maine's most famous news magnate was mentally weighing a significant portion of his beloved newspaper's reputation in his brain. Marsh had turned in a hell of a lot of columns, good columns, ones that did make the transition to the Associated Press to be published in newspapers all across the country. Marsh had paid his dues in full, and in a time that saw the slow transition of the clattering newsroom floor to the quiet desolation of cubicles to the modern era of lazy journalism, where staff writers submitted their columns from a table in Starbucks Coffee shops on their laptops and iPads and smartphones. In his own career, R.H. Cummings had seen all the signs on the wall about the downfall of printed news. Losing Erik Marsh was not doing his newspaper any favors.

"Kid, I can't afford to lose you," Cummings said, almost in defeat. "When I hired you, it was because you were among the last of the real breed of journalists. You've never let me down. I'm honestly grateful as hell to still have you here." Cummings reached down and pushed a button on his intercom panel. It buzzed momentarily, and then was met with the sound of his secretary's cold, nasally voice.

"Yes, Mister Cummings?"

"Miz Burke? I'm going to be making a few changes. I'm taking Erik Marsh off the crime beat column and giving him a shot as a staff writer for *The Beacon's* local and society desk. Starting tomorrow, he'll be reporting to Beverly LaChance. Please let Bev know, and please contact Luis Alvarez. He'll be stepping up to the crime beat desk first thing tomorrow morning. Understood?"

There was a short pause, as if Ms. Burke's world had suddenly been turned upside down. In his mind, Erik could picture that old biddy scribbling notes madly on her legal pad with a dour frown on her face. After a few seconds, her nasally voice retorted, "Yes, Mister Cummings. Those changes will be arranged immediately."

Erik moved toward the desk and held out his hand for his employer to shake. "Thank you so much, Mister Cummings. I know I won't let you down. This is exactly what I needed."

Cummings made no move to return the handshake. "Sit down, son."

Erik sat in his chair, the ache in his head finally starting to give up the ghost. What had felt like an all-out migraine was now ebbing to a dull but manageable throb. A handful of ibuprofen and a large cup of water would be able to push the pain away. He'd had no way of gauging how much stress he'd placed himself under until the burden was lifted and he could breathe freely again. The feeling was night and day. The feeling was ecstasy.

Cummings raised his eyebrows as he stared hard into Erik's eyes. "Now, about your drinking… This is the *last* time you show up to my newsroom all shitty under the juice. Do I make myself clear?"

Erik Marsh dropped his head in shame, and the ecstasy slipped away as quickly as it had come. "It won't happen again, boss."

The late afternoon sun was still high in the June sky when Erik left the newspaper office at One City Center. It shone with pleasant promise and generosity, unlike the later summer sun that only scorched and took away, leaving the tourists with skin as red as boiled lobster instead of brown and attractive. For now, only weeks from the summer solstice, it melted away the final cobwebs of the late spring thaw. The city was alive again, and here in Monument Square, people were enjoying June's First Friday. On the first Friday of the summer months, Monument Square opens to the public. The local denizens of the art community hauled out their works for display and hopefully make a few sales to sustain their muse. There was a farmer's market, where fresh produce was trucked in and sold by local growers. There were hot dog carts and pizza vendors and peddlers of popcorn and sweets. The aroma of fresh coffee from the city's cafes filled the air. And now that the business day was over, local musicians and street performers were hustling for change as crowds gathered to watch.

Erik's headache was now a dull ghost in his skull, fading fast with every footfall away from the *Portland Beacon*. He glanced around Monument square, watching all the people milling about: lovers walking hand and hand past the statue of Henry Wadsworth Longfellow, whose bronze visage kept watch over the concourse of red brick and stone and families with small children in tow, the latter constantly pronouncing their wants in whines and screams as they passed by the vendors. Seagulls bobbed and weaved among the humans, eyeing them suspiciously as they collected spilled popcorn and crumbs. Every now and then a child would pull free from his mother's grip and chase them off into flight. Some things never changed.

Erik found his way to an open bench beneath a tree and sat down under its freshly blossomed boughs. He placed his palms against his temples and began massaging until the last of his headache slipped away for good. He smelled sausages cooking somewhere nearby, and they made his stomach rumble. Erik glanced around to see if anybody nearby had heard this indiscretion, but it looked as if most of the people in his vicinity were gathering in a huge circle to watch one of the street performers. From his spot outside the ring, he could only hear vaguely what was going on until a PA system hummed on and the voice of a young woman elevated above the hustle and bustle.

"Ah, t'ank you all so much for coming out dis afternoon," the girl's voice carried over the crowd. "I hope you are all enjoyink dis beautiful day."

Erik could hear the absolute joy in her voice as she spoke and found himself wondering which part of Eastern Europe she hailed from. Russia? The Czech Republic? Her accent had that choppy, broken flavor to it, where syllables tumbled over themselves phonetically in their mission to sound resolute. Yet even with the imperfect dialect, her voice sounded beautiful. Like a drunken angel.

"And now, who's ready to have some fun, huh?" she asked, and the crowd clapped and cheered in reply. "I can't hear you. Are you vit me?"

The crowd cheered harder.

"Okay, yes, excellent. My name is Svetlana, and I am performer from da Carpathian Great and Tiny Circus—"

There was a moment where the crowd burst out in laughter, with hands clapping in approval. Erik found himself suddenly irritated that the crowd refused to part for him so that he, too, could watch the spectacle. He stood and clambered up onto the bench so he could peer down and see the show.

Svetlana wasn't stunningly attractive as her voice had led him to believe. She was cute, bordering on pretty, but his first impression of her was that she was nothing more than an awkward teenage gymnast who had somehow time-warped from the 1980s. She was wearing a pink camisole and a purple knee-length skirt; rainbow-colored leg warmers covered the rest of her legs. Her hair was filled with spikes of small, meticulous braids fastened with hot neon ribbons. She was tall and slender, the kind of woman that his ex-wife would have declared "perky," if she'd still been by his side—or "whorish" if she'd noticed Erik admiring her a bit too much. But her smile…that smile of glistening white teeth behind hot red lipstick. It was a smile that promised a glimpse of ecstasy just beyond the fires of hell.

You're a fool, he told himself. *That's just the writer in you conjuring metaphors and lapsing into college student prose. No wonder you were never published.*

Svetlana reached down and pushed a button on her portable CD player, and then the plaza filled with raucous East European carnival music. Erik could make out the balalaikas thrumming in silly cadence to the tambourine, pennywhistles, and percussion. The sound was almost dizzying, but the rest of the crowd had already begun clapping along in time. The young woman never lost her smile as she picked up a hula-hoop and began swaying her hips along with the music, and then she was pulling three smaller rings out of nowhere and juggling them as she gyrated the bigger hoop around her torso. As the beat of the music picked up, so, too, did the speed of the clapping from the audience, and then Svetlana was juggling the three smaller rings with one hand and lifting the hula hoop up around her body with the other. She passed the hula-hoop gently beyond the juggling rings, flipped it over her head, and with one quick fluid motion, she did a front flip—the juggling rings still flying perfectly—and landed with both feet back inside her hula-hoop. There was a split second of adjustment, and then she had the hula-hoop going full-throttle around her waist again.

The crowd screamed and whistled in awed amusement. Even Erik found himself clapping his hands in approval.

The show continued for about ten minutes, with Svetlana introducing new props and new tricks. At one point she'd set up a miniature pogo stick and a tiny trampoline and was vaulting herself far above the crowd, doing occasional front and back flips to the cheers and applause from the circle of onlookers. More rings were produced, and then she was performing contortionist tricks to fold and bend her body through seemingly impossible spaces. She was captivating, and yet it was her smile that Erik could not take his eyes off of. The smile never left her face, and he found himself wondering how the hell anybody could look so happy in a world that was so cruel and ugly. Perhaps if she'd seen the things he'd seen and known the things he had learned about humanity. Erik found himself realizing that if sharing this darkness with her could wipe that smile away, he'd rather lie to her and damn himself for eternity. Some folks were just meant to bring lightness to the world. Svetlana of the Carpathian Great and Tiny Circus was one of them.

"I have one last trick I vant to share vit you all today, but before I do, please give yourselves big round of applause, okay? I'm too tiny to do you all justice so you must clap for yourselves and know that my heart claps with you, for you are very kind." That smile was still on her face as she glanced around the crowd of clapping, hooting, and whistling spectators. There was a moment when Svetlana turned his way, and then she was looking directly up at him from his perch atop the park bench. The two made eye contact, and for the briefest second, her smile faltered, curling downward just around the edges of her lips. The moment passed, and as she once again surveyed the crowd, she smiled as full and wide as ever.

Erik had the sensation of free-falling; he felt as if he'd stepped into an elevator only to have the car's cable snap, sending him plummeting down a stories-high chute. He leaned backward and placed his hand on the bench, waiting for the vertigo to cease. Eventually, it did, but her final act—one that included two volunteers, a jump rope, and three chain-saws being juggled—floated before him as if he were in a dream until the music had run out and Svetlana was taking her final performance bow.

"T'ank you all so very much for watching. If you enjoyed the show, I hope you will show your appreciation by dropping some moneys in my hat here. If you're wondering what to give a girl to bring her happi-ness, I highly recommend portraits of dead presidents. You can help me start my own private museum, no?"

The crowd lined up as if on command and began dropping tips into an old top hat. Svetlana bowed politely a few more times, and then proceeded to load her props and belongings back onto her hand truck. Erik reached into his pocket and found his last three crumpled-up dollars waiting at the bottom. He'd meant to use the cash to buy a hot dog and a Coke from one of the street vendors, but instead he found himself climbing down off the bench and waiting at the back of the line. The vertigo had passed, but a small part of him—the part that somehow knew his marriage with Kelly was destined to fail long before he placed the ring on her finger and said, "I do"—was telling him that this was all a big mistake. He'd seen it in her eyes, and the way her smile had faltered when they'd made eye contact.

The line moved quickly, with many smiles and compliments to the petite girl in the rainbow leggings. She curtseyed once or twice when she spotted anything larger than a one dollar bill, and she even took a moment to kiss an older gentleman in a wheelchair on the cheek as he pushed his way through the line and dropped his offering in her hat. Erik could see the bright red lipstick on his cheek, just above a plastic tube that carried oxygen to the man's nostrils. It was tender to watch, endearing, particularly as the old man blushed and smiled as he rolled himself away.

Erik was last in line, and by the time he dropped his last three dollars into her hat, Svetlana had her gear packed up on her cart. She smiled at him, but her smile still seemed to falter around the edges of her mouth as she picked up her hat.

"I really enjoyed your show," he said, watching her as she tipped the currency out of her hat and into a small canvas handbag with sunflowers embroidered on both sides. "I hope I didn't somehow catch you off guard or anything. You seemed a tad distressed when you looked up at me. I was the one over on the park bench." Erik turned and nodded to the bench beneath the tree.

Svetlana smiled politely. "No, not at all. You get…how you say? Accustomed? Yes. You get accustomed to strangers looking down on you. I am pleased you like my show. But if you'll excuse me, I really must be on my way."

She flipped the hat up onto her head, casually pressing the braided spikes of hair under the brim. When she turned to go, she accidentally dropped the canvas purse onto the red-brick concourse. The bag opened, and some of the dollar bills tumbled out and fluttered away in the warm spring breeze. Svetlana knelt down and tried to snatch up the money and stuff it back inside her bag. Erik watched, mesmerized, and then found himself running after a crumpled dollar bill, possibly one that he'd donated, as it floated off toward the statue of Longfellow. He chased it down in a few exaggerated steps that made him look like an old Vaudeville comedian and found himself grinning as she stood with her hands on her hips in mock-annoyance until he handed her money back.

"You are very noble to help out a poor young lady," she said as he held out the bill to her. "Some boys would have kept the money and run away."

"I'm not 'some boys'," he answered. "And my name is Erik. Very pleased to meet you." He held out his hand for her to shake after she stuffed the rogue dollar back into her purse. She extended her hand tentatively and shook.

"I'm very glad to meet you as well," she replied, and the smile was there on her face again, genuine and radiant. "But here— I cannot take your last three dollars. You should really get yourself a bite to eat." Svetlana opened her purse again and went to retrieve three singles from inside.

"No, please, it's really okay. I can just…" Erik recoiled for a moment, and the feeling of vertigo crept back up on him. "How… How could you possibly have known that was my last three dollars?"

Svetlana had the three singles in her hand. "Are you sure you won't take dis back? I feel terrible you might go hungry tonight because of me."

Erik glanced around the square. The crowd had dispersed by now, moving on to the next attraction or the next food vendor as the sun slowly sank over the western horizon behind the city. He felt certain that there had to be some kind of hidden camera that had captured him as he perched on the bench; he imagined some other member of the Carpathian Great and Tiny Circus speaking to her through a hidden ear-bud. Even street performers weren't above using technology to work a crowd nowadays.

"Is somethink wrong? Did you lose somethink?" Svetlana waved the dollars before him one more time before shoving them back into her purse. Her smile was wider than ever, and it made him feel silly.

"It's just… I was just…" he stammered. He took a moment to clear his mind, and then his eyes met hers for the second time that evening. "That *was* my last three dollars, although I have no clue how you could have possibly known that. In fact, I think your back was still turned to me when I dropped my money into your hat. How did you *know?*"

"It is long story," she said with a wink. "One I don't believe either of us has time for this evenink." Svetlana slipped her purse into one of the boxes on her luggage cart. "I have prior commitments to keep, and you should be getting home to call your son and tell him goodnight. He won't be able to sleep until he hears you tell him you love him."

A stunned look spread across Erik's face. "How are you doing this? Are you a mind reader or something?"

"Kind of. Let's just say that I wasn't sure that you were safe until you shook my hand. I can tell you are good guy, and that puts me greatly at ease. So I promise you, next time we meet, I, the Amazing Svetlana of the Carpathian Great and Tiny Circus, will allow you to buy me a real dinner. Provided you are still employed at your newspaper job, of course."

Svetlana bowed, tipping the old, faded top hat on her head just enough to darken her lovely eyes, and then she was hauling her cart behind her across the red-brick concourse. Erik watched as the setting sun stretched her shadow across the bricks into a lovely puddle of serendipity. He had an idea that he was going to be spending a lot of time on the park bench, waiting for her to return and perform again.

Chapter 3

Saturday, June 4th

Svetlana Barnyck dreamed of her mother's death.

It was a dream that haunted her over the past fifteen years, one that always left her sobbing and hiding beneath her blanket. The dream rarely deviated in details and events over the years, giving it more of a feeling of repressed memory than of some fluid fictional dismissal of random thoughts and images. Svetlana had only been six years old when her mother, Ivana Barnyk, was murdered in cold blood somewhere near the southern border of Ukraine, on the opposite side of Romania, after a sideshow carnival act her family was performing in went sour.

The dream always started the same way: her mother, a fortune-teller, had been inviting guests onto the stage for her to "look into their pasts and discover their futures." Madam Ivana had the *Omniscient Eye* that was somehow capable of penetrating deep into the souls of men to uncover their darkest secrets. The talent was supposedly hereditary and handed down for generations in her family lineage. Before Ivana Barnyk, it had been Celeste Fiore. Before Celeste, Katerina Janst. Somewhere in her father's private stock was a scroll with the entire family tree of descendants dating back close to Year One on the Great Roman Calendar. Next to every female gifted with the *Omniscient Eye* was an inked sketch of a human eye enshrined within a circle, although the sketch looked more like an upside-down question mark with an X in the center of the arc. The last name on that scroll—if it still existed—was Svetlana Barnyk.

In the dream, it was a warm early-summer evening, and Madam Ivana was inside a great canvas tent illuminated by gas lanterns in front of large mirrors. It was a throwback to early gypsy theater, and her father, Mikhail Barnyk, had insisted on the old ways in spite of the easy supply of gas generators and electric lights. "Ambiance and romanticism always pack 'em in," he had told her in his gruff, vodka-soaked voice. There were folding chairs separated into two sections; each section was eight seats wide and ten rows back, with an aisle directly down the middle. The seats were packed with farmers and factory workers and what Americans would refer to as the "working class." There are no business suits or banker attire among the crowd of weary countrymen in spite of the fact that the Cold War had been over by a decade and capitalism was still trying to sweep through Eastern Europe.

The previous act, Aldo Barnyk, Svetlana's brother, was a knife-thrower. Both Aldo and their older sister, Shimi, were part of the show, with Shimi performing a belly dance/striptease act to close the carnival. Aldo, at least ten years older than Svetlana, looked more like a full-grown man than a teenager. He was already capable of growing a full beard on his square jaws, making him look like a younger version of Papa. She could remember his face, and she could recall with frightening accuracy the way he, too, would pull members of the audience up onto stage with him, and the look of terror on their faces when he would instruct them to stand against the wooden wall and not move a muscle until his act was over. Then Aldo would launch a stream of six long-blade throwing knives, each razor-sharpened before every performance, until they formed a ghastly silhouette arching around the living target. The crowd would offer a chorus of "oohs" and "aahs" as the target stood deathly still, with that look of absolute dread plastered on their face until they heard the *THWUK* of the final blade entering the wooden backdrop. Aldo would ask them to step forward and take a bow, but every single time, without fail, they would turn first and stare at the wall where they'd been standing and see just how close those blades came to hitting them. They always smiled, always bowed graciously, and always left feeling as if they had stared death in the eye.

Those goddamn blades. Aldo always took his bow, and then vaulted off the stage, leaving the knives embedded in the wood until the family performance was over.

Aldo was never a part of the dream, but those knives were.

In Svetlana's dream, the stage belongs to Ivana, and she's already had a handful of guests with her on stage. Always the same faces, all of them present on the night Ivana Barnyk was murdered.

The first woman onstage was a common housewife with dreams of one day becoming a poet. Her mother had gripped the stranger's hand firmly, and then unlocked a series of secret girlish fantasies the woman had harbored all through her life. The woman giggled nervously and nodded her head with each premonition that Madam Ivana brought out of her. In the end, her mother had promised that one day the woman would work up enough courage to submit the poetry she'd written in all her spiral-bound notebooks to a real publisher and her work would be read and shared worldwide.

"*Sérdeñko* (dearest heart), many of my predictions," her mother confided to her weeks before her death, "are really just self-fulfilling prophesies. I merely point zem in zee right direction, and zey do all the work demselves. You understand, no?"

The six-year-old version of herself did not understand.

"Zees people don't want zee truth. Zey just want reassurance. Zey just want to hear that der future holds something good for them. Zey need to realize dat der future is what *dey* make of it. Once zey know I can really see their past, dey will believe anythink I tell dem."

The second person on stage with her is a young man from Russia. He is old enough to be a soldier and is waiting to see if he will be taken into the Russian army. He wants to know if that is where he is supposed to be in life, if *his* life was meant to be a soldier like his father before him. Madam Ivana takes his hand and sees into his past; she sees that the man is actually terrified of his father, that his father somehow knows, *knows* that the man is a homosexual in spite of him hiding it and lying to his father. The young man is suddenly very uncomfortable, especially now that he has been outed in front of a tent full of his fellow countrymen, but Madam Ivana's voice is calm, soothing, and then she's telling him what he already knows: that he has no real desire to become a soldier, and that it will never bring him happiness. "You need to escape from your controllink father's clutches and do vat makes you happy," she tells him in a sultry whisper. "Your life belongs to you. Escape from dis place and go live your life."

Even at six, Svetlana can still feel the bittersweet sting as the young man gets up and hugs her to the sound of thunderous applause inside the tent.

By now, deep within the dream, she can detect a dark presence there with her inside the tent. There is an intruder present among the farmers and factory workers that has other business than taking in a gypsy carnival. Svetlana begins to scan the faces in the crowd, trying to spot the alien and discover what he's up to, but all she sees is tired faces trying to look happy. She sees prematurely gray hair and missing teeth and wrinkles and worry lines. A small part of her feels terrible that her family is here to con as much money out of them as they can, but the Barnyks and the other families traveling with the show need to eat.

And then *he's* climbing the steps and onto the stage with her mother. Madam Ivana can tell something is already wrong and is fighting to keep the smile on her face.

In the aftermath of what happened, she could remember her Papa half-screaming, half-sobbing, "*Why?* Why did dat man not believe your mother's talent? Why did he have to test her?"

It took less than a second for her mother to yank her hand away from the old man who climbed up the wooden steps and sat down across from her at her table. In the dream, Svetlana can still see the way the gaslight reflects on the man's face, illuminating the man until he looked more like a beast as his dubious smile turned murderous.

Madam Ivana had time to utter one terrified sentence, "You murdering Nazi scum!"

And then the old man was up on his feet, racing toward the blades in the wooden wall that Aldo had failed to remove when his act ended. Shimi is watching from backstage the whole time, and she can do nothing but scream at the top of her lungs as the scene unfolds. The old man grabs only one knife, and then he is stabbing it into her mother's heart. The old man is screaming, "You're a witch!" over and over again until Mikhail and some of the other gypsy roustabouts wrest him away from her and pin him to the ground while the tent quickly empties itself of the terrified spectators.

Svetlana could tell the intruder was still there among them. It had not been the old Nazi that was so scandalously outed and then carted away by an angry mob of gypsies. That man, who they later found out was an upper-echelon officer in the SS, was beaten within inches of his life before the local constables could intervene. No, the sinister phantom is still in the tent with her family as her mother lay bleeding to death.

"Zee Eye! Vee must pass on zee eye while Ivana's still alive!" Her Papa, crying, was brushing his wife's long, black hair. "Please, before it's too late."

And then Mikhail was beckoning to his daughter. "Come here, Svetlana. Do not be afraid."

She feels a pair of large, coarse hands on her shoulders, gently pushing her forward toward her mother. She hears the ragged breathing still sucking and gurgling from Ivana's dying bosom. There is blood around Mama's lips now, dribbling unmercifully down her chin and onto the sawdust. Ivana looks up pleadingly at Mikhail with tear-filled eyes. Her words come out ragged and choppy, with hisses of death escaping her vocal cords.

"Please...*please* let it die vit me. Don't do dis to our child."

And then that feeling of evil she'd perceived earlier was standing right beside her. It had been that tall man, the one everyone in their camp referred to as *Zee Doctor*, as if he were somehow familiar to them all, but for the life of her, Svetlana could not remember what family he came from or in which van he traveled. He was merely a presence, and one that only popped up in times like this.

This was the intruder. She had always known it.

Zee Doctor removes the knife from her mother's chest, and then he is slitting the bare patch of skin on her forehead, almost directly between Ivana Barnyk's eyes. When the incision is complete, Svetlana gasps in horror.

An ancient, jaundiced eyeball rolls forward and drops out into *Zee Doctor's* palm.

"Come here, quickly, my dear child."

Blood gushes down over her mama's face. It runs in sanguine splashes down her cheeks and lips as each deteriorating heartbeat pumps it out of her.

"*Sérdeńko*...my baby," she whimpered. "I'm so sorry!"

With one final, labored inhalation, Ivana Barnyk closes her eyes and drifts away into that great, blackened void of nothingness.

The dream ends just as *Zee Doctor* gouges the knife blade into Svetlana's forehead and shoves the toxic organ inside her with his long, bony fingers, and then she lurches awake and screams in terror.

When the fear subsided and her heart rate dropped back down to normal, she got out of bed and slipped quietly into the bathroom. The rest of her apartment was silent, save for the electric fan humming in the frame of her bedroom window. Svetlana finished her business and flushed, and then stopped to examine her reflection in the vanity mirror. Her eyes were barely slits, and in the bright shine of the light bulb overhead, she could barely see her pupils gazing back. She forced her eyes open wider, feeling tears forming in the corners of her eyelids. When her eyes focused, she gazed up at her forehead, looking for the telltale scar that she had known was always there, would always be there, but she saw nothing. Only smooth, clear skin pocked by nothing more than an occasional freckle.

This happened! she thought to herself. *I know it did. Dat man came out of nowhere, and he cut me open. He took dat eye out of Mama and put it in me. It really happened.*

Svetlana had felt the presence of the intruder the evening before, back when she'd performed for the crowd in Monument Square. She was certain it had been the young man standing up on the bench watching her, but her suspicion had passed once she shook his hand. That man was safe. The *Omniscient Eye* never lied. Still, the intruder had been present, watching.

Normally, the silence did not bother Svetlana, but after the dream recurred she found that she could not stand it. She slipped back out of bed and switched on the transistor radio on her armoire. The room filled with the sound of oldies music as she climbed back into bed and pulled the blankets up around herself.

She was still trembling as she sank back into slumber.

"Hey, boss, there's a colored fella upstairs who wants to see you. Says he used to play the blues here back when your daddy ran the bar."

Roy Higgins looked up from the invoice sheet he'd been poring over. Cooney Distribution Services would be arriving later that afternoon to deliver crates and boxes of hard alcohol for the weekend, and that ratty little bastard Dixon they always sent to Velvet Mojo wouldn't unload a goddamn thing unless the paperwork was completed. Roy set his clipboard down on his desk, sat back, and folded his arms behind his head.

"Didja get a name from him, or did he just mesmerize ya with some kind of Jedi mind trick? Jesus, Hank, I got work to do, and I hate being interrupted."

Hank ran a hand through his short blond hair, offering a sorry smile. "He said, Sumpin-sumpin Walton, but I can't rightly remember. The guy looks like a goddamn homeless person. And he's got the strangest damn eyes I ever seen, I tell you what."

"What does he want?"

"Shit, I reckon he wants to audition to play gigs here. At least that's the vibe I'm gettin'." Hank Willis, the daytime bartender of Velvet Mojo, seemed amused rather than serious, as if this were nothing more than a practical joke. Perhaps this colored fella hadn't heard of a thing called "booking agents" or "the internet," where the rest of the known music industry was putting together business relations and applying for concert gigs. Velvet Mojo might not be the premier blues club on the Memphis scene, but it was still a respectable juke joint, and blues and jazz bands were always jockeying to play this venue. It had been that way since his daddy, Mel Higgins, opened the club in the early sixties.

"Didja explain to him that we only got openings for a dishwasher? Ever since Laverne quit, Denise has been pulling double-duty between minding the bar and soaking glasses. And that's a recipe for drunken clients to try and rip us off."

Hank stared down at his cowboy boots for a moment and ran his hand absently through his hair again. "He said that as long as your office ain't changed since your daddy ran the joint, his picture would still be up on the wall. Third from the left, right between W.C. Handy and Ernie McCoy."

Roy Higgins stood up and hustled around his desk to the wall next to the stairs where Hank was speaking to him. The "Wall of Blues," as his daddy used to call it, contained portraits and snapshots of dozens, perhaps a hundred, of the old-time Delta bluesmen. Black and white celluloid phantoms of men like Robert Johnson and Furry Lewis and Willie B., all with that same serious gaze, with their guitar necks held like talismanic idols next to their smooth, black faces. Roy moved over to the left and gazed at the photo, and his chin dropped comically in disbelief.

"What is it, boss?"

"I'll be damned," he whispered, and then he was pushing his bulky, sweaty frame past the surprised bartender and hustling up the stairs.

Joe Walton watched him burst out into the hallway beside the stage and barrel toward him, his white hand outstretched for him to shake.

"Roy, is that really you, son?" Joe grinned. "I don't think you were more than ten years old the last time I saw ya. You were sittin' with your daddy behind the bar, watching me play over on that yonder stage. Look at you all grown up now!" Joe grasped Roy's hand and shook it vigorously.

"They finally let you out, huh? I can't get over it. 'Smokehouse Joe'

Walton is standing right here in my bar!"

The smile dropped instantly from Joe's face, as if Higgins had just dropped an enormous insult on him. Higgins tried to pull his hand away, but Joe squeezed his hand tighter, causing his knuckles to crack and the white flesh of his hand to turn pink.

"Y'all know that ain't my professional name. I've always gone by 'Tobacco Joe' Walton."

Hank, who had blundered up the stairs behind his employer, looked confused. "You know this guy, boss?"

Higgins turned, annoyed. "Boy, this is one of the best guitarists that ever set foot in this here bar." He turned accusingly back toward the black man in the faded suit and bowler hat. "Except that the only venue *you've* been playing in lately is prison. Ain't that right, *Smokehouse* Joe?"

Hank still looked puzzled. "Why do they call him 'Smokehouse Joe'?"

Higgins squeezed his own hand against Joe's smooth, black skin. Joe had assumed the boss of Velvet Mojo had soft hands, money-counting hands, and found himself surprised at the strength now crushing back with equal force. Joe had remembered him as a boy with a chubby, sun-freckled face and a peach-fuzz haircut. Now he was a man with a receding hairline and tobacco-stained teeth and a crazed look in his eye—the same look he remembered seeing in the eyes of Ol' Scratch way back when.

"They call him 'Smokehouse Joe' on account of those white boys he murdered. Leon and Rufus Hickey. This ol' boy here stabbed them to death with a sling-blade, and then skinned them alive and stuck their carcasses in the smokehouse on his daddy's farm. Ain't that right, Joe? What was y'all fixing to do with them? Eat them for Sunday dinner?"

Joe Walton pulled his hand away. He could feel the sweat from that cracker still on him, and it made him feel dirty. That was the damnable thing about whities; they lived and breathed hypocrisy as if it were a religious sacrament. How many brothers had they dragged out and hanged in the middle of the night, kicking and screaming and praying to the very same God for help and justice? How many black women had they raped and tortured into silence? He could still hear his Mama's cries as the Hickey brothers beat her and molested her after his Daddy was gunned down in cold blood and left her for dead on their kitchen floor. Even after his Daddy's body was removed, nobody ever came by to check on him and see if he was okay. Nobody wanted to dirty their hands helping him clean up the blood.

Murdering those two boys was never about justice. It was about something deeper. More sinister.

Hank's eyes widened, and he emitted an audible gasp, followed by an obligatory, "Lord, have mercy," in a slow Southern drawl.

"That ain't up for discussion. You know damn well what them boys did to my family, and you'd have done the same if you was me. I remember how you used to watch your Daddy back when *he* ran this place. You idolized him. And rightly so, cuz' yo Daddy was a decent man. He was one of the few white folks that would let us play in his bar way back when white people was discovering the blues. I used to pack this place in when I was a young man, and I'm ready to do the same right now."

Higgins gave an amused glance to Hank and then turned back to the black man in the bowler hat and blue suit.

"You think you can pack this place in? What, did they let you have a guitar in the slammer so you could brush up on your scales and practice your licks?" He and Hank both laughed out loud as if this was all some comical farce, one they would be joking about long after the nigger turned tail and went on his crazy, white-folk murderin' way. When Joe refused to blink, Higgins stopped laughing. "You're really serious about this? You think just because you're outta jail that people still remember you and are going to suddenly flock into Velvet Mojo to hear you play? A lotta people only remember you because they know what you did. They's still mad at you, ol' boy. Now, I know you got talent. At least you had it way back when, but look at you now. You ain't nothing but a skeleton in a suit and hat, walking around like you don't even know you ain't dead yet. If I let you play here, there are people gonna be mad as hell at me. They gon' think I love white-boy-murdering niggers or something. How's that gonna look for my business?"

Joe took a deep breath in through his nose and then exhaled slowly through his mouth. This whole thing had been a bad idea, but other than this, he had nothing. He had to eat. He had to be able to bring in some money, and do so legally in case the law was watching him. And, of course, his guitar was still somewhere way the hell up in Maine. Options were beyond limited. They were a matter of connecting the dots, and those dots were already preordained by Ol' Scratch.

There was no fighting the Devil's plans.

"Roy, I ain't askin' you to make me your star attraction on Saturday night. Hell, I ain't even askin' for sympathy or understanding. I know damn well you got a business to run. But if you're anything like your Daddy, I'm guessing you're a bettin' man."

Higgins and Hank both chuckled again.

"Well, whatta you got in mind, 'Smokehouse Joe'?"

"This place used to have an outdoor P.A. system. If it still works, and you want to lend me one of your house guitars, I'm betting I can have this place packed in ten minutes flat."

Hank laughed again, but this time Higgins kept quiet. He looked around Velvet Mojo, noting the fact that there were only three people currently sitting and drinking in his establishment, with one being a local drunkard who never seemed to leave, and the others a black couple that might have been a pimp and one of his call girls hashing out business in a booth by the window. There were at least half a dozen other juke joints around the block that were already packed with white folks listening to the modern version of the Delta Blues. Right up the street, cats like Mississippi Clay and "Screamin' Dave" Banks were pulling in the tourists. His own establishment *should* have been jumping right now, but Mojo was understaffed and not prepared to take on real business until after 5:00 p.m.

Higgins gave Joe a cold, deep stare. "All right, killer. If you really think you still got it, my boy Hank, here, will get you set up to play. You got ten minutes. I'm gonna go back down to my office and take care of some business. If this place ain't full and jumping when I come back up, I want you gone. And you never come back again. You hear me?"

The expression on Joe's face never faltered. "It's a deal."

Higgins laughed and shook his head. "You used to be something special, Joe. I can still remember the way you played from back when I was a boy. Your music has haunted me for decades now, and I can't even say why. Hank, you get this man here all set up. There's a Stratocaster up on the wall behind the stage. You just get 'Smokehouse Joe' Walton set up to play, and if he does pack this place in, you come downstairs and get me."

The owner of Velvet Mojo turned and went back down to his office in the basement.

"Well, alright 'Smokehouse Joe'," Hank said. "Y'all just follow me."

Within ten minutes Velvet Mojo was packed. The moment Hank flipped on the house P.A. system and Joe Walton started strumming and singing, people started turning heads. Joe laid down the opening chords to his song "Homesick Blues"—a murderous little ditty that he'd written long before the Hickey brothers had shown up and committed their crimes—and began wailing into a rusty old microphone about "Ma still cookin' her alligator pie." The response was almost immediate. It was if everyone within proximity of the bar suddenly decided that they needed to hear about his mother's apron, still bloodied with alligator offal, and his cheating daddy's innards. Joe followed up with "Enough of Yo' Cheatin' Ways" and "Ol' Scratch," which was the song that made him famous, just after the Devil came to call while he was out working his Daddy's tobacco fields. By then, Velvet Mojo was wall-to-wall filled with customers, white and black alike, ordering drinks and listening to the old, skeletal black man with the Fender strutting about the stage and dripping with sweat, smiling and wailing away on his guitar, wringing every single note out of it like he was seducing a lover.

Hank didn't have to go down to the basement to fetch the bossman. Roy Higgins could hear the crowd stomping along and clapping and wolf-whistling between songs. By the time Joe finished playing "Ol' Scratch," Higgins was standing beside the stage with that same bugeyed whitey look he'd had when he watched Joe play as a boy. Joe tore through two more songs—"Delta Blackbird" and "Gonna Burn That Old House Down"—before tipping his hat and taking a final bow to his audience and retreating behind the curtain. Within seconds, Roy Higgins was backstage as well and shaking his hand again. This time, his grip was lighter and far friendlier.

"I don't know how you did it," Higgins shouted among the crowd's cheers for an encore, "but I was apparently dead wrong about you. What the fuck just happened out there?"

Joe lifted his bowler hat and wiped the sweat from his brow with the sleeve of his jacket. He set the hat back on his head and smiled politely. "Let's just say I still know how to pack 'em in."

"You never even told me what you were betting for," Higgins said. "But I'm guessing I already know. You're looking for a steady-paying gig. And by the look of you, y'all need money up front. How much are we talkin' about?"

"Honestly, I don't even know how much you payin' house bands nowadays. I've been gone a long time, and by the look of things, a lot of shit has changed since I last played here. But you offer me a square deal and let me hold onto this here guitar, I think we can work something out."

Higgins cocked his eye. "You really think you can keep drawing in crowds like this every afternoon? Maybe they don't remember you now, but they will. Especially if I start advertising that you're my daytime gig. Bad blood is bound to come out sooner or later. It always does."

"Honestly, son…" Joe Walton looked directly into Roy Higgins's eyes. "If it had been your Mama and Daddy, what would you have done if you were in my shoes? Those two boys shot my father dead and then had their way with my Mama. If I'd been born white, would people hate me or would they say I did the right thing? I never hid behind the color of my skin. I did my time in prison, and I put all my past behind me. I just wanna move on now." Joe tipped his hat at the owner of Velvet Mojo. "With all due respect, your Daddy would have understood, and he wouldn't have been hassling me about it. He'd have just welcomed me back and let me play, the way he did with *all* the bluesmen that came through here. I hope his boy has the same good sense."

Higgins stood up straight in his shoes, looking the old bluesman in the eye. "My Daddy wasn't all that fond of niggers. Let's just be clear about that. You're giving him way more credit than he deserved. But he loved the blues, and he loved the money that kind of music brought in. If you really think you can keep packing 'em in, I'll give you three hundred a week, with food and drinks on the house. And you can hold onto that guitar as long as you play here exclusively. And if I ever catch wind of you playing elsewhere, you're out the door on your scrawny, black ass. You catch my drift?"

"Smokehouse Joe" Walton extended his hand. "Deal."

Roy Higgins felt like he was shaking hands with the Devil himself. Never in his dreams would he have realized how close to true that was.

Chapter 4

The elevator door opened on the third floor, and Erik found Beverly LaChance standing there waiting for him.

"I understand they call you *Erik the Black*. I can only imagine what *my* staff will end up calling you now that you're here with us."

She held her hand out politely, and Erik shook it, feeling immediately entranced by the editor of the local section of the *Portland Beacon*, primarily with the perfume she was wearing and the way her white sateen blouse revealed her impressive cleavage. Beverly looked to be at least a decade younger than he was. With her long blonde hair neatly done up in a bun and her large-framed reading glasses, she reminded him more of a librarian than the matriarch of Maine's biggest newspaper's social scene.

"It's nice to see you, too, Beverly. Mister Cummings told me to report to you this morning for my new assignment."

"I've read almost every single column you've written. I have no idea how anybody can write about such ghoulish topics and make them sound so—exciting. You have a real talent, Mister Marsh. I have to admit, I'm really surprised to see you up here on our floor." And then, in a conspiratorial whisper, "The most excitement you're gonna cover around here is the annual 'Flower and Garden Show' at the Civic Center. C'mon, let's go into my office where we can talk in private."

Erik followed her down the carpeted corridor, past the row of cubicles where other columnists were typing away about art exhibits, celebrity sightings, and reviews of local plays and concerts. There was a radio on playing acoustic versions of the latest pop songs, and as he walked past the eye-level wall barricades, Erik could feel eyes peeking out at him. The walk felt more like the Death Row march of an inmate on his way to the chair than the new reporter making his way to the boss's office.

"I haven't heard from Mister Cummings directly, but I've been told you're looking for a temporary change of pace. I suspect the difference of reporting about rape and murder will seem like night and day compared to covering the things we do around here." Bev stopped short of opening her office door to face him. "Gossip columns and charity events don't carry the same gravitas as a body found in a dumpster. None of the things we write about here are going to win you a Pulitzer Prize. I'll be honest with you, Mister Marsh, I truly don't understand what you're doing here. You'll be wasting your talent working for me."

Beverly opened her door and stepped aside so that Erik could enter her office. It was much tinier than R.H. Cummings's "War Room" office, but it was serviceable nonetheless, with an adequate desk, an over-sized event calendar on the wall, and rows of color photographs of what was presumably her husband and children. When Erik was seated in the uncomfortable guest chair across from her desk, Beverly smiled politely again and sat down.

"This is awkward," she sighed. "And it's only a formality, but I have a memo from Mister Cummings to ask you directly if you are sober this morning. From the way you've been presenting yourself, I assume you are. Do you have a drinking problem, Mister Marsh?"

Erik was taken aback by the question. Cummings was obviously scrutinizing over his investment with the newspaper. Of course, he'd ask, and of course, Ms. LaChance would report back to him if he'd been slurring words or showing signs of belligerence or discontent. The truth was that he managed to fall into the easiest slumber in years after his meeting with Cummings and his subsequent phone call with his son to say goodnight. Getting off the crime beat had felt like a weight had been lifted from his chest. He'd managed to avoid the series of nightcaps with the bottle of *MacAuley Brothers* bourbon that he kept in the cabinet under the sink and settled for the cool ocean breeze blowing through the windows of his studio apartment on Lisbon Street.

It was the first night in eternity without nightmares about the things he'd seen over the years.

"I'm completely sober. I promise." Erik held up his pinky, kissed it, and rubbed it across his heart.

He thought of Owen and how his son's voice had sounded so much older than the last time he'd spoken to him. Erik smiled to himself as his only son rambled on about how close summer vacation was, and how his mom had agreed to become a Den Mother for his Cub Scouts troop, which meant camping trips and merit badges and making new friends over recess. "I still want to spend time with you, Dad," Owen mentioned with a hint of accusation in his voice, and Erik could not blame him for it. "I know it, Tiger," he said back. "And I promise we will. My job is going to change, and I'm going to make sure I do a better job of being your Dad."

"Good," Owen said. "Because Mister Allen says he's gonna be my new dad once he marries Mom in October. He says he's not replacing you because you'll always be my dad, but he also says he wants us to be best buddies because it will make Mom happy."

None of this was out of the blue. Kelly mentioned that she'd been dating Allen Rogers almost a year ago and that they were very happy together. Allen was an insurance agent out of Hetfield—the same hometown he and Kelly shared a house in, once upon a time—roughly half an hour north of Portland and was already financially secure with a successful practice. That was fine with Erik; it meant that alimony would drop significantly, if not completely, and all that would be left was child support payments to make sure Owen's needs were being met. And truth be told, Kelly deserved to be happy. All the lonely nights he'd put her through while snooping around the city to follow up on murders and rapes and vulgarities of humanity. It had created an impenetrable wall between them.

As well as his drinking, he couldn't forget that.

"I'm going to be honest with you," Beverly said, leaning across her desk so that her clear blue eyes met his, her cleavage suddenly growing into a vast canyon beneath her blouse, almost daring him to break eye contact. "I'm very familiar with your work, and I feel that you are a wasted talent working here in the local section. Your coverage of the Chin-Bok crime syndicate's murder spree back in 2007 was Pulitzer Prize material. How a Caucasian with a New England accent penetrated the Chinese Mob and practically handed it over to the Feds is stupefying. You're giving all of that up to drop columns about art exhibits and socialite events is a flipping waste of talent. Everyone in my department would kill to pick up where you've left off. At the very least, you could be covering politics up at the State House or something more vital to *The Beacon's* success. Quite frankly, I just don't get it."

Erik sighed. "Look, Bev—" He'd dropped to the more casual address of his new boss, which he wasn't entirely sure would be appropriate considering that he'd have been canned immediately if he'd shown the slightest trace of intoxication at this interview. He was not a stranger to Beverly LaChance; he'd sat in long board meetings with her as R.H. Cummings chewed out his staff when circulation was low or when he praised them with the deepest sincerity when they nailed a lead that led to worldwide internet hits on *The Beacon's* website, the Chin-Bok story being one of those moments. Erik knew who she was, had passed her a thousand times in the course of his tenure with the newspaper, but she had remained something of a footnote, not important enough to stop and talk to as he flew through the halls of the *Portland Beacon* to his cubicle or on his way out the door to the next horror show waiting to be reported on.

She was another pretty face with fluff to report about.

Now she was his boss.

"—I can't do what I was doing anymore. I can't explain it any better than that. I've seen too much horror to continue and still consider myself a part of humanity. People are insane. Everywhere. I had to walk away from it before I became insane myself."

"And you're sure this is really what you want? Reporting throwaway stories meant for grandmothers and pretentious art lovers and judgmental Christian scrutinizers? Because we get letters by the sackful telling us that we're going to burn in hell for reporting about fundraisers to support Planned Parenthood or the Portland Gay Men's Chorus. You haven't seen hatred until you've read a letter from Grandma Public damning those queer musicians to Hell."

Erik laughed in genuine amusement. "Believe me," he said once he caught his breath. "Indignation is a far cry from watching the State Police removing severed body parts from a crawl space in a condemned building."

Bev scowled, a wave of unexpected nausea washing over her pretty face.

"I'm not kidding. I have nightmares about festering body parts, parts of children who were abducted and murdered. I asked to be reassigned for a reason. I need a change. Or I need to leave. *The Beacon* has been my home for years, and I'm loyal to it. So, pretty please with sugar on top, give me a fucking assignment so I can go back to work."

An almost comical expression of shock passed across her face, and her lower lip quivered for a fraction of a second. Her scowl lingered for a moment as she composed herself, and then Beverly LaChance was leaning back in her chair and scrolling through a computerized calendar of events, looking for stories for the new guy to cover. "Okay, let's see… I've got an art exhibit at the University of Southern Maine opening up. A local artist named Danny Evarts. I've got a reading event at the Portland Library, a writers group called the Tuesday Mayhem Society doing a symposium on ghost stories. Up in Topsham is the first Cruisin' Night of the summer. You know. Where they haul out the classic hotrods and jack up the fifties music? The Shangri-Las and Jan and Dean. What else? Oh, here's something."

She clicked on a hyperlink on her computer, and the screen exploded into a web page dedicated to an independent movie release. Erik glanced around Beverly's chest to get a better look.

The page read:

*THURSDAY, JUNE 9*TH *AT THE MERRILL AUDITORIUM, Join us for the premiere release of the new DownEast Cinema film debut, DEATH'S LAST CARESS, starring C. James Roberts and Gail Silvers. Filmed in Southern Maine, this independent motion picture explores two young lovers caught up in a deadly game of crime, lust, and mortality in a society of morbid voyeuristic fascination. This film has not yet been rated by the Motion Picture Association of America.*

"That's the one," Erik pointed emphatically toward the computer screen. "Get me a press pass to that event and let me cover it. I promise I'll give you a killer report and have that auditorium packed for the premiere."

"I can get you a press pass," Beverly answered. "But you still have the rest of the week to fill in. I'll tell you what. Consider this your initiation week. One column every day—and I don't even care about what you choose to write about. Just make sure you impress the hell out of me. If you think you can do that, I'll have my contacts arrange for an all-access pass that includes private time with the actors and the director. And I expect it to be *serious* reporting. I don't want innuendoes or tabloid fodder, okay? That stuff's got no place here at *The Beacon*."

"Yes, mother."

"And can the back-talk. This is *my* department. I earned it through experience and hard work, not from leveraging through nervous breakdown theatrics. Cummings may have a soft spot in his heart for you, but I don't. You're good, Mister Marsh, but only as good as your last column. If you can't carry your weight here, I'll send you back to Cummings so quick your head will spin. Got it?"

A stunned look swept across Erik's face, followed by the first unexpected wave of really wishing he'd had a drink or two before coming to work. He could feel his teeth slowly grinding back and forth in his mouth, enamel jags clashing around his dry tongue. Erik took in a deep breath and nodded at his new boss. "Sorry, Miz LaChance. I was out of line."

"Good. Now go hit the streets and find something newsworthy to write about."

Gus Bickford was standing just outside the door of the Hetfield Hardware and Agriculture store, grabbing one last cigarette before the store opened for business. The sun had already burned off the last of the morning fog, and the coolness of dawn was nothing more than a distant memory. The only thing cool at the moment was the half-empty Dunkin' Donuts coffee cup he'd left back by the register, and Gus was kicking himself in the ass for not finishing it while it was still hot.

He watched with mild interest as the white van pulled off Route 196 into the Hetfield Hardware parking lot. It was one of those old Ford Econoline deals, made for commercial use but invariably maligned as being a "pedophile van." You could distinguish it by its lack of windows behind the cabin and around the rear. This particular van had no business stencils or markings to indicate that it was a commercial vehicle, and Gus found himself a tad surprised when the driver rolled up to the parking spot directly in front of where he was standing, killed the transmission, and threw the door open.

He'd been expecting an old man with a baseball cap and dark sunglasses—his own mental picture of a sex offender or child abductor—but it was a middle-aged woman in cutoff denim shorts and a blue gingham shirt buttoned down her chest and tied off in a knot just above her belly button. The woman should have looked attractive but didn't. Her long blonde hair was funneled into a loose ponytail, and her bony frame was wrapped in grossly over-tanned skin.

A pretzel stick, Gus thought to himself. *She looks like a goddamn pretzel stick with eyes.*

"Good morning," he said politely, dropping his cigarette into the ash receptacle and pushing the door open for her. Gus couldn't help but notice as she walked past that Ms. Pretzel Stick reeked of liberally doused perfume to hide her body odor. She looked as if she hadn't bathed in weeks.

"Anything I can help you find?"

Ms. Pretzel Stick smiled politely, absently brushing a loose strand of blonde hair out of her face. When she spoke, it was slowly and calmly, as if she was delivering rehearsed material. "My husband and I just bought some land up here. We're looking to start a farm and raise some livestock."

Gus nodded politely. "Okay, what are ya thinking of raising? Chickens? Pigs? Sheep?"

"We're gonna need some animal pens," Ms. Pretzel Stick continued absently, as if she hadn't heard him. "The house we bought already has a barn on it, and some of it has already been converted into stables, but I don't think we're going to be owning anything big like cows or horses."

Her voice sounded as if it was on the verge of quivering and falling apart. He was already wondering if this lady was insane or perhaps under the influence of an illegal substance. Her eyes darted nervously around the store, looking to see if someone or something was trying to spy on her. Her hands were gripping the ring of keys she'd entered with tight enough to cause the brown skin on her knuckles to turn pink.

"Oooo-kay, let's try this again. What kind of animals are you thinking of raising?"

Ms. Pretzel Stick turned sharply and stared at him as if she'd suddenly been slapped awake. "Oh. Oh, my. We're going to be raising goats. Goats, and a handful of dogs. At least to start."

Gus tried to smile back, but this lady was making him terribly uncomfortable. It wasn't like she was going to be a physical threat to him. Even in his late fifties, Gus Bickford was still in damn good shape. He still had his army physique beneath the surface of the three decades of post-service civilian life that led him to jockeying a cash register in this Podunk hardware store. Ms. Pretzel Stick was obviously unarmed—there was nowhere to stash a piece in those shorts—and it looked as if a strong wind would strip her arms and legs right out of their sockets the way it would strip limbs off a dead tree. But she looked crazy, and crazy was incalculable. "Well then, let's get your dogs figured out first. We've got some crib kennels right over this way. What breed of dogs do you have?"

"Labs. We've got six right now, and they're awful big," she stammered. "And we'll probably be taking in more over time."

Gus led her around a corner to a display of metal-framed pet cages. They were placed in order of size, from smallest to largest. The smallest ones looked fit for terriers or pugs, the breeds Gus's wife called "yip-yip dogs." The largest looked like it could house a full-grown lion comfortably, with room to stretch its paws and swish its tail without hitting the top.

"Those are perfect," Ms. Pretzel Stick said, pointing to the largest cage. "I'll take six of those."

Gus Bickford nodded politely. "What about your goats? Do you want to look at our line of pasture fencing? We actually have it marked down right now, if you're interested."

"Some other time. For now, I just want the cages."

Ms. Pretzel Stick was twitching. Gus understood her body language right away. The crazy lady in the pet aisle was now jonesing hard for a fix. Best just to get her cashed out and send her on her way.

"Let me go grab a hand truck and get your cages loaded up. I'll meet you at the register."

Gus thought of zipping out to the stock room and phoning the police, but by the time they got here, Ms. Pretzel Stick would probably be long gone, and the truth was that he really preferred to not get involved. He had his own stash of reefer in his lunch pail, which he planned to smoke just before lunch so that his meal of leftover barbecue chicken would be that much more enjoyable. His wife knew her way around a stovetop, but getting the munchies always made her cooking more desirable. He didn't like the thought of Johnny Law showing up with the K9 unit only to bust *him* rather than the crazy lady. What she did when she left the store was *her* business.

He returned with the dolly and loaded six boxes containing the extra-large cages. Gus chuckled as he noticed the words ASSEMBLY RE-QUIRED stenciled in the lower right corner. *Hopefully, her husband will be sober enough to put these together because she ain't got a snowball's chance in hell.*

Ms. Pretzel Stick paid in cash. She never said a word as she forked the bills over the counter. She was carrying a lot of green, way more than someone who looked like she was living off food stamps and most likely crystal meth. The old man politely helped load her purchase into the "pedophile van" and sent her on her way.

All the warning signs were there, but Gus Bickford never caught her real name and never told anybody that he'd ever had contact with her when he saw her dead body on the news later that week.

"You don't recognize me, do you?"

Erik had returned to the bench in Monument Square, not entirely sure what his next move was going to be. Part of him was already questioning his own judgment concerning the lateral change in his job at *The Beacon*. The social scene required having connections, a true interest in *the arts*, and being a "people person." Beverly LaChance had given him a real ultimatum by sending him out to bring in his own stories, only it was beginning to feel like she was setting him up to fail. Now here he was, with a notebook and pen on his lap, trying to hash out some kind of list of people he knew in his own social circle, and all he could come up with was a list of names from the police force. People he'd interviewed hundreds of times about murders and rapes and robberies. Erik wondered if any of them were planning some kind of bizarre art exhibit based on forensic evidence.

Erik saw the woman with the canvas tote bag walking toward him from across the concourse. She was absolutely stunning in her flowered summer dress, and he couldn't help but notice how it billowed around her thighs in the cool breeze coming off the ocean. It wasn't until she called out to him that her voice registered in his memory.

"Svetlana?"

The woman smiled, and it was as if the whole world suddenly grew radiant, dazzling.

"Ah, I vas hoping you hadn't forgotten me already. I must look very different from zee last time you saw me, huh?"

"Yes!" Erik practically tripped over his own tongue to reply. "Different is good, though. I just, I…"

Svetlana chuckled. "That's vat you men *all* say. But tell me… Why did you come back here to dis spot? Were you looking for me?"

"Would you be impressed if I said 'yes'?"

"I vould be wary. If you came back here just to see me, you'd be trying to intervene with fate, and dat is no good. I'm a firm believer that serendipity cannot be manufactured. And if I touched your hand again, I vould know if you vere telling zee truth." She sighed. "But I see you also have your homework with you." Svetlana nodded toward the pen and notebook. "I think you must be on assignment right now. You are working on your newspaper column, no?"

Erik blushed. "I've been trying to write a column, but I have no idea what I'm going to write about. This has all been a great big mistake. I came back here to this bench pretty much because I have nowhere else to go. I suppose I was hoping a story would just fall into my lap from out of nowhere, but that never happens."

"Now *DAT* is serendipity," Svetlana smiled. "You are in luck, my friend. I, the Amazing Svetlana of the Carpathian Great and Tiny Circus, will grant you a story."

The stunning woman in the flowered dress set her canvas bag down on the bench next to Erik and pulled out a checkered tablecloth, which she spread across the red bricks of the concourse. When she was satisfied, she returned to rummaging through the tote bag.

"What are you doing?"

"I'm politely inviting you to lunch, and you vill not say 'no.' I hope tuna fish sandwiches are okay."

Svetlana drew three Crayola crayons and a hair-elastic from the bottom of her bag. With a quick flicker of her fingers, she wrapped the elastic around the cobalt-blue, chartreuse, and hot-pink crayons, forming a tight bundle out of them. She reached back into the tote bag and produced a CD case (Enya's Greatest Hits collection), set the case down in the middle of the tablecloth, then placed the bundle of crayons on top of it so that they were standing up.

"Do you have a lighter or some matches?" she asked politely.

Erik reached into his pocket and produced a cigarette lighter. "What are you doing?"

"I'm providing ambiance, you silly man," she replied. "When vas the last time you ate tuna by candlelight?" She flicked the strike-wheel and lit the points of the crayons until they caught fire. The flames flickered in the hue of the crayons' respective colors. Erik watched her body as she moved, mesmerized at just how beautiful this woman truly was.

Svetlana dove back into her tote bag and produced two paper plates, two sandwiches in plastic baggies, and two bottles of water. She laid the items neatly on the picnic blanket, taking care not to tip over the crayon candle she had created. When she was satisfied, she stood, held her hands out to him, and hoisted Erik to his feet. "Come, sit vith me and ask me your questions. I know that you've been curious about me since the last time vee met."

The two sat across from each other on the picnic blanket. Erik turned a page in his notebook to start fresh. He picked up the ink-gel pen and scribbled the name SVETLANA. "Um, could I start by asking for your last name?"

Svetlana had already taken a bite of her sandwich. She chewed and swallowed, then uncapped her bottle of water and took a swig. "Barnyk. B-A-R-N-Y-K. It is Slavic word for 'ram.' At one time my family vere shepherds, but dat vas generations ago. And dey vere also gypsies. My entire family belonged to a traveling caravan of carnival performers. I spent my childhood traveling all through Europe performing in tents. I vas very tiny back then and could do little more than juggle rings and scarves. Papa used to clasp his hands together and thank God that I was pretty because I vas so clumsy back then. It took many years to perfect my talents."

Erik scribbled all of this down in his notebook. "Where are you from, originally?"

It was Svetlana's turn to blush. "I honestly do not know."

"You made it into America. You have to have a birth certificate or something, don't you? To enter the country?"

Svetlana's eyes grew comically wide. "Ooooh, I have birth certificate, but it's as phony as any of my illusions, I promise you. In actuality, I do not know where I am originally from. Nor do I know where my brother and sister were born, or my parents for dat matter. Vee are, how you say? Hodge-podge citizens. My birth certificate says I was born in Serbia, but only because dat vas easiest country to obtain documentation. I'm sure my papa paid handsomely in Dinar to make sure I vas documented. Papa vas very smart man. I can claim citizenship in Serbia. My brother Aldo is citizen of Romania. My sister Shimi is a citizen of Ukraine. Vee had many safe havens throughout Europe, but never a place we called 'home.' Does that make sense?"

Erik scribbled and nodded. "Yes, it makes a lot of sense. How old were you when you came to America?"

Svetlana took another bite of her sandwich and chewed slowly, deliberately. When she swallowed again, she said, "I vas eleven when I came to America. It vas a few short years after my mother died."

"I'm very sorry," Erik uttered, looking up from his notebook. "I'm starting to feel awkward for prying."

"It is for your story, no?" Svetlana smiled politely, and Erik noticed a small gob of mayonnaise on her lip. He reached into his pocket and pulled out a handkerchief, leaned forward, and wiped the offending blob from her face. He performed the task so quickly that he hadn't even noticed he was doing it, and then found himself mortified as he tucked the handkerchief back into his pocket.

"Oh my god, that was extremely rude of me," he stammered. "I apologize. Sincerely."

Svetlana smiled again, and again that feeling of radiance seemed to illuminate those darkened parts of him that kept him brooding and unhappy. This was turning out to be the strangest interview he'd ever conducted.

"You worry too much," Svetlana said. "I am not offended. So many women in dis country are vorried about 'feminism' and 'equality' dat dey cannot see a favor being given to dem. Vat you just did for me was genuine. From da heart. My honor is still intact, thank you very much."

"You are unlike any woman I've ever met, Svetlana. You were saying about your mother passing away. What disease did she die from? Had she been sick for a long time?"

Svetlana set her sandwich back down on her paper plate and folded her hands across her lap. The smile vanished from her face, and it had felt like the clouds had passed before the sun. The crayon candle in the middle of the picnic blanket began to flicker, making Enya's face in the CD tray appear sinister and accusing.

"Mama vas murdered in the middle of a performance," she whispered. "She vas a fortune-teller. She had the same gift I have. She could see into a person's past. Da man that got on stage with her dat day—"

"We don't need to talk about this if you don't want to," Erik interjected. From her body language and the look on her face, this interview was quickly falling apart. He'd been asking questions geared less toward a newspaper interview and more toward a fact-finding mission from a possible suitor. Erik was shocked to discover how much the lines blurred when the interview concerned the living rather than the dead.

"It is okay, really—"

"No, it's not. I've obviously upset you."

"You did nothing wrong," Svetlana insisted. "Curiosity is not a crime. You need a story, and I vant to give you one, and I tell you it is okay." Svetlana smiled again, but this time it looked manufactured, the way Erik understood her birth certificate had been manufactured. "Vat you really want to know is how I could see into your past, no? I know *I* would be curious myself if a stranger was able to see into my memory and tell me things about myself. It is a scary prospect." Svetlana's voice dropped to a range of conspiratorial projection. "My Mama died because of it. She had seen terrible things about dat man on the day she died. Mama went to her grave seeing his crimes and inhumanities."

"Can I ask you a personal question?" Erik put the notebook and pen down on the picnic blanket, indicating he was now going off the record.

"Of course."

"When you saw me up on the bench, you looked at me as if I couldn't be trusted. Why? Did you think I was *that* man? Did you think I was some aberration in the crowd that was there to do you harm?"

Svetlana folded her hands and placed them over her mouth as she searched for an answer. When none came, she dropped her hands back down across her lap. "I don't know vat I thought," she finally replied. "I could see on your face that you vere hurting, and most probably I assumed the worst. I cannot lie, though. I saw that man that killed my mother, and you had the very same look on your face. I vill never know why he came forward dat day. Maybe he just vanted forgiveness, or perhaps some form of reckoning dat he vas not the terrible human being that vould have done all those atrocities. Whatever it vas he vanted, my mother vas not prepared to give to him. She only saw his darkness."

Svetlana shivered, and Erik noticed the goose pimples rising up and down the skin of her bare arms in spite of the warm summer sun.

"I have to know," Erik asked, leaning forward so that his eyes were looking into hers. "Did you see that same darkness in me? When you touched my hand, I mean. When you saw inside me, was it awful? Am I damned to hell?"

Her real smile returned again, and when it did, it felt like salvation.

"I only saw sadness and confusion, Erik. If I'd seen anything wicked, I would not be here with you right now."

Erik smiled. "It makes me happy to hear that. Still, now that I know you have some kind of gift of sight, I want to know how you got it. How is it that Svetlana Barnyk can look into the souls of men and see their past? Where did this power come from?"

Svetlana shoved the last bite of her tuna fish sandwich into her mouth, chewed, swallowed, and told him as best as she could about the *Omniscient Eye*.

Chapter 5

Saturday Evening

It had felt like the first time in forever that Erik Marsh didn't feel a burning need to swing by the Agency Liquor Store on his way home and grab a bottle of whiskey to help him through the night. He never even noticed that his Honda Civic had sailed right past the store on his commute up Route 1, or the voice in his head constantly whispering *don't forget to stop*. Erik's mind was still on Svetlana and how he couldn't seem to take his eyes off her, and what a striking transformation it had been between the girlishly cutesy street performer and stunning young, professional woman who offered him an impromptu interview for his very first column in *The Beacon's* social section. Svetlana Barnyk, it had turned out, was also an exchange student at the University of Southern Maine and worked part-time as a day counselor for special needs citizens there in the city's east end.

"Zee whole 'street-performer' thing—zat just puts spending money in my pocket and keeps me from letting my skills go to waste," she'd confided to him. "I do it because I still like performing in front of people. I like putting smiles on their faces. The whole world needs a smile, you know."

Mostly, though, he'd been thinking about her explanation as to how she could see into his past. Erik had hung onto every word she said, but even now, hours after he'd typed up his column and emailed it to Beverly LaChance back at the Portland Beacon, he wasn't entirely sure she was being truthful with him.

But why doubt her? Why would she lie about it? What would she gain from it?

For starters, having that kind of supernatural power almost begged the worst of humanity to come forward and try to force her to use it for their own gain. It would be over simple things at first—how to get a foot in the door in the career world or how to solve woes of the financial, marital, and emotional persuasion. It would only grow darker from there. Erik wasn't sure if the skepticism behind this rationale was coming from all the years he'd spent reporting the crime beat and seeing first-hand what bad people can do, or if it had all just been a question of common sense in a world where the thirst for power was *de rigueur,* from politics to religion to the local school PTO meetings.

It's human nature to want an edge on people, he thought. *If she really* does *have this supernatural* Omniscient Eye, *why would she share it? Why wouldn't she keep it to herself and use it to her own benefit?*

That was the conundrum of Svetlana Barnyk of the Carpathian Great and Tiny Circus. She had not used her magic—if you could call it that, and Erik was certain there would be people who would call her a witch if they'd seen her use it—during her act, but she'd used it to make a judgment about him, to be sure that he was safe before she confided in him about it. But she also allowed him to write about it in his column. What did it all mean?

"You vill only write nice things about me in your column, no?" Svetlana had asked him before saying farewell for the afternoon, but not before taking both of his hands into her own as if to read his answer telepathically before he'd had the chance to reply.

"Of course," Erik answered. "Cross my heart and hope to die."

She smiled, but there was the briefest trace of sadness in it, and he'd caught it just as it evaporated into the ethereal. "I know you've thought about dying in the past, Erik Marsh. I can see it in your soul. Part of you thinks Kelly and Owen will be better off with you gone, and maybe the world will be as well, but dat is not true." Svetlana let go of his hands. "I believe happiness is right around the corner from you, and that you've already taken your first steps in trying to find it."

"Will you be a part of that happiness?"

He'd blurted the question out before he knew he was even thinking it. Erik watched as her cheeks reddened, and then her smile grew into something much happier than before and he felt that sunshine-radiance spreading out from it.

Her smile is like a supernova, he'd thought back at that moment. *It has the warmth of the stars within it.*

And now that he'd had time to think and rethink the memories he'd shared with her that afternoon, another thought occurred. *A supernova marks the death of a star. It's the atomic heat of something enormous collapsing and dying from the inside-out.*

As he pulled his Civic into the parking lot of the River Mill Apartments, the words she answered with played in his head, and it was as if she was sitting right next to him, answering out loud with her sweet, choppy European voice.

"I am firm believer in both fate and serendipity. Serendipity blessed us with introduction. She pulled us together in some cosmic ballet for her own delight. But that does not mean we are supposed to be coupled romantically. Only fate can decide that."

"I don't see the difference," Erik said.

Svetlana sighed. "Fate is inescapable. It is a conclusion, rather than a muse. The *Omniscient Eye* does not allow me to see those conclusions nor understand their significance. You are sweet man, and I hope serendipity allows for us to keep crossing paths, but there are no guarantees." She noticed him frowning. "Dis is not a bad thing, Erik Marsh. Don't look so sad. Vee have plenty of time to let serendipity engulf us and enjoy what it chooses to share. In the meantime, go write your column and get it done. I have to get to work."

"Can I at least have your cell phone number? Can I call you?"

Svetlana Barnyk chuckled over her shoulder as she made her way across Monument Square toward Congress Street. "I don't own a cell phone!"

He wrote his column on his smart-tablet there on the bench in Monument Square. He had decided to omit everything she'd told him concerning the *Omniscient Eye* and concentrate on her dual personality of exchange student and street performer. For Svetlana's protection, of course. He proofread and revised it over a cup of coffee at a table in Mr. Bagel across Congress Street and emailed it up to Ms. LaChance in her office at Once City Center. He was nearly certain he could see her office window when he stepped outside the bagel shop and glanced up at the building that Maine considered the heart of the state's financial market. Somewhere in those offices, Beverly would be watching her inbox like a hawk and would undoubtedly forward his column to Cummings for approval.

Erik parked the Honda in an empty spot over by the flower boxes that formed the island between the parking lot and Route 196. The red and yellow crowns of tulips waved lazily in the late afternoon breeze while cars sailed by behind them. A handful of smokers were perched over at the end of one box, puffing and laughing and enjoying the sunshine, and why not? It felt like just two weeks ago that morning frost still covered the ground and May showers still threatened to turn into snow squalls when the Canadian winds had their way with them. He waved at the cartel of smokers and wasn't the least bit surprised that they took no notice of him.

The light on the answering machine was flashing when he entered his apartment, indicating two missed calls. Erik tossed his car keys on the coffee table and pressed play on the machine.

The first voice-recording was obviously Bev LaChance.

"I've got to admit, I'm very impressed with the column you sent in today. It's not the award-winning material I might have expected from somebody of your talent, but then again, it really captured something I thought for certain you wouldn't be able to convey—humanity. I've seen that street-performer you wrote about, and I think you did a terrific job in character study and exposition. The column will run tomorrow morning. Oh, and I also wanted you to know that I've set up your press pass for the movie event Thursday evening. Four more columns like this one and it's all yours. See you tomorrow morning."

The machine beeped to next message.

It was his ex-wife, Kelly. Her voice sounded terrified.

"Hi, it's me. Call me as soon as you get this message or as soon as you see tonight's newscast on television!"

The machine beeped to indicate there were no more messages.

Erik picked up the remote control from the coffee table and switched his television onto the Cable News Channel. Truth Carson was sitting behind his anchor desk, his eyebrows parked on his forehead in an expression of grave seriousness. Carson was in mid-sentence when the audio feed on the television came to life.

"…in a city that has been besieged with what appears to be *another* occult sacrifice, this time the crime scene happens to be in an elementary school in a sleepy little suburb called Hetfield. Local sources are reporting that the Hetfield Community School's cafeteria has been turned into what looks like the scene of a satanic ritual. We take you live now to Hetfield, Maine, where Paula Drake is standing by. Paula, what can you tell us about the crime scene and what evidence has been uncovered so far?"

Owen's school.

"Jesus Christ," Erik whispered, his shaking hand fingering the volume-up button on the remote control.

The screen switched over to a stationary camera just outside the school, where a young woman in a navy blue pantsuit was standing between the flagpole and the entrance of the building. There was a line of yellow "crime scene–do not cross" police tape circumscribing the doors, extending out around the flagpole, and coming to an abrupt end somewhere behind the line of squad cars parked where the school buses normally lined up to drop children off in the morning and carry them back home after the final bell rang. Behind it, Erik could see the wooden bench by the entrance doors, where he used to sit and wait for Owen to finish kindergarten for the day. Seeing the empty bench behind the fluttering line of yellow tape was disconcerting.

"Truth, I'm standing here outside of the Hetfield Community School, which has now become the latest crime scene of an alleged devil-worship ceremony that just might have a grizzly connection to the serial killer that local authorities are now calling 'Le'Sinestre'."

The live feed switched to a pre-recorded montage showing footage of the blood and carnage in the hallway outside the cafeteria where his son ate and commiserated with friends ever since kindergarten. The reporter's voice continued narrating the news piece.

"Warning: some of what you are about to see is shocking and upsetting," the voice spoke matter-of-factly. "At some point earlier today, the Hetfield Community School was broken into, and what looks like a Black Mass was held in the very heart of the building. The perpetrators entered through a back door and vandalized the building with graffiti drawn in blood, which at this point the State Police are waiting for the State Medical Examiner's report to verify whether the blood belongs to an animal or a human being."

Erik watched in horror as the camera panned the cafeteria, showing a pentagram drawn on the floor in what looked like powdered chalk. The ring around the star was surrounded by candles that looked as if they'd burned right down to their bases. Surrounding this was what looked like the bloodied carcasses of dead animals: mutilated dogs and cats and presumably a groundhog. On the walls were archaic symbols drawn in blood, along with words that formed satanic lyrics and incantations. The camera panned by too fast to read the script, but several words popped out that he understood immediately. Erik yanked the notepad from his pocket and began scribbling them down furiously, his exodus from the newspaper's crime beat totally forgotten.

Exalted One.

Apocalypse.

Gates of Hell.

And the most frightening of all:

Suffer the children to come unto me!

Erik shut off the television, grabbed his keys, and flew back out the door to his Honda.

On the occasions when people asked Warren Pembroke about the nature of his deformed hand, his responses varied in a stream of lies grand enough to form an ocean. And each lie came from behind a mask that concealed a haunting of shame and self-loathing possibly greater than the world itself. Wasn't that, after all, how all of humanity worked? Wasn't it a long line of generations that put on fake faces as they examined themselves in the mirror, never understanding that they were seeing themselves backward? And didn't they thrust that inversion of understanding upon every generation after themselves, in the forms of philosophy and religion? In Warren's eyes, the world was a damned, doomed monkey gritting its teeth in hostility and throwing shit at everything in its path.

At twenty-seven years old, Warren Pembroke was tired of the world. Warren was ready to kill the monkey once and for all.

He turned the Ford Econoline onto the entrance ramp of Route 295 South and stepped on the gas. Charlene Tibbets sat in the passenger seat, rocking back and forth and mumbling incoherently. The fingers of her hands clasped together in front of her chest, where they twitched and fidgeted in unending chaos. In the back of the van, Caroline Stork sat on top of the boxes containing the pet cages that Charlene had purchased earlier that morning from Hetfield Hardware and Agriculture. When Warren turned the wheel and forced the van onto the entrance ramp, the boxes shifted without warning, sending Caroline crashing into the tire well directly behind him.

"Hey, couldja take it easy up there? It's not like I have a seatbelt or anything to protect me back here."

Warren glanced at her in the rearview mirror and smiled. Caroline was attractive as hell and could give an amazing blowjob when she was turned on. Her halter-top and jeans were still covered with blood from the Jack Russell terrier she'd ripped apart before the ceremony. With no bra on underneath, her nipples pushed through the bloody fabric like pencil erasers.

"I need to get high," Charlene muttered from beside him. Her blood-shot eyes pierced ahead through the windshield in a hypnotized gaze. "You said we could get high after we were done in the school. You promised us!"

"Where's Abby?" Caroline commented from behind. "I thought she was coming with us tonight." Caroline pulled off her halter top and chucked it on the floor by her feet. Her bare breasts were coated with dog's blood, which was still tacky enough to smear over the myriad tattoos on her body as she hoisted off the top. For a moment Warren contemplated changing plans and heading directly back to Tibbets Manor so that both women could get cleaned up before entering the next phase of the evening's events.

"We're picking Abby up down at the Bayside Hilton in Portland. She's had some changes in her schedule that had to be dealt with. And then we need to convene for tonight's *real* sacrifice."

Warren glanced at the watch on his left hand. The time read 7:47 p.m. His eyes fell upon the highway again, then dropped to the deformed hand on the steering wheel.

In his mind, he was four years old again, and his father was once again angry as hell.

"Pull his fucking sleeve down, will ya?" Colin Pembroke barks at his mother, pointing to the rolled-up sleeves of his gray hoodie. "For Christ's sake, I'm sick of people looking at our kid like he's a freak."

Janis Pembroke sighs heavily and squats down next to the toddler version of Warren, where she takes the sleeve of his hoodie—the one with the New England Patriots emblem ironed on across the front; Warren will never grow up to play sports, but as a kid, he can still be a fan—and unrolls it so that the cuff extends halfway across his palm.

"He's just a boy, Colin," his mother answers. "It's not his fault. You can't keep treating him like there's something wrong with him. If the world thinks he's a freak, it's *their* problem, not ours."

The four-year-old version of himself is fighting back tears. They are at the Cumberland Fair, and some old woman in the 4H building has just noticed how badly Warren's right hand is deformed. She gasps audibly and begins making the sign of the cross right there in front of the rows of vegetables with blue and red award ribbons beside them. Once upon a time, when Colin Pembroke was a child, this very carnival used to have a freak show, where human oddities with deformed limbs and exotic medical conditions thrilled the crowd of onlookers brave enough to pay the fifty cents to enter the tent. Those days have passed by the time Colin's only son is born, but it is a true story that senior Pembroke is only too happy and too quick to pass on to his child.

"You could have made a fortune for us," Colin Pembroke will tell his child one night after dinner and a few cold brewskis. This would have been around when Warren was seven. "You could have been 'Warren, the Goat Boy'! People would have come from miles around to see you up on stage with the other freaks."

"Colin, stop it!" his mother responds for him. Warren can still smell the scent of Bois de Violette perfume as she wraps her arms around his trembling body to protect him from his father's drunken outbursts. It is a fragrance he will later discover was a bit more expensive than a school-teacher can really afford, but that is not a reason to hold a grudge against her. Staying with her drunken, abusive husband, however…

"Warren, you said we could get high!" Charlene tugged hard on the sleeve covering his deformed hand, and for a split second he wished the hand worked well enough to reach out and choke the life right out of that burnt-out cunt.

"We'll get high after we pick up Abby, okay? We'll stop back at the house, and you can smoke all the meth you want. But for now, you need to just fucking shut up. Can you do that?"

By thirteen, Warren found an avid fascination with American carnival freak shows. The now-teenage version of himself spent his free time at the Portland Public Library pulling books on P.T. Barnum and Tom Norman and a literal cast of thousands of human marvels and oddities. Part of it was a quest to understand his identity. A deeper, more sinister part of him was really charting a path of all the people to blame, and at the top of that list were Colin and Janis Pembroke. Colin, with his never-ending bottle of scotch, and Janis, with the genetic cocktail of chaotic chromosomes that she'd inherited from Vernon and Doris Lange. Those messed-up chromosomes have, of course, passed on to the last vestige of the Pembroke family. With no brothers or sisters and no cousins, this cursed existence ends with Warren. At this stage of his life, Warren has been called a freak by nearly everyone he's ever encountered in the South Portland school system, bullied by all the jocks and hoodlums, and mocked by the girls that found his hand repulsive.

"I don't mean to be rude in asking," Clara French, the manager at the McDonald's that gave him his first paying job had asked him during his interview, "...but what on earth happened to your arm? Were you born like that?"

Warren Pembroke—the seventeen-year-old version, the young man that lost his mother less than six months before to an unexpected "freak accident"—smiles a handsome grin back at the plump woman with her blonde hair in a neat ponytail beneath the navy blue sun visor of her fast-food uniform. The woman is stuffed into a bench in the dining area with his job application splayed out in front of her. Seventeen-year-old Warren sits across from her. His smile is almost handsome, and that is the damnable thing about his deformity; it spoils what otherwise might have been a perfect package. At seventeen, Warren is growing into a handsome young man hauling around what looks like an animal leg. It is cosmically unfair. It's a fucking curse. Other seventeen-year-old boys are standing in front of their mirrors, looking at their backward reflections as they squeeze zits until they pop or comb their oily hair for the hundredth time before picking up their best gals in their daddy's cars and doing all the things that Warren would never get to do.

"I rescued some orphans from a burning building," he answers Clara French, looking deep into her brown eyes and seeing nothing remotely human about her. "I got my arm caught when the floor above caved and fell on top of me. The doctors did the best they could to save it, but..." Warren closes his eyes, and the smile slips away. "I'm sure I can still flip hamburgers with my left hand. I'm not disabled."

The van was almost at the Portland exit. Warren hit the turn signal with his good hand and steered the van onto the exit ramp. When he did, the boxes in the back of the van shifted again, sending Caroline sprawling toward the other side of the vehicle.

"Ouch! Holy shit, man! Could you please slow down on the turns?"

"Sorry," he said to nobody in particular.

Warren steered the van through Saturday night traffic, weaving through headlights and taillights until the Econoline pulled up outside the Bayside Hilton. Abby Silverstein was standing there in a long blue dress and white cotton sweater, waiting. She had her *Coach* purse slung around her neck so that the strap passed directly between the cleavage of her bosom. The jewels on her necklace and earrings reflected in the street-lamps, giving her the appearance of something between a princess and a call girl. She smiled and waved as the van came to a halt and Warren shifted into park.

He leaned over and spoke into Charlene's ear. "Get in the back with Caroline."

"I'm gonna be sick if I don't get high soon,' Charlene sobbed. Her chin was now quivering, and he could tell that withdrawal was beginning to kick the shit out of her insides.

"You will," he answered in a cool, soothing voice.

Charlene opened the door and jumped out. Abby unslung the purse from her body and scooted into the passenger seat. She closed the door and yanked her seatbelt down around her body. Warren leaned over and placed his deformed hand on her chin, turning her face until she was looking at his.

"We missed you today," he said with a smile, and then his lips were mashing into hers. Abby resisted at first, and then she found herself returning his kiss. Their tongues met briefly, and then she was pulling away.

"Sorry, but things have been busy this week. Once I get through this weekend, I have whole big bunches of free time."

"Did you get the stuff I asked for? Did you take care of business with Rhashan?"

Warren shifted the van back into drive and took off in the direction of the Tibbets bungalow, where the junkie in the backseat's husband was currently decomposing in the basement.

"Yeah, I got it." Abby was still clutching her purse, which she patted with her right hand as if to verify. The diamond tennis bracelet on her wrist sparkled under the passing street lamps. "You know I don't like visiting your dealers. It would be very bad for my reputation to get pinched by the cops on a drug charge."

"It would be very bad for your reputation to get caught helping us dispose of dead bodies, but you do it every now and then, don't you?" Warren's smile grew grotesquely wide. Abby hated it when he smiled like this; it was another sign that their acquaintanceship was due to be severed. She could go on just fine without him, and if she really needed to, she knew ways to murder him and make it look like an accident. Of course, there were the other two women in the backseat, the junkie and the topless vagabond, whose role in their association was still yet to be determined. If they witnessed anything, she would have to off them as well. Things were now beyond complicated and tiresome. If things didn't change soon, drastic measures would *have* to be taken.

"Rhashan said he didn't like what he had to go through to get the shit you wanted," Abby patted the Coach purse again. "He said if you want any more of it, you'll have to go through a different dealer. What the hell do you have me carrying around here?"

"Do you have drugs up there, Abby? Do you have meth?" Charlene was groaning in agony from somewhere in the darkness of the van.

My hand was bitten by a shark when my family vacationed in Florida, Warren once told a teacher in junior high school.

I damaged my hand when I stuck a butter knife into an electrical outlet when I was three, he told Pastor Marcus Dietz after Sunday School, when Pastor Marc, as he told all the kids in the United Church of Christ to call him, as if they were all somehow "buddies" in God's name, asked him about it.

I got bit by a rabid fox.

I was abducted by aliens, and they experimented on me.

I was a leper in a past life. I'm reincarnated, as a matter of fact.

The last thought slapped him awake as Charlene continued to rant from behind him about narcotics, opiates, and hallucinogens.

This has all happened before. I'm almost sure of it, and I can't even say how, but I know that somewhere, maybe in a past life, I've done this shit already. And now I'm doing it again.

"It's a drug called 'Devil's Breath'," he said, his eyes looking at Charlene through the rearview mirror. "If Rhashan was put off by obtaining it, it must be something more powerful than I calculated. We can't afford to waste any of it. We're going to need it to carry out our plans."

"It damn well oughtta be powerful, for the amount of money you paid for it," Abby said. "What exactly does it do?"

Warren Pembroke smiled that terrible smile once again. "You'll see."

Chapter 6

"Holy shit, it's Erik the Black!"

Sergeant Richard Mendel was standing by the flagpole at the Hetfield Community School, smoking a cigarette and looking bemused the way those jocks on the high school football team always did whenever some freshman geek tried out for the team. It was the look of scornful dismissal. Erik Marsh recognized it immediately, but approached the yellow caution tape anyway.

"Up yours, Dickie. I need to get inside. Has the crime scene been secured enough that you can give me a walk-through?"

"I don't know what you're talking about, son. The *other* guy from *The Beacon* has already been through here, along with reporters from plenty of other news outlets. He had one of them fucking wetback names. Alvarez, I think. Little Mexican guy with long hair and a goatee. He said you weren't covering the crime beat anymore. Is that true?"

Erik felt his cheeks instantly flush. That loose-lipped little Latino motherfucker was already badmouthing him to gain credibility. Had he done the same thing back when he started reporting? Did he throw someone else under the bus to break his first big story? For the life of him, Erik couldn't remember, but that didn't necessarily mean it wasn't true. The guy that ran the crime beat before him, Lou Malone, had been in journalism longer than Erik had been alive when he arrived at the *Portland Beacon*. Old Lou made Erik think of the old Ross McDonald character, Lew Archer, but Archer had been a private dick in a string of old noir detective stories. Lou Malone probably could have been a private investigator, had the knack for following leads and sniffing out evidence until perps were forced from the shelter of "alleged" to the world of "guilty." Lou's reporting somehow always aided the police as if he was doing their job for them. How many thugs had been collared and sentenced to life in Thomaston Prison because of Lou? How many crimes did Erik ever help to solve in his own tenure? While he was cutting his teeth on the crime beat, Lou Malone was being awarded the Key to the City by Mayor Kane. Three short years later, Lou was gone from *The Beacon,* and Erik was covering all the local crime stories.

What the fuck ever became of Lou Malone?

Who did Lou screw over to get the crime beat desk?

"Sergeant Mendel, I understand that *The Beacon* sent the newbie up here to report, but I have a feeling I can be of greater use to you. Luis is new at this gig, and he's got no fucking clue what to look for at a crime scene like this. You know me! You know I might be able to spot a few bits of information that he may have missed." Erik thought back to the report that Paula woman gave to Truth Carson on the Cable News Channel, hoping to glean an edge of omniscience that would convince the representative of the Maine State Police that his presence was vital.

The Omniscient Eye, he found his mind remembering. *If only Svetlana were here with her gift of sight…*

"You're looking for a guy that calls himself 'Le'Sinestre'," Erik added. "Dick, walk me through the crime scene and let me take some notes. Give me a chance to help you."

By now the school's principal, Monica Hammond, and the school's Superintendent, John Durocher, were huddled together with various teachers and PTO committee members over by the flagpole, whispering amongst themselves and casting dour glances toward the entrance of the building. It was a cinch that several of them were sending text messages and posting reports on Facebook about what was going on inside the elementary school in the heart of their hometown. Most of that information was going to be based on generalizations and speculation until the State Police could issue their official report, which wasn't going to happen until at least Monday morning.

Another voice hollered out from behind him.

"Is that Erik the Black? Holy shit! What the hell is *he* doing here?"

Erik felt his face flush all over again. Officer Anderson had just parked his cruiser over behind Erik's Honda and was making his way toward the tape. By now all the exterior school lights were lit, illuminating the parking lot of the campus, along with the growing line of school officials and concerned citizens, as if it were daytime. Beyond that, one of the other state police officers in an SUV had backed up a sodium arc light so that it pointed toward the façade of the school, and when he flipped the "on" switch, the whole front of the school burned in faux illumination. Erik Marsh could feel the heat from the lamp warming the cool, clammy skin on his neck. The early summer sun had been warm, but once it set, the temperature began to drop steadily. Before long, the evening fog would roll in off the river and settle like a blanket all over the town.

Sergeant Mendel leaned in close to him so that they were face to face. "Convince me why you really want to help. Tell me, honestly, why you actually give a fuck. 'Cuz Alvarez tells me that you ain't even working the crime beat anymore and that makes me suspicious as hell of your motivations. Alvarez says you're working the local section now, covering tea socials and charity walk-a-thons. Is that true?"

Erik met the big man's gaze. He knew the state trooper extremely well from all the cases he'd responded to while reporting for *The Beacon* over the past decade. The fact that the trooper was making him feel inferior solidified the fact that Erik Marsh was no Lou Malone. Lou would have been invited in already to examine the crime scene, and in all likelihood, he would have found a clue or two the police had overlooked. Erik had to practically beg for it. It felt degrading. It felt like his request for a transfer was more than justified; it was mandatory.

"Richard, my boy Owen goes to school here. I don't give a flying fuck about the story. I want to help you capture the sonofabitch that did this and put him away for life. I want to make sure my son is safe here."

Sergeant Richard Mendel stared long and hard at Erik's face. There was a brief moment where Erik was certain Mendel would cry "bullshit" and send him on his way without setting one foot inside the school. The moment passed, and then the big officer—Erik had him pegged at 6'4"—was lifting the yellow crime scene tape to allow him entrance.

"Hey, Pete." Mendel turned toward Officer Anderson as the smaller trooper approached the police line. "Take this guy inside and let him have a look at the cafeteria. If he asks any questions, I want you to fill him in with the facts as best as you can. Got it?"

The inside of the Hetfield Community School was a bloodbath. Erik was used to the smell of death and decomposition from all the crime scenes he'd reported on, but the halls of the school alone gave the impression of walking through an abattoir. There were chunks of animal offal strewn across the walls of the main foyer, some defying gravity and sticking where they'd splattered upon impact, while others had tumbled to rest on the floor in tacky puddles of crimson. There were evidence flags strewn everywhere in numerical sequence, only the sequence Erik found himself walking into was already in the sixties. The first fifty or so led in reverse order toward the back of the building, where the assailants had broken in. The numbers persisted forward as Officer Anderson led him toward the cafeteria.

"I sure hope you ain't eaten anything in the last few hours or so because you're liable to upchuck once we get inside." Officer Anderson turned toward Erik and grinned. The guy looked like he was on the fringe of becoming a lunatic himself. It really didn't take all that much, Erik knew from first-hand experience. There's a fine line between sanity and madness. A tiny switch nestled in the cerebral cortex or some other soft spot in the brain. Trip it once, and there's no coming back. There's only a lifetime of broken reality once it's been flipped. "Oh, and watch your step. All the overhead fluorescent bulbs have been smashed out. Move slowly, and try not to kick too much glass around."

Officer Anderson used his sleeved elbow to push open the cafeteria door. The scent hit Erik the hardest.

"Oh, my God," he whispered as the funk of splayed offal hit him. "I can't breathe!"

"You're gonna want to smear this under your nostrils." Officer Anderson pulled a small jar of Vick's VapoRub out of his pants pocket and tossed it to him. "It'll help. And just remember that it's only animal carcasses inside. We don't need no fucking coroner's report to confirm that. Mostly dogs and cats. The bodies were mutilated and discarded right in the center of the cafeteria, and then the suspects used them to mess up the halls on their way out. The bitch of it is that whoever did this knew how to dismantle the security system the school had in place. Based on that information alone, we suspect that this had to have been an inside job. Someone who either worked for the school or was present when the alarm system was originally activated. You don't just break into a school without appearing on video surveillance or triggering alarms to the local police department."

"You don't, unless you've spent enough time casing the joint or happen to be an expert on disarming surveillance systems," Erik answered. "For all we know, it could be a disgruntled parent or a bunch of dumb teens that just got lucky. Let's get inside the cafeteria and look around."

The light from the sodium arc lamp outside radiated through the glass windows and lit up portions of the cafeteria, but not well enough to see perfectly. Fractals of glass sparkled in reflective piles underneath the damaged ceiling fixtures. The piles formed comically neat rows on the bare floor where the dining tables had once been. The tables had been collapsed and now leaned haphazardly against the walls. A few had toppled onto the floor, their stiff legs protruding at unnatural angles, making them look like large, dead animals.

The chalked pentagram on the floor looked even bigger in real life than it had on his television set. If Erik had to hazard a guess, the diameter had to have been at least six feet across. The circumference was eerily perfect, as if someone had taken the time to run a protractor from the center and arc a complete circle. The pentagram inside was also perfect; a star whose points fell on perfect angles and uncanny symmetry. Somebody methodically cut precise lines and angles to create the perfect blasphemy. Erik did not need to squint his eyes to protract the goat head the star created. It practically leaped up off the floor and hovered above the burned-down candles and blood puddles.

Directly in the center of the star was a ceramic chalice, filled with blood and swarmed by flies that darted and hovered about the rim. Somewhere outside, under the cover of darkness, were people who had sipped of this unholy communion. This was not the work of disgruntled citizens or bored teenagers; this was something that lingered in the realm of wickedness, something that reflected the antithesis of purity and sanctimony.

"Whoever made this wasn't the least bit in a hurry," Erik spoke out loud. "They were precise. Complete. They took their time to get it right."

"Which rules out teenagers," Officer Anderson agreed. He was shining his flashlight into the darkened valleys and corners of the cafeteria while Erik examined the floor. "We've already picked up on that. High school kids would have done it in a hurry, afraid they'd get caught. And even the lowest high school thug wouldn't have killed the animals in here so precisely. If you look at the carcasses, they were killed in such a way that the least amount of blood was spilled before they were hauled in here. Most were probably carried in here whole and butchered outright by the perpetrators." The officer pointed to a cat's body splayed out on one of the dining tables. Its calico fur was matted with congealed blood.

Erik was only half-listening. His eyes had fallen onto the syntax painted in animal blood around the walls of the cafeteria. The text had appeared fragmentary on the report from the Cable News Channel, but now that he was observing it up close, he was able to absorb the words more clearly. On the wall next to the window where the staff from food services prepared meals for his son and his schoolmates was the beginning of some bizarre text. It read:

SUFFER THE LITTLE CHILDREN TO COME UNTO ME,
THAT THEY WILL FIND TRUTH, WHERE THE GOSPELS
HAVE LIED.
FOR I, ALONE, WILL TEACH THEM THE TRUTH ABOUT LIFE
AND DEATH AND EXISTENCE.
THE LORD JESUS IS ALL A LIE.
I WILL SHOW THEM THIS!

Moving clockwise to the northern wall of the dining room, to where a white projection screen—the one that digital film projectors, those vessels that replaced the old reel-to-reel projectors of the past, amused the children with videos from Walt Disney and Dreamworks and such on special occasions—dangled just out of the kiddies' reach, the message continued.

I AM THE TRUE WAY.
THE DARK LORD TRUSTS ME ALONE TO OPEN THEIR LITTLE
EYES TO THE TRUTH!
BEHOLD, GOMORRAH, FOR YOU HAVE PROVED
YOURSELVES SINNERS,
AND I, ALONE, AM THE SALVATION.
THE CHILDREN ARE MINE, AND WILL PAY THE PRICE OF
GENERATIONS.

More animal offal, only now there were bloody marks below the text on the walls, as if someone took the time to coat themself in blood and press their body against the plaster. Erik could tell easily that the body that formed the bloodied prints was female, as the breast marks pressed against the ivory paint were a C-cup approximation.

He closed his eyes and tried to imagine the Satanist that could coat herself in animal blood and writhe around against the school cafeteria wall where his only child ate his lunch every day. Would she have been the same person to mathematically chart a perfect pentagram on the floor? Probably not. The woman with the bloodied breast prints was probably following orders, and by the appearance of her work, she was less about precision and more about flaunting her sexuality.

"You're seeing it, too," Officer Anderson announced, his voice echoing off the cafeteria walls. "There's obviously more than one person at work here. The person who sketched the pentagram is deliberate, methodical. I'm guessing most likely male. The person whose body prints are on the walls is obviously female."

Erik turned to the third wall, the one that separated the cafeteria from the outside hallway. The text continued.

I AM THE LIGHT OF LUCIFER,
AND I WILL GUIDE THE CHILDREN HOME.
YOU WILL KNOW ME BY THE NAME...
LE'SINESTRE!

"Le'Sinestre," Erik repeated out loud.

"It sounds French, doesn't it?" Officer Anderson was now shining his flashlight on the signature on the wall. "I think it means, 'The Evil One' or something."

"It's not French," Erik answered. "It's Latin. It translates roughly to the 'left-handed'." He turned toward Officer Anderson, who immediately lowered his flashlight. "There are books in the Old Testament that clearly dictated that people who are left-handed are somehow affiliated with the Devil. Leviticus or Deuteronomy. I don't quite know. The guy we're looking for, the one who orchestrated all of *this*, I'm guessing he's predominantly left-handed, and he takes it as some kind of sign that he's somehow special."

Erik looked back at the perfect pentagram in the center of the floor. The flies buzzed madly about the chalice in the middle, their hum a monotonous drone of cold finality in the otherwise quiet room. "Whoever drew that made a perfect circle and a perfect star, and he did it with his left hand." He stood quietly for a moment, observing the significance of the act alone. "This wasn't an act of vandalism. This is an actual calling card."

"A calling card, huh?" Officer Anderson raised his arm and shined his flashlight into the darkened space just behind where they'd entered the room. "Then what the hell would you call *that?*"

Erik turned to see the dead goat that had been crucified directly into the wall. Long iron spikes poked out of the beast's legs, forming bloodied punctures just above each hoof. Gravity had already taken its toll, as the animal was sagging forward—almost ready to topple—in an arch that suggested the joints of its front haunches were dislocated. The goat's head dangled, its tongue lolling out of its open mouth. Tendrils of blood and saliva stretched toward the floor from the tip of the dead beast's chin.

"Look at its belly," Officer Anderson said. "They slit it exactly how the Romans pierced our Lord Jesus so that he'd bleed to death. That poor fucking animal was alive when they did this to it. Now, we didn't let Alvarez or any of them other news people take photographs of that. We're not going to cause a public panic. As far as we're concerned, we want people to *believe* that all this shit is just vandalism until we catch these sick fuckers. Do you read me? These people are the real deal."

"I read you. So what's your plan for catching them?"

Svetlana Barnyk sat at one of the patio tables outside the Meridian Café. The café was directly across Congress Street from Monument Square, where she'd just finished tonight's street performance. She finished her show to the usual chorus of cheers and applause, packed her gear back onto her handcart, and brought her show accoutrements back up to her lime-green Volkswagen Beetle. After locking up most of the evening's take inside her glove compartment for safekeeping, she flitted her way to the corner crosswalk at the intersection of Congress and Temple Street, where she nearly tripped over Ernie, the homeless guy who occupied the entranceway to one of the empty buildings. Ernie, like herself, had a collection hat out, only his performance consisted of a chorus of drunken snores where he laid out on the ratty blanket beneath him. Ernie had a cardboard sign behind him that read, *Jesus is watching, please help if you can!* Svetlana recognized her own handwriting, as she had helped him make the sign the summer before. Ernie had watched her perform on many occasions and had always smiled and clapped for her as she took her final bows. It made her heart ache to see that he still had it, and she found herself near tears as she passed.

Ernie coughed and hacked for a few seconds, changed positions on the hard sidewalk, then fell back into his drunken slumber.

At least you survived another winter, she thought. Svetlana reached into her canvas tote bag and retrieved her wallet. She pulled out a few singles and dropped them into his hat. *No performance necessary tonight, my friend,* she thought as she turned away and sauntered on toward the café.

She could afford the donation and was happy to give it. The Carpathian Great and Tiny Circus was always profitable on Saturday evenings, and tonight's performance had been no exception. Her meal of lentil soup and corned beef Panini came courtesy of some old geezer who dropped a ten-spot in her collection hat. He had blushed and smiled a grin of stained dentures as he tried to rub her lipstick off his cheek while his ancient wife glared in disapproval. At the Meridian, there were a handful of other tables set out on the sidewalk outside the café—white wooden tabletops on wrought-iron legs, each built for an occupancy of two. The tables came complete with Mason jar candles flickering precariously in the breeze rolling in off the waterfront. Only one couple was dining outside, and the ambiance seemed to be turning their innocent flirtations into something more romantic. Even the music floating lazily from the solitary speaker below the canvas awning by the café's entrance suggested amorous liaisons, leaving her feeling lonesome in spite of the unending ebb of people still milling about the concourse of Monument Square. The formidable parade of cars moving back and forth on Congress Street, each looking for that coveted empty spot to park in and join in the evening festivities, added to the ambiance.

Svetlana had been thinking about Erik all afternoon, long after their chance encounter when he came out of the office building across the street looking for his journalism piece to write about for his new column. She'd given him his story about her life as a street performer and told him about the *Omniscient Eye,* already knowing full well that he would never write about it and put her in possible jeopardy. Svetlana wasn't sure if she'd been testing his virtue, or whether it was even fair of her to do so, but she had established honesty up front, and that was enough. Erik seemed interested in her in a sincere way. Much of it had been curiosity, and Svetlana was sure that mutual attraction was definitely a big part of it. He was older than her by a good amount of years—enough so that her brother would not have approved—and he was divorced with a son already in grade school, which Papa would not have approved, but she saw decency in him. The *Omniscient Eye* never lied. Erik had flaws, but so did everybody. That made him human.

After their brief encounter, Svetlana coasted through her day job at *Bayside Assisted Living*, where she spent her afternoon working with Daisy Leonard, a septuagenarian with Down Syndrome, who loved to paint with water colors and acrylics but had enormous difficulty with her physical health and personal hygiene; Dylan Pensky, a mentally retarded twenty-three year old who wet himself frequently and rambled on about how he wanted to be God; and Da'Quell Nye, a thirty-year-old African American veteran who came home from Afghanistan missing his right leg and a good portion of his torso, both from an improvised explosive device that he stumbled across after his company's explosive ordinance disposal unit somehow missed it when securing a base of operations outside Kabul. Da'Q also suffered from Post-Traumatic Stress Disorder, which rendered him incapable of socializing in public places without a constant dread that something around him was about to explode. The cherry on top of his dog shit ice cream sundae came in the form of a divorce notice from his wife after she discovered what happened to her man while he was overseas. Svetlana had spent a lot of time worrying about Da'Q, but whenever she managed to touch his hand, the *Omniscient Eye* saw only a fighter and a survivor. The man still had a long life ahead of him, and just like she'd felt about her own honesty with Erik, it was enough.

The amplifier above the door had been playing "When a Man Loves a Woman" by Percy Sledge, and when the next song came on, Svetlana found herself frozen in her seat. The candle in the Mason jar flickered in the cool tidal breeze, but the chill on her skin from hearing the lyrics caused her flesh to break out in goosepimples. It was by a very young Cher. The opening notes of the song plinked out carnivalesque calliope notes from the speaker, and then the darkened evening air filled with the lyrics to "Gypsies, Tramps, and Thieves," and Svetlana felt her mind tumbling back to Eastern Europe, where her Mama was now dead and buried in a plot of earth somewhere near the southern border of Ukraine. In her mind's eye, she could see *Zee Doctor,* the phantom that had traveled in the caravan of gypsies that her own family belonged to although he had no known origin or kin to place the rogue apothecary within their tribe. *That* reality never escaped her. After her immigration into the United States, she had come across a copy of Bram Stoker's novel *Dracula* and had seen the cursory sketch of the real Vlad Tepes; she had shuddered to see the very likeness of *Zee Doctor* in the flowing hair and mustachioed scowl of the man who had sliced open the flesh of her forehead and pushed the *Omniscient Eye* into her cranium, as if the bone of her skull was nothing more than clay to his touch.

But in the night all the men would come around, and lay their money down.

"T'ings aren't safe for you anymore," Aldo had told her. She could recall how handsome her older sibling was, with his long, flaxen hair tied in a ponytail and the soft whiskers of his beard perfectly trimmed and groomed. He wasn't in his show wardrobe of clean white silk shirt and black leather vest, but in denim jeans that seemed too bulky for his frame and a black t-shirt with the *White Zombie* logo stenciled in crooked red letters across the front. Aldo had spent a great many nights dreaming of escaping to America to embrace the culture of heavy metal and musical rebellion.

Svetlana Barnyk had just turned thirteen years old and fallen victim to the curse of womanhood for the first time. The hemorrhaging began in a camp somewhere in Serbia, and Svetlana, thinking she was dying, shrieked in terror as she wiped after using the toilet in some two-bit hostel inside the city. Aldo had been in the room next door watching television when he heard the screaming; he'd thought perhaps an intruder had meant to do harm to his younger sister.

"Shimi should have told you about dis," he said almost apologetically after she came out of the stall and thrust her arms around her older brother. "You are a woman now. You can get pregnant. The tings Papa is going to ask of you to do aren't fair. No, not at all. Der are going to be men dat are attracted to you and vill vant to have zer vay vith you. And dey vill pay good money for it. I vish tings could be different, but dat is something I cannot change. You're menstruating, and dat means you can carry a baby now. Do you understand?"

The tone in his voice was one of sheer heartbreak.

The younger version of Svetlana shook her head in shame.

"Da men vill vant to have sex vith you," Aldo said, lowering his eyes to the ground. "Zey von't see you as a girl anymore. Zey'll see you as a woman. Sister, zey'll vant to put their man-parts inside you." Aldo's cheeks flushed as he said this, and his eyes welled with tears.

The younger version of Svetlana could sense the absolute agony and shame radiating off her brother's skin, and it made her feel dirty and ashamed as well.

"Papa knows all this, and he doesn't care. Sister, you are old enough to know da truth. Papa used to let strange men have zer vay with Mama because zey paid good money for it. And now, look at you! You are old enough to grow breasts and be thought of as attractive by the old men who come to our shows. It has already happened to Shimi. You've seen the vay the men stare at her ven she dances. Da men all vant her, and those that have money get to have her." Aldo was now crying, as if his tear ducts had let loose an arroyo that could flood the whole of the fields where their caravan had camped. "I don't vant this for you, Svetlana." Aldo dried his cheeks with the sleeve of his shirt.

"I'll find a vay!" he whispered, his penetrating hazel eyes meeting hers once more. "Little sister… I'll find a vay to get you out of here. I don't know vere life will take you, but I pray it isn't here because zere's nothing here for you but shame." Aldo hung his head. "*Zee Doctor* gave you the *Omniscient Eye*. I vatched him do it. He took de eye out of Mama and put it inside *you*. I'll find a vay to get you out of here, but once you go, you vill be on your own. You'll have to use *The Eye* to find a vay to safety. It vill tell you who you can trust and who to stay away from. Do you understand?"

The younger version of Svetlana was crying now. Seeing her brother weep in shame was almost more than she could bear. And the truth was, this world of traveling carnival attractions was all she knew. Svetlana understood Papa selling homemade distilled whiskey and Aldo with his throwing knives and Shimi belly dancing with lavender and turquoise veils around her face and beads around her neck and her bosom barely covered. That was the whole world to her, and it made sense. Papa had money to put food on the table and keep their caravan moving from bloc to bloc across Europe, and it kept the crowd happy in spite of the poverty and the threat of violence in the changing face of the war-torn continent.

The Barnyk family had not known prosperity, but it thrived and moved on with frightening efficiency. And that, like everything else in her life, had been enough.

Unbeknownst to Mikhail Barnyk, his son began skimming revenue off box office tills, and Shimi began hoarding tips from the men that "came around to lay their money down" on her so that the youngest of the Barnyks could escape Europe permanently and find passage to the United States.

On a cold November morning, when their caravan had found their way into Italy, Aldo secured barter to send his younger sister aboard a freighter that would pass through the Mediterranean Sea and dock in London, and then set sail across the cold, winter Atlantic Ocean for New York. There would be one last performance for the youngest of the Barnyk family in a street carnival outside Tuscany, where Svetlana would perform her silly slight-of-hand illusions and quirky acrobatics that she'd later perfect for The Carpathian Great and Tiny Circus. And once the act started and she noticed Papa at the far edge of the audience whispering with *Zee Doctor*, she knew things were about to go terribly wrong.

All she could truly remember of the Old World was *Zee Doctor* and how much he looked like a vampire as he performed haphazard surgery on her to impregnate her brain with the *Omniscient Eye*. Somehow, she'd known all along that he had been an evil entity, and no matter where she went, she could feel him close by.

The song ended, and Svetlana Barnyk looked up from what was left of her dinner. Half of her Panini remained uneaten, and she immediately thought of Ernie laying on the sidewalk only a few storefronts away. At least she could make sure the old man had food in his belly for the night. She turned toward the plate glass window and rapped on the glass. A waiter who had been standing nearby noticed her and came outside.

"Is there something I can get you?" the young man asked. In his neatly pressed white shirt and black trousers, he reminded Svetlana of her brother. How handsome he had looked the last time she saw him alive.

"Yes, please. I'd like to get the rest of my dinner wrapped up to go."

In her peripheral vision, she watched a white Ford Econoline van cruise down Congress Street and stop at the intersection and wait for the traffic light to change from red to green.

"Sure, no problem." The waiter slipped back inside the Meridian Café, then returned moments later with a small plastic container and a designer paper bag with the initials *MC* and the words *Portland's Number 1 Bistro* stenciled over a mosaic of colored blocks. The waiter picked up her plate, slid the remaining half of the sandwich flawlessly into the plastic container, and then bagged the container neatly for her.

"Here you go, ma'am. Enjoy the rest of your evening."

Again, in her peripheral vision, the white van had apparently done a U-turn and was now charging back down the boulevard in the direction it came from.

"T'ank you very much, I will," she replied, pushing a handful of singles into his free hand as he turned to take her table settings away. And then she was pushing her empty chair back underneath the table and making her way up Congress Street toward the Temple Street intersection.

When she arrived at the entrance to the storefront, Ernie was gone. She stood, confused, looking down on the ratty old blanket and the empty bourbon bottle and the filthy old hat that still held the dollar bills she'd dropped in for him. The old man, however, had disappeared. And with no family or friends to concern themselves about him, it was as if he'd never existed at all.

In the pit of her stomach, just as she had way back at her final performance in Tuscany, that gnawing feeling that something was about to go terribly wrong made her blood run cold.

"He's coming around."

Abby Silverstein was kneeling on the bum's feet in the back of the Econoline, keeping his legs from kicking and struggling. Caroline and Charlene were each pinning one of the old man's arms down to the floor of the van. They'd already removed the old man's grimy jacket and shirt, leaving him topless and exposed to their terrible plans. Ernie O'Malley's torso stank of body odor and excrement, and the pale pallor of his skin was coated with a muzzy layer of offending funk. Even the wisps of white chest hair were tainted from neglect.

Ernie opened his eyes.

Seeing the bloodshot eyes make the transition from swimming in disorientation to lucid understanding had an almost comical effect. Abby found herself biting her lower lip to refrain from laughing out loud.

"Please, please don't hurt me," the old man whimpered. "I got nothing to give you. Please just let me go. I'll do whatever you want!"

Warren Pembroke appeared from behind Abby, holding the craft knife in his left hand. "Oh, you will *anyway,* my friend. You don't have a choice. But if you can hold still long enough, you'll have a fighting chance of living through this unfortunate little episode."

Charlene and Caroline both laughed as the old man struggled.

"Hey, keep still, handsome!" Caroline, still topless and coated with dog blood, leaned forward and allowed her bare breasts to plop down onto the old man's face. She wiggled her body back and forth for a few seconds, mashing her bloody breasts against his cheeks until they, too, were tacky with blood, and then sat upright again. "There. You look much better now. Did you enjoy that? Do you like girls' titties in your face?"

Warren had allowed Charlene and Caroline a quick line of cocaine after parking the van behind the brick train trestle that extended over lower Congress Street. That particular section of thoroughfare forked into one-way traffic back at the St. John Street intersection, so that the vehicle was perfectly concealed in the enveloping darkness. The closest establishment now was a Denny's restaurant a quarter mile away, far away enough that whatever sounds coming from the back of the van would not be heard over the din of traffic and the noise of the occasional freight train that ran on the tracks above them.

Warren Pembroke smiled. He raised the instrument in his good hand above his head and spoke in a cold, emotionless tone. "Father Lucifer, I desecrate this soul in your holy name—"

His good hand came down, and the blade slashed across the old man's chest with surgical precision. Ernie O'Malley screamed into the darkness as pain gouged into his inebriated senses.

"—that he shall carry *your* message to the waiting world of sin and darkness."

A second slash across the old man's chest, and blood was now pouring out all over his filthy skin. The Harpies pinning him down laughed and taunted him as his body and soul became one with perfect agony.

Chapter 7

Sunday, June 5th

Joe Walton slipped out the back door of the Velvet Mojo for a quick cigarette to calm himself down before his matinee gig began. He'd been nervous enough just getting to the bar that morning, and when he saw the posters Higgens plastered all over the plate glass windows out front, reading *"Matinee performances only: 'Smokehouse Joe' Walton, direct from Luttrell Prison"* with his face photocopied from the picture that hung on his office wall, he damn near lost his cool and walked away. The Tennessee sun was already making the air swelter until it felt as if the paint on the tired, old bricks of both the bar and the building beside it—a Laundromat called Southern Suds—could just turn to dust and blow away. The concourse between the two buildings was narrow and reeked of centuries-old piss, and breathing in the caustic odor on top of the stifling air made Joe think of prison life in Mark H. Luttrell. It made him think of having to hear the prisoners on either side of his cell taking a shit as he lay on his bunk and tried to sleep through those hot summer evenings. He could stand the heat, even with his black suit and hat on, turning his nearly-bald head into a boiling kettle, but the scent and the memories that came from the alley made him nauseous.

He slipped down to the parking lot in the rear of the joint and pressed a cigarette between his lips, and then fumbled open a book of matches sporting the Velvet Mojo logo he'd snagged off the bar. With the fumes clogging out the piss stench, he could almost think again, and that felt like a relief. Higgins had paid him three hundred dollars the day before, and that scratch was half gone already. By Saturday night, Joe had bartered a room at the YMCA over on Elvis Presley Boulevard. It was a one-holer with a two-burner electric countertop stove and a mini refrigerator that could hold little more than a six-pack of beer and a cardboard Chinese takeout box. Joe knew this, as this was his big "First-Night-Outta-The-Joint" dinner. Even now, here on Sunday morning, there were still three bottles of Coors and a congealed version of sesame chicken on fried rice waiting for him if he could stomach it. Lord knew, he couldn't stomach it last night. There'd been too much grease and cheap beer and too many bad memories. The quiet solitude of civilian life drove him half-crazy, and that was *with* the wail of police sirens outside his window and the two junkies arguing down the hall from him.

Saturday's blessings allowed him a trip to the nearby Wal-Mart, where Joe purchased new underwear and socks and clean, white tank-top under-shirts. He bought himself a new leather belt and new shoes and a few t-shirts and shorts he noticed on the discount racks. He never even bothered to try them on, preferring to move through the store quickly and make sure nobody was paying the slightest bit of attention to him. That was another reality of prison life—that nagging feeling that everybody who lays eyes on you just knows you're guilty of something. A final stop in the pharmacy aisle to buy some disposable razors and shaving cream and a toothbrush, and then Joe was hustling back to the Y to wash up and get ready for his first real gig back in the free world.

He thought he'd be more nervous about it, but standing up on the stage and playing the blues again to a real, living crowd; it had felt like heaven. It felt like...

"It feels like *déjà vu*, doesn't it, boy?"

The blood in Joe Walton's veins went cold, turning the beads of sweat on his forehead and dripping from his armpits into daggers of ice.

"I ain't got no business with you." Joe took a long, deep drag off his cigarette, and then dropped it onto the macadam. He picked up his foot and ground the toe of his new leather shoe onto the butt and rubbed it out with fierce deliberation. He could feel the Devil practically right be-hind him, Ol' Scratch just as he'd appeared in the tobacco fields when he was just a boy, all white-skinned and burning eyes. Joe was certain that if he turned around and faced him, the Devil would not have aged the slightest bit, even though he himself had gone from a scrawny black boy to a worn-out old man with gray around the ears and white in his whiskers. *Time stands still in Hell,* he heard in his brain. *Eternity don't mean nothing if time stands still.*

"We both know that's not true, Joe. Your soul belongs to me."

"Only when I die," Joe whispered. "Until then, my life belongs to *me.* I got *free will.* That was never part of the bargain, was it? I can come and go as I please and do whatever the fuck I want until God sees fit to put me down. Ain't that right, you lying ol' bastard?"

Laughter from behind him. The sound of fingernails dragged down a chalkboard. He hadn't realized it, but Joe was suddenly *terrified* to look behind him. The truth was that he wasn't certain if the Devil was in human form after all, or if he was a demon with bat-like wings and goat horns on his head. The presence of evil was enough to put real fear into his heart.

"Oh, son. God doesn't work like *that.* He doesn't follow humans around and point his finger randomly when he 'sees fit'." More laughter. "You're all alone in this world. You're disposable. God doesn't *care* if you die. That's what makes you humans so…so compelling. You have *free will,* and you used it to murder the Hickey brothers. Tell me, did you see God standing nearby? Did he point a finger and say, 'Smite those two no-good mother-fuckers'?"

"It don't matter," Joe said. "The fact is, if you was gonna take my soul to Hell, you'd have done it by now. You already know I ain't gonna be your slave. I ain't gonna do your dirty work for you in the time I got left. Y'all just wasting your time on me, so you just go on back to Hell."

The laughter behind him grew deeper, more sinister. "You *will* do my bidding before your life is over. Everything is already in motion, Joe Walton. Stop wasting your time here. Your guitar is waiting for you up in Maine. Go up and find it, and I'll teach you how to play the most beautiful music."

Joe Walton spun around, not even realizing that his body was in motion, not even knowing if his eyes could handle the shock of facing the agitator of his damnation. There was only blind rage and adrenaline. There was only guttural instinct and curiosity.

Oppressive heat and the stench of piss billowed in from the alley-way. Joe peered down toward the busy street and saw the white folks standing in line by the door to the Velvet Mojo. Here it was on Sunday, the Lord's day, and the sinners were flocking to hear the blues rather than traipsing off to church to be saved.

The bar's alley door opened and Hank Willis popped his head out. From a distance, the bartender looked more like a prairie dog poking his head out of a hole in the desert sand.

"Roy said to get your ass back in here. You're on in two minutes and— Hey, are you okay? You look like you've seen a ghost or something."

Joe lifted his hat off his head and wiped the sweat away with the sleeve of his jacket. "I'm coming," he sighed. He locked down at the butt of the cigarette he'd just smoked. There was a long trail of blood trickling from the filter-end where his toe had mashed it into the ground.

"How y'all doing?"

Joe walked out from behind the red velvet stage curtain, picked up a power chord from off the chair that had been set out for him, and plugged in his Fender. He dialed the volume knob up and strummed twice, listening to the open strings ringing out from the amplifier behind him. The amp was one of the old house pieces, a Marshall with ripped fabric covering the woofer and tweeter and a line of knobs and switches along the top bar. The painted stencils indicating each knob's function had been worn completely off through the years of use and abuse in its life at the Velvet Mojo, but Joe had figured it all out with little difficulty. And of course, Joe had already run his sound check back at eleven, making sure the guitar was tuned perfectly so all he had to do was turn the amp on and plug in.

When Joe stepped on stage, he was ready to boogie. The round of whistles and applause in response made him smile.

The Velvet Mojo was full once again, and even with the stage lighting taking away most of his depth perception and ability to focus, he could still make out random faces hovering over beer bottles and hamburgers and chicken wings. Joe scanned harder, nearly certain that Ol' Scratch was out there sitting at one of the tables. He could feel in the pit of his stomach that something was still amiss. The daggers of frozen sweat had melted off again, trickling down his ribs somewhere beneath one of the new tank-top undershirts he'd thrown on after showering that morning. He strummed again with his fingers—the real bluesmen almost never used a pick—this time letting his fret hand tug and strangle the strings into a meld of harmony.

"Let's feel some blues, people!"

He'd spoken into the microphone and got a quick blast of feedback, and then Joe Walton was offering a throaty growl of lyrics while the notes he plucked on his guitar jangled through the amplifier behind him.

"I got my walking papers,
my baby said she don't want me no more!"

The crowd clapped and whistled from the sea of tables in front of him.

"I got my walking papers,
my baby said she don't want me no more!"

His long, bony fingers issued back and forth between bar chords and finger-picking notes up and down the fretboard.

"That woman just fired my ass,
and sent me packing out her door."

The room erupted into hoots and hollers, and Joe found himself smiling in spite of that sinking feeling that still gnawed at his gut. *The people haven't changed,* he thought. *Even after all these years, the people still relate to the blues. They still feel good about songs that should make 'em feel bad.*

His index finger slid up the B string, and he launched into a solo of notes that wailed like broken-hearted mistresses, while his eyes pierced once again through the veil of the stage lighting into the darkness of the crowd. The room was filled with local blue-collar stiffs and tourists and college kids and unemployed folks drowning their sorrows. Their faces were white and black and brown. There were two Japanese men at the end of the bar, older guys that looked like they had no earthly business in a joint like this, but there they were, clapping along with the rest of 'em. Joe leaned toward the mic to deliver the next verse.

"Another man gonna do the job,
of loving my baby tonight!"

He could smell the scent of piss. It came suddenly, obtrusively, and for a fraction of a second, Joe almost lost his place in the song.

"I said, another man gonna do the job,
of loving my baby tonight!"

The scent grew stronger, fouler, and the droplets of sweat on his skin
were daggers again. Somewhere in that sea of black and white faces, Ol'
Scratch was watching. He could feel that presence of evil, and he forced
himself to concentrate on the song and the people in the audience.

*Just keep your shit together. Keep it together, and then you can get the fuck outta
here and get yourself some whiskey. You still got some cash left in your wallet to get
good and drunk tonight.*

"My broken heart is now unemployed,
and I'll be crying 'til the morning light!"

He was still pulling through the notes, but his fingers were beginning
to fidget. He could tell in how the jangle of notes from the amplifier behind him was quickly growing shaky with tremolo. It was when he heard
the voice from the audience that his guitar playing fell apart.

"It's that nigger! That murdering nigger that killed us!"

Joe's eyes flashed toward a table by the window at the front of the
bar. The Velvet Mojo's red curtains had been drawn across the bar's plate
glass windows, turning the bar into a darkened theater, but Joe could still
manage to discern the person whose voice had brought the room to silence. There was no skin on the man's face, nor on any part of his cadaverous body. There was only a map of crimson muscle tissue and blood
vessels forming cable networks up and down his extremities. But the
voice was instantly recognizable: Rufus Hickey, the older of the two redneck boys—and coincidentally the less intelligent one—was now standing
up and pointing toward him. His snaggletooth jaw was etched forever into
a hideous, lipless grin, with teeth stained brown and rotted from tobacco
and beer that he'd been too young to drink when he died.

"We're gonna getcha, nigger," the other cadaverous audience member
agreed. Leon Hickey, two years younger than Rufus but taller by a good
four inches, had only been fifteen years old the day he pulled the Colt 45
on Charles Walton and shot him dead. The bullet put an enormous, gaping hole in his father's forehead where his thoughts and feelings could
leak onto the hardwood floor of their kitchen in a puddle of blood and
chunks of gray matter. Leon then held the pistol on Mabel Walton as the
older Hickey brother tore off her apron and summer dress to rape her.

"Yer gonna die, 'Smokehouse Joe'!"

He'd stopped playing altogether, his heart jackhammering in his chest as his face looked out upon the crowd. They'd stopped clapping and whistling, but none of them seemed to be turned toward the table by the window where the two ghosts taunted and threatened him. It was as if they didn't even know his antagonists were there among them. Surely, somebody would have seen their bloodied faces and screamed in fright.

"Don't just stand there! Play something!" Roy Higgins had crept over to the side of the stage and hollered at him from somewhere behind the velvet curtain. "What the fuck is wrong with you?"

Hearing Roy's voice jarred him back to consciousness. Joe strummed again on the guitar and leaned into the microphone.

"I know a thing or two about Ol' Scratch,
When it comes to his bad business, there's always a catch."

The trance on the crowd broke again, and more hooting and whistling issued from the sea of darkness in front of the stage.

"We're gonna drag you down to Hell, nigger!" the phantom version of Rufus insisted at the top of his cold, dead lungs. "You just wait and see. We've got your mama down there, you know. We still take turns on her."

"Her dead pussy feels like old leather now," dead Leon agreed, ramming the balled-up muscle tissue of one closed fist into the opened other as if to signify something dreadfully lascivious. "She feels like a cold football now. We still fill it with our seed, though. It's like we just can't say 'no' to it."

The older Hickey laughed at that, the teeth of his eternal grin clicking and clattering as his dead jaw opened and closed.

"Y'all go back to Hell, motherfuckers!"

Joe jumped off the stage with his guitar still wrapped around his shoulder and torso. The power chord was still plugged into the amplifier, and when the chord went taut as he rushed toward the front of the bar, the line held fast, yanking the ancient Marshall amplifier over until it toppled onto the stage. When that happened, an explosion of sparks flew through the amp's front, setting the ripped fabric of its facade on fire.

"Tobacco Joe" Walton closed the gap between the stage and the table at the front of the bar in seconds. He'd already removed his instrument and had started swinging it at the two phantoms sitting at the table. It never even registered to him that the people he was bludgeoning with the Fender guitar were *not* the fleshless corpses of Leon and Rufus Hickey, the two boys he'd murdered to avenge what they'd done to his parents. They were actually a couple of newlyweds who had stopped to have a bite to eat and a few drinks before going off to tour Graceland. The side of the young man's head had caved in under the weight of the guitar's body and was spewing blood down onto his *Elvis is STILL the King!* t-shirt. The wife was clutching at her rib cage and gasping for breath as fractured ribs dug into her lung tissue. Tears flowed from her eyes and blood spattered from her lips as she coughed and gagged.

It also never registered to him that the Marshall amplifier was now burning and that the sparks from the amplifier had jumped over to the red velvet curtains and that fire was now spreading through the bar at the speed of catastrophe. Had Joe turned around for a second, he'd have seen Roy Higgins screaming and running toward the door to the alley, his shirt and pants engulfed in flames that were quickly ascending toward the hairline on his neck. The bartender, Hank Willis, was already long gone.

"It's time to go, Joseph Walton," the Devil's voiced oozed from every corner of the burning bar. "You will do *MY* bidding before your time here is through."

Joe dropped the guitar on the floor, wiped the tears away from his eyes, and bolted toward the door to the alley.

Velvet Mojo burned to the ground as Joe Walton fled into the hot Tennessee sunshine.

Ol' Scratch watched and laughed with delight.

✲ ✲ ✲

Caroline Stork woke up to an enormous hangover. The pain was so bad that the first kiss of sunlight felt like salt on her eyeballs. As she squinted hard and rolled over onto her side, she felt the room spinning around her.

What the fuck happened last night?

As the room gradually stopped spinning and the subsequent nausea subsided, her mind began to travel back to the night before. They had parked the van behind the train trestle, that much was perfectly clear. She could remember seeing the Denny's sign off in the distance and wishing she wasn't slopped up in dog's blood so that she could have wandered over and grabbed some food.

I wanted breakfast, she thought. *I wanted one of them pancake plates, the kind named after the baseball phrase. What the fuck do they call that? The* Big Home Run? *I wanted pancakes and bacon and eggs and toast like my grampa would let me get before we'd go fishing on Saturday mornings.*

Delbert Stork was long retired from the car dealership when his son, John Stork, passed away from clogged arteries from big, greasy meals that included the baseball breakfast she wanted, which gave him all the time in the world to spend with his only grandchild. Caroline was ten when Daddy collapsed in a quivering heap in the middle of Crossgates Mall, and she watched helplessly as some pimple-faced security guard tried to resuscitate him. It was a memory she very rarely attempted to recall, but in the times she did remember, she was covering her weeping eyes with her hand and peeking through the way she had the first time she watched *Scream* on cable television. Her mother, Jocelyn Stork, was clutching her father's hand and screaming at him at the top of her lungs to "Cut the shit, John, this isn't funny!" In the end, the pimple-faced guard had fractured a couple of her father's ribs from overly ambitious compressions. The guard, a kid really, couldn't have been long into his twenties. Caroline remembered how his face had gone ashen as the fat guy on the floor died in front of his family, and then he sat there on the floor and wept. He was still crying when the EMTs arrived and took the body away.

He tried, though, she remembered. *That kid gave it his best.*

And so did Grampa Del.

The old man, who had taken to wearing sweatpants and oversized t-shirts in his early sixties, tried to be a father figure to her. At ten, her whole world was *Harry Potter* and *Lord of the Rings*, and Grampa Del did his best to adapt to her world of fantasy and literature. As her mom seemed to regress into a world of alcohol after her husband died and no longer seemed to care about her, Caroline and her grandfather had shared movie nights and book release parties, which had meant the world to her. But he also tried to open her world to his own interests, and that meant dragging her out in his flat-bottom boat on Saturday mornings, out on the Mohawk River where he taught her to fish for bass up and down the river's muddy banks. And Caroline *did* enjoy it. The thrill of feeling the tug on the line, and then hauling in a real, living animal that tried to fight and escape. Hauling a fish back into Grampa Del's green Coleman boat meant that *she* had greater power than that animal. It had felt god-like. That feeling had never escaped her.

Something snagged my Daddy on a line, and he fought to escape, but whatever was pulling from the other side reeled him in.

Before she hit puberty, Grampa Del tried to be a parental figure. But as her breasts developed and she became a young woman…

The old man in the back of the white Econoline van…

Another animal that fought and tried to escape.

She'd rubbed her bare breasts in the homeless guy's face. Her chest was still coated with the blood of the dog she killed, the Jack Russell terrier that Charlene spotted wandering around off its leash over by Summer Street. Warren had insisted that they make the drive up to Hetfield to visit their new "headquarters," as Warren had so elegantly put it, his good hand and his deformed hand making an air-quotes to drive the point home. But the trip hadn't just been about scouting their new digs. Charlene's old house was bound to be discovered sooner or later, with her late husband's corpse still decomposing in the basement. Mr. Tibbets had not reported to work for over a week now, and Charlene had abandoned all her own personal responsibilities and connections as well, and sooner or later the police were going to have to look into it.

Charlene Tibbets.

Oh, fuck! Oh, fuck, Charlene is dead!

The homeless guy had been subdued in the back of the white van, and Caroline had thought that he was to be the ritual sacrifice to appease Lucifer. Warren had carved the pentagram across his belly and had performed the Moon Ritual as planned, but he hadn't killed him. Caroline could see in her mind's eye the old man—who now looked very much like Grampa Del—with the inverted pentagram carved into the flesh of his naked torso, his face contorted with agony and acceptance as Warren's knife made its final bloody slashes across his skin.

"There is still a chance for you to live," Warren told Ernie O'Malley in a whisper after the final cut was made. "I'm not going to kill you. I'm going to let you go." Warren turned to Abby. "Where's that envelope? I need it."

Abby reached into her purse and pulled out a letter, grasping it gingerly with her fingernails as if trying not to get any fingerprints on it.

"You are only a messenger, my friend. Do your part, and you will live." Warren grabbed a roll of duct tape from the floor of the van from somewhere between the boxes of animal cages that Charlene had bought earlier, ripped off a piece, and taped the envelope onto Ernie's belly just above the line of his pants. His chest was bleeding profusely where the knife's edge had carved the Devil's Star into his skin.

"Let him go!" Warren had ordered. The Harpies removed their weight from his extremities.

The old man sat upright in a flash. "Why are you doing this to me?"

Caroline once again thought of Grampa Del on the day she slit his throat with his own fishing knife. That wicked, old sonofabitch was now taking her out on his boat just to molest her, cop his cheap, greasy feels of her private parts as if her body belonged to him. Caroline had ended his abuse with one quick, fatal stab and watched his life end in a pool of blood that collected at the bottom of the faded green flat-bottomed boat. In the end, Grampa Del was just one more cold, dead fish, and she remained a goddess of all things living.

It was as if Warren had understood all along. Warren had found her and had understood her for what she was. Caroline Stork was the *Goddess of Retribution*.

"Your sins have dragged you down, my friend," Warren told the old man as the two stared eye-to-eye. "And now you have to pay for them."

At some point Warren snatched a pouch out of Abby's hand, a pouch she'd pulled from the same purse containing the envelope now taped to Ernie's torso. Warren reached inside the pouch and then raised his good hand to his lips and blew a cloud of dust into the old man's face. "You're a zombie," Warren whispered. There was a moment of terrified clarity in the old man's eyes, and then his pupils rolled back into his head and Ernie O'Malley began to twitch and convulse in a zombie-like state.

"Open the door," Warren commanded.

Caroline opened the rear door of the Ford Econoline van, and the zombified version of Ernie O'Malley was pushed from the vehicle. He limped and convulsed back out onto Congress Street, his limbs flailing at the night air in cataleptic thrusts. The drug had snatched away his brain the way those fish hooks had snatched away all those fish she'd hauled in back from her own childhood. Ernie O'Malley was nothing more than bait. With the envelope taped below his bleeding chest, someone was bound to come upon him accidentally, and then the cops would find Warren's message. And they would pass it along to the right hands.

Lucifer told him it would be so.

Caroline pulled the van's door closed after the old man scampered off in his zombie trance. "Now what?" she asked Warren.

The man with the deformed hand rounded on Charlene. "You've become too much of a risk," he told the withered old junkie. "We no longer need your services."

Warren Pembroke picked up the crafting knife in his good hand, the one he had used to trace the pentagram on the old man's torso. He raised it up and shoved the blade directly through Charlene's right eye until the end of the hilt came to rest beside the bridge of her nose. Her pupil erupted in a spray of blood and jelly that splashed across Warren's beautiful young face. Both Abby and Caroline watched as the blade passed through her eye and embedded itself somewhere inside Charlene's drug-addled brain, and then Warren yanked the blade out again, and her lifeless body toppled onto the bed of the van.

"Father Lucifer, accept this sacrifice from your humble servants. Take her willingly, as she had so willingly served your true purposes."

Warren had murdered Charlene.

The memory forced Caroline to sit up in bed, her heart thudding in real terror and cold sweat coating the bare patina of her flesh.

Charlene's corpse was lying beside her on the mattress, her naked body still covered in blood from the night before and her one good eyeball staring in wretched disbelief up at the ceiling tiles above. The other eye was completely gone, dug out of its socket to leave a permanent void in her skull.

Charlene's telltale eye had the same accusatory look as her father's had after the EMTs pulled the pimple-faced security guard off of him, and Grampa Del's had after she severed his jugular while the bass he'd snared continued to tug and pull at the line of his Zebco fishing pole. Caroline looked down at the corpse she'd cuddled next to all night in her unconscious abandon. Flies were now collecting around the gaping wound of Charlene's empty eye socket. The smell of piss and shit emanating from the nether regions of the late Mrs. Charlene Tibbets was enough to make Caroline turn away and vomit.

When she finished, she looked up and noticed Warren watching her from the doorway.

"Get up. We still have lots of work to do."

Chapter 8

Monday, June 6th

Kelly Marsh was cooking breakfast when the doorbell rang. A tray of bacon sizzled inside the old Kenmore oven and a pan of fried eggs was ready to be flipped, and for all she knew, her fiancé, Allen, was still up in the bedroom getting dressed for work in the Men's Warehouse suit she'd laid out for him. She could hear their dog, Cricket, barking and scratching at the front door, ready to lavish whoever was ringing the bell with a wet, slobbery round of licks if said ringer was foolish enough to bend down and pet her.

"Allen, honey, can you get that?"

The pan of eggs was beginning to smoke, so she lifted it off the burner and set it on one of the cool burners on the back of the stove. She could hear the television in the living room; Owen was still camped out in there in his pajamas, watching some cartoon or other and reveling in the fact that school had been canceled for the day. The Hetfield Community School had issued a mass cell phone text message stating that the school had been vandalized over the weekend and that the custodial staff needed extra time to clean up and repair damages. Based on what she'd seen on the news, she'd actually expected the school to be closed for the whole week, and wouldn't *that* have been a colossal inconvenience? As it were, with her own schedule at the Downeast Credit Union permanently fixed and with Allen's constant business travels, Owen's summer afternoons would be spent at her mother's farm in Topsham. Part of her was hoping that Erik would step up and take his son for a few hours a day, but with his drinking…

The doorbell rang again, and Kelly sighed. "Don't worry, I'll get it!" she hollered, hoisting the tray of bacon out of the oven and plopping the oven mitts in frustration on the kitchen counter.

When she opened the door, she nearly gasped. "Erik! I wasn't expecting you."

Cricket squirmed past her legs and scooted into Erik's embrace

"Hey, baby! Did you miss Daddy? I missed you, too, sweetie." As she suspected, the dog gave her ex-husband a series of licks and laps that left his clean-shaven face wet. When the dog finished, Erik stood up, and their eyes met. "Good morning, Kelly." He tried to smile, but there was a flicker of awkwardness below the surface that kept him from looking happy.

"Is someone at the door?" a man's voice issued from the hallway, and then Allen was standing behind her. "Oh. Hello, Erik. It's good to see you."

It was as if the awkwardness intensified immediately, and why not? Her fiancé was living in the house that she and Erik had bought together after they were first married. The house, situated on the corner of Main and High Street, was a gambrel with brown clapboard siding adorned with pink shutters and trim. When they'd first seen it, Kelly had declared, "It looks like a gingerbread house!" She'd had an enormous grin on her face. "I could spend my whole life living here." During the divorce proceedings, Erik never contested her wanting to keep the house. The truth was that he actually hated everything about it. Wrong color, wrong location, wrong everything. The only thing that made it *right* was how happy it had made his new bride. And it was a solid, real home for their future children to grow up in; well, Owen, at least.

Erik looked up at Allen, still framed in the doorway behind Kelly. With him in his navy blue suit and Kelly in her cotton blouse and skirt, they looked more like business associates than future bride and groom.

"Good to see you, too."

"Allen, why don't you check on Owen and get him moving. I need to drop him off at my mother's place in half an hour."

"Sure thing, honey." He bent down and kissed her cheek, a performance that made Erik think of the way Cricket would squat down and tinkle on every corner of their lawn as if marking her territory. The thought gave him his first honest smile of the day.

"You never called me back Saturday night," Kelly said icily after Allen ducked back inside the house. She folded her arms across her chest, a posture of annoyance that he easily recognized from their marriage. What he hadn't expected was that she had trimmed down all the mommy-weight she'd put on from carrying Owen. In fact, she looked as slender and pretty as the day he first met her back at the University of Southern Maine. Noticing it now made Allen's property-marking kiss sting all the more.

"I'm sorry about that," he said. His gaze dropped to the sidewalk of the home that had once belonged to him. Weeds crawled up between the walkway's squares of cement, and he immediately hated Allen for it. "I haven't been able to pay my cell phone bill lately. And by the time I got home, it was late, and I didn't want to bother you."

"Do you know what happened?"

"Yeah, I was there and got to see what happened inside. It was a real mess."

"I should have figured as much. You must have written a column about it for the paper."

Erik smiled. "I'm off the crime beat. I told Cummings I needed a change. I'm doing a column for the social pages now."

"Now? After all this time, you finally let it go? Why didn't you do that back when *we* needed you? Seriously, Erik…" She let her arms drop to her sides, her fists clenched into bony wrecking balls. "You made *me* the villain by making me choose to keep our son out of *your* world of darkness. And now that we've moved on, you finally decided to come out on your own? Thanks a lot."

He thought her reaction would have been one measured in either relief or mild happiness for him, and when her annoyance grew deeper, he found himself growing defensive. Here they were, under the eaves of their once-upon-a-time front door, and they were already back to the same old argument. And here was Kelly, almost reciting verbatim what she'd told him back when she finally dropped the word "divorce" on him. *Everything was* his *fault, and yet* she *was the bad guy.* The drinking. The mood swings. The distancing himself from family events and responsibilities. Erik owned those things, had them thrown in his face on every occasion.

Quit blaming yourself, honey, he told her on the day he walked out, his breath still heavy with bourbon. *I was BORN to be the monster. You can blame me for EVERYTHING.*

"I didn't come here to fight, Kelly. I just wanted to spend a little time with my son. I already know the school is closed for today. I just thought maybe I could spend a few minutes with him before I head down to Portland and go to work. Would that be okay?"

As if right on cue, Owen came darting past his mother's legs, down the steps, and then his son was wrapping his arms around Erik's waist.

"Hi, Dad! What are you doing here?"

Erik picked up his son and squeezed him in a tight embrace. "I've been missing ya, Owen. I can't believe how big you've gotten."

In his peripheral vision, he watched Kelly's hands slowly unclench and fall limply to her sides. Her head was hanging down in accepted defeat; even the anger was beginning to slowly trickle away as it radiated from her. And then Cricket was bouncing up and down, her front paws pushing into Owen's rear end as if to say, "I want in on this."

"I promised my mom I would drop Owen off at her place by eight-thirty. If you'd like to drop him off for us, be my guest." She turned to go back into the house, took a couple of steps, and then turned back around again. "Is the school safe? They still have four more days of classes, but his attendance record has been very good this year, and I have no problem keeping him home if they think…"

"It's safe. The Town Police are going to issue two more resource officers to watch the school grounds until classes end for the summer. And the reality is that there is almost zero probability that the people who did it would return to the same place and target it again. They'll be looking for a new target with minimum risk and as defenseless as possible. The reality is we lucked out. Our school was only a calling card."

He set Owen back down on his feet. "Go inside and grab Cricket's leash. We'll take her for a quick walk, and then I'll drop you off at Grandma's house."

Erik watched as his son scrambled back up the steps, past his mother, and into the house. Lurking somewhere behind the door was Allen, most likely listening just out of his line of sight. It didn't matter.

"Is it… Is it the serial killer?"

"Most definitely. And it's a good bet there's more than one."

"Are you going to help the police find them?"

"No. I want nothing to do with this one. The only reason I went out to the school was to see what happened and be sure our son is safe. They'll have the mess all cleaned up before lunchtime this afternoon, and then life will go on there as if nothing ever happened. Scout's honor." Erik held up his pinky finger and crossed it over his chest.

Owen and Cricket came darting back out the front door. Cricket's tail was wagging hard enough to thump Kelly in the stomach and push her nearly off the top step as she passed. Erik had to stifle the grin from his face.

"Kelly, for what it's worth, I'm sorry. I truly am. I wish you and Allen every happiness. I know you'll be an even prettier bride the second time around." He took the leash from Owen's hand, and then he knelt down beside his son. "Go give your mom a hug and kiss goodbye, okay, champ?"

"'Kay, Dad." Owen ran back up the steps, hugged and kissed his mother, and then was grabbing Cricket's leash back from his father's hand.

They turned up High Street and ascended the uphill macadam into the face of the glowing morning sun. The lawns on either side of the street were still soaked with dew, the moisture on the blades of grass reflecting like shimmering emeralds. Some properties had been neglected of that first spring lawn-cutting, and in the longer patches of grass were tussles of spider webs, also coated with morning dew. When Owen was five or so, Erik used to tell him that those patches of webbing were actually "Fairy Beds," where wood nymphs and pixies would slumber after the stars came out. "On the nights when the moon is full," he told his son at bedtime one night, as if reciting from a storybook, "those pixies and nymphs come out and throw *big* parties with cake and ice cream and lots of yummy food to eat." Looking at how big his son was now, nearly five years older and wiser, the notion of pointing out the "Fairy Beds" seemed silly.

I've lost time, he thought. *I've thrown that time away, and I'll never get it back. I don't even know how to start a discussion with him.*

It was as if Owen had read his mind, and saved him the awkwardness of starting a conversation. "Dad, how bad was it at my school? The people who vandalized it… What did they do?"

It had been awhile since they'd walked up High Street together, and it was slowly registering that the climb was steeper than he remembered and that it actually felt like work forcing his legs to continue. When Owen was a baby, it was an evening ritual for Erik to push him in the stroller up High Street, through Hillside Cemetery at the top of the hill, and then back down to their house again. That was *his* wind-down time, after his column had been written and delivered, and he begun transitioning into writing fiction during the evening. The walk gave him time away from the telephone and the computer and the police scanner. It also gave him time away from Kelly, with her unending list of chores and gripes and drama, which allowed him to dive into his stories. The walk meant ironing out plot points and character arcs and shaping the imaginary world inside his head. Walking here, right now, was beginning to have that same effect. Only now the people and problems in his head were *real*, and being the author of his own life meant unraveling and sorting them out and finding his own happy ending. The realization was frightening. Even Cricket, in her old age, was not trotting as fast as she used to. She was too busy sniffing and glancing and barking at anything that resembled motion.

"It was pretty bad. I won't lie about it. Lots of broken glass and damaged property. I wouldn't worry about it, though. The police will catch the people who did it. They almost always do. And when they're caught, they'll go to jail for a long, long time."

Hillside Cemetery was less than a hundred yards ahead now. Erik could see the entrance flanked by the cyclone fence surrounding the property. The driveway through the cemetery formed a massive horseshoe, with a series of smaller one-lane strips leading from High Street to the back of the horseshoe. From overhead, the graveyard resembled a large, crooked comb, with headstones, obelisks, and statuary scattered across the land. The entrance on the far side of the cemetery was nothing but forest, which stretched out in a blanket of pine, maple, birch, and oak.

"Mom was really upset about it," Owen said, almost to himself. "She was more scared about it than I was. I just wish we could have had the whole week off and started summer early."

"I bet." Erik smiled and patted his son's moppish hair. Had he still been living at home with them, he'd have already dragged the boy to see Rachel at Hairs-To-You down on Main Street for a trim. As it were, spring semester portraits had been shot back in April, and Kelly would have made sure that Owen's hair was perfect for his shoot, and that was probably the last haircut the boy had received. Somewhere in a stack of unopened letters on his desk was a letter from Kelly containing a wallet-sized portrait of his son, but alcohol and stubbornness had prevented him from finding it. "I think it's going to be a great summer this year. I was thinking that maybe you and I could start spending a lot more time together. I've been missing you, and I've been a terrible dad. I want to fix that before it's too late. Do you understand?"

Cricket had noticed a squirrel digging through a birdfeeder at the base of one of the headstones inside the cemetery, and began bounding toward it. She was pulling hard enough to nearly yank the leash out of Owen's hand, but the boy held fast and found himself being tugged toward the cemetery entrance.

"Cricket! C'mon, down, girl!" Owen shouted as the Golden Retriever woofed and struggled to reach the surprised critter. The squirrel turned and bolted down the horseshoe lane, rounded the asphalt corner, and then darted up into an oak tree on the inside patch of grass. The sun overhead was casting long, crooked shadows off the headstones around them. Cricket pulled at the leash until the elder and younger Marsh were standing in the shade of the oak, both panting from trying to keep up with the dog.

"Dad," Owen said between pants.

"What, son?"

"Nothing." Owen stroked Cricket's head and tried to soothe the still-animated animal. "C'mon, Cricket. It's just a stupid ol' squirrel. Let it go." Owen tugged firmly on the leash, and Cricket woofed back at him in agitation as she trotted back out onto the asphalt. Erik followed, quietly wondering if his son even heard him at all. There was definitely something brewing in his son's mind, but trying to stir it without permission seemed like asking for trouble. Erik found himself hoping that it had everything to do with Allen and that his son quite possibly hated the man who was currently planning to marry his mother. *Has to be it,* he thought. *It just has to be. If he was upset with me, he would have said so by now.*

They rounded the far part of the horseshoe, and way up ahead at the far edge of the lane, Erik saw the white van crawl to a halt and park. The van was less than fifty yards ahead, and he could just see the figure of a woman piling out of the cab and making her way around the vehicle. She disappeared behind the van for a few seconds and then reappeared at the rear doors. She was tall, skinny, with wild red hair and wearing a gray tank top and pink Capris pants. Even at a distance, Erik could see the tattoos that ran up and down the exposed skin of the woman's frame. The woman moved slowly, like a wounded animal, and he found himself temporarily alarmed. Only ten minutes ago he promised his ex-wife that his son was safe as can be, but the closer he and Owen came to the white van, the more he realized just how vulnerable he was. Once upon a time, when his job at the newspaper exposed him to some spectacularly crazy people, he'd considered purchasing a handgun, but in the end he always talked himself out of buying one because the line from "depressed" to "suicidal" was just too damn thin. Owning a gun would be the grain of sand that toppled him over into the world of statistics and forgotten names.

The woman threw the rear door of the van open and hauled out a large, white bucket. She pulled the bucket free and slammed the door shut, and then she disappeared again into the area behind the van. Erik, Owen, and Cricket were now close enough to see the van's windshield. The top part was tinted, but the bottom was visible, and across the dashboard was a series of maps, folded newspapers, a half-roll of toilet paper wedged between the glass and the dash to the point where the cardboard cylinder was crushed, and scattered fast food wrappers wadded up into balls. The woman's head reappeared from the front of the van. Her back was to them as she walked toward the tree line at the perimeter of the cemetery. The sun above splashed her shadow across the grass like a fallen ghost between the rows of headstones.

She must work here, Erik thought. *She must work here at the cemetery, and she's just—*

"Dad, about the school getting vandalized… I dreamed it was going to happen."

Erik froze in mid-stride and faced his son. He turned his face just before the woman with the bucket passed through the last line of headstones and plodded off into the woods at the perimeter of the cemetery. "What do you mean, you dreamed it would happen?"

"A few nights ago. I dreamed that some bad people broke into the school. They brought in some dead animals, and then they drank the animal blood like they were vampires or something. And they had a goat with them. They led it in on a piece of rope, and then they nailed it into the wall of the cafeteria." Owen stopped for a moment, and Erik could see the tears welling up in the corner of his son's eyes. "I wanted to look away, I really did, but it was just a dream, and I couldn't turn my head. They nailed the goat into the wall, and the goat was screaming the whole time, only it was screaming in a human voice. And then they stabbed it in the belly with a big knife, and its guts spilled all over the place. Dad, I think they killed it the same way the Romans killed Jesus in the Bible."

Erik kneeled down in front of his son. "Did you tell your mom about this?"

Owen shook his head solemnly. "No. Mom and Allen were watching the news when the story about my school came on. She was so upset that I was afraid to tell her. Dad, I've been really scared about it ever since. I need to know… When you went into my school, was there a goat inside?"

Erik looked back toward the van and watched as the woman reappeared from the tree line. The bucket was gone. She half-walked, half-staggered back toward the cabin of the van, opened the door, and climbed inside. The white Ford Econoline roared to life, and then Erik found himself guiding Owen and Cricket out of the way as she drove past, never giving any indication whatsoever that she had seen them. Erik watched as the brake lights came on, and then the van was turning down one of the single-lane causeways back toward High Street.

He turned his face toward his son again. "No," he lied. "There were no goats inside the school. Only broken windows and spray-paint graffiti. Now, c'mon. Let's get you to your Grandma's house before she starts to get worried about you."

❧ ❧ ❧

Erik noticed the squad cars surrounding One City Center the moment he turned onto Congress Street. The pulse of the blue LED strobes immediately registered as State Police vehicles, and there had to be at least six of them cordoning off the entranceway to the building where the *Portland Beacon* conducted business. He drove his Honda down to Temple Street, found an open spot at one of the parking meters, and whipped into the vacant space.

His gut reaction was that there must have been a bomb scare at *The Beacon* this morning. It had happened in the past on numerous occasions, usually politically motivated after a certain headline ran or after Cummings left a blistering editorial reply to some news event or other, but as he approached the building and realized that none of his colleagues had been evacuated, he suspected something deeper. Erik entered the building and pushed the button for his floor.

Beverly LaChance was waiting for him the moment the elevator doors opened. "Where the hell have you been? Have you checked your cell phone at all this morning? You need to get down to Cummings's office." Her voice was a throaty croak from the moment the doors parted, and she had that same icy posture that Kelly met him with a few hours earlier. "They're all waiting for you down there."

"Who's waiting?"

"Everyone! Cummings, the state police— Hell, Truth Carson is down in Ron's *War Room* right now, waiting to talk to you."

"What the hell happened?"

Bev pushed him back into the elevator as the doors began to close in front of him. "Just go!"

Beverly LaChance was right. The area outside R.H. Cumming's office was crowded with troopers in their navy blues and the plain-clothed dicks in suits and ties. In the far corner by the water cooler was an area set up with a Cable World Media camera pointing toward an empty folding chair bathed in floodlights. The shine off the metal was bright enough to make Erik squint as one of the detectives rushed over and grabbed him by the arm.

"Is this our boy?" an obese fellow in a white shirt and tan raincoat that reeked of stale tobacco asked as he led Erik by the arm over to Cummings. Erik could see the gun in his shoulder holster protruding through the fabric as if the jacket had been shrink-wrapped around his bulky frame.

R.H. Cummings looked annoyed but kept his composure. "Yes, that's Erik Marsh. He *was* working our crime beat column, but we just recently—"

Another man pushed through the crowd, only this one held the meticulous dazzle of Hollywood and Sleaze. The furrowed brow on his high forehead and the trace of blemish concealer on his perfectly shaved cheeks was all the introduction Erik needed. Truth Carson was extending his hand, trying to grasp Erik's as the detective continued to lead him into Cummings's office with his iron grip.

"Everybody, just hang on for a moment," Carson bellowed as his soft, manicured hand fell into Erik's. "This kid just might be the link we need to find the killer. If you're going to question him, can we please do it in front of our camera? You know—for posterity? If the kid has information, we can help get the word out and maybe you can finally catch this creep." The edge in Carson's voice seemed both accusatory and authoritative.

Erik pulled his hand away. "Boss, what the hell's going on?"

Cummings opened the door to his office, trying to allow the heavyset detective, who was now sweating harder than Cummings was, if that was possible, to pass through. He could feel the guy's perspiration sopping through the sleeve of his shirt where his fingers were gripping Erik's arm. The detective tried to usher Erik through the door, but Carson was suddenly grabbing and tugging at his other arm, trying to haul him back into the hallway as if he was nothing more than a bad dog on a leash.

"Kid, I need to talk to you," Carson said above the growing din of policemen, who were now closing in and whispering heatedly about the rising spectacle. "You're the key to unlocking the mystery behind Le'Sinestre. Let me help you open the door. Do you know who I am?"

Erik looked at Cummings, whose face was now crinkled in absolute disgust, and then gazed back at the cable news magnate as if he was nothing more than a pile of dog shit. "Yeah, I know who you are. You're Harold Kirsch. My boss told me all about you. If it's all the same, we'll break the story here at *The Beacon.*"

The last thing Erik heard as the door swung closed behind him was the sound of R.H. Cummings laughing behind the detective's shoulder and whispering, "Son, you're getting a raise for that."

"My name is John Barrett," the large man said. "I'm a senior detective with the Maine State Police." He reached into a pocket of his raincoat and produced a pair of purple rubber gloves that immediately made Erik think of being in the delivery room on the day his son was born. Erik remembered feeling overwhelmed with a sense of wonder and panic at the same time and worried that he might just manage to pass out onto the cold, sterile tiles of the delivery room floor before his only son could arrive. Now, here he was with that same feeling, the surgical gloves being that final grain of sand that tipped the scale.

Cummings rounded the desk and plopped himself down into his chair. Perspiration marks had flowered from his armpits hours before they were due on his normal daily schedule.

"This letter did not arrive with the morning mail," Cummings said dryly, then pushed the envelope across his desk. "If it had, the last thing I'd have done was call these bozos in and turn *my* office into a carnival."

Erik sat down across from him, went to pick it up, and then pulled his arms back. "This is evidence, and I'm not allowed to touch it." He looked up at Detective Barrett. "Isn't that how it works?"

"Our lab team has already processed the envelope," Barrett uttered behind him. "But all the same, this will be easier if I handle it." Barrett nodded at the envelope on the desk. "The killer knows you've been covering the crime beat for the newspaper. That's why he addressed the envelope to you. Your boss has already informed me that you've personally requested a new detail here at *The Beacon.* I don't believe your involvement with the newspaper is as important to our suspect as getting his message across. Is this the first time, to the best of your recollection, that he's tried to contact you?"

Erik looked down at the envelope and studied the rough scribbling. His name and the newspaper's address were done in black crayon on the envelope, as if written on by a child, and highlighted with red. Erik thought at first that the red was also crayon, but upon closer inspection, he noticed the red splotches were actually dried blood. There were also diabolical sketches that matched the ones he'd seen back at his son's school, archaic symbols that resembled both animals and weapons. For a return address, only the word LE'SINESTRE in block letters, followed by the numbers 666.

"I'd have remembered if he'd tried to contact me. You guys would have been the first to know. Can you please open it and read it?"

Detective Barrett picked up the envelope gingerly with rubber-gloved fingertips, carefully slid the letter out, and placed the empty envelope face-up on the desk. Erik fished his cell phone out of his pocket, switched it on and into camera mode, and photographed the envelope as Barrett cleared his throat and read words written in what looked like the scrawl of a child. There were more caustic black crayon strokes forming both letters and symbols on standard printer paper. The letter read:

Mr. Marsh,

I've been waiting for you to discover me and embrace my darkness. I've been leaving my calling cards at every scene, but you have not deemed me worthy enough to cover my work in your column. Why are you not captivated? No matter. In the end you will seek me out. You will be greatly interested as my plan is unveiled. I have been chosen, and I shall answer the call. I am the new shepherd and I shall eschew my parade of goats unto the earth to deliver a thousand years of darkness. And you shall know me by name and beg for my forgiveness and mercy before the final sunset.

Yours in Lucifer,
Le'Sinestre

Detective Barrett folded the letter and slipped it neatly back inside the envelope.

"So, Mister Marsh, if this guy has been leaving crime scenes around the state for the past few months, how is it that you've managed to not report on *any* of them?"

"I honestly don't have an answer," Erik said, feeling his cheeks flush. "I suspect I *have* covered a few of them, but I also suspect they were long before he escalated to murder. And the murders I did cover never portrayed any evidence of Satanic activity. If this is really our guy, maybe his calling cards fell short of taking any notice."

"Erik can always go back and pull up his old columns and see if there are any clues that stand out." Cummings's arms were now on his desk, his hands folded neatly on the hardwood top. It struck Erik as almost comedic just how presidential the man looked behind his desk in his *War Room,* with the awards and framed newspaper clippings surrounding him. "This is the first time we've heard the name *Le'Sinestre* here at the *Portland Beacon.*"

"Carson already ran it on his news channel," Erik said. "Le'Sinestre was the one that vandalized the Hetfield Community School this past Saturday. My son goes to school there. Alvarez covered the story for us. It's a good bet his column went out in the Sunday edition."

Detective Barrett stripped the rubber gloves off his hands and tossed them in the trash can beside the desk. "If that's true, then our suspect has probably seen it already. It's a good bet that any further correspondence will go directly to Alvarez."

Erik looked at the detective, and then back at his boss. It felt like a light bulb went off inside his head. "If this letter didn't arrive in the mail, how *did* it get here?"

Jamal Ellis had the trip timed out down to the exact minute. He would punch off the clock at the USPS Southern Maine Processing and Distribution Center in Scarborough at 11:00 p.m. He'd have his Chevy Camaro revved up by 11:02, be northbound on Route 295 by 11:04, and get off Exit 5, the St. John Street exit, by 11:08, give or take a few minutes depending on existing traffic situations from miscellaneous events, like a late baseball game at Hadlock Field or a concert at the Cumberland County Civic Center. Of course, if the Po-po was in force, it meant not gunning the Hemi engine anywhere above five miles over the speed limit. Black skin meant long, drawn-out pullovers, the kind where Johnny Law kept one hand hovering over his holstered Taser while the other took his license, registration, and insurance card. And on a warm June evening like this, the police were bound to be out and looking because summer was breathing life back into the city.

Jamal called in the order to Ma La Dragon, a fast-food version of Chinese cuisine over on St. John Street in Portland. Because the restaurant was across the river from Scarborough, it meant the restaurant's drivers weren't going to deliver to his place of employment, and that was fine. Once Jamal was off the clock, he could steal himself off to the privacy of his car and light up a joint once he was off postal property and not worry about hidden surveillance cameras catching him doing anything he wasn't supposed to be doing. And sparking up would help give his appetite a boost, making the General Tso Chicken and fried rice that much more delectable. So somewhere between 11:02 and 11:04 p.m., he lit the joint he kept in his glove box and took a few hits while he drove, then stubbed out the burning cigarette in his ashtray before rolling onto the highway.

The buzz had kicked in full blast as he sailed the Camaro off the highway and onto St. John Street. He could see the pink and green neon of the Denny's sign as his car's stereo blared out some new reggae artist that was trying desperately to sound like Bob Marley. *It's all about the percussion, mon!* Jamal thought and then laughed as if the phony Jamaican accent in his brain was the funniest thing he'd ever heard. The shit he was smoking now was some damn good stuff, purchased from a new connection he'd made a few short weeks ago. Some cat named Rhashan, whom he'd met through a friend while barhopping through the Old Port. *That dude was Jamaican fo sho!*, Jamal thought, and then found himself laughing again. *Once them white folks find this guy, he gonna be a millionaire.*

Jamal saw the figure ahead in the distance and stopped laughing. The figure looked like something out of a horror film, the kind you see on cable television at night where the dead come back to life and saunter after the living in an attempt to devour them. Even from a few hundred yards away, Jamal could tell that the dude was old, white, and injured. Bleeding, in fact. The old dude was topless, and his chest was bleeding profusely. The dude, however, seemed unaware of it. He was half-loping, half-staggering toward him down the middle of St. John Street, with his head at a bizarre angle and his arms clawing at the dark as if he was trying to catch some invisible animal from midair. From a hundred yards away, Jamal could almost make out the bloody pentagram inscribed into the flesh of his abdomen. From fifty yards away, he could see the old man's knees buckle and tremble from somewhere below his waist. It never occurred to him to slow the Camaro down. The mental clock in his brain was still keeping tabs on the digital clock on his dash panel, making sure that, even though he was still high, he was on schedule so that he could be back to work and punch in from lunch on time. As long as his brain was still working, as long as he still comprehended that the artist on the radio was ripping off the late, great Bob Marley and that he had to be to Ma La

Dragon in three minutes to pick up and pay for his order, then be back on the highway by 11:22 p.m., this phantom honky meant nothing to him.

With less than thirty feet separating them, Jamal noticed that the old man's eyes were rolled up somewhere into the backs of his eye sockets, and that his mind—stoned out from Devil's Breath from the very same dealer that sold him that killer weed he'd just smoked—was floating in some parallel universe. And the Devil's Star across his chest was perfectly defined in the headlights of his Camaro.

"Holy shit, it's the muthafuckin' zombie 'pocalypse," Jamal uttered. And when the old man noticed that the headlights were shining directly on him, he meandered further out into Jamal's lane and began clawing and raging at the metal beast that was quickly approaching.

Jamal Ellis stepped on the gas and ran down Ernie O'Malley in cold blood. The dude was stone-cold dead by the time the police arrived. One of the waitresses from Denny's had been outside smoking a cigarette and talking to her boyfriend on her cell phone and had witnessed the whole thing. She hung up on her boyfriend and immediately dialed 911 to report it.

The letter Warren Pembroke had taped to his belly was still intact. It was addressed to some staff writer at the *Portland Beacon*. And while the shaking, blubbering young black man from the postal service was cuffed and booked—his order from Ma La Dragon completely forgotten, and supped on by the hungry Chinese family members who owned Dragon sometime after the restaurant closed for the night—one of the officers removed the envelope and handed it to his superior. The letter climbed the chain of command until it reached Detective Barrett.

Joe Walton felt both disoriented and terrified as his eyelids flipped open, filtering in a long vertical stream of light from the crack around the boxcar's doorframe until it blinded him. He'd been dreaming again, although this time he was standing somewhere foreign, somewhere he'd only heard about in legends of the old Delta bluesmen. There was a crossroads where two dirt paths intersected in the middle of nowhere. In the distance, he could hear the screams and wails of humans in terrible agony, but from which direction they came from he couldn't be sure. There was a sense of non-reality all around him; dead trees stood like angry skeletons in an accusing roadside jury, with their twisted limbs pointing in every direction. The smell of sulfur and brimstone fell all around him, trickling from the sky in burning embers that flecked on his face and arms until hot, white blisters formed on his black flesh.

A noise crept up from one of the dirt avenues. It sounded like wild, wretched bleating, like a herd of crippled farm animals awaiting the slaughter. He turned, aghast, ignoring the infuriating pain on his skin to see what beasts brought forth such a din.

Far from his vantage point, Joe watched as the line of horns and hooves trod toward him up the lane to the Crossroads. It was a parade of goats, nudging and staggering onward, moving closer and closer to him. Some dragged long lines of iron chains from their necks, carving trails in the dirt beneath them. Others snuffed and snorted in rage, and nipped at the beasts in front of them to keep them moving on. All of them had been blinded, their eyes carved completely from their sockets, leaving bloody trails down the thick, dirty fur on their faces.

They're diseased, he thought to himself. *I don't know how I know, but I can feel it radiating off of them.*

He heard the sound of laughter. It echoed all around him, penetrated him, filled his mind with madness. It wrung the hope right out of his soul in one long, miserable twist.

I'm so close to Hell. God have mercy on me!

"These are my children," Ol' Scratch spoke, his voice undulating in ancient and terrible frequencies.

The vibrations in Joe's ears caused him to lose his balance and stagger. The old man held his hands up to his ears to silence the voice, but it had already clawed and burrowed inside his head, a poisonous rodent sent to feast on his mind.

"I have called you here to lead them home for me. I have called you to be my shepherd and deliver to me what is mine!"

The dream ended as quickly as it came, and by the time Joe's eyes grew accustomed to the light, he discovered he was crying.

A few minutes passed, and when the tears subsided, he sat up, pulled a wrinkled pack of cigarettes out of his pants pocket, and fished one out. He placed it between his lips, lit it, and inhaled deeply. He'd heard the stories of the old boxcar hobos, jumping cars and riding the rails from place to place, always searching for something better. Running away. Starting over. There were scattered memories of old black-and-white television programs and the occasional picture show his Daddy had taken him to at The Bijou, where old white men with stubbly faces and dirty clothes staggered around like they were drunk. They wore baggy pants and faded hats and carried long sticks with their possessions bundled in a hand-kerchief on the end. Which illustrated just how little *he* had at the mo-ment—not even a pauper's bundle on a stick. Joe had the clothes on his back and the remainder of the cash Higgins paid him before the Velvet Mojo burned to the ground. The rest of his belongings—the new clothes and toiletries—were still back at the Y, where they'd be discovered shortly after Claud Lambert, his parole officer, came to call and obtain his requisite piss test. Once they put two and two together—the murders and fire at the Mojo and his sudden absence—there would be all-points bulletins for his immediate arrest.

The sunlight stopped stinging his eyes, so he got up, walked over to the boxcar's door, and threw it open a bit further.

It was hard to tell exactly where he was. It had been a good twenty-four hours since the fire, and since he made his big escape in the Chase Atlantic Railway boxcar. It had occurred to him back when he was shopping at Walmart that the world had changed for the worse somehow while he was locked up in Luttrell. Prices had grown sky-high for food and clothing. Cars moved at breakneck speeds, and those driving them had tempers that burned even faster. And after that whole terrorist attack on New York City, citizens could no longer be trusted to be who they said they were. Joe had visited the bus station first, had held the remainder of his cash in his sweating palm as he tried to purchase a ticket for any-where, but without a driver's license or any form of identification, nobody was going to sell him anything. And perhaps that had been for the best.

He caught the boxcar on a whim after panic took over the controls of his adrenaline and rationality. Joe didn't even know which direction the train was heading. He saw only shelter and escape, and that seemed like the best he was going to get without Johnny Law kicking the shit out of him and slapping the cuffs back around his wrists. But even in the twenty-four hours he'd been traveling, he could tell that he'd made it a good distance away from Memphis. The air already felt cooler, less humid, and the hot, swampy feel of the rivers had given way to more tem-perate forests and mountains. The train was heading north. In fact, even with all the stops the train had made, there was a good chance he'd crossed clear into Kentucky already.

Joe thought about his guitar. The old acoustic relic that he bought with his own money after practically slave-farming on fields owned by stingy old white men who dropped pennies into his hands after laboring until those same hands puffed with blisters and scabs. All the old bluesmen named their guitars after women: Lucille, Maybelline, Betty Jean, Charlotta. Joe never gave his guitar a girl's name. The only name he ever called it was "Mine." There was something romantic about giving the instrument a woman's name, but at the age he learned to play, and the age Ol' Scratch bestowed talent upon him in return for promising his soul, the only girl Joe really cared about was Liliana Page, a pretty sixteen-year-old on one of the farms he'd worked to raise money to buy the guitar. And she didn't give a shit about him. Lili was far too content with the older boys who played pool in the hall on Kasmir Street to notice the sweaty boy picking tobacco leaves out in her father's fields. And on those lonely nights when Joe fantasized about her, he picked up his guitar and played the blues until those strings wept with sorrow.

Ol' Scratch was indeed calling the shots. Everything that had transpired so far happened to *His* design. Joe had seen the ghosts of Rufus and Leon Hickey out there in the crowd, had heard their threats and insults as clearly as if they'd never died. In his mind's eye, he could still see the bloodied meat of their muscle tissue in the footlights and stage lights, how it glistened wetly even after death had enveloped them all those years ago.

All those years ago.

Joe reeled backward and sat down hard on his ass, feeling the world moving around him as the floor of the train pushed on in its unending chorus of groans and clacks. Somewhere below him, cold iron wheels spun on metal, and ancient brakes screeched out in protest whenever the train needed to stop. They squealed loud enough to wake the dead, just as those two boys' screams had done when he stuck the blade inside them and began to saw off their flesh.

They were barely conscious as he flayed them, their eyes wild and limbs secured tight in the same bailing wire Daddy used to tie the tobacco stalks.

"The only reason they didn't lock y'all up for what you did to my folks is cuz your skin is white," he'd whispered just before the blade fell into the younger boy's bare abdomen and started to hew away. "So I'm gonna fix that. I'm gonna take your skin right off yo' body, and then you won't get away with hurtin' nobody no more."

Daddy had taught him.

When he was eleven, an alligator had discovered the waterhole on the south side of their farm and had occupied it as her own. Soon after, chickens began disappearing. It was only a few at first, and since the gator hadn't been discovered, Daddy decided that there must be some wild predator out there hunting them down, which meant their free-range days were over. Under a blistering Tennessee sun, he and Daddy had constructed a fence around the coop using old cane chutes and chicken wire. A few days later there was a terrible racket outside the coop. He and Daddy had out been harvesting tobacco leaves when the ruckus started, and the two could hear the hens clucking in reckless abandon.

Daddy rounded the barn first, and when he saw the gator poking and pushing at the fencing while the birds spread their wings and cackled in terror, he stopped dead in his tracks. Joe could remember the younger version of himself catching up to Daddy and stopping cold at the senior Walton's side.

"Don't move, boy," Daddy told him as the alligator turned to examine them. The beast had to be at least ten feet long, with its mouth pulled into an amused snaggletooth grin. Its long, green tail flicked for a moment, and then the gator turned back to the chicken wire and pushed at it again with its snout.

"Oh, you brazen motherfucker," was all Daddy said before bolting back to the house to grab his shotgun. When he returned, he pointed the barrel at the reptile and pulled the trigger, and the deer-scatter cartridge made the beast's head disappear in a geyser of blood and green scales.

"We want to keep the pelt," Daddy explained, pulling his hunting knife out of the sheath on his belt. "We can take it to the market and sell it. People will buy it and make boots and belts and wallets from it, so we can't spare any of it. We need to strip the skin off as perfectly as possible, and then we can dry it up in the smokehouse. Do you understand, Joe?"

"Yessum, Daddy."

Joe Walton wasn't going to sell the hides of the boys who killed his father and raped his mother. He was going to tan them until their hides were as dark as his own skin, and then he was going to keep them as a souvenir, a lesson that folks couldn't get away with murder, a lesson that justice meant something deeper than an old, white judge leading a young, white jury to decide that their own kind had greater rights and privileges than he had.

The alligator had been looking to eat. To survive.

The Hickey boys had been out to amuse themselves. To raise hell without paying any dues to the Devil. They would have gotten away with it if Joe Walton hadn't avenged his Daddy. And all of it came at the price of fame and fortune, which he'd already promised his soul to Satan to obtain.

Everything has happened according to HIS design. All that time I spent in jail. MY lifetime. If I could have forgiven them— If I could have done what the 'Good Book' said—

"You couldn't forgive them," a voice called out from one of the darkened corners of the boxcar. Joe spun around and saw the figure huddled in the far corner, just underneath an old painted sign that read "Chase Atlantic Railroad; Shaping American Commerce Since 1937" in faded red paint. Joe had thought the car was unoccupied, and the voice had taken him completely by surprise. When his eyes adjusted to the darkness of the corner, Joe saw that the man speaking to him looked exactly like the hobo he'd recalled from his memories of the old black-and-white movies. He had on dark trousers, a dirty white shirt, and an old gray vest buttoned down over his enormous gut, with a tiny pink carnation poking jauntily from the vest's lapel. The hobo even had on the old felt hat and the pauper's sack tied around a sycamore branch at his feet.

"You couldn't forgive them because they were unforgivable." The bum sat up, his face a beam of radiant friendliness, as if he'd known Joe for years and years. "You did what you had to do. An eye for an eye, am I right?"

Joe turned away, a solitary tear falling from his left eye. He looked at his hand, and at the numbers 666 tattooed on the flesh beneath his fingernails. His tears made the numbers blur in his vision.

"It was always your design. But back then I was a child. I saw through the eyes of a child, and I followed in my childish ways. Now, I'm a man. And I ain't your slave. I don't *need* to play into your plans. I don't have to go to Maine if I don't want to, and I don't have to find my guitar if I don't want to. I could just jump off this here train any ol' time I want and figure things out. And if I have to go back to prison, then so be it."

The old man in the corner of the boxcar smiled. "You never named your guitar because you never cared about finding love the way those other guys did. You were too concerned with the 'Cult of Joe' to really give a damn. The only thing that mattered to you was *you*. I gave you talent, and all you cared about was where that talent brought you. And that was what was so amazingly fun about you, Joe Walton; you took the lazy way out. You felt like people owed you because you knew how to play the guitar. You thought they needed to hear you and praise you and give you their love and devotion. And yet, once you had talent, you had no message to give anyone. Ya had nothing to say, Joe! You could have changed the world for the better if your songs were about peace and harmony. But they weren't, were they?"

Joe said nothing. He merely watched the hobo in the corner smile lasciviously and stare him down as if he were nothing more than a whore waiting to be dealt with. This was the game Ol' Scratch played—pointing out the truth and then relishing in the lies that ensued.

"I ain't proud of what I done," he said at last. "And I know that I can't undo my past. But that don't mean I have to play your game. I don't have to follow this here boxcar north to Portland, Maine, and find my guitar if I choose not to. And for the moment, I choose not to. The next time this train stops, I'm jumping off, and wherever I go, it will be by my own design."

"Fair enough," the hobo said. "But don't say I didn't try to help you."

The homeless man evaporated into thin air, filtering away in the warming summer sun like a phantom from the spirit world. Seconds later, the train's engine blasted a warning whistle, old brakes screeched in protest, and then the train was lurching to a halt somewhere north of Lexington, Kentucky. The unexpected slow-down caused Joe to stagger, his long legs buckling just enough to let gravity have its way with him. He toppled hard onto the floor of the car, and the scent from his dream was replaced with the warm, sweet smell of tobacco leaves.

Dried flakes of tobacco littered the floor of the car. They poofed out from under his body in a dark cloud and then flittered all around him.

Joe got to his knees and crawled to the door of the car to see what was going on outside. When he saw the rows of flashing blue strobe lights up near the engine, he knew that the police were looking for him. And just as easily as he'd hopped aboard the Chase Atlantic Railway car, he slipped off again, crawled underneath the car, and ran off into the woods on the other side.

Chapter 9

Abby Silverstein noticed that Caroline had picked up a slight facial tic after Charlene's death. The muscles beneath the skin around her left eye now flicked occasionally in rebellious contractions, making the redhead's eye squint uncontrollably. Neither of the women had known that Warren intended to murder Charlene in cold blood, but Abby understood it to be a clinical, rational decision in order to move forward with their plans and not get caught. Charlene was a junkie, useless and desperate for that next fix. And that was dangerous. Hell, even dealers like Rhashan wouldn't flip her a dime bag because it was so blatantly obvious she was using. That kind of shit was bad for business.

Whereas Abby viewed the older woman as a cheap sexual gratification, and very easily expendable, Caroline had taken to thinking of her as a mother figure. Way back at the beginning of it all, the redhead had sought her out and bonded with her. Charlene had battled endometriosis and subsequent ovarian damage that left her and her husband diagnosed with infertility. Charlene had very much longed for a daughter similar to Caroline, and Caroline was looking for something more maternal than her own mom had turned out. It was as if Warren had known what each woman was looking for and facilitated that missing part in each of them. The drugs helped.

So where do I play into all of this? What did he see in me *that made him trust me enough to fit into his plans?*

Warren had moved their operation to the new place in Topsham, a small farmhouse just outside the border of Hetfield. The property—a sheep ranch owned by Herb and Karen Mueller—had acres of green hillsides surrounded by electric fencing. Warren took Caroline up here to scout the place out just the week before, back when Charlene was still alive but not really living, and just yesterday Caroline had returned to pay a visit to the couple and introduce herself. Karen Mueller answered the door, polite as you please, in a blue gingham housedress and apron. Her gray hair was drawn up in a ponytail, and her eyeglasses were attached to a silver lanyard by black loops around each earpiece. The chain dangled down her face and around her jowls before slinking off to hide beneath the ponytail.

"Can I help you?" the fifty-seven-year old asked, looking down at the young woman with the fiery red hair and the tattoos.

"Sure can, grandma." Caroline smiled as she pulled the butcher's knife out from behind her back and lunged forward before Karen even realized what was happening. There was a comical moment somewhere in there once the blade pierced the old woman's belly all the way to the hilt and her glasses slid off the bridge of her nose and dangled precariously from the lanyard. The old lady took a step backward, and those goddamn glasses started rocking back and forth like a pendulum, as if old man Mueller was suddenly fucking her from behind. Caroline pulled the blade back out of her abdomen and watched in fascination as the old woman dropped down to her hands and knees, blood pouring from the wound, those glasses still swinging wildly.

"Honey, who's at the door?"

Herbert Mueller rushed in from the hallway, his denim bib overalls and work boots still grimy from the morning chores even though Karen reminded him so many times not to wear them goddamn boots inside her house? Didn't he have the brains God gave him to know that he had sheep shit stuck in the treads? Herb plowed into the living room and noticed his wife of nearly forty years rolling around on the floor, clutching the gaping wound in her belly and struggling to breathe.

"What the fuck did you do to my wife?" The old man stormed through the room toward the redhead with the tattoos, his giant farming hands, also grimy from the morning's chores, stretched out as if to strangle this terrible intruder. Once again, the butcher's knife was quicker, only this shot was given out of fear. The blow was more forceful this time, pushing the blade between ribs and directly into Herb Mueller's heart. The old man was gone long before his wife succumbed. Seven more minutes would pass before Karen Mueller joined her husband somewhere in posthumous eternity.

Twenty minutes after that, the white Econoline pulled into the driveway, and Warren claimed the property as his own.

Caroline's eye had twitched the whole time. She just hadn't been aware of it.

Now, here they were inside the Mueller house, and Caroline was cleaning the blood from the hardwood floor with a bucket of soapy water and a sponge. The suds on top of the bucket had turned sanguine from the blood, but the wood was nearly spotless. One more round of sponging and the last traces of the Muellers would be gone completely. Warren was out for the afternoon, running his own errands and making his own preparations for what was still to come. Abby wasn't exactly sure what time he'd return, but he'd expect the mess to be gone just as he'd commanded, or there would be hell to pay.

Caroline was still on her knees, her hands occasionally wringing out the sponge into the vat of crimson suds, but her mind was obviously elsewhere. And her eye, her goddamn eye kept on twitching. It reminded Abby of that Edgar Allan Poe story, the one where the old man with the bad eye was stabbed to death. *What the hell was it called?* The young guy living with him had stabbed the old man and buried his heart under the floorboards, only the heart came back to life.

The redhead stopped squeezing out her sponge and looked up at her. "We're going to die, too, before this is over."

Abby walked over to her and ran her fingers through Caroline's long, red hair and was shocked to discover just how much her locks looked like an eruption of blood.

"Shhhh. Don't talk like that. You know he still needs us."

"You don't *know* that. Did you see how easily he killed Charlene? He looked like a goddamn snake, just waiting to strike when she least expected it. He put the knife right into her fucking eye!"

The tears came suddenly, and then Caroline was pulling herself away from Abby's touch. She buried her face in her hands and sobbed. To Abby's horror, Caroline's gasps and hitches almost sounded as if she was laughing rather than crying.

"Look. We need each other. We've come this far already. But you also need to understand that Charlene became a danger to us. She was too hooked on drugs to be trusted any longer. All it would have taken was an undercover cop offering some meth and she'd have been selling us down the river."

"He could have let her go," Caroline retorted somewhere from beneath her folded hands.

"Oh, honey, no. She had nothing left. Her husband was already dead, and any life she had before Warren arrived had been washed away. I'm hurting, too. I hated to see her go. But she went fast, and now she's resting in a better place."

Caroline stopped sobbing and looked up at her. That goddamn left eye was still twitching, making her long, black eyelashes look like a Venus flytrap. "She's burning in hell. And so will *we* by the time Warren is done with us."

Caroline stood, picked up the bucket of crimson soap water, and hauled it out the door to dump it.

Abby watched silently. Her heart was suddenly pounding in her chest. *It was* The Telltale Heart! *And, in the end, it drove the young guy mad.* Caroline was right about everything. Sooner or later, Warren Pembroke would also consider *them* as expendable, especially if it meant carrying out his plans successfully. And if the police stumbled onto him, he would definitely kill them without hesitation, and then quietly move on to some new hunting ground. That was what predators always did.

I need to find out what he's thinking. If there was only some way I could see inside his head.

The answer came to her in a light so blinding that her eyes lost focus momentarily. The LSD tabs, the ones embossed with the red serpent illustration, which he took every time he communed with the Dark Lord. She could steal one and finally see for herself just who Warren was taking orders from. Perhaps Satan had a message for *her* and could guide her and Caroline to safety.

Abby looked at the front door of the Mueller farmhouse. Warren had already been gone for at least two hours, and there was no way of knowing exactly when he'd return. Warren told her something about visiting a construction site for supplies he needed, but as always, he didn't get too specific. Caroline was still outside somewhere, perhaps rinsing out the bloodied bucket with the garden house over by the barn. Or perhaps she was curled up in a fetal position somewhere, still lamenting Charlene's death. It didn't matter. What mattered now was getting answers while she had the chance. Her heart pounded even faster as she opened the door to the master bedroom, where the late Herbert and Karen Mueller once slept as husband and wife. The bed was still disheveled, the patchwork quilt and yellow afghan sprawled across the bottom in a tumultuous heap. There were still wet spots on the fitted sheet where Warren and Caroline had copulated the night before, and it made her glad once again that she'd managed to decline his sexual advances.

Caroline is hurting because she lets him fuck her when she doesn't even trust him.

Abby hastily examined the room, looking for the Altoids tin that Warren kept his LSD tabs cached. She started with the dresser drawers. All the Muellers' clothing and personal effects had already been discarded. Caroline had removed all their identification and dumped it somewhere out past the Hetfield cemetery yesterday or the day before. Abby pawed through the loose shirts and underwear that Warren called his wardrobe. He owned only two pairs of jeans that she was aware of, and he was wearing one of them right now. The other pair was in the third drawer down, along with a collection of firearms that she suspected weren't even registered to him. There were boxes and boxes of ammunition in this drawer as well, making her wonder exactly when he'd purchased all this firepower when it seemed like he never even left his headquarters at all unless he needed to. Warren was too smart to purchase anything online and have it delivered, and he was strictly all about paying in cash anyway.

In the distance, she could hear a car rushing down Route 196, and her heart froze. When the car zoomed on toward Hetfield, her breathing returned, and she continued searching. It was when she noticed the half-empty package of adult diapers on top of the dresser that she figured things out. Old lady Mueller was, apparently, incontinent, or at least concerned enough about accidentally wetting her drawers that she'd lined her panties for protection. The package wrapper on the dresser looked alien to the rest of the quaint little farmhouse bedroom. Shit like this just reinforced to her that Warren wasn't nearly as clever as he thought he was. She'd spent her youth hiding her diary in a half-empty package of tampons, and then her stash of reefer when she was older and Daddy decided he needed to snoop through her belongings to make sure she wasn't up to anything illegal. Abby slipped her hand inside, fished around nimbly, and pulled out the Altoids tin.

She listened again for the sound of passing cars. When she heard none, she opened the tin, slipped out a tab of LSD, and popped it under her tongue.

When she was satisfied, she placed the tin back inside the Depends package and went back down to her own bedroom to close her eyes and wait for the Dark Lord to appear.

By the time the meeting in Cumming's office was over, Truth Carson and his crew from Cable World Media had already left the offices of *The Portland Beacon,* their mission to capture Erik Marsh on film and get insight into Le'Sinestre an absolute failure. Erik walked out of Cummings's War Room feeling as if he'd been ambushed, and seeing the remaining troopers huddling around the hallway and whispering back and forth seemed a reminder that even the law was nothing more than an old hound dog sniffing and waiting to pick up a scent. Erik walked past the mob of troopers in their perfectly ironed blue uniforms and black ties, wondering just how much information they had on the state's biggest serial killer since John Joubert had been put to death in 1996. He could smell the starch and desperation in their perfectly pressed collars and pleated pants as he made his way to the elevator. Those boys and girls—Erik counted at least three female troopers in the hallway—were nothing more than bloodhounds waiting for someone to hold up a dirty pair of britches under their noses to pull a scent. They were anxious to get a trail on Le'Sinestre and pull him away from society as if he were nothing more than a raccoon hide. As he passed, the only thought that made any sense was that he couldn't wait to get out of the office and find a bar where he could get absolutely hammered for the afternoon, his latest society column for Beverly LaChance be damned. Even as he boarded the elevator and hit the "Lobby" button, he could picture that bitch up in her swag upper office waiting for him to send his latest article so that she could pass her judgment over it before committing it to the *Portland Beacon*'s society page. People like Beverly LaChance had no fucking idea just how cruel and terrible Maine's real citizens could be. In her eyes, the social scene was all perfectly rosy, with the art district cognoscenti fawning over the latest exhibition in the Portland Art Museum or the latest spoken-word poetry event out in the Old Port. For Beverly, any mention of life's inhumanity made no reference to her as a progenitor to the arts.

Somewhere far away from One City Center was a bar that would be close to hosting Happy Hour, and that was where Erik Marsh was prepared to find solace and begin to consider just exactly what was happening in his unaware city.

Deep down, he was praying he would run into Svetlana along the way, and she would talk him out of it. In his deepest fantasy, she would be there waiting to rescue him from all of this.

"Baby, you okay?"

Da'Quell Nye had removed his prosthetic leg and was lying down on the couch, the sweat still dripping out of his warm, black skin and through the fabric of the New England Patriots t-shirt he was wearing. Physical therapy had been brutal earlier that afternoon, but Da'Q was every bit the warrior he'd been back in Afghanistan. Up until that point, Svetlana had been her normal, chatty self, all positive energy and exuberance as if the white girl with the funny accent was actually the Fairy Princess of Happyland. It was annoying on the surface, particularly on those bad days where Da'Q reverted to memories of Tikrit, where his whole world exploded in gunfire and mortars, and enemies in long, flowing cloaks screamed for him and his platoon to die. But deep down, the girl had been an angel—his angel—constantly soothing him and helping him put the puzzle of his disheveled life back together again.

On those moments when Svetlana went quiet, there was a problem.

He'd had the evening news turned on while Svetlana whipped about his tiny assisted-living apartment, tidying the place in a fastidious whirlwind that almost reminded him of his own mother when he was young. Svetlana was talking to herself as she moved, as always, making comments like, "Okay, *dat* goes *dere*," or "*Dis* needs to be washed and sterilized," or "Da'q, vee need to do a better job of teaching you to be independent. Dis is all stuff you could be doing on your own."

Which was true. And was usually responded to in the patented Da'Quell Nye retorts of, "Uh huh," and "You're right 'bout that," and "I'll do better next time." Just as he told his mom as a child, and told his ex-wife back when his body was all still in one piece. Back when the notion that the *worst thing that could happen* was their Toyota Corolla needing a new transmission when they could scarcely afford to pay their mortgage.

The local news was playing a segment about some homeless, old white dude in the Old Port being run down by a brother out on Lower Congress Street. Svetlana had been chatting a hundred miles per minute before then, and then she was stone silent as she watched the news report, her face turning ashen, more so than usual, if that was possible. The girl was as white-bread as they came. It was after a few seconds of awkward silence after he spoke that she replied.

"I know dat man!" She raised a trembling hand up to her face and rested it across her chin, her mouth, her nose, as if she were a child peeking in fear at something terrible. Seeing her making this gesture reminded him of being a kid and watching *Night of the Living Dead* with his father. Of course, Reggie Nye laughed as his only son peeked through curtained eyes as the little girl in the basement came back from the dead to eat her mother, but the fear in him was as cold and real as hearing mortar blasts exploding around him in the middle of the desert. In the heart of battle, there was no time to cover one's eyes.

"Dat man is Ernie O'Malley. He is homeless person dat hangs around Monument Square sometimes."

"Not anymore," Da'Q said, holding up the remote control to increase the volume on his Panasonic flat-screen television, the only thing of *real* value Kitty Nye allowed him to keep after the divorce settled and the dust cleared. Kitty got their house in Biddeford, their car, most of their bank account, and the wounded warrior from Afghanistan got a fucking television. God was truly dead. As the footage played through, showing video surveillance of the darkened boulevard where the actual assault occurred, the reporter continued speaking in his nasally, condescending tone. He gave the impression that the story on the homeless guy was a throwaway piece that he'd been handed against his will.

"Police officials have confirmed that the driver, a Postal Service employee from Scarborough, was definitely under the influence of a Schedule One narcotic at the time of the incident and has already been booked and processed by the State Police. Prosecutors have already stated that they will pursue a murder charge along with a laundry list of other charges linked to the drug usage and vehicle operation violations."

The surveillance footage played through again, this time in slow motion, and there was Ernie O'Malley, bare-chested and bleeding all down his ribcage in the pale light of the street lamps. There was a big, white blotch around his belly, like a discarded napkin had stuck to his skin, but she couldn't tell what it was in the brief clip. Ernie was jerking and twitching as he staggered down the street; the pupils of his eyes rolled somewhere to the back of his head as if he'd been doing nothing more than sleepwalking. The oncoming vehicle's headlamps fell somewhere down around his knees and then inched upward as the car hurtled faster toward him. And then the old man's body was being propelled backward under the force of the car's bumper, a noiseless blast that knocked the old geezer clear out of his shoes while his bones and organs crumpled and ruptured inside his body. There was a shower of darkened droplets in the night-vision footage that washed over the car's windshield and body-top before the car moved far enough to be out of camera's range, and then the street was empty again.

"Meanwhile, State Police will continue to examine information and try to discover the identity of John Doe, the latest homeless person in the State of Maine to fall victim to such inhuman brutality. They are asking anyone with knowledge of this man's identity to please come forward and help bring justice and closure to his family."

The screen filled with a still shot of Ernie, his face frozen into the unmistakable contortion of emptiness, as if his soul had already fled his body and left it for dead. Svetlana could feel her eyes stinging from the tears that began to fall. Seeing his face reminded her of her mother on the day she was murdered.

"I have to go," Svetlana whispered. "I have to talk to da police. I know dis man. Something happened to him long before that car ran him down. There was dis white van…"

If I could touch his hand, maybe there's still time to see what happened to him. Maybe I can still see through his eyes and find out who did this to him.

Of course, there was no way of knowing if this was true. She'd never turned the *Omniscient Eye* toward a dead person, had never touched a cold, graying hand and seen through cadaver eyes, but in theory, it had to work. Didn't it? Did there need to be electrical brain impulses or senses and feelings, or was it all just a veil of the ethereal she was peeking through all this time? There was no telling until she found out where they were keeping Ernie's body so she could hold his hand and see if the visions came to her. And even then, how long would his visions haunt her once she'd seen them?

It didn't matter. What mattered was catching and putting away the bastards who had done this to him. Not just the young black man who ran him down, but the people who had taken away Ernie's conscience and rendered him a walking puppet with a bloodied chest and flailing arms.

Before Da'Q could protest, Svetlana Barnyk was fishing her car keys out of her pocket and hustling toward the door. The moment her back was turned toward the television, the screen filled with the face of a terrified young black man whose worst crime unto humanity had previously been getting stoned out in the parking lot where he worked and accidentally missorting letters in a postal letter case and giggling like mad when the Reefer Express landed him in Buzz Town.

Da'Quell lifted the remote and switched the channel as Svetlana pulled the door closed behind her. The flat-screen television landed on a station where young white women in swimsuits frolicked on a beach some-where far south of Maine, their long blonde hair blowing in a warm oceanic breeze while the cameras zoomed in on their cleavage. In his mind, though, another young black man was about to spend a lifetime in jail, and why in God's name did he get his own self blown up in a foreign country de-fending *that?*

As the world around her began to transform, Abby Silverstein felt her eyes slowly growing accustomed to the blurred lines of reality, where the walls of the farmhouse turned into wavy columns of flame and burn-ing sulfur and the cheerful pattern of flowers and watering cans leeched into monstrous backdrops of skulls and cadavers all around her. The world inside her head was spinning now, growing opaque with sanguine spatters of crimson and burgundy. Abby held her arms out before her and recoiled in horror as her right hand shriveled before her eyes, grow-ing monstrous the way Warren's deformed arm always appeared, twisted like a wounded animal's paw after being snared in some form of inhumane trap. Terror struck her heart as she witnessed this terrible manifestation, and she wondered if she would ever return back to normal once the trip she was taking had faded. Her dainty fingers shriveled and gnarled in the hue of the raining embers of sulfur falling around her, and when her eyes came back into focus, she was standing in the center of a crossroads.

She could tell that Hell was close by.

"Why have you come here, my child?" a faceless voice asked.

"Warren is out of control," she answered, looking down at the grow-ing hoof where her right hand used to be. She felt dread creeping into her soul as if her body and Warren's now shared something far more sinister than if she'd fornicated with him. That fucking bastard was really, *really* in line with Satan, and far deeper than she ever could have under-stood. For Abby, her acquaintance with Warren had begun with a mutual fascination with the occult. She'd been in a rebellious relationship with her own father, who had acquired a global financial empire by exploiting the lower forms of humanity in countries with names she couldn't even pronounce. And in his own hubris, Carl Silverstein had devised his own form of reality where *he* was a god and could get away with fucking young Taiwanese boys while Abby's mother poisoned herself in a haze of vodka and sedatives, leaving Abby to practically raise herself. Even at the heart of the crossroads, she could feel the spirit of Carl Silverstein floating by down the road on his way to Hell as she tried to bargain for something better for herself. Had something happened to her father back on earth, something terrible she hadn't even found out about yet? It didn't matter. If her father burned for all eternity, she really didn't care. After all, hadn't she caught him stealing glances at her as her own body began to develop with puberty?

Abby could feel the height of the LSD pulsing through her now, the reality of her situation now melting into this terrible vision. The trees on either side of the crossroads were coming to life, moving and pointing toward dangerous and unknown paths all around her. In the distance, she could hear the constant wailing and gnashing of the teeth of the damned, her now-obvious and resolute future based on the choices she'd made and the fate she'd already accepted. She was sure that somewhere deep in that wicked chorus she could hear her own voice pleading for mercy. The sound of it terrified her.

"You are desiring to know how to deal with Warren Pembroke," the faceless voice proclaimed. "You want a glimpse into his mind so that you can tell what he is thinking and whether you are pertinent to his plans or if you are expendable."

"I need to know," Abby cried from the heart of the crossroads. "I need to know what's going on inside his head, and whether he plans to kill me and Caroline to see his plans through."

There was an eternity of silence from the beast where she could hear nothing but the low howling of the damned all around her. Hell was real, that much she understood now. The world of religion back on earth was all fables and superstitions, but here in the netherworld, it was all an eventuality. If heaven existed, it could not be seen or experienced from this place, and Abby found herself damning her father even more for whatever sins he'd committed to push her that much farther away from it.

Seven generations, she remembered. *The Bible said somewhere that the wage of sin will be paid in seven generations. Daddy's sins, MY sins. I don't even know how far back and how far forward my birthright lies.*

"You want to see into Warren's mind, my child?" the beast sang to her. "You want a glimpse through Azezel's Eye .. The *Omniscient Eye*."

Abby turned and saw a figure strolling up the dirt road toward the crossroads, a man with long, flowing hair and a mustache that crept down his sinister chin into two knotted vessels of permanent history. The younger version of Svetlana Barnyk had known this man as "Zee Doctor," who had taken the *Omniscient Eye* from her mother's head and placed it into her own at her mother's deathbed. To Abby, the young immigrant was as foreign and disguised as her own feelings toward Warren Pembroke, but the manifestation of *Zee Doctor* now promised to uncover all of this. This abomination had something to offer her that she had not been promised before: Insight. Insight that she had been so fundamentally missing ever since she'd come in contact with Warren Pembroke.

"I can help you find her," the man with the flowing hair and mustache soothed. "I know who she is, and I can help you take from her what should rightfully be yours."

Abby could feel her acid-induced trip slowly fading around her. In in the distance, she could hear the sound of the Ford Econoline van sweeping into the driveway that once belonged to Herb and Karen Mueller, two middle-aged people who had abandoned the world of commerce and progress for a life of agriculture and simplicity. With their own children raised and delivered unto the unjust and uncaring world, they only had themselves and a collection of livestock of unwitting sheep waiting to be slaughtered to chronicle their tragic existence.

Warren had already stripped everything away from them. And as her high wore off, Abby Silverstein now understood her place in the grand illusion of existence; hers was to strip Warren of his title and authority under Satan's wing. Hers was to inherit the darkness of humanity that Warren was supposed to bring.

"I will lead you to her when the time is right," the figure with the flowing hair and mustache said as the crossroads slowly spun beneath her feet and fell away from under her. The man's eyes burned red, and as he smiled at her, Abby could see the glistening fangs and the forked tongue that slithered between them. The last thought that crossed her mind as the image faded and the sound of the door slamming in the living room below was that this man was some kind of vampire, and he would feast upon her. Not just on her body or the blood that flowed through her veins, but on her very soul. Abby pushed her finger between her teeth and clenched down to suppress the rising scream.

The sound of footfalls below turned into heavy clomps as Warren Pembroke started climbing the stairs.

Abby left her bedroom and darted into the bathroom, locking the door behind her.

Erik Marsh made two passes up and down Monument Square looking for the beautiful European street performer with the rows of pretty braids tied up in ribbons. There had been hope that she would be performing her Carpathian Great and Tiny Circus to a full crowd of tourists and locals, folks from the business district and students from both the University of Southern Maine and the Maine College of Arts, but the plaza was nearly empty. At first Erik dismissed it as a typical workday, but deep down below the surface the truth was finally exposed and festering. People watched the news, and the story of the hour was that some batshit crazy serial killer was operating in the name of Satan. And now that the killer had named himself—

Le'Sinestre. This fucking lunatic thinks he's the Left Hand of the Devil.

—people were going to react as they always had when baddies let themselves loose on the public. The Hillside Strangler, The Zodiac Killer, Son of Sam, BTK. Throw in a clever and disturbing nickname to sensationalize their insanity and you create a panic. Hadn't that been his job, after all? Christ, could he have even come up with a better nickname for this screw-loosened freak if he tried? The guy had obviously grown tired of waiting for his attention and actually sent a letter—while killing the messenger in the process, can't forget *that* particular bit of information—to introduce himself. How fucking thoughtful was *that?* Some homeless guy was taken to the Chevrolet Grill, as Sergeant Mendel would aptly quip while spreading that absorbent sawdust shit on the still-fresh pools of blood. Ol' Dickie never lost his sense of humor, as that was his go-to defense mechanism that kept him from spewing his dinner all over the macadam while cleaning up the latest mess.

After making his second pass down the concourse and not seeing Svetlana, Erik made his way to the Nickelodeon Cinema, turned right, and pushed down the block until he came to the city's thoroughfare of bars and taverns. A quick jaunt down Fore Street led him to the Old Port Tavern, where a wooden sandwich-board sign unfolded neatly out on the sidewalk by the entrance way boasted the daily menu specials in pink, green, and blue chalk and proclaiming tonight to be karaoke night beginning at 9:00 p.m.

I can skip the singing, Erik thought as he pushed the door open and stepped into the darkened room. *I'll just grab a couple of drinks and try and forget about today and the column for Bev that I never got around to writing after getting ambushed by the State Police and—*

"Erik Marsh, is that you?"

I really didn't think today could get any worse, Erik thought as he watched Truth Carson leave the entourage at his table and stride across the bar with his right hand out for him to shake.

"I know we got off on the wrong foot earlier," Carson said as he closed the distance between them and grasped Erik's hand. "Please, come join us. We've got a lot to talk about. I truly believe that if we work together, maybe we can just bring down this nutjob before more innocent lives are taken."

Carson's hand was smooth, manicured, and oily with lotion, and it had all the firmness of an underbaked cake. Erik had to resist the temptation to raise his hand up to his nose and sniff it to determine which scent the King of Cable Newscasting preferred.

"Pretty please, with sugar on top. Come join us at my table. I can fill you in on all the information my own team has collected since we arrived here in Portland."

Erik looked back at Carson. Even with the last rays of daylight going down over the western horizon, the man had failed to produce any trace of five o'clock shadow. In fact, even in the dim light of the tavern, he could detect the remnants of the makeup job his assistants had applied to his face, probably back before he'd even set foot in the *Portland Beacon.* Carson still looked perfect, ready to go on the air at a moment's notice. Another quick glance over to Carson's table—his eyes were quickly adjusting to the dimness inside the tavern—and he could see two separate video cameras and a boom mic parked on the floor nearby. It was a safe bet that Carson's crew were interviewing Portland residents and asking how they were feeling knowing that a psycho killer had invaded their otherwise demure city.

"That's very tempting, but the truth is that I'm waiting for someone. I'm off the clock right now and would prefer to be left alone."

"Are you crazy?" Carson's eyes immediately lost their softness, and Erik could almost see the fierce determination of a cobra waiting to strike. Guys like Truth Carson almost always clawed their way to the top and would fight with every last breath to stay there. Yeah, his hands were soft, but so what? You didn't need your hands to read off a tele-prompter and tell the world about the latest ISIS attack or the tsunami that wiped out an entire city somewhere in Southeast Asia. All one really had to do was look good and sound sincere. *He couldn't have picked a more ironic pseudonym,* Erik thought. *Truth may look pretty and all, but just underneath the surface, it's bitter and angry and unpredictable.* "Right now you're sitting on what is probably what is going to be the biggest story of your career. Let me just point out to you that the big headlines from Maine don't amount to jack shit to the rest of the country. People aren't sitting in their homes and saying to themselves, 'I wonder how life in Maine went today.' You know why? Because this state, even on its worst day, ain't a fucking hot spot for sensational news. Now, I've spent *my* afternoon reading up on your columns over the past two years, and there are only a few real stories that you've managed to break that would remotely draw my attention. I can count on one hand how many I would have aired on my show. And even if I did, those stories would have done nothing to boost my ratings. What does that tell you?"

"It tells me I live in the right state," Erik answered, his eyes never breaking contact with Carson's, and even then he found himself wondering if the television anchor's eyes were really *that* blue or if he wore contact lenses. It wouldn't have surprised him in the least if there was a demographic of women between 30 and 50 who watched his show just because they found his eyes attractive. Hell, there was probably a demographic of gay men who also found him irresistibly sexy.

"Your problem is that you're full of shit," Carson retorted. "You've done some great journalism over the years, but the stories you were dealing with were such small potatoes that you never learned to think outside *The Portland Beacon.* The newspaper era is over, son. Don't you get it? You're sitting on a goldmine with this Le'Sinestre guy. He's your ticket to leaving all this behind and pursuing *real* journalism. Now, you've been to his latest crime scene. You probably have stuff stored up there in that vacuum you call a skull cavity, stuff that could be pulled out of you with the right line of questioning that could offer insight to helping capture this dude before he kills again. Let me interview you. I've been in this business a long, long time, and I know how to aim questions to get real answers."

Erik glanced toward Carson's table again. One of the cameramen he recalled from earlier at the office of *The Beacon* had already shouldered his video unit and was on his way over. Likewise, another guy had switched a button on a small electronics pack and lifted the boom mic into the air. The sharks were already circling, hoping to catch a sound bite or perhaps something more significant.

"Really, your offer is tempting, but this was a mistake, so I'll just be leaving n—"

"Ah, Erik. Der you are!"

Erik spun around and noticed Svetlana standing right behind him. "I was beginning to tink you had forgotten about me completely. Come. We go someplace else vere vee can be alone." And then to Carson, whose face was growing red with both embarrassment and exasperation, "I recognize you from zee television. Vat is your name again? Truth Fargone? It is very nice to meet you, Mister Fargone. Velcome to our great State of Maine."

The laugh erupted from Erik's mouth like a freight train.

"It's 'Carson'," Erik corrected her. "And Mister Carson was just saying goodnight. C'mon, let's get out of here."

Erik Marsh could hear Carson swearing at his entourage and demanding whatever footage they captured to be deleted as he and Svetlana walked out the door.

Part II

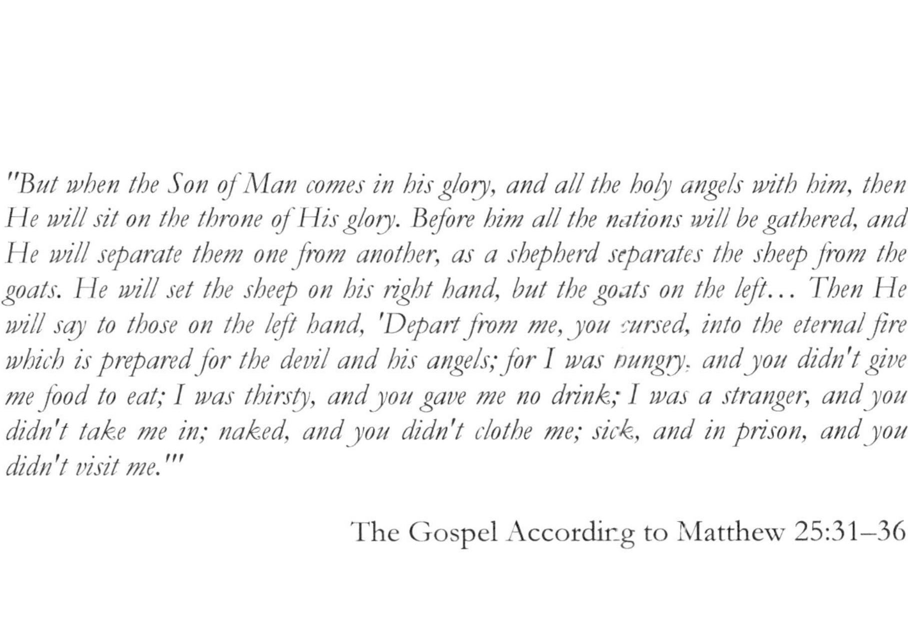

"But when the Son of Man comes in his glory, and all the holy angels with him, then He will sit on the throne of His glory. Before him all the nations will be gathered, and He will separate them one from another, as a shepherd separates the sheep from the goats. He will set the sheep on his right hand, but the goats on the left... Then He will say to those on the left hand, 'Depart from me, you cursed, into the eternal fire which is prepared for the devil and his angels; for I was hungry, and you didn't give me food to eat; I was thirsty, and you gave me no drink; I was a stranger, and you didn't take me in; naked, and you didn't clothe me; sick, and in prison, and you didn't visit me.'"

The Gospel According to Matthew 25:31–36

Chapter 10

Tuesday, June 7th

Even in June, the West Virginia mornings could be cold and unforgiving. Joe Walton had only been sure he'd crossed the Kentucky border when he'd seen the billboards on the side of the highway reading:

WEST VIRGINIA DESERVES BETTER
29 COAL MINERS DEAD
PROSECUTE MASSEY!

Had he stayed on the train, he'd have passed clear through this state and moved directly into Virginia, where the billboards were more apt to read:

SMOKING KILLS!
HOLD BIG TOBACCO ACCOUNTABLE

After all, Richmond was the central nervous system for cigarette rolling. Even as a child on his Daddy's farm, Joe understood the tobacco stalks he'd helped his Daddy roll and dry would be placed in a boxcar like the one he'd ridden in and shipped to where white folks would unload it, roll it into cigarettes, and ship it back out across the nation, but not before lacing it with chemicals and toxins to make each coffin nail as addictive as possible. Joe murdered the Hickey brothers and that poor couple back in Memphis, but that was nothing compared to the genocide Big Tobacco had launched on America. Somewhere under the cover of darkness, Ol' Scratch was laughing.

Joe told the Devil that he wasn't going to do his dirty business, wasn't going to seek out his old guitar, and in the bottom of his heart, he'd meant it. But in those quiet moments when he tried to clear his mind and think of a real, honest-to-goodness course of action—that one was a hoary old saw of his Mama's. *Son, you gotta decide what's the best course of action to take. And you ain't gonna find it unless you put it all into God's hands!*—but the bottom line was that *any* course of action he could fathom was not going to rescue him from damnation. There was a crossroads beyond death, with dirt paths leading in opposing directions, but the truth was that, in one way or another, they all led him down to Hell.

Choices had already been made for him. He thought he'd still had *free will*, but that was as much an illusion as believing one of the paths at the crossroads would lead him to the Pearly Gates of Heaven. There were no best courses of action. No choices. Only acceptance.

The road had taken him to an old, rundown motor lodge outside of Huntington—the Sleepy River Motel, named after the Ohio River, which was neither sleepy nor tranquil as this ramshackle inn's name would suggest. In reality, the river was tempestuous, particularly when the hard spring rains forced its banks to flood, and on occasion knocked down old culverts and washed away large patches of asphalt on those back roads through the sticks.

After ditching the train, he traveled mostly on foot, walking until the soles of his old leather shoes grew thin and he could feel the jagged macadam poking through into the skin of his feet. Once that happened, he found himself holding his thumb out, the same one he used to plant on the neck of his guitar as the fingers of his right hand ran up and down the fretboard, to hitch a ride. He was sure that nobody in Kentucky was going to pull over for an old black man in a dirty suit and bowler hat, but eventually a red Ford F150 rolled to a stop on the shoulder, and a young black man was waving him to climb inside the cab.

"Where ya heading, Old Timer?" The kid—and he had a hard time calling him "kid" when he sat cramped behind the steering wheel like a fat sardine in a shallow tin can. The boy was enormous—was all smiles, as if he'd just won the state lottery or been selected to be the first Negro astronaut to go to the moon.

"I'm traveling north for now. Can y'all give me a lift?"

"Sure. Hop in, grampa!"

Joe climbed into the passenger seat of the extended cab and marveled at just how much room there was. His Daddy's pickup truck was minuscule in comparison. He could remember his knees crushing into the glove box as he and his father drove a full bed of tobacco to Chelmford Square, where that no-good, white bastard Ritchie Millhouse would have them weigh their haul on a broken Old Will Knott scale, and then pay roughly half the real value of the crop in cold, hard cash. "It ain't like you can afford to say 'no'," that fat fuck with the low sideburns and crooked grin would remind them. "If you can find a better deal elsewhere, y'all are free to take it."

"The name's Dante. Dante Moses," the kid behind the wheel said, offering a hand to shake. Joe offered his own hand and was surprised at just how easily the kid's hand enveloped his own. "Just finished my senior year at LSU. I got drafted by the Baltimore Ravens. I'm on my way to the NFL!" Dante smiled, exposing a gap between his middle teeth wide enough for Joe's Daddy's truck to drive through. It was a genuine smile, the kind that Joe himself could scarcely offer nowadays, and it made his heart ache with jealousy. He might have had that same smile back when he used to play in front of crowds of enthusiastic blues fans, but that felt as much an illusion now as his *free will* seemed to be.

"Is that so?" Joe answered. "Good for you, son. I bet y'all's folks is as pleased as pie."

Dante flicked the turn signal and pulled back out onto Interstate 64 East. "Aw, hell. It's only me and my Momma. I never knew my Daddy. But yeah, she sho is proud of me. I broke the LSU record for quarterback sacks during my junior year. We beat Texas A&M that year." The kid's smile grew wider, if that was possible. "And then we beat Iowa in the Outback Bowl. That's when the scouts started calling our house phone and wanting to talk to me. Can you believe that?"

Of course, he could. This kid had been born to be a linebacker the way he, himself, had been born to sing the blues.

"Well, I wish you the best with it. You just remember to keep yourself safe. Them big boys in the NFL don't care about college bowl records or campus trophy cases. They only care about division championships and Super Bowl rings." Joe Walton remembered this from decades of Februarys back at Luttrell, where the convicts gathered to watch the final game of America's favorite pastime. It wasn't until the Houston

Oilers moved to Nashville in 1997 and switched their name to The Titans that the inmates in Mark H. Luttrell suddenly became rabid football fans and doubled their workload around the prison to retain their right to convene in the cafeteria and watch the game on a projection-screen television. Only, Joe Walton didn't give a shit about football and volunteered to work kitchen duty instead. Doing so was a badge of sacrifice that led the other inmates to offer a cigarette or two in return. "And they'll mow you down to the ground to get it. You be expendable, and if you get hurt, they'll replace you with somebody else that's just as hungry as you are for success."

Dante chuckled, and the paunch he was hiding behind the truck's oversized steering wheel shook with delight. He carried himself with a level of confidence as large as his bulky frame, as if he knew some cosmic secret that he kept hidden beneath the surface of his cocksure smile.

"Aw, shit. I ain't got nothing to worry about," he said, lifting his left hand off the steering wheel and wiping a line of sweat that was forming across his forehead. "I got talent. And you can't hold back talent, Joe. At least that's what my Momma always says."

Joe felt his insides turn to ice. Did he tell this kid his name? It had been on the tip of his tongue to throw out a different name, one he could stick with now that the law was going to be on the lookout for "Tobacco Joe" Walton. Back in the boxcar, he'd thought of The Swinging Foot, the three-piece house band that accompanied him whenever he gigged as a teenager. Willie "Stump" Simms on piano, Del Grier on the upright bass, and Collie Gray on drums. Back in the boxcar, Joe had decided to go with Del for his pseudonym. He'd like Del best. Del Grier, at 6'4", was the tallest member of the band. And that cat could place his long, black finger on the top of his instrument and twirl his bass around is if it were a lover on the dance floor, and then shift his fingers around the frets as if he were sliding them right up her dress to her black velvet honeypot. All the while, that razor-sharp mustache above his lip wouldn't flick a whisker as his lips curled into a smile.

Dante dropped his left hand back on the steering wheel, and Joe was suddenly, dreadfully certain that Ol' Scratch owned this boy's soul already. It was a safe bet that, once upon a time, Dante Moses was right-handed, just as he had been as a boy. Something in that deal with the Devil changes things, turns things opposite. Joe could recount too easily the number of folks he'd seen as the decades flipped by like pages in the old Sears and Roebuck calendar his Mama hung on their kitchen wall, folks who were known as left-handers, whose lives were burdened by tragedy. Joe had already been serving time in prison when that black kid from Seattle went to England and became famous, only to die of a drug overdose after returning to America and headlining the closing day of Woodstock. A few quick decades later, another Seattle luminary changed the face of rock and roll just before blowing his brains out with a double-barrel shotgun. How many had given their souls, only to succumb to tragedy after realizing what they'd done? How many continued to keep going, without even caring?

"Yessir, I'm ready to make my mark on professional football," Dante continued, both hands now grasping the steering wheel as if he wasn't just driving a pickup truck, but driving his life into something better, something more permanent than schlepping a backpack of textbooks around and pretending to give a damn about education while an easy and lucrative future lay ahead, waiting to be taken. "I'm gonna break all kinds of records once I get that Ravens jersey on and hit the gridiron. This is what I was *born* to do."

Perhaps it had been a trick of the mind, but Joe could almost smell the odor of brimstone oozing out of this kid's pores. Dante stared ahead at the road, the smile never leaving his face, as if all of this was truly just a dream, and if it *was* a dream, then this kid would probably rather die than have to wake up and see and understand exactly what he'd given up when he bargained with Ol' Scratch.

When Joe saw the sign at the edge of I64 reading

NOW LEAVING KENTUCKY, COME BACK SOON!

he turned and looked at Dante Moses.

The young man driving the truck had sprouted horns; tiny nubs were peeking through the short, curly hairs of his scalp. Joe didn't think the kid had been aware of it, as Dante's eyes never deviated from the highway or the reel of film projecting in his head of each and every tackle the kid had made on the field after offering his soul for talent and success. There was only a void between reality and fantasy, a veil that Joe had come to know after years of pondering the matter after his own success had been stripped away.

"You can let me off here," Joe said coolly, his eyes fixed on the left-handed driver.

"Aw, c'mon, gramps," Dante replied from somewhere in his dream state. "Let me take you up to Portland. I got time. Let me help you find your guitar."

A shiver ran down Joe's spine. "I ain't going to Portland. I already made myself clear about that."

"You're gonna go wherever *He* tells you to go," Dante said, the smile never leaving his face. The kid's smile was frightening. "Haven't you figured that out yet, Joe?"

"You can just pull over now."

"You know I can't do that," Dante said, taking his left hand off the wheel and wiping the sweat from his brow once again. "I have to follow *His* directions, and so do you."

There was a break in the median up ahead, with the ubiquitous NO U-TURN sign directly behind it. The turn was separated by a patch of asphalt between the long, unending island of grass that divided the east- and westbound lanes of Route 64, one where the State Police either parked and set up speed traps or reversed direction to respond to an emergency. Today, the arterial was empty, as if some unseen force had kept it so. Joe's heart was pounding in his chest as Dante, at first, stomped on the gas pedal, and then at the last second slammed on the brakes of the F150 so that he could turn onto the arterial, and then navigate the over-sized pickup truck into the direction of oncoming traffic.

"You're going to do as *He* says, aren't you?" the face of the still-smiling young black man on his way to play Baltimore Ravens football asked. The first of the oncoming vehicles lay hard on the horn before shifting a sharp left onto the shoulder to avoid the head-on collision.

"I'm gonna do what's right," Joe responded, the image of the cross-roads already in his mind's eye. "And if that means both of us going to Hell, then so be it. He's gonna cheat you outta playing football and being famous just like he cheated me. And I don't give a fuck. If we die right now, it'll be *you* that's cheated out of your future."

More cars zoomed past, the faces of each driver stricken with both surprise and terror. Later, after all of this was over, a string of white motorists were going to be filmed on the five o'clock news stating how that young colored fellow behind the wheel of the pickup truck was out of his mind, probably on drugs, and had caused the kind of accident that leaves lots of innocent folks dead. Wasn't that how the white world worked, after all?

Joe had been staring out at the oncoming line of cars and tractor-trailers. Fate wasn't going to forgive them easily, as Dante Moses had already cast the die into motion. Each passing vehicle caused a ripple of vibrations in its wake, shaking the hell out of the red F150 as they flew by. A quick glance at the speedometer showed that Dante Moses was hurtling at the oncoming traffic at nearly 80 miles per hour, and parting the steel beasts like the Red Sea. Had Joe not been terrified, he would have laughed at the coincidence of the boy's name and biblical reference.

"Son, please don't do this." Joe reached out his left hand and placed it on the boy's shoulder. He could feel the heat of the kid's body through the LSU Football—GEAUX TIGERS—t-shirt he was wearing. Dante Moses felt like a volcano, and his body's reaction to Joe's touch proved it as tiny pinholes of burning sulfur blistered through the cotton fabric. The edges of the shirt smoldered just as Joe yanked his hand away, and then the fifth-round draft pick out of Louisiana laughed as his shirt actually caught fire. The smile never left Dante's face.

"Let's forget all about Portland, Joe. Let me take you home instead. Let me take you down to Hell and deliver you in person."

His hands turned the steering wheel forcefully to the left, and then to the right. In his peripheral vision, Joe watched as a green Subaru station wagon cocked its tires sharply to the right and went careening into the copse of trees surrounding the outer edge of the highway. More cars behind that one pulled hard maneuvers and managed to stay on the neck of the road and not lose control. On the opposite side, a motorcyclist swerved and caught the guardrail, and then he was somersaulting in mid-air, only to land in the passing lane on the other side of the highway. Seconds later, the cyclist was run over by an eighteen-wheeler.

Joe could feel his heart pounding in his chest and began to see his life flashing before his eyes. He'd thought that phenomenon had always been a myth, but here he was, remembering the alligator eating his Mama's chickens and holding that old, beat-up acoustic guitar in his hands the first time, and the way it felt the day he'd murdered the Hickey brothers and tacked their hides inside the old smokehouse, and then lit the logs inside the firebox and closed the door.

This was how his life was going to end.

And almost hilariously, he found he didn't care. He was tired of running.

"Alright, son. We'll go together."

Joe Walton stretched his calloused fingers out, grabbed the steering wheel, and gave it a hard yank toward the trees. By now the oncoming traffic had already slowed way down to a crawl, most pulling over toward the side of the road and standing still to see how this would end. Joe could already hear the helicopter hovering somewhere overhead, and he could see the flashing blue lights of the State Police approaching from both directions. Guns would be pulled, and shots were most likely going to be fired before this was over. And if Dante Moses survived all this, he was going to look right at the authorities and tell them that he had no idea Joe was an outlaw when he picked him up at the side of the road and forced him to take evasive actions out of fear for his life.

Only, the kid was fighting back, trying hard to push the steering wheel back toward the road.

"Your soul is *Mine*, Joe," an unearthly voice issued from Dante's lips. "Did you really think you could get the upper hand on me?" The kid's t-shirt was now fully ablaze, and smoke was beginning to fill the cabin of the pickup truck. It smelled of burning flesh, and it again made Joe think of the Hickey brothers and the way the flies hovered around their flayed carcasses while their skins turned brown in the heat of the smokehouse.

Joe turned his torso around and swung his right hand with all his might. He felt his knuckles crushing into the big kid's nose, and the crunch of exploding cartilage underneath his hand was proof enough that Dante's nose was broken. Dante reeled backward against his seat with a surprised "Ooof," and then blood was gushing down his lips and chin. Dante took his hands off the steering wheel and clapped them over his now crooked nose, and Joe jerked hard again at the wheel. The red F150 flew off the gravel and into the grass, and then it smashed into the trunk of a pine tree; fir-covered limbs cracked and flew as the bumper collided, and then the airbag was exploding into Dante's bloodied face just as the windshield shattered and fell inward.

When Joe opened his eyes and discovered that his body was unharmed and relatively intact, he unbuckled his seatbelt, opened the door, and rushed into the woods before the police could navigate the gridlock of traffic and make it to the scene.

"You look like hell, buddy. Are you alright?"

Joe looked at the white-bread dude at the counter of the Sleepy River Motel and nearly broke into laughter. The guy was easily in his forties and looked like a rube you'd see at a carnival midway. His balding pate was covered with an unconvincing comb-over that started from somewhere on the back of his head, and unlike Del Grier's mustache, his was a tangle of whiskers that looked more like pubic hair he'd seen on almost every white inmate back at Mark H. Luttrell. If Joe looked like hell, this dude was no bargain, either.

"Yes, I'm fine. Just had a bit of a rough spell in my travels. Y'all got any rooms available?"

"Sure do. I'm assuming you want a single occupancy?" The guy was wearing a heavy-duty plastic badge just above the left breast pocket of his Dockers button-down. The badge read SRM in a light blue oval, with the name Skip K. just beneath. Skip K. reached back to a card table behind him, lifted a guest registry book, and began leafing through the pages.

"That'd be fine," Joe said. "Whatever's cheapest."

"Oh, the rooms around here are very competitive," Skip K. said, dropping the opened registry in front of him on the service desk. The book landed with a plop that startled Joe for a moment, and then he got a hold of himself again. He had to play this cool. There was no way of knowing if the helicopter above or the squad cars that arrived on the scene of the accident had video footage of him darting into the pines, or if the news was already privy to Joe's being in the pickup truck that had caused so much catastrophe on I64. Skip continued droning on in his nasally white-bread voice. "I'm just gonna need a driver's license and valid credit card."

"Look, son, all I got on me right now is cash. My car just died, and I never fished my wallet out of my glove box before the tow truck hauled it away. I just need a room for the night, and then I'll be on my way in the morning. I'll even pay up front, if that he'ps."

Skip K. looked at the registry book, and then at the black man in the filthy suit and bowler hat. There was no doubt in his mind that this was all about to go sour. Even if this dumb-fuck whitey gave him a room, he could almost count on the police paying him a visit long before the sunset. That was how things worked. Right now, Skip K. was sizing him up as some kind of criminal or drug addict. The fact that he was paying in cash was immediately suspect; how did a black man in a filthy outfit come across hard-earned American dollars without somehow breaking the law to get it?

"Let me ask you something?" Skip K. leaned across the desk so that he was staring eye-to-eye with Joe Walton, never knowing what crimes this colored fella *was* responsible for. "What towing company took your car away?"

Fucking shit! Rube or not, Captain Comb-over, here, is on the ball. He's a sharp one, and shame on me for not having a better story ready for him.

"I don't rightly recall. I called Triple A, and they arranged ever'thing. Look, I ain't gonna beg ya or nothing, and I ain't gonna raise a stink about you bein' a racist white prick for not giving me a room. Either you will, or you ain't, and I'll be on my way. I'm not looking for trouble. I just need a place to sleep tonight."

Skip K., a.k.a. Captain Comb-over, leaned back and thought for a moment. When he came to a decision, he reached forward and closed the registry and placed it back on the folding table behind him. Afterward, he reached to a pegboard behind him, hauled down a diamond-shaped key fob, and placed it on the counter in front of Joe.

"Normal rate is thirty-nine ninety-nine per night. You wanna stay, you can pay me eighty. And you're gone before we even roll out the continental breakfast in the morning. No questions asked, no visits from the police. Are we understood?"

Joe reached into his pants pocket and pulled out the billfold and what remained of his advance from his gig at the Velvet Mojo. As he peeled off four twenties from the wad, he thought about Roy Higgins and wondered if that fat fuck burned to death when his bar went up in flames. Or if Dante Moses had burned to death when the airbag trapped him behind the steering wheel of his crumpled pickup truck as his shirt continued to conflagrate.

Just before sleep finally overcame him, Joe watched the evening news on an old 19-inch television screen on top of his room's only dresser. The Zenith even came equipped with the old-fashioned rabbit-ears antennae. Of course, the big headline had been about Dante Moses, the LSU linebacker who had been on his way to Baltimore to join the Ravens for summer practice, only to crash his truck after losing his mind and crossing into oncoming traffic. Naturally, the young black man was dead behind the wheel, and when they pulled the responding State Police lieutenant to give details, a bag of suspicious white powder magically appeared as evidence in part of their "ongoing investigation." Thankfully, no mention of Joe Walton, the fugitive from Memphis, was made.

"I'll be damned," Joe whispered as the story ended and faded back to the anchorwoman behind the news desk. He'd almost fallen completely asleep when the young, attractive blond purveying the news switched stories to the incident on the Chase Atlantic Railway line from the night before. Joe Walton sat up on his bed, picked up the remote control, and turned up the volume.

"We take you now to John Wilson for an update on the bomb threat that shut down one of the eastern seaboard's biggest freighting lines. John?"

"Tonya, I'm standing here in Northern Kentucky where officials have finally concluded their search of each car on the Chase Atlantic Railway's northbound service after threats were phoned in to local authorities that a bomb was going to wipe out all the cars affiliated with Petrol-Plus Oil. The company, owned by financial titan Barry Silverstein, has come under close scrutiny by political action committees and protest groups after being linked to Saudi oil interests that have alleged ties with the Islam extremist group, ISIS."

"Motherfucker," Joe whispered, picking up the remote control and turning off the television set. "They wasn't even looking for me."

The bluesman lay his head down on a faded blue pillow and immediately fell sound asleep.

And on that cold and unforgiving Wednesday morning, before the sun could reach above the Appalachians with the first rays of light, "Tobacco Joe" Walton woke up, quietly got dressed, and hit the road, making sure to leave the diamond-shaped key fob dangling from the door to his room.

※ ※ ※

"You *still* owe me a column from yesterday!"

Erik was sitting across from Beverly LaChance in her tiny office, immediately wishing he'd never asked R.J. Cummings for the new position. His mind was still stuck on yesterday's surprise letter from Le'Sinestre and the upheaval of police activity that had descended upon the *Portland Beacon* because of it. He'd had his share of letters from the local crazies during his tenure as the crime beat reporter; death threats, hoaxes, and lunatic ramblings were nothing new to him. But this one had been different. This one had rattled him enough to snap-capture an image of the black crayon scribblings and sketches on his otherwise useless cell phone, and he'd spent half the night examining them when he should have been sleeping. He'd ruminated for hours—long after he'd left Svetlana's studio flat and went home for the night—on how the hard-sloped lettering had matched the bloody letters on the elementary school walls, and Googled the satanic glyphs on the PC in his living room to see what they meant. It had been a miracle that Svetlana had found him earlier that evening, before he could get himself blind, stinking drunk and let it all go.

It had felt as if she'd *known* to look for him. It had felt as if she'd used that *Omniscient Eye* of hers to see inside him and know that he was on the brink of some kind of self-destructive path and had intervened. Erik had never believed in angels, but the East European gypsy girl felt more and more like something Heaven-sent. Even here in Beverly's office, his mind was wandering off to wondering where she was right now, and if she was thinking about him.

"You didn't *really* vant to drink dat whiskey anyway, did you?" she asked in her bubbly European voice, the same voice she used to cajole the audience that gathered to watch the Carpathian Great and Tiny Circus out in Monument Square. "Dat stuff is no good for you." She'd wrapped her arms tight around him as they walked back up Exchange Street toward the Congress Street intersection. He was already awash with relief after she broke up the interaction between him and Truth Carson back at the Old Port Tavern, and to a greater degree that she'd found him at all after his lousy day, but as they approached the Meridian Café on Congress Street, Svetlana grew quiet. She stopped dead in her tracks when they reached the empty glass grotto of the storefront where Ernie O'Malley had last been seen sleeping on his ratty old blanket. By then, the blanket and old hat that held his donation money had been snatched away by some other homeless person in the city, and whatever vestiges of the old man's existence he'd had left were gone. Taken. It was if he never existed.

"I have to tell you sometink," Svetlana whispered as her eyes began to well with tears. "I had to go to da police station today—"

"Have you even heard a word I said?" Beverly LaChance had her hands planted firmly on her hips, her face contorted into a look of exasperation. "If you want a paycheck at the end of the week, you actually have to earn it."

"Yeah, I know. I tried, I really did, but yesterday unraveled way too quick for me. *You* try having a serial killer drop you a letter attached to a dead guy's body and see if *you* feel up to writing about celebrity sightings in the Old Port. It's not my fault. I wasn't expecting this." Erik shifted uncomfortably in his chair, his mind still flashing back to the satanic glyphs on the note from Le'Sinestre. Svetlana had brought him back to her apartment, and over a cup of tea, she shared her experience of identifying the body of Ernie O'Malley after nobody else in the state of Maine could trouble themselves to give his photograph a second glance. Officer Anderson had been the one to drive her to the State Medical Examiner's office to see the old man's body and make the identification. In return, Erik showed her the photograph on his cell phone of Le'Sinestre's letter. She used her thumb and index finger to enlarge the image on his phone, and then she examined each symbol, nodding and making "hmmmph" sounds as her eyes penetrated each obscene angle and arc. It was the seventh glyph that made her gasp and put her hand over her mouth.

"What is it?"

"I know dis one! Dis is called 'Azezel's Eye.' *The Omniscient Eye*! Dis is what allows me to see into people's pasts."

Erik glanced down at the image. The symbol was a circle, the orb of an eye, with what appeared to be an upside-down crucifix curving into an also upside down question mark directly in the center of the circle. And within the center of the question mark's curve was an X, forming the pupil of the eye.

"It's just a coincidence," Erik answered, looking into the unblinking eye. It felt almost hypnotic to look at it.

The cell phone rang in his hand. It happened so unexpectedly that Erik actually jumped backward, nearly dropping his phone onto the floor.

"I thought you said your phone was deactivated," she whispered, staring at the phone in his hand as if it were a poisonous snake waiting to strike.

"It is. I haven't paid my bill in two months."

The phone continued ringing. Erik held it up and glanced at the caller ID screen. The screen simply read PRIVATE CALLER, NUMBER UN-AVAILABLE.

"This is insane. I don't understand." Erik's thumb hovered over the icon that would answer the call, but he couldn't bring himself to push the button. The phone rang and vibrated in his hand for the fifth time.

"Let it go to voicemail," Svetlana insisted. "Dere's no need to answer it. You are here vith me, and you're going to give me all your attention tonight. Do you understand me?"

"Yes."

The phone stopped ringing. There was no beep to indicate any message had been left in his voicemail file. Erik stood and stared at the cellphone in his hand for a long while, until Svetlana put her hand on top of his and said, "Just turn it off for the night and put it away. Vee von't go looking for any answers tonight. Vee don't need to invite any demons in to speak to us. It's been a long day for both of us already."

Erik nodded, turned off the cellphone's power, and shoved it into his pocket.

"Good. Now, how about dat tea?"

Erik could tell that she'd been deeply rattled as she turned away and sauntered into her tiny kitchen to put the kettle on the stove. The normally bubbly, charming, young street performer was now somber, nervous. It had been a jarring transformation, as he'd always found comfort in her confidence and her aloof style, a feeling he'd never felt all the time he'd been with Kelly. He'd considered his ex-wife his equal through most of their marriage, but Svetlana had felt like a higher power to him. Even with her being much younger than he was, it felt like she had all the answers and had taught him more about life and living than Kelly ever could. Watching her now felt as if she'd had that *joie de vivre* taken from her, the same way some faceless figure had removed all her homeless friend's personal belongings once he was gone. Seeing her go through that made him feel angry and terrified at the same time.

But the glyph… *Azezel's Eye.* How prevalent had that been in the culture of Devil worship? What had been Le'Sinestre's purpose in adding it to his note? Had it been for show? Was this guy merely drawing satanic images to induce fear, or was he really buying into the whole "black magic" angle? Erik pondered these things until Svetlana returned from the kitchen with two cups of tea. At some point, her smile had returned, and Erik felt certain once again that she was some kind of angel sent to protect him.

"Look, the movie premiere is only two days away," Beverly LaChance scowled. "If you really still want it, you get out there and find a story to report about. And it had better be a damn good column, let me be clear on that. Otherwise, you can kiss your opportunity for the premiere good-bye, and I'll give it to one of the interns from USM. Do you understand?" Beverly stood up and walked over to the door. She opened it in a grand, sweeping fashion as if to punctuate the fact that she was finished with this meeting whether he was ready or not. Erik couldn't help but admire her. There was a reason Beverly was running the department. She exuded authority with laser precision, all the while maintaining that feminine mystique that made her both desirable and despised by her underlings. Even the girls who penned columns on wedding shows and garden parties at the Portland Expo Center had it in for her, gossiping quietly about her around the Keurig coffee machine whenever her door was closed.

It's all just a big game, Erik thought as he slipped past her and plodded off down the corridor to the newsroom. *Everything is for show. It's all about impressing people and keeping up appearances and knowing our roles. I've been at this shit far longer than she has, but* she *knows how to play the game, and I don't. That's why she's the boss.*

And then a final, upsetting thought flashed through his mind as he made his way down the lower hallway of One City Center. It made his blood run cold so that even in the warmth of the late morning sun he felt himself shivering.

Svetlana possesses black magic. What power she has came from the Devil. How the hell am I supposed to trust her? It's not like I can see into HER past.

Erik stopped dead in his tracks, his mind a jumble of profound confusion. *She knew how to find me last night. She came right into the Old Port Tavern and rescued me from Truth Carson. What if she's a part of all of this? What if she's been working for Le'Sinestre all along and is using me to get information? Jesus Christ, she can touch my hand and know everything about me. What information has she stolen from me already?*

The hands on his wristwatch weren't even at 10:00 a.m., but the hackles on his neck and shoulders were rising in desperation for that first drink of the day, that tumbler of whiskey that would steady his nerves and bring his heart rate back down to normal before that second tumbler could make him feel numb.

"Get that story first," he told himself as he darted past the blonde tart at the reception desk, who'd been eyeing him suspiciously ever since he'd appeared in the Social Pages offices. "Get your column written and submitted to that bitch Beverly, *then* you can drink the rest of today away."

Erik found himself exiting One City Center through the parking garage rather than through the front doors that opened into Monument Square. For all he knew, Svetlana might have been waiting outside for him, and he wasn't ready to face her until he'd figured things out.

Chapter 11

Wednesday, June 8th

Dawn had broken up in Hetfield, and a young couple was sitting in an idling car on the corner of Main Street and Goddard. The woman in the passenger seat was barely awake and had to keep rubbing the crust out of the corners of her eyes. It was as if every time she flicked away the little pebbles of sleep, the sun would cause her to squint again, and moments later, new tears would trickle out like lava, forming new islands of crust where the old ones had taken root. Her fiery red hair was still disheveled in spite of the ponytail she'd wrapped before leaving the old farmhouse.

"You still ain't told me what we're looking for yet, or why we have to be out so goddamn early this morning," she announced in an irritable voice.

The man with the deformed right hand sat behind the wheel, watching Main Street through his rearview mirror. The car's radio was belting out an old Rolling Stones number, "Gimme Shelter," and at the moment Keith Richards was delivering some blistering guitar work. Concentration broken, Warren Pembroke found himself wondering if Richards was left-handed. When Caroline spoke, it jarred him from the daydream he was having.

"We're on a recon mission," he said. "The school bus will be coming by any minute now. We need to know its precise route. Every stop, every cluster of little faces, every corner where concerned parents are waiting with their children. The school year ends on Friday, so we've only got a couple of days to get things perfect before we make our move."

Caroline yawned for the umpteenth time. Then she fished a pack of Camels out of the purse by her feet, pulled out a cigarette, and lit it. The Volkswagen Jetta's cabin filled with a light blue haze, until she cracked open the window and began fanning the smoke out with her hand.

Warren Pembroke ignored her and listened to Jagger spouting off about how rape and murder was just a shot away. The female vocalist—her name being Merry Clayton, although Warren Pembroke would never know that; he would only know her as "that black girl" whose voice made him both lustful and afraid—was howling in the background for all her worth, and it once again made goosebumps rise up and down his flesh. When the song ended, he looked down at his watch.

7:20 a.m.

Caroline took a few more drags off her cigarette, rolled down the window a bit further, and tossed the butt out onto the sidewalk. Her head was still heavy from the cocaine she'd snorted the night before, and she already found herself wanting a few "pick-me-up" lines just to get her brain back into working order. If Warren wanted her to be paying the same kind of attention he was, he was going to have to offer a helping hand because she was miles away from the corner of Sober and Alert. The school bus could have passed twenty times by now, and she wouldn't have noticed and couldn't have cared less. She thought about asking him for a hit but decided to stick to wiping the new mounds of crust out of her eyes.

Which was good, because Warren appeared to be deep in thought, and disturbing him when he got that way was just asking for a slap in the face—with his deformed hand, no less—and a verbal rebuke that would probably leave her in tears.

Warren took another glance in the rearview mirror, then checked his watch again.

7:23 a.m.

Somewhere far up the street from where they were parked, the front door to a tall, white colonial opened, and two Chinese sisters in shorts and t-shirts stepped out onto the top riser of the brick stairway. The older one adjusted her backpack, turned back toward the open door, and stepped back onto the jamb to kiss her mother goodbye. The younger one followed suit, adjusting her backpack onto her shoulders, before turning to kiss mommy. *Good.* Good for these two little brats who still think mommy was the light of their world.

The memory crawled into his brain like a poisoned worm; one where his daddy, Colin Pembroke, had already left their house in Brunswick to head north on Route 1 to the Bath Iron Works, and Janis, his mommy, was getting him ready for his last day of school back in fifth grade. His friends, Tommy and Dave, had gotten permission that morning to ride their bicycles the mile and a half to the Harriet Beecher Stowe Elementary School, but Janis Pembroke wasn't going to budge. The world's biggest "helicopter mom"—a phrase Warren wouldn't hear until long after he began college—would take him by his deformed hand and hold it up in front of his face.

"Oh, honey, don't you get it? Don't you see that you need BOTH hands to work your brakes properly?" She was alluding to the hand-brakes on both sides of the handlebars on the 10-speed bike Colin bought for his son's 10th birthday, the ones she had pointed out to his dad that were as useless as tits on a bull if he couldn't open his right hand far enough to engage the metal lever so that his rear brake operated at the same time as his front brake. And as if her nagging hadn't been enough, Warren had managed to flip his bicycle over on at least three different occasions that spring, with the last time causing him a bloody nose when his face hit the cold spring macadam. Warren had come home with his face and shirt crusted with blood, and his handlebars once again knocked out of alignment. The boy was lucky he was even allowed to ride a bicycle at all.

Jump-cut to homeroom, long after Tommy and Dave had padlocked their own 10-speeds to the iron bike rack outside the school and made it safely into homeroom.

"Didja have a nice ride on the school bus?" Tommy Malone rubbed it in immediately. "What's the matter? Didn't mommy think you could make it to school without flattening your nose again?"

Dave Pfeiffer laughed as well. "Maybe there isn't a handicapped parking spot on the bicycle rack."

Both boys, even though he still called them "friends," spent the morning lambasting Warren over the fact that he didn't get to ride his bike to school. Their jibes were cruel, but they were true, and that was the thing that hurt him the most. Janis Pembroke was *always* going to hold her only son hostage to the terrible, big, wide world as if he would never be able to survive on his own. And Colin Pembroke would *always* look at his only son as an abomination, a freak of nature that brought shame down upon his family. Even at ten years old, there had been an acute awareness of his role within his family, and within life itself. He could remember his tenth birthday, after Colin Pembroke had brought him out to the garage to show him the black-and-white Avocet 10-speed with the red ribbon and birthday tag dangling merrily off the handlebars. And he could remember the discussion he'd overheard when his parents thought he was asleep.

"How *could* you? How could you buy him that bike when you know goddamn well his hand won't be able to work the brake?"

"Honey, he's ten years old. He needs to learn how to adjust. How to compensate. If he wants it badly enough, he'll *learn* how to use his hand and make it work."

"Jesus Christ! I swear to God, I think you want him to have an accident. You'd just fucking love it if he pedaled out into traffic and then his hand didn't work when he needed it to, and *then* he flips that bike when coasting into an intersection. You'd love a neat and tidy little accident that put your poor, deformed son into a coffin so that you wouldn't have to deal with him. And knowing you, you'd love the wave of sympathy that would pour in afterward. You'd love our neighbors spouting off about how you tried to be the best daddy ever when you bought him that goddamn bike that's too big for him to begin with. You'd love the fucking casseroles the other moms would drop off to the house after Warren's funeral, and how all our neighbors you're so sure are thinking of our son as a freak would suddenly see differently. They'd only see our struggle and how hard we tried, and they would take pity on us rather than judge us. That's what you want, isn't it? To stop being looked at as if we're raising a monster and be looked at as if tried our best to treat him as if he were a normal boy?"

Warren could remember with perfect, icy clarity the sound of his father slapping his mother somewhere off in the sanctity of their bedroom. The sound of flesh smacking across flesh, and then his mother crying out in surprise, long after he'd been tucked in and his own bedroom light had been turned off.

"You just mind who the fuck you're talking to," Colin Pembroke told his cowering wife after delivering the blow. "Warren is what he is, and he ain't going to change. But that doesn't mean we need to keep treating him as if he was different than anyone else. I bought him that bicycle because that's what fathers do. They raise their sons to stop being afraid of the world around them and learn to live in it. And I ain't raising Warren to be no goddamn pussy. If I did, I'd be a failure as a father."

The ten-year-old Warren Pembroke had overheard all of this. And he remembered the hatred he felt for his daddy after hearing the senior Pembroke slap his mother. It would be a good six years before the "accident" that would give Warren the vindication he wanted against the man whose sperm mixed with his mom's bad batch of chromosomes and gave him life, deformed or not. Even in his deepest dreams, he could still see his father with the family's Chrysler LeBaron jacked up out in the garage, and Colin Pembroke on the roller-skid underneath trying to fix a damaged U-joint, and his own deformed hand suddenly reaching out to the jack's handle and giving it a good, sharp twist as if there had never been a thing wrong with his hand to begin with.

In the rearview mirror, the school bus had emerged on the corner down by the Hetfield Library and turned onto Main Street. He could see a handful of houses behind the parked car where groups of children had come outside to wait for the bus to pick them up. Up ahead, the Chinese girls from the colonial were now down on the sidewalk, their backpacks nestled neatly down their posteriors as they waited to board the school bus. And all up and down Main Street, not a single parent was standing with their children. After all, this was their final week of school, and they all knew the drill by now.

Warren turned toward Caroline only to discover that she'd dozed off again. His hand was fast, in the same manner that Colin Pembroke's hand had been fast to lash out and strike his mother.

"Wake up, you fucking cunt," he demanded after his misshapen hand slammed across her sleeping face.

Caroline sat bold upright and shot her hand up to cover the already blossoming red mark on her cheek. "You didn't have to do that, you asshole!"

"The bus is coming. The driver's route begins around four houses back. You're going to need to remember this for Friday."

The man with the deformed hand watched the two sisters turn on the sidewalk and wave back up at their mom, who was standing in the open doorway. The school bus zipped past the car they were sitting in, and the car shook from the vibration waving off the bigger vehicle. A few seconds later, the bus's red flashing lights were coming on as the vehicle squealed to a stop at the curbside. The door opened, and the two sisters climbed dreamily inside and hustled toward the back of the bus. Warren watched as the younger of the two sisters unslung her backpack and dropped it into the seat as the red flashing lights were turned off. There was a brief moment when the girl looked out the back window of the bus, noticed him watching, and offered a bright, cheery smile and accompanying wave at him.

Warren Pembroke lifted his deformed hand off the steering wheel, smiled his friendliest smile, and waved back at her. In his mind's eye, he could already see her pupils oozing into cloudy onyx puddles and goat horns sprouting from her forehead. When the girl took her seat, and the bus started moving forward, he wrapped his bulbous fingers around the gearshift, pulled it into drive, and followed.

"Tobacco Joe" Walton hardly slept a wink from the time he left Kentucky to the moment the train pulled into Albany, New York. The smell of burning diesel and the constant chug and clack of the boxcars grinding along the rails now set his teeth on edge and kept him from getting too comfortable. The scream of rusty wheels on cold, firm iron sounded a bit too much like two young, white brothers who had their skin flayed off while their hearts were still beating. Every time the train slowed down, he could hear Rufus and Leon Hickey pleading for mercy while his Daddy's knife removed their redneck skins from their carcasses. The car he was riding in now was half-full of scrap metal that looked as if it had been mined from a demolished building. Girders and rods lay flat along the length of the car's floor, their rust spots and imperfections giving evidence to being exposed to the elements for a long period of time. Joe could feel the coldness flowing off the metal and biting at his extremities as he huddled in the front corner of the boxcar. Even in June, Appalachian mornings were cold around the base of the mountains until the morning sun could crest the stony summits. Time ticked away mercilessly as the train rolled ever forward, and Joe found, to his surprise, that he longed for the other car, the one leaving Memphis that smelled of stale tobacco bundles and made him think of his childhood. At least *that* car smelled like home.

Landscape passed by in grand vistas, but Joe took no notice. The rolling hills of Kentucky, the majestic mountains and valleys of the Appalachians, the long, green forests of Pennsylvania, the lakes and rivers, the cavernous tunnels through mountains of stone where sunlight was all but swallowed up, and the burning diesel smut filled his lungs as he rode alone in the dark. All these things passed by, but Joe was too preoccupied with his circumstances to care. He was a prisoner of his own mind, wallowing in paranoia and dread even though the miles between him and the place he'd escaped from continued to grow. All those miles meant nothing when damnation was the only thing waiting in his future.

It never escaped his mind that Ol' Scratch was guiding him forward. Even when he jumped this new train, he knew without question that it would be heading northbound toward Maine, toward the place where his old guitar would be waiting for him. The question was *why?* Why was it so goddamn important that the old bluesman, the convict from Mark H. Luttrell Prison in Tennessee, travel all the way up the Atlantic coast just to be reunited with a block of wood with strings? How did it all figure into *His* evil plans? Now that he had committed murder for the second time in his life, either he was going back to jail, or the law was going to gun him down in cold blood the moment he was recognized. Joe wasn't sure if racial tensions were as bad in New England as they were down south, but he was certain that he would eventually be found out and would have to face his destiny one way or another.

So why bother with all this trouble? Why not just give in to the police and screw over that old Devil?

"Because I gotta know," he announced to the empty boxcar; he was surprised at how his voice echoed back to him off the car's wooden walls and how his steaming breath in the cold morning air made him feel like a cadaver already. The sudden realization that the acoustics in the car were better than half the juke joints he'd played as a young, free black man made him laugh. It rolled out from his throat in small chuckles at first, and then Joe threw his head back and howled with lunatic guffaws. More steam floated from his lips and nostrils as he laughed until he was gasping and slapping his calloused black hand across his kneecap in total hysterics. The walls of the boxcar laughed back at him. If he'd had his guitar with him, he'd have been singing the blues for all his worth, just to hear that wonderful reverb bouncing back at him.

So this is what insanity feels like.

The sound of the engine's whistle dand the clang of alarm bells from a crossing gate somewhere up ahead told him that the train was rolling through some new city and approaching its next stop. Tires below the boxcar screeched their protest as the train decelerated. As always, he heard the sounds of the Hickey brothers as the younger version of himself stripped their hides off the way his Daddy had done to that alligator.

I gotta destroy it, Joe thought. *He wants me to find my guitar; and I don't know what for, but I gotta destroy that motherfucker until there's nothing left of it. He means for me to have it, but I don't really want it. So fuck him and his plans!*

The train rumbled to a halt, and Joe stood up. His stomach ached, and he had to move his bowels desperately. It had crossed his mind to just pick an empty corner of the boxcar, drop his drawers, and defecate right there in the car, but pride would not allow him to do so. That was for two-bit drunks and hobos, and he was neither. Back in Mark H. Luttrell, he wasn't allowed to take a shit unless some bull-screw told him he could, so he'd learned how to hold it in. And the train couldn't go on forever anyhow. The engineer and freight conductors would also need a rest stop eventually, as well as take on fuel and more boxcars. Besides, he preferred not to occupy a car reeking of his own shit, and he definitely wanted to leave no evidence behind that he'd been there.

He pushed open the door to the boxcar and jumped down into the late afternoon air. By now, the mountains were long behind him, and the air felt warm and luxurious. The train had stationed at a yard adjacent to the Hudson River. Cars zipped by going both north and south and east and west on Routes 787 and 90, and he could see a green road sign nearby reading ALBANY and EAST GREENBUSH. The city itself sprouted upward from the Port of Albany on the Hudson riverside into a series of skyscrapers and towers, churches and museums, apartments and ghettos. The air echoed with the noise of construction work and car horns and men up ahead in the train yard shouting directions to each other.

Prob'ly best not to stand around and wait for someone to notice you.

Up ahead on one of the roads leading into East Greenbush, Joe noticed a Burger King sign and started walking. He still had a few dollars left in his old rawhide wallet, which meant he could still afford to eat after he did his business in their restroom. With any luck, he could be back on the train before it departed and moved on.

He froze in his tracks and put his left hand on his back pocket.

His wallet was gone.

"What the fuck?"

Joe put his right hand on his other rear pocket and noticed that it, too, was empty. His wallet, a brown leather accessory—brown leather ancestry, because really, in the right light, it looked like the skins of the Hickey brothers after he'd let their hides cure up in the smokehouse—

he'd bought after his first paying gig as a bluesman, had disappeared. Vanished as if it had never existed, along with the last sixty dollars Roy Higgins had paid him.

I know a thing or two about Ol' Scratch. When it comes to his bad business, there's always a catch.

Joe turned and looked at the boxcar, and then found his feet running toward it at full steam, hoping and praying that he had simply dropped his wallet when he stood up. He scrambled up into the boxcar and moved over to the corner he'd been huddled in. The corner was empty.

No, not quite empty. There was a small piece of paper lying in the corner where the two walls of the boxcar joined. It was half-covered in dust from the car, but it was there nonetheless. Joe picked up the paper and unfolded it. It was a note from Ol' Scratch.

I CALL ALL THE SHOTS. DO THINGS MY WAY OR I'LL MAKE YOUR LIFE A LIVING HELL.

Joe felt his bowels release, followed by the hot tears of shame falling down his cheeks.

Up ahead on the railroad tracks, the diesel-engine blew its whistle. The serpent of iron, timber, and diesel let out a groan, and then the rusted metal wheels once again shrieked the agony of those two white boys he'd murdered as the train continued its jaunt northbound. Somewhere in Chelsea, Massachusetts was an iron foundry waiting for the scrap metal, and Joe Walton would need to either find a new boxcar or abandon the train altogether, but at this point, it felt like all his choices had already been made for him.

"Hurry up, honey. The bus will be here any minute."

Kelly Marsh dropped her son's lunch bag into his backpack and zipped it closed. The morning was already off to a shaky start with Allen oversleeping by a good thirty minutes. Once again, he'd forgotten to set the Quartz Mickey Mouse alarm clock, the one he'd brought with him when they'd mutually decided that he should move in. After all, once her divorce had been finalized, she missed having a man in the house—for her and Owen's safety, as well as other reasons. Had she not set the alarm on her cell phone, they would all have overslept, and the day would have been a disaster.

Beyond that, the nightmare Owen had sometime around 2:00 a.m. had been a doozy. It was the kind that Kelly associated with night terrors, where her otherwise quiet, mostly happy child suddenly turned into a screaming, crying ball of terror. She'd been sound asleep when it started—the two bottles of merlot she and Allen had put down the night before with the lasagna dinner she cooked from scratch had something to do with that, and probably with Allen's forgetting to set the alarm clock—and his whimpers and cries had incorporated themselves into her own dream. And then he was screaming, and she made that perilous climb through layers of dream-sleep back into the land of conscious lucicity. The wine had left her with a throbbing headache, and when she turned on the lamp on her nightstand, the pain radiating from behind her eyeballs was extraordinary. Kelly glanced at the Mickey Mouse clock, never noticing that the alarm button on top wasn't popped into duty mode, and then over at her sleeping fiancé. When she had her orientation, she turned the lamp off again and hurried into Owen's room.

Her child was sideways on his bed, with his new *Star Wars* blanket and sheet set rumpled into a mess around him. Kelly flipped on the light switch and noticed that the sheets were soaking wet. Owen was still screaming and thrashing about, and to see it upset her. After all, wasn't this all probably a manifestation of the boy's mother and father getting divorced, with his mom bringing a new man into the house? Was this how little boys processed? She knelt down beside the bed and gently nudged Owen awake.

"C'mon, Honey, it's all right. Mommy's here now. C'mon, baby, it's just a dream."

Owen opened his eyes and immediately lifted a hand above his brow to shield out the light.

"It's too bright in here," he whimpered.

Kelly stood and walked over to turn off the light. Then she was kneeling beside him again.

"Owen, baby, I think you wet your bed. I'm going to have to get you some new sheets and a blanket. Will you be okay for a minute?"

His ten-year-old hands thrust out and caught her by her nightgown. "Don't leave me. Mommy, I'm scared."

Kelly ran her fingers through his long blond hair, the hair she'd passed down to him through the miracle of genetic predisposition. He had his father's eyes, though, and wouldn't *that* haunt her every time she looked into his hazel-blue orbs?

She nuzzled her nose against his cheek. She could feel the tears still flowing from the corners of his eyes as she brushed some stray hairs off his face. "Sweetie, it was just a dream. You're awake now, and you're okay. I promise."

She could sense the boy's heart rate finally slowing down, and his labored breathing was now entering and leaving his body in controlled rhythms rather than gasps.

"I dreamed— I dreamed there was this really scary man, and he was trying to turn me into a goat. Like the kind you see at the petting zoo at the Topsham Fair. He gave me horns in my head and made my ears stick out. And the man told me he was going to steal all the love and happiness out of my heart so I couldn't feel pain and hurt anymore. Mom, I was so scared."

"Oh, honey." Kelly gathered her son into her arms and held him close. "It was just a dream, and it's over now. I'm sorry you were scared. But it can't really happen, you know, for real. Nobody can turn you into an animal."

"I want to talk to Dad," he said, his wet face now nestled into her bosom.

Kelly sighed. "We can try calling him later this morning, before you get on the school bus."

And now here she was, practically pushing him out the door, the phone call to Erik Marsh long forgotten. Kelly watched as Owen zipped down the granite steps, still adjusting the red L.L. Bean backpack until the straps squared across his shoulders, his blue denim shorts giving way to winter-pale skin that wouldn't be tan until mid-July. She watched as the bus rolled up Main Street and came to a stop. The red lights flashed and the octagon STOP sign arched outward against oncoming traffic, and then the door swung open. Owen climbed up the steps and found a seat somewhere off in the zone in the middle, where his fifth-grade friends were waiting. When the door swung shut, Kelly turned and went back inside her gingerbread house, never noticing the car with the bad man from her child's nightmare following it.

I need to find a story.

Erik Marsh was wandering through the Old Port looking for a slam-dunk column to type out and send to Beverly LaChance, but his mind was already careening toward where and when he could get a drink. It had occurred to him that this jaunt he was making was taking him right past the busiest bar district in the city, and part of him had his eye on each and every watering hole doorway, hoping some news story would jump right out and lure him in. This newfound paranoia toward Svetlana weighed him down, made him wonder if the girl he was falling in love with could even be trusted. Even as he wandered down Exchange Street toward the waterfront, he could hear the questions bubbling up in his mind about just how trustworthy that cute little immigrant girl really was and if she'd really been on the level with him. He'd made it all the way to the East-wyck Hotel off Commercial Street when the story he'd been hoping for came to him.

He saw the limousines glide into the roundabout and park just in front of the hotel doors; the first one was an old-fashioned black Cadillac with fins stretching out all the way to the rear, and the second was a modern white deal with no make or model markings to discern its history. The old-fashioned one parked first, and its driver proceeded to get out from behind the wheel and open the door for the car's inhabitant. An older man with long, curly hair, designer sunglasses, and what looked like a scarf or an ascot, floated out, nodded to the driver, and slipped some cash into his hand. The second car's driver followed suit, only in this vehicle was a dashing younger fellow in a razor-sharp suit and tie and a stunning brunette woman in a red Gucci dress. The woman took the hand of the driver as she slid her long, lovely legs out of the car and joined Mr. Suit.

"Ah, James. Gail. This is one of the finest hotels in the city. I think you'll be quite comfortable here for the rest of the week."

"That's very kind of you, Mister Kramer, but I'd have been perfectly happy staying back home. My wife and I live right here in the city." Mr. Suit turned and looked at the young brunette woman. "And I'm pretty sure Gail lives around here as well. Isn't that right? Didn't you say your folks own land around here?"

Ms. Brunette blushed and smiled. "You know I prefer not to make a big deal about that, Jim."

"Well, just the same," Mr. Ascot said—Kramer, he'd heard the young-er man call him, and Erik could tell that Kramer's smile was manufactured. "We've got the premiere right around the corner, and it's nice to have a home base outside of New York. Platinum Reel Pictures has already picked up the tab until we leave for Manhattan on Friday, so we might as well en-joy their hospitality."

By then, bellhops were rolling luggage from the limousines' trunks and trolleying them inside the hotel. Erik had to agree with Mr. Ascot that this was truly the most opulent hotel in the city. Probably for the whole state, for that matter. It was built on Yankee splendor in the early 20th Century, back when the textile empires made their riches during the first World War. The Eastwyck managed to survive the Great Depression, although ownership had changed hands from at least three different families between the stock market crash and the Second World War, and it remained the bastion of upper-echelon elitism in a state that now waged survival on food stamps and government supplements. It was where celebrities and dignitaries stayed when their yachts reached port in Casco Bay while the rest of the city feasted on burgers at Three Dollar Dewey's and drank cheap bottled beer until their paychecks were gone.

Erik had heard most of their conversation before the enormity of what was going on clicked in his brain, pushing all his thoughts about Svetlana and that tumbler of whiskey he'd been craving out of his mind. These were the actors he was *supposed* to be meeting with on Thursday for the movie premiere. He struggled to recall the film's title and was already watching Mr. Ascot wrangling the lead actor and actress into the hotel's lobby.

Death's Last Caress. The title popped into Erik's brain as if someone had flipped a switch and it was suddenly buzzing in bright neon letters. He remembered leaning across Beverly LaChance's breasts to get a better look at her computer screen and read the information about it. *Starring C. James Roberts and Gail Silvers.* Erik was already racing toward the lobby's revolving door, nearly knocking one of the bellhops on his ass to catch up with the trio.

"James, Gail, could I please talk to you for a moment?"

Ms. Brunette had already passed through the door, but she still jumped in surprise at hearing her name called out. She looked ahead at Mr. Ascot and Mr. Suit, smiled politely, and then was coming back out through the revolving glass door again.

The woman returned to the concourse and stared at him, her lovely red dress flapping in the waterfront breeze. "Um… Do I know you from somewhere?"

Erik watched, transfixed, as she used her hands to smooth the fabric down against her thighs. If Svetlana had ever seemed attractive to him, this woman eclipsed her beauty tenfold. "Not yet," Erik grinned back. "Hello, I'm Erik Marsh. I'm with the *Portland Beacon.* I'm not actually supposed to be interviewing you until Thursday afternoon. I have a pass to your press junket and your movie premiere."

"That name sounds familiar," Gail said. "Are you sure we haven't met? I'm almost positive I know your name from somewhere, Mister Marsh."

"Oh, believe me. I'd remember if we'd met before." Erik extended his right hand, nearly dropping the camera bag out of it before switching his gear to his free hand. "Anyway, it's very nice to meet you."

Gail took one of her hands off her thigh, allowing the dress to billow around her again. "It's nice to meet you, too." Her smile faltered for a moment. "You're not stalking us, are you? You're not going to go all paparazzi on us, right?"

By now, Mr. Suit had also revolved back out through the glass door and was standing by her side.

"Jim, this is Erik Marsh. He's a reporter from *The Beacon*. I'm guessing he's here to do a story on two hometown kids making it into the movies."

The handsome young actor held out his hand for Erik to shake. "Pleased to meet you, Erik. But there must be some kind of mistake. Aren't you the guy who writes the crime beat columns? I'm pretty sure everything with our picture is on the level. No actors or animals were injured while filming *Death's Last Caress*. I'll swear on a whole stack of bibles on it."

There was a slight moment when Ms. Brunette's face went ashen, as if she was actually in shock to hear that a crime beat reporter was coming to talk to them, and Erik felt a genuine trace of embarrassment.

"Oh, no, no, ma'am. I'm not here about any crime stories today. In fact, I've taken a lateral job at the paper. I'm not covering the crime beat anymore."

"Cross your heart and hope to die?"

"Scout's honor." Erik slung the camera back over his shoulder. "This was very forward of me, and I apologize. I don't mean to put either of you off. I was just hoping I could maybe catch a quick interview with you both since I'm already here. You know—to help build excitement for the movie premiere."

Mr. Suit looked at his watch. "I'm really sorry, but I need to get checked in and then go meet up with my wife for lunch. Then I have to be at my day job. We're not celebrities just yet, but at least this is a step in the right direction."

"Can I quote you on that?" Erik was already flipping a notebook out of his back pocket and preparing his pen to scribble notes.

Mr. Suit laughed. "Yeah, sure. Look, if you've got a press pass for Thursday, I'll be happy to sit down and talk with for you as long as you'd like. Seriously, I apologize, but I really have to run." And then to Gail. "I'll catch up with you later on. If you don't have any plans, maybe you could join me and Molly for dinner."

Ms. Brunette was smiling again, her hands back to pressing her dress to her thighs. "No promises. You know what a hard-ass Kramer can be. God only knows what hoops he'll have us jumping through before all of this is over."

Mr. Suit glanced at his watch again. "Now I'm *really* late. I gotta run." He turned and pushed back through the revolving door, leaving Erik standing with Maine's newest starlet.

"What do you say, Miz Silvers? Do you think you can give me a couple minutes of your time?"

"I think that can be arranged. We can go up to my room and maybe have a drink if you're up for it. Do you like Mimosas, Mister Marsh?"

"Please, call me Erik. And that sounds terrific."

Ms. Brunette wrapped an arm around Erik's and guided him in through the revolving door into a lobby of white marble and crystal chandeliers. "Well, Erik, since we're on a first-name basis now, my real name is Abigail Silverstein. My friends all call me Abby. But for now, please keep that *our* little secret."

Svetlana was long forgotten by the time Erik and his interview subject made it onto the elevator. The only thing left in his mind was that Erik felt serendipity finally opening up to him.

Something is very wrong!

Svetlana was in the home of her client, Dylan Pensky, when the dark cloud passed in front of her *Omniscient Eye*. It had felt exactly like it had back when she'd had her first menstrual cycle, and her brother Aldo had warned her of things to come if she'd stayed on as part of their traveling caravan. By then, she had *Azezel's Eye* already planted within her forehead for at least three years by *Zee Doctor*, but how much had she really understood about her new gift back then? In fact, had it even occurred to her that her sister Shimi had refused to touch her or have any kind of contact with her once Mama died and she inherited the gift of sight? Was it so difficult to believe that Shimi had become afraid of her and of what she might have seen if Svetlana touched her hand and looked into her past? What had Mikhail Barnyk done to Shimi?

Those answers were obvious. Aldo had told her just before swearing to help her escape to America and find a life of freedom from fear and exploitation under Papa's hands. Shimi had become what people in America called a prostitute. She danced for strange men to get them aroused, and then she took their money as each, in turn, had their way with her, all while the younger version of Svetlana took to the stage and juggled silk scarves and bowling pins, and later on, as she improved, the same sharpened knives Aldo had used in his blade-throwing exhibition. Even then, a small part of her had noticed how the crowd had thinned out of the enormous canvas tent once she took to the stage for her act, but had she ever really understood that the men, the ones not with wives and children in tow, were lining up for a few minutes with the buxom gypsy dancer?

Papa knew something was amiss when Svetlana took the stage for her performance for the last time. *Zee Doctor* had known as well; she'd seen him standing next to Papa at the back of the tent, *Zee Doctor* pointing at her and whispering to her father. Did he have *Azezel's Eye* as well?

Svetlana didn't think so.

No. Most assuredly, he did not, or things would have played out differently, and Aldo and Shimi would still be alive.

Dylan Pensky was at the dining room table in the apartment that assisted-living had set up for him. He'd been officially diagnosed with a toxoplasmosis-based congenital infection as a fetus in his mother's womb, leaving him with a moderate form of damage that left him at around forty-five percent cognitive ability. Dylan was a bright, cheery twenty-something that was never going to be able to do more than recite lines from *Scooby Doo* or *Jonny Quest*, and even then his enunciation was hampered with slurs and mistakes.

"Mizz Lana, you look sad," he announced from the table, a mess of crayons and computer-printed coloring book pages scattered about in front of him. The picture he was working on was a runoff of an old Saturday morning cartoon classic, Hanna-Barbera's *Hong Kong Phooey*. The character was of a dog in a karate outfit that was normally orange—Dylan had colored it in with green and purple—and a mask that slipped just over his eyes and beneath his long ears. The dog's face was carved into a permanent sculpture of Zen happiness, his eyes closed knowingly and his jowls stretching into a satisfied grin. Dylan's crayon scribbles somehow gave the dog a perverse, unnatural look. The cartoon had been voiced by a well-known character actor, Scatman Crothers, but even the actor's old, friendly black-man voice—a scratchy mixture of Uncle Remus and Dick Van Dyke—couldn't make this beast seem amicable. Dylan's version of the clumsy, unassuming Kung Fu hero looked more likely to tear out one's throat than to save anybody anytime soon.

Svetlana turned from scrubbing the inside of the microwave oven and tried to smile. "I am okie-dokie. Scout's honor. I just have lots to do before I leave for today." In her mind she was still racing backward in time, trying to figure out this sudden eclipse of her inner eye. Svetlana thought of Erik and how their evening the night before had ended. Erik, of course, had wanted to stay. He'd been vulnerable when she found him, and he'd had a lot to say about the murderer that was now stalking the streets of Portland. Le'Sinestre, this baddie had called himself, and Svetlana could still see the sloping crayon handwriting and the satanic symbols he'd left on the note for Erik. Just how Erik's situation related to her own exile from Eastern Europe eluded her, but perhaps that had been the reason for the eclipse.

"You're not upset?" Dylan asked quietly from the chair at his kitchen table.

"Not even a little," Svetlana lied. Something was definitely wrong, and every time the retarded boy with the close-cropped haircut and over-sized eyeglasses interrupted her, it broke her train of thought and left her frustrated. Things were about to go very bad, indeed, if she couldn't figure out how to protect Erik Marsh, and she was growing frightened that she'd lost him already. If only Erik could be there now… If she could just touch his hand for a second and see what visions leaped into her mind.

"My drawing is finished, Mizz Lana. Come see. Come see my pick-toor."

Svetlana dragged the sponge across the top of the microwave oven one last time and closed the door. She set the sponge down on the counter-top, slipped off the latex gloves, and dropped them into the trash can. "I'm coming, Dylan. Show me your picture—"

The instant Svetlana placed her hands on the retarded boy's shoulders, the images came fast, shooting to her brainstem in lightning bolts of neuron synapses. The cloud was lifted, and the *Omniscient Eye* was looking at the preadolescent version of Svetlana Barnyk up on a stage somewhere in Bulgaria, where the younger version of herself was giving her final performance. The image flashed to Papa, who had been standing next to whoever was having this particular vision, and Papa's face was drawn into a rictus of absolute fury and disgust.

"I vill *not* allow her to leave! Svetlana belongs here vit *me!*" Papa was saying, the heavy Romanian accent biting through his choppy English like a wolf feeding on its prey. Moments later, as her act came to a close, Aldo was bounding onto the stage. His flaxen hair and beard made him look so much older than he really was, but here in the image, her brother looked more like a child than ever. And a disobedient child at that.

"Folks, tank you so much for coming out to see us tonight. Ve regret to inform you dat we have to close tonight's performance a bit early, but ve vill be here for da rest of the week and ve promise bigger tings in da nights to come."

In the vision, Shimi was there as well; she had her hands on the younger version of Svetlana's shoulders as if to drive her out of the back of the tent. Svetlana had forgotten that Shimi had even been there. She was surprised to learn just how much she'd forgotten about the event; all those little details that swam away like frightened minnows from her subconscious, and seeing the look of absolute terror in her older sister's eyes made her skin run cold.

"You two stay vere you are!" Papa screamed at her older siblings from across the big top, but Shimi was already pushing the younger version of Svetlana past the confused spectators and out through the back flaps of the canvas tent. Aldo was pushing forward in the last vision she could recall of her older brother. He was moving toward Papa to talk to him, but by then *Zee Doctor* had disappeared, and Mikhail Barnyk had pulled the bone-handled knife he'd kept in the sheath on his hip and was lunging forward at Aldo.

In this new vision, she saw exactly what happened. She watched as her father rammed his dagger into Aldo's heart, and her older brother fell to his knees, his eyes wide with disbelief.

"Ve're sending Svetlana away," Aldo's lips quivered. "Ve're sending her far away from *you* and *Zee Doctor*, to where she'll be safe." These words hissed and bled out in his final breath, and then Aldo fell dead at their father's feet.

Svetlana saw all these things and then yanked her hands off Dylan Pensky's shoulders.

"Look at what I drawed," the mentally retarded boy, who was not much older than she was, said.

Svetlana looked down at the coloring book picture.

The cartoon character was a mess of scribbles and blobs of color. What made Svetlana cover her lips in terror was the black, crayoned symbol in the corner. Just like the one from the picture that Erik Marsh had shown her on his cellphone.

Azezel's Eye, with the orb and the upside crucifix and question mark. The image was an exact replica of the character in Le'Sinestre's letter.

Dylan Pensky turned around to face her. "I vant it back!" the boy growled, only it had been the voice of *Zee Doctor* rather than Dylan's. "You've had it long enough. I'm coming to get you and take it avay, and you are going to die!"

Svetlana bolted for the door and left her client to fend for himself. When Dylan's body was discovered many hours later, after the ungodly scent forced Iris McCann, the woman in the apartment next door, to call the police, the twenty-something victim of toxoplasmosis would be found with a steak knife sticking out of his chest, directly through his heart. The steak knife seemed to have no viable prints the police could use to determine the murderer.

Somewhere in the night, Ol' Scratch laughed his terrible laugh.

Erik knew he'd been drugged. He could feel reality swimming around him as he glanced back and forth at the pad of paper and pen in his lap to the beautiful woman sitting in the fainting chair in the corner of her suite. She'd allowed the hem of her dress to sneak up her thighs, and the shoulders of her dress had slipped down enough to expose her bosom. At some point, Abby Silverstein had unzipped the back of her dress and let it slip down just enough to distract him. At least long enough to drop something in his Mimosa, anyway.

"Tell me—do you like what you see, Mister Marsh?" She smiled and seductively ran her tongue across the top of her lip. "Would you like to see more?" Abby slipped her hands behind her and unzipped further, allowing her dress to flutter open, exposing her bare breasts.

"What did you do to me? Did you slip somfink in my dring?" He lifted his right hand and watched as his fingers doubled, then tripled. He shook his hand back and forth before his eyes, watching them fan out in slow motion. Dozens of fingers clawed and splayed before his dilated pupils, his hand now a horde of spiders dancing in midair. He tried to get up, the pad and pen falling to the carpet. "You fucking bitch, you poisoned me!"

He collapsed back into the chair, and moments later, his eyes rolled back, and he fell to the floor, unconscious.

Abby pulled up her dress, zipped the back, and smiled. "I have a friend who's going to want to meet you," she said to the unconscious figure. "This is going to be just the distraction I needed."

Abby picked up the phone and dialed.

Chapter 12

By the time they returned to the Mueller farm, Caroline had picked up where the late Charlene Tibbets had left off, with the desperate need to get high. From the moment they stopped tailing the school bus and turned back onto Route 196 toward the farm, she was sobbing quietly and chewing on the flesh of her left thumb. Her eye was still twitching as well, which made her look partially insane. Warren tried to maintain his patience with her, had understood that she was detoxing and probably hurting quite badly inside, but the reality was that he didn't care. What he *did* care about was that he still needed her to carry out his plans. Caroline's role in all of this was vital; if she couldn't drive the school bus and keep her shit together, everything he'd been planning would come undone.

"We'll get you high as soon as we get back to the farm. I promise." Warren dropped his deformed hand into her lap, nuzzling his bulbous fingers back and forth across the tattooed skin of her thigh. He steered Herb Mueller's station wagon cautiously around the twists and turns of Route 196, only allowing his eyes to stray to the ink illustrations still partially concealed by the fabric of her cutoff denim short-shorts. Of course, after all their rounds of lovemaking, he knew all the details of her tattoos intimately, but seeing his deformed fingers float across them so tenderly as they moved toward her vagina caused his penis to engorge and throb beneath his jeans. At first, Caroline squirmed at his touch, but then she forced herself to relax to his advances.

"Warren?"

"Yeah, baby?"

"You have to promise not to murder me when all of this is over. Swear to me that you won't kill me. I don't fucking care about Abby, but you have to promise me on your own life that you'll let me live."

Warren lifted his hand off her leg and placed it back on the steering wheel. "Why on earth do you think I'd murder you?"

Caroline's facial tic was coming on harder than ever. The muscles around her eyeball contracted and relaxed in rapid spasms, sending tears flowing down the side of her left cheek. Seeing it made Warren want to belt her as hard as he could until her eye sat dead and motionless in its socket, a useless pool of jelly and fluids that would never see him pull the gun on her, even if her other eye did.

The feeling of *déjà vu* burned through his mind again, bright enough to almost make him veer off the road and crash the late Herb Mueller's station wagon. He took his foot off the gas pedal, allowed the car to slow on its own, and when he could see again, he gently guided the car onto the road's shoulder and shifted into park.

All of this had happened once already. Warren Pembroke was certain of it. It was as if he was reliving somebody else's past, and that feeling left him filled with dread. There was so much confusion now, as if all he'd learned and read and experienced was bringing him up to some giant meta-physical echo of a past that did not belong to him. Warren thought about Abby and how he'd met her in the book section of some new-age spiritu-ality store up in Boothbay Harbor. The place was called *Enchantments*, and it had an extensive literature section dealing with witchcraft and the occult. Abby had been busy learning all about Aleister Crowley and his no-tions of astral projection. He'd been looking for works by Nikolas Schreck concerning the power and legacy of the Left Hand. Abby Silverstein was young and attractive and extremely rebellious toward the life her family had carved out for her. It had been so easy to manipulate her, to be fasci-nated by the things that fascinated her, to offer a convenient friendship based on mutual interests. Back then, in the beginning, he knew that if he made sexual overtures toward her, he'd lose that trust and friendship, so he pretended not to be interested. That worked to his advantage because she had confided in him that she was a lesbian and only fucked guys if it could upset her parents or gain her the things she wanted. Time and time again she reminded him that sex with him was something she *didn't* want. It didn't bother her that he often watched her having sex with Caroline and Charlene, had caught him masturbating on several occasions—with his deformed hand, no less—but if he indicated that he wanted to join in, she would excuse herself from the orgy and find something else to do.

Abby knew how to keep Warren at bay, but before this was all over, he was going to fuck her. He was going to rape that little daddy-hating bitch and fill her womb with his seed. Warren had communed with the Dark Lord over it on several occasions, and Father Lucifer had promised him when the time was right he could have her and impregnate her. And the fact was, now that he'd come across this new shit, this Devil's Breath, he would be able to contain and control her as long as he wanted to. The only factor now was her growing status as a celebrity, what with her new movie's premiere on Thursday. And even that was merely an inconvenience. The Dark Lord had already told him that her little independent film was going to be a blip on her life's radar screen; the film would garner a bit of local attention, but it was going to flop once it hit the Tribeca Film Festival in New York City and then evaporate into thin air as if it never even happened. And then Gail Silvers, a.k.a. Abby Silverstein, was going to fall back into obscurity; she would only be known as the daughter of a global billionaire who fucked little boys in third world countries and an alcoholic mother whose liver was nearly a lump of necrotic tissue at this very moment.

Warren and Abby would have a child, though. That much was promised. And he was going to be the Antichrist upon his birth.

Warren turned to Caroline. "I'd never harm you, sweetie. I need you." He placed his deformed hand on her cheek and turned her face toward him. "I need both you *and* Abby. I can't do this alone. Now, let's get back to the farmhouse and we'll get high together. Just calm yourself down until we get there, okay?"

"Okay."

He shifted the car into drive and sped off toward the farmhouse he now called his own.

Warren heard the telephone ringing just as the two entered the house. He wasn't going to pick up the phone, but something inside his brain urged him that it was important, that it would be worth his while to do so.

It was Abby.

"You remember that guy you keep talking about? The one who used to write the crime beat columns for the *Portland Beacon*? I've got him in my hotel room right now. I've drugged him up good. He's unconscious right now. What would you like me to do with him?"

The nagging feeling of *déjà vu* refused to release him.

I think I'm reincarnated. All of this has happened to me already in a previous life. I must have fucked up the first time or Satan wouldn't be sending me back to do it all over again. I have to get it right this time, or I'm damned to Hell.

"I can be there in half an hour. Don't fucking move him or do anything to him until I get there. Do you understand me, Abby?"

"Totally. I'm in my usual suite. Knock twice, and I'll let you in."

Warren Pembroke smiled. The Eastwyck Hotel belonged to Abby Silverstein's father, and Abby's actual residence was a suite near the rear of the hotel. They would be able to carry Erik Marsh out without any staff or patrons noticing. It would mean pulling the Econoline van out of the barn and risking the drive down to Portland and back, but Warren could play it cool when he wanted to and knew beyond a doubt that he wasn't going to be caught.

At least not yet.

But more than that, Abby could still be trusted. He'd had his doubts after finding her locked inside the bathroom yesterday. had, in fact, concerned himself that she might be planning suicide or phoning the police to let them know he'd taken her hostage. She'd shouted through the locked door that her stomach was in knots and that she was just nervous about the movie premiere and not to worry, but the stakes were now too high for that.

Everything had been set into motion.

Now it was all about dealing with that cowardly little prick from *The Beacon*, the one who had refused to write a single column about what Le'Sinestre had been up to.

This motherfucker was going to pay for his transgressions.

Erik Marsh felt consciousness flooding into his brain like a tidal wave.

The first thing he noticed as his mind swam back into the world of the living was that he was sitting in the dark and that somebody had gagged him. The fabric they used left a sour taste in his mouth. But when the smell hit him, he became completely alert and felt himself retching against the cloth that kept him from screaming for help. Never, in all his years of reporting on death scenes, had he smelled an odor so pervasively foul. Even with the lights out, he knew he was surrounded by dead bodies, and as the dry heaves continued, he found himself seriously worried that he would asphyxiate.

More than that, as he became alert, he discovered that he was bound to the chair he was sitting in, with his hands tied securely behind his back. The red flag shot into his head that the ropes were way too tight; his right hand was beginning to tingle from blood loss. If he stayed in that position, it was very conceivable that he was going to lose his hand permanently.

Fear filled him, and he struggled in the wooden chair, trying to shake himself free and call out for help between the dry heaves. The darkness was oppressive. It weighed down on him like a coffin lid.

It was that bitch from the hotel. She'd drugged him and brought him here.

What was her name?

Gail Silvers?

My friends all call me Abby.

Why would she do this to him? That gorgeous piece of ass had brought him back up to her suite for drinks and an interview, and she'd taken him hostage and brought him here.

The smell of decomposition entered his nasal cavity again, and he felt his gorge rising. He was going to vomit shortly, and with the gag in his mouth, it was likely to filter out through his nose, or possibly choke him. He could already feel the tang of stomach acids burning into his throat.

Where the fuck was he?

The light came on, and Erik glanced wildly about the room. He was in a basement, that much was evident. An oil tank and furnace were parked in the far corner, along with an old Maytag washing machine and clothes dryer. On the adjacent wall was a metal shelving system that held paint cans and toolboxes and other domestic accoutrements. It wasn't until he turned his head to the left and saw the severed remains of William Tibbets and the decomposing body of his wife, Charlene, that panic truly set in. The male corpse was a jumbled piled of limbs, grey sloughed-off flesh, blood, and spindly bones. The woman had been laid out on her back, her head resting on the dead man's legs. Her bare skin was pale, almost greenish, in the fluorescent light above. She had an upside-down pentagram carved into her belly, between her sagging breasts and her navel. Both of their bodies lay atop an old vinyl tablecloth. Their blood had long since puddled off the vinyl and onto the concrete floor, where it congealed into a dark crimson lake. Flies were buzzing around madly in the air above them, and maggots wriggled on their festering meat. Erik

Marsh screamed around the gag in his mouth.

From somewhere above, a door opened, followed by the sound of footsteps coming down the stairs. And then Erik looked upon Le'Sinestre, seeing the damaged right hand attached to the man who was otherwise perfect. The man's fingers were so grotesque that Erik had to close his eyes as the fiend rounded the landing and walked over to him, stopping just few feet away from the woman's body.

This was the Left Hand of Satan.

"So *you're* 'Erik the Black.' The guy from the newspaper. The one who has refused to report anything about me since I ascended into glory. Look at me!"

Erik opened his eyes and craned his neck to look at his captor. The guy was still just a fucking kid. How old was he? Right out of college? Not more than his mid-twenties. If his hands were free, Erik was certain he could have kicked the living shit out of this guy, his tingling right hand be damned.

Erik turned away and looked at the bodies on the floor. The corpse of Charlene Tibbets was still fresh enough to see the gaping wound within her eye socket. Her body was sprawled out onto the tablecloth a few short feet away from where Le'Sinestre was standing, with her head gazing upward toward the ceiling and her useless eye socket staring at the light bulb in the metal cup dangling from the rafters. Erik had no way of knowing that she had once been one of his Harpies, had danced naked with those other women in the kitchen on the floor above just a few short days ago. The other corpse, the one belonging to her late husband, was now a putrid mound of decomposition beneath her. One quick glance from his eyes caught the pools of flesh that had dripped off the cadaver onto the basement floor. Even now, bluebottle flies were buzzing everywhere near the corpses, feasting upon the offal and laying their eggs in the rotting flesh.

The stench was intolerable.

Erik struggled, but the ropes held fast, and the gag was keeping him from speaking.

"Abby, get down here!"

A second person crept down the stairs into the basement, and once she stepped into the light, Erik saw Abby Silverstein; she was wearing a summer dress and still in the makeup from earlier in the day. Abby crept around the landing and glanced at him, her pretty fingers pinching her nostrils closed, but the smile never left her face.

"Hello, Mister Marsh," she said. "Sorry we never got to finish our interview."

"Abby, we have no real use for this piece of shit anymore," Le'Sinestre said. "He's not even working the crime beat. But—" He held up the index finger on his good hand, as if to prove a positive point. "—we still need a sacrifice for the Full Moon. We can use Mister Marsh as our bloodrite for our Solstice Ritual. And then, when Father Lucifer is appeased, we can launch the Goat Parade."

Le'Sinestre smiled in victorious satisfaction. "Everything Father Lucifer has promised me has come to fruition. With Mister Marsh's death, we will evoke an Age of Darkness. And then we shall send forth our own flock, and they shall blaspheme the world in word and deed. They shall cripple humanity with sin and blight. Everything is coming forth according to *His* design!"

Abby Silverstein crept around the bodies of the late Mr. and Mrs. Tibbets and approached Erik Marsh. He could almost recall the way she flashed her breasts at him to taunt him as the drugs she used to subdue him began to take effect.

"I know you don't yet understand, Erik, but you will. *His* powers are just too great to deny. You could have been a part of all this, if you could just understand."

Once again, she lowered her top to expose her bare breasts. She rubbed them across his face, pushing her hardened nipples into his cheeks. "That's as close as you will come to Heaven," she whispered. "I do hope you enjoyed it."

Le'Sinestre watched until he was satisfied. "Abby. Come! We've got work to do. Leave him for now; he's not going anywhere. When the time is right, we'll kill this nonbeliever and spill his blood and be done with him."

Abby Silverstein bent down and kissed Erik hard on the cheek. "I'm so sorry," she whispered. "You really seemed nice enough. But we've got work to do, and you no longer suit our needs."

Le'Sinestre stepped forward. He held his hands to his lips and blew something into Erik's face. "You are now a zombie," Warren whispered. "You will only do MY bidding."

Erik tried his hardest not to inhale, but he was already panting in panic, and the fine, white powder filled his nasal passages. Its effect wasn't immediate, but when it came, his eyes rolled back into their sockets, and he felt his memory tumble away into nothing.

All that was left was a burning hunger for flesh.

There were cadavers still near him, their raw meat exposed and waiting, maggots and all. Erik tugged hard on the ropes, trying to break free so he could run to them and feast.

After Svetlana Barnyk fled her client's home in absolute terror, the only thing she could think to do was to find Erik and tell him what had happened. She ran to Monument Square and marched up and down the concourse, hoping to find him lingering about somewhere, or maybe even looking for *her*. It was now pushing six o'clock. Even though Tuesday evenings were normally busy in Downtown Portland, with families coming to dine in the local restaurants and college kids now on summer break heading out to grab a few drinks at Happy Hour or catch a Red Sox game at one of the local sports pubs, there were very few people to be seen here in the heart of the city. Maine now had a phantom in Le'Sinestre, and urban paranoia was spreading. She could see it in the faces of the people who passed her, walking quickly to their destinations or getting to the parking garages to find their cars and drive home as soon as possible. That evil son of a bitch could be on another continent right now, merely sending letters to the *Portland Beacon*, and people would still be cowering in fear and scurrying like scared animals.

He could be back in Romania, she thought. *He could be traveling in a gypsy circus, selling potions and telling people their futures.*

Svetlana stopped cold in her tracks, the world around her dancing in some strange cosmic ballet that she'd only now become aware of.

He could be disguised as Zee Doctor, *cutting into some new child and giving her some terrible new demonic gift.*

"*I vant it back. You've had it long enough. I'm coming to take it avay, and you are going to die!*"

Svetlana placed her trembling hand to her forehead, to where *Zee Doctor* had once upon a time sliced open her flesh and pressed *Azezel's Eye* into her head. Beneath her hot skin, she felt the cursed orb rolling about, trying to see past the thick skein of tissue, trying to see where that terrible man might be.

He's not a doctor at all, she thought. *He is the Devil. And now he's here to kill me.*

People continued to pass by, giving her strange and uncomfortable glances. She could feel their eyes staring at her, reading her face and her body language before scurrying away. Svetlana could feel the blind mistrust radiating off these pedestrians, all racing away to keep out of the shadow of the evil intruder that now held the city hostage. Svetlana was a foreigner to them, so it came to no surprise that they should find her suspect. And why shouldn't they? After all, Svetlana was discovering her misfortunate connection to him; one that could see into all their pasts if she could reach out and touch their hands.

The Omniscient Eye was never a blessing. It was always a curse. Mama died because of it, and now I will, too.

Svetlana looked up at One City Center, to the offices of the *Portland Beacon*. Perhaps Erik was still at work, getting the column he owed his new boss written and delivered. In her heart, she knew better, knew that he'd perhaps fallen off the wagon and was right now getting drunk in one of the local bars, but she could no longer stand around and wait for him to appear out of nowhere.

In her heart, she knew that time was running out.

The sun was finally setting as the train pulled into Chelsea, Massachusetts. Joe Walton had left the boxcar door open enough to watch the sun going down over the western horizon. There had been a moment of sheer terror as the freight workers finished swapping out cars back in Albany and one walked right past *his* car as he was removing his soiled underwear and trying to clean himself up. He could hear the guy outside, whistling some old Bob Dylan number and occasionally hollering out to the younger workers to "Mind your fingers and your fucksticks once you hear the whistle blowing!" In the end, once the train blew one long, baleful whistle signaling dispatch, Joe held his shit-filled boxers out the door and dropped them into a culvert leading into the Hudson River; a farewell to a city he'd never see again.

There were several more stops along the way, just as there had been between Kentucky and New York, and with his belly rumbling and aching for food, he decided to make one quick departure. Somewhere between Lee and Adams, Massachusetts, the train stopped to swap out an oil car, and before he even knew he was in motion, Joe hopped off and darted into a Circle K and broke the law once again. This time, the old convict shoplifted a pre-wrapped Italian sandwich as the young Vietnamese girl working the cash register was assisting two young white boys buying cigarettes. From behind, they looked very much like Rufus and Leon Hickey, and even though he was halfway out the door with the sandwich tucked in the armpit of his suit jacket, he still froze and did a double-take. As the glass door swung shut behind him, he could hear the two brothers laughing their scratchy, dead guffaws.

The afternoon had warmed up nicely, and he could smell the fragrances of spring wafting through the boxcar door—fresh pine, grass, wildflowers, and weeds. The train passed through the Appalachians once again, and a sense of tranquility overcame him. It flowed through his black skin and deep into his soul, and it occurred to him that he was ready. This last journey was more than he'd ever dreamed about back at Mark H. Luttrell, and now here he was, free as any animal God, Himself ever placed on earth. Ol' Scratch may have been the author of his journey, but that didn't mean shit. Not with the world passing by outside his boxcar. Not while his eyes were taking in land and lakes and rivers and mountains far away from Tennessee. This land was as alien to him as Mother Africa, who forfeited his ancestors to be brought to America as slaves.

Most of all, Joe knew there would be no going home from this journey. The Devil would deal his death card once he made it to Maine, and that was fine. He owed a debt whether he liked it or not, and he meant to pay it. But it would be just fine by him to screw over that old Devil good and proper, maybe teach Ol' Scratch how to sing the blues before his eyes closed one last time.

The Chelsea switch-out went relatively fast compared to Albany. Once again, the sound of the freight worker crunching gravel with his work boots and whistling Bob Dylan songs, and once again admonishing fellow railmen to "watch their fingers and their fucksticks." Joe smiled and held up the remaining portion of his sandwich. He closed his eyes, bit into it, and chewed. It was the best sandwich he'd ever eaten.

The train whistled long for dispatch, and "Tobacco Joe" Walton was moving closer to Maine.

※ ※ ※

Caroline Stork was high as a kite when Warren returned to the Mueller farm. She was lying on the couch in a pair of gray sweatpants and a black Motörhead concert shirt. Her tattooed arms protruded from her sleeves and folded tight across her chest, the way a corpse would in a casket. Her eyes were glassy and vacant. Except for the twitch, which remained the sole trace of evidence that she was even alive. Perhaps the pills and the powdered lines on the coffee table were going to kill her before he would.

"Caroline, get up. We have work to do."

Her gaze never left the ceiling. "I don't want to, Warren. I'm tired, and I'm so, so cold."

Warren stormed across the living room and toppled the coffee table over in one furious sweep. The cocaine and the pills went flying in every direction as the furniture crashed into the wall. His deformed hand reached out and grabbed a handful of her long, red hair and yanked her up into sitting position. Caroline's eyes went wide, but the vacant expression lingered. A runner of bloody snot dribbled out of her right nostril.

"We're gonna get you sobered up, and then we've got a lot of work to do. And if we can't, if you're too weak and fucked up to carry your own weight, I'm going to slit your fucking throat and leave you outside for the coyotes to eat. Am I clear?"

She nodded weakly, her hair pulled tight in his iron-gripped fist. He released her, and there was a brief moment where he was certain she was going to fall face-first onto the hardwood floor, but Caroline caught herself.

"Can I please have a drink?" she mumbled. "I need a glass of water." The corners of both her eyes welled with tears. They slid down her cheeks in hot, miserable trails. "I hate you for what you've done to me."

When she was sober, the two walked up the hillside to the barn. Warren slid the eye-hook from its loop and pushed open the heavy track-door. The Econoline was parked inside. A John Deere tractor slept peacefully behind it. Behind that, a wooden staircase led up the back wall to the hayloft. Once they were inside, Warren pulled the door shut and led Caroline by the hand up the stairs.

On the upper floor, the animal cages that Charlene purchased had been assembled and placed along both lengthwise walls. The room itself now looked more like a prison than a barn. The remaining bales of hay had been stacked neatly at the front of the barn, obscuring the two glass window frames enough to leave the room extremely dark.

Good.

In his mind, Warren could already picture the cages filled with children. There would be screams and tears, of course, but the Devil's Breath would erase that quickly enough. In his vision, their little eyes would roll back up into their heads, their chins quivering as they bleated like baby goats.

Suffer the little children to come unto me.

Sheep go to Heaven and goats go to Hell.

Warren Pembroke was going to send a lot of people to Hell before he was finished. The Goat Parade was almost ready.

He looked at Caroline. "Come forward."

Her eyes were no longer vacant, but those pretty hazel orbs were still glassy, still wet with tears. She closed them and stepped to the center of the room.

Warren pulled the dagger from behind him and slashed a small slit into her left forearm. A fatal wound opened across the fairy's belly as the ink of her pixie tattoo parted and blood gushed hot down her hand and onto the floor. Warren returned the dagger to its sheath behind his back, grabbed her arm, and twisted so that more blood spilled onto the floor.

"Father Lucifer, we consecrate this place as your own hallowed ground. Protect us from intruders and non-believers as we do thy bidding."

Caroline's eyes gritted shut as the wails and sobs bellowed out of her.

Erik's hands no longer tingled.

The only thing now in his mind was a desperate hunger. It made his mind go white with fury and panic. All that meat so close to him, so appealing and attractive and waiting for him. He no longer saw human forms on the tablecloth, nor understood that they were even dead. For the moment, he understood nothing in human terms at all. Words had vanished. Concepts unraveled. For the moment, he had no comprehension that he was salivating into the gag in his mouth, or that the chair beneath him was buckling and wrenching every time he lunged forward.

His fury rose until Erik was pushing himself up to a standing position, the rope holding the chair tight to his body. His hands were still clasped behind his back. His right hand was now white clear up to his elbow. Erik never felt a thing. He closed his eyes and ran headlong toward the corpses on the floor. When his shoe hit the dried patch of blood from the dead couple, he lost his balance and went sprawling downward onto the late Charlene Tibbets's belly. With the gag still in his mouth, Erik tried over and over again to bite into her stomach and breasts.

The white fury in his brain now burned red.

Nora Pearson could tell something was wrong. She never considered herself a nosy neighbor in her own mind; she and Griffin Pearson had lived in Portland since their honeymoon two years ago, and they still had yet to really get out and meet anybody on Ocean Avenue. Nora was aware of the older couple next door, had offered a friendly "hello" to them once or twice when she got home from working the night shift at Maine Medical Center and the woman was leaving for her own morning job. Nora was pretty sure that the woman's husband worked from home, so if he came and went during the day, it was while she and Griffin slept. That was the thing about night owls; Nora and Griffin only seemed to pay attention to their neighbors if they were making a racket and preventing them from sleeping. Even then, it wasn't like they could do much more than gripe about it.

At least the older couple tried to be respectful. They never seemed to make a lot of noise. In fact, it seemed at least a month or two since she last saw either of them. Probably back in April, when that last snowstorm of the year dumped six fresh inches on the city, and What's-His-Name was out there with his goddamn snow blower just after she drifted off into a deep sleep. Not that she could blame him for that one. Shoveling driveways had to be done, and if it wasn't him, she'd have been woken up by the snowplows grinding by anyway.

But yeah, the couple seemed nice enough, and seemed to respect the Pearsons' privacy, so Nora tried to do the same out of courtesy.

But there had been a smell coming from next door over the past few days. It seemed to grow worse as the weather got warmer, and it seemed to carry farther, too. Griffin had commented that maybe the What's-Their-Names forgot to put their trash out on collection day or something. That had been two days ago. Now, here she was getting ready to head to Maine Med for her shift, and the smell was making her sick to her stomach. Griffin was also getting dressed for his own job at Hannaford's. She could tell by his denim jeans and flannel shirt that he would be stocking the freezers again, which meant she'd hear a lot of bitching and complaining come morning about his aches and pains and how that asshole Kenny almost *never* has to stock the freezers.

When they opened the front door to leave, they could hear the commotion. It sounded like something terrible was going on in the What's-Their-Names' basement.

"Should we go over there and ring their doorbell?" Nora asked, her eyes wide with fear.

"Seriously? What if someone broke in and attacked them? There could be some drug addict in there or something. What if he's got a gun?" Griffin eyed the house suspiciously.

"Let's call the police." Nora turned to her husband, almost pleading. "Something is very wrong. And that smell! That smell is just getting worse. What if they're both dead inside? Maybe from carbon monoxide or something?"

"Then what's making that noise?" Griffin froze. "What if it's that serial killer they keep talking about on the news? Jesus Christ, he could be over there inside right now."

Nora pulled her cell phone from her pocket and started punching 9-1-1. Griffin stood back and waited, watching the house next door and seeing nothing and everything in the shadows. It was amazing how the eye could play tricks on you, how a tree branch passing in front of the street lamp could cast human shadows on aluminum siding.

"If we report this, we're going to have to wait until the police get here. They're going to ask a lot of questions, and we'll be considered witnesses. Both of us will end up late for work, and you know Lynette has it in for you. You know, the one you always call 'Nurse Ratched'?"

There was a brief pause as she envisioned Lynette running right to the human resources office to rat her out. That bitch never got over the fact that Nora had seniority over her, even though they were both hired the same day, and Nora nearly pushed the "end call" icon on her phone's touchscreen. The thought passed, and then an operator was speaking into her ear.

"Nine one one, what's your emergency?"

Nora looked at Griffin, and then at the house next door. If there had ever been a sense of respecting privacy, this was probably going to push that over the cliff. If the What's-Their-Names were just having wild sex or a domestic dispute, the last thing they'd want is the police knocking at their door, especially since their next door neighbors called it in.

"I— I don't know what exactly to report," Nora said, her voice just above a whisper. "I think my next door neighbors are being attacked."

Chapter 13

Thursday, June 9ᵗʰ

Svetlana called out sick from her job and spent all morning hovering around the entrance to One City Center, waiting for Erik to show up for work. She spent the hours listlessly pacing and watching the horde of hump-day working class citizens hustling up and down Congress Street: bankers in their suits and dresses; merchants heading off to Exchange Street and Commercial Street, ready to open their stores for the day; lobstermen and fishermen coming back from their morning trawls of trap-setting and net-hauling. Further up Congress Street were City Hall and the Courthouse, where the important people were grabbing a last cigarette before commencing with the lawful duties of Portland. Even around the corner in Monument Square, police officers stationed themselves in somber authority, keeping a close surveillance after Wednesday's doings.

It made her think of passing through parts of Croatia as a child and seeing all the men with their rifles slung across their shoulders, looking as if they almost *wanted* something to happen. There was always the thought of escalation, and then retribution in the form of bullets and clubs. The thought scared her.

At a quarter past eleven, she knew decidedly that Erik wasn't coming. Just as the evening before, she walked away from One City Center and traveled uptown on Congress Street.

Svetlana saw the commotion from a block away. A crowd of people stood around one of the storefronts ahead, watching some crazy old black man arguing with what had to be the shop's owner. As she approached, Svetlana noticed the sign above the store's front window, reading, "Second-hand Blues: Used Guitars and Instruments." The black man looked tired, feeble, and his dark suit and bowler hat were filthy. Perhaps the guy had been another homeless man, like Ernie O'Malley and so many others, and was being politely asked to sleep somewhere else. The tone of their argument suggested otherwise, and she was now picking up more words the closer she moved toward them.

"That guitar belongs to *me,* motherfucker! Now, I don't know how y'all got your hands on it, but you's got stolen property, and if I don't get it back, I'm gonna report ya ass to the police."

"Go ahead and call the police," the owner, presumably, shouted back. He was a younger fellow with a thick beard and a rainbow-colored tie-dye t-shirt covering his pot belly. The man looked more like he'd follow the Grateful Dead than listen to the blues. "We'll see how they feel about some homeless vagrant disturbing the peace and making threats. Now get your ass outta here and don't let me catch you around my store again. I got video cameras rolling twenty-four-seven back inside, and I got a Magnum behind the counter. It's *my* right to protect myself and my store, and I won't hesitate to use it. Do you fucking understand me, pops?"

"You're gonna need your gun when I kick the shit outta you, boy." The black man was advancing toward the store owner, and now the crowd was *aaahing* and whispering and pointing fingers. A sickening feeling of excitement and expectation hovered above them. Two or three people were holding their smartphones up in video mode.

Where the hell are all those policemen? The ones patrolling Monument Square as if they were an army detail?

The black man's fists were clenched, and he was swinging, but the store owner was quick, surprisingly faster than Svetlana would ever have believed. A solid right hook caught the black man on the chin, and then his knees were buckled beneath his lanky body. The man twisted and fell down hard onto the sidewalk, his bowler hat toppling to the cement. More cell phones were now in the air as the onlookers snapped pictures and pointed at the guy on the ground, who was now crying and holding both his hands against his jaw.

"Everybody here saw it!" the store owner bellowed at them. "That guy was going to hit me, and I had to defend myself. I'm calling the police. If you've got it on your cameras, then you're holding evidence. Don't anybody go anywhere." The man went inside Secondhand Blues to make the call.

Svetlana pushed through the crowd and bent down next to the old black man. She threw an angry glance at the crowd of onlookers as she moved closer to him. "All of you just stood dere and vatched," she hissed. "Vat is wrong with you people? Dis man is not here for your entertainment."

"Hey, you get away from him, lady!" the owner yelled from the doorway, his hand clutching the receiver of an old-fashioned telephone, the kind with the kinky spiral of chord connecting it to the wall.

Svetlana reached out her hands to the black man. "Are you okay, sir? Let me help you up."

The man took his hands off his face and placed them into hers.

The *Omniscient Eye* opened as their hands connected, white skin on black. And then Svetlana was looking at a young black boy with a terrible grin carved into his face as the blade of his knife punctured the white boy's belly and pulled upward. The boy's body was bound with rope to a support joist in a barn, with his hands secured behind the post. The boy was screaming in agony as the blade sliced him from abdomen to throat, dropping his organs and innards onto the barn floor. The squishy plops of entrails caused dust to rise up off the wooden floor in tiny clouds. On the next beam over, the boy's younger brother was already dead, his skin flayed completely off him. The corpse was nothing but meat and blood and bone. Even his face had been taken from him.

Svetlana let go of the man's hands, and the stranger fell back down onto the sidewalk. "You're a murderer," she screamed. "You killed those boys. I saw it. I saw everytink!"

The black man snatched up his hat off the ground and was on his feet again. "Shut your mouth, bitch," he said. "That's a goddamn lie. I ain't never hurt nobody.

"You did. You murdered them. I saw it!"

The crowd was larger now, and from down Congress Street came the sound of police sirens approaching, fighting through the afternoon traffic to the little guitar shop on the corner of Congress and Oak Street.

"Get outta my way, you crazy bitch." The black man shoved her aside and started running down Oak Street while the crowd of onlookers shot their videos and looked on and did nothing. He was out of eyesight before Svetlana could pick herself up off the ground, and long gone by the time the police cruisers pulled up to the curb.

Joe Walton didn't stop to catch his breath until he was safely ensconced in the trees of Deering Park. He hurried past the duck pond and over to the row of bleachers at the baseball diamond, his heart pounding in his chest and the voice of that crazy white girl still echoing in his ears. The park was alive with activity: joggers and rollerbladers zipping past on the walking path, a rumor of mommies sharing gossip while their toddlers frolicked on the playground, sunbathers stretched out on blankets with books in their hands or headphones atop their heads. The morning was absolutely perfect for all these things as the summer solstice drew closer. He'd felt that perfection the moment he jumped off the train as it chugged past the waterfront and into the city. It had been just after 7:00 a.m. when he arrived, and the sun was rising and kissing the green Maine landscape good morning. It was about as good a day to die as any day he'd ever lived. And yet even then, Joe could feel the temperature changing around him. The summer heat felt almost too hot, and the cool breeze coming in from the waterfront was tainting the sky with hints of darkness.

"You're a murderer!"

How could that tall girl with the pretty hair and the foreign accent possibly know that? Could she have recognized him from his past at a glance, after all these years? Definitely not. He'd felt it the moment she placed her hands on his own. She saw right clear through him, had looked into his very soul and saw through his own eyes. Joe didn't know how he knew this, but it felt right. That girl was a witch. Ol' Scratch had sent her as sure as he'd sent the ghost of the Hickey brothers to haunt him and keep him on the move.

When it comes to his bad business, there's always a catch.

Only that didn't feel right at all. That crazy bitch wasn't mocking him or provoking him. She tried to help him, had given her hand to him out of pity and mercy.

But she saw the real *me. She saw that I killed those boys, and if I hadn't yanked my hand away, she'd have seen that couple back in Velvet Mojo as well.*

Everything up to that point had felt way too easy. From the clean break from the boxcar—it had even slowed to a crawl as it shambled its way along the outskirts of the very park he was sitting in—to the walk uphill toward the heart of the city, Joe felt as if his feet knew exactly where to carry him, as if his guitar was calling out his name in ringing chords and open strings that his soul could feel rather than hear. Joe had wandered up Forest Avenue past the old brick Postal Service building, past watering holes called Bubba's Sulky Lounge and Zoots—the thought crossed his mind that if he actually *did* get his guitar back, those would be the first venues he'd audition at for gigs—and all the way up the hill to mid Congress Street. And for no reason whatsoever, he turned left and crossed at the intersection, walked one block, and found Secondhand Blues. His guitar was right there in the front window.

Seeing his instrument made him weep, right there on the sidewalk. Big, salty tears spilled from his eyes as he gazed at his own reflection in the glass. Only, the boy who was once called "Tobacco Joe" Walton was long gone, a ghost trapped somewhere at the crossroads. Joe could almost see the boy's eyes gazing back at him in the reflection. It was the same wide-eyed stare that watched his Daddy jab the alligator in its belly and strip the beast of its scaly green coat. It was the same wide-eyed stare that watched Judge Albert Jackson bang his gavel and dismiss the case against Leon and Rufus Hickey. He stared as the all-white jury found those good ol' boys to be "not guilty" of the murder of his father and rape of his mother. All the other Negro farmers knew for a fact that Jackson and half the jury were Klan members, but to the fifteen-year-old Joe, it destroyed any notion of justice and equality. Leon and Rufus Hickey walked out of that courtroom as free men—even though they were still only boys, just a few years older than he was—and the younger version of Joe Walton spent the next few years plotting his revenge.

And then that cracker sombitch with the beard and the tie-dye shirt noticed him staring through the window and decided to confront him before he'd even set foot in the store.

"Beat it, pops. There are laws against you homeless people camping out in front of the city's stores and eating establishments. You're scaring potential customers away and hurting my business. And I ain't gonna fucking put up with it. Take your sorry ass someplace else."

"I ain't going nowhere. That there is my guitar hanging in your store window, and I want it back."

What the hell had he been thinking? With his wallet gone and no money to dicker with, what had his plan exactly been? Just show up and announce that "Tobacco Joe" Walton had come for his six-string with the expectation that some white-bread asshole would just hand it over without question?

It don't matter now. You been found out. Them folks in the crowd was snapping pictures and looking for scars and identifying features and you wasn't about to get away with anything. By now the police community is on the lookout for yo' ass anyhow. There was people back at Velvet Mojo giving statements to the police. And if Roy Higgins made it outta that fire, he's identified yo' ass for sure.

So now what?

"Tobacco Joe" Walton watched the children playing on the playground, their inattentive mothers laughing and sharing stories about foolish husbands and small-town scandals and which wines were best to serve with white-people dinners. Joe watched and shook his head.

These cracker pieces of shit don't know nothing about singing the blues.

Joe had come all this way for his guitar. And now he discovered that he was ready to kill for it if he needed to. That hunk of wood and strings was the last thing on this earth that truly belonged to him, and he wanted it back. Joe had come here to die, and if they gunned him down while trying to steal back his guitar, so be it.

The crowd of onlookers in front of Secondhand Blues had mostly dispersed as the first-responders parked their squad cars and came over to speak with the fat, bearded storeowner ("Rusty Perkins," the man said as he shook hands with the officer. "This store has been in my family three generations now."). The few who lingered were clutching their smartphones in their hands and waiting to show the law what they'd captured during the episode. Svetlana Barnyk had remained as well and was surprised to see Officer Anderson once again. The young, handsome cop nodded at her as he approached the owner of the guitar shop to take his statement. Afterward, he turned to the crowd of stragglers and asked if anybody had any information to give or if they had any photographic evidence of what happened. Svetlana waited patiently, watching as the officer moved from person to person, examining video and camera footage on their cell phones. The officer had a notepad and pen out and was scribbling notes furiously as he observed over and over again what had transpired out in front of the guitar shop.

Svetlana never saw the couple emerge from the crowd behind her. There was only a fraction of a second when she felt the hypodermic needle slip into the fatty area of her hip, and then two sets of arms were guiding her away from the storefront.

Svetlana turned to the dark-haired woman on her right as the woman whispered, "Are you sure this is the right girl?"

Her eyelids were growing heavy fast. Whatever drug she'd been pricked with was dragging her into unconsciousness with sinister precision.

She turned to see the person on her left, the one who had jabbed the needle into her skin and pushed down on the plunger.

It was *Zee Doctor.*

"Hello, Svetlana," he smiled through his long, terrible mustache. "You didn't think you could keep *Azezel's Eye* forever, did you?"

She was almost asleep as the couple led her over to the Ford Econoline van and shoved her into the rear of the vehicle.

Erik Marsh felt himself moving within a dream.

In it, there had been dead bodies all around him. More than he'd ever seen in all his years as a crime beat reporter. He recognized many of the corpses from sight, famous people who held some influence or affection for him. Others he knew more intimately. Erik saw the faces of belated family members and friends and old teachers and neighbors and church members from St. Paul's Cathedral, where his mother had dragged him and his sister every Sunday after their traditional fare of corned beef hash and eggs. Eileen Marsh never drifted far from her Irish roots. Their bodies lay out like a putrid wasteland before him. Once living figures, capable of love and hate and guilt and remorse, now scattered across the landscape, and some were piled atop one another like fallen trees as far as his eyes could see. On the horizon, a blood moon hung over the wastelands, staring back at him in sanguine accusation. Its presence turned the whole skyline red, and when the wind blew, the air filled with flakes of burning brimstone.

> *The moon, in its languid stroll across the sky,*
> *Tore a hole in the earth and watched it die.*

As he stepped forward, the corpses ahead rolled over on their rotting haunches, allowing him passage. Brittle bones snapped, and gases hissed and released from festering bodies. The smell was intolerable. Erik retched and pinched his nostrils shut as he cautiously moved forward. More bodies rolled away until up ahead, in the bloody moonlight, Erik could see a copse of crooked trees forming a path. Erik moved farther still and discovered that the wasteland of dead bodies ended at the side of this new path. He also discovered that the temperature here was rising rapidly, enough to make his bare skin prickle on his face and arms. When he turned back to look at the corpses, he gasped in terror.

The bodies were now engulfed in a raging sea of fire. Its flames soared way into the blood-red sky, like a volcano, sending more burning embers spewing forth into the night.

Erik stepped onto the path before him and started to run. He could feel dread deep in his belly. His heart pounded in his chest until he could hear his pulse jackhammering in his ears. He could see something up ahead in the distance, something like an oasis, and he found himself running faster.

There was a crossroads ahead. He could see it perfectly now, less than a hundred yards away. Limbs dangled in threatening clusters from the branches on either side of the path, but the trees seemed to open up and lose their imposing dread the closer he got to the intersection.

Erik's head felt as if it was on fire. This place was Hell, he was sure of it.

From nowhere and everywhere, a voice spoke to him.

"You belong to us now, Erik. You don't know it yet, but you belong here. Come forward and face your judgment."

Erik's eyes flew in every direction, trying to discover the author of these words. "I don't belong here," Erik screamed back. "Please, there must be a mistake!"

"Erik. Erik? Erik!"

He felt the hands on him, gently rocking him back and forth, and his mind swam upward, through the blood-red sky and the frizzled ashes of brimstone until he came into light and the dream-world broke through to reality. Erik opened his eyes.

A doctor was standing over him, shining a penlight directly into his pupils. The light stung, forcing him to wince and recoil. After a few moments and a few swear words, Erik lowered his hands from his face to examine his surroundings.

He was in a hospital. The doctor examining him, an older fellow with skin and features that looked of Indian or Pakistani ethnicity, slipped the penlight back into the pocket of his lab coat and smiled. Behind him, two nurses were doing busy work evaluating vital signs on a computer monitor and replacing a bag of clear fluid that dripped from a bladder into tubes that fed into the crook of his left arm.

"Ah, you're back, Mister Marsh. Tell me, how are you feeling?"

Erik leaned back against his pillow and tried to recount how he'd gotten there, but found that he couldn't. It was as if there had been a long blank spot filled by one of the most realistic and terrifying nightmares he'd ever endured. His temples pounded, forcing him to flinch in pain. It felt like just the act of thinking was causing his brain to swell up inside his skull.

"My head hurts. Bad." He looked at the doctor. "Can you give me some painkillers or something?"

The doctor turned to the nurse next to him, a petite woman wearing flower-printed hospital scrubs, and whispered something. She set down the clipboard she was holding and left the room. The other nurse, a much taller woman whose face looked both nervous and mesmerized, finished replacing the saline pouch and moved quickly behind the doctor.

"We had to give you a blood transfusion, Mister Marsh. When they brought you here, we immediately suspected that you'd been poisoned by some kind of illicit drug. We're awaiting the toxicology to return to see what the culprit was. In the meantime, there are some officers waiting outside to speak with you."

The petite nurse returned with some pills in a paper cup and a glass of water. "Let's sit you up so you can swallow these," the nurse said. She turned to the other nurse and motioned with a slight nod to come help her, but the other nurse remained stationary. She was watching Erik with wide, frightened eyes, had been from the moment Erik woke up. The doctor noticed this and intervened.

"Here, let me help you," he said, slipping his arm behind Erik's body and propping up both him and his pillow.

Erik took the paper cup of pills and the water, and then looked at the doctor. "What is this?"

"It's just Tylenol. It'll help you with your headache.

Erik popped them into his mouth and washed them down. When he finished, he handed the empty cups back to the nurse.

"Now if you're ready, I'll send the police in to speak with you."

Erik lay back down and watched Inspector Barrett—the plain-clothes detective who had visited him back when Le'Sinestre's letter turned up at the *Portland Beacon*—enter the room, followed by a uniformed trooper Erik didn't recognize. Barrett nodded at the doctor as he passed by and sat down in the only chair in the pod. "Is he going to be okay, Doc?" Barrett asked, looking up and down Erik's frame. Even with the blue hospital blanket on, Erik realized he still felt naked and vulnerable.

"Yes, yes. Mister Marsh is going to be fine."

"Does he remember anything?"

"You know, you can ask *me* if you want to, Inspector. I'm right here."

Barrett glanced at him and smiled. He then turned toward the doctor and the two nurses. "Would you give us some privacy, please? We need to talk."

"Of course." The doctor—the name on the pin over his jacket pocket read Abnacki—signaled to the two women, and they filed out into the hall.

"I apologize. Are you okay? Do you remember what happened to you?"

That part was still a complete blur. There was no recollection whatsoever. There was only…

"I remember being hungry. But not just hungry. I felt absolutely famished, as if I'd been starved purposely for a long time." Erik sighed. "I guess that isn't very helpful. It doesn't even make any sense."

The trooper finally spoke. "No, it makes a lot of sense. When we found you, you were trying to bite into—"

"When they found you—" Barrett intervened sharply, glaring at the officer. "—you'd been kidnapped and drugged and left in somebody's basement. You were bound with ropes, your arms behind your back and your torso and legs tied to a wooden chair. Now, we're not sure what they used to drug you, but we think it may be a new form of hallucinogen called Devil's Breath. Can you remember anything at all about someone blowing some kind of powder in your face?"

Erik closed his eyes. The image came easily once the scenario was described. "He had one hand," Erik opened his eyes. "He was left-handed. His right hand was all messed up. And he—" His eyes went big. "It was him. It was Le'Sinestre. Only, he wasn't the one who kidnapped me and drugged me. It was that bitch. The brunette from that new movie that's going to premiere on Thursday. Her name was Gail something. Gail…" Erik closed his eyes and thought back to Beverly LaChance's computer screen when she offered him the story. "Her name is Gail Silvers. Only, she said her friends called her Abby because her real name is Abby Silverstein." He felt elated that he could recall all of this information. It was empowering to be able to name the person who had victimized him. Just remembering made him smile in triumph. "We were at the Eastwyck Hotel. She brought me up to her suite to do an interview, and the next thing I knew, everything got fuzzy and I passed out. When I woke up, I was down in the basement." The smile disappeared immediately. "There were two dead bodies down there with me. I was tied up and gagged so

I couldn't speak. I saw Le'Sinestre and Abby in the basement with me. Abby Silverstein is one of them. She's part of all this."

Inspector Barrett turned to the uniformed Trooper. "Go bring her in. I don't care if her father owns half the state of Maine. I want her in for questioning *today*!"

"I'll call you as soon as we find her," the trooper replied. And then to Erik, "I'm glad as hell I didn't shoot you earlier. But the way you were carrying on, I thought you were— I thought you were rabid or something. I didn't know."

When the trooper was gone, Erik looked at Barrett. "What the hell is he talking about?"

Inspector Barrett stood up and slapped his hands up and down his torso, an action that made him look like an umpire dusting himself off after the big play at the plate. Bottom of the ninth and the bases were loaded. "When the cops broke down the door at the Tibbets's house and found you in the basement, you were trying to eat one of the dead people on the floor. Charlene Tibbets, in fact. She even had a pentagram carved into her stomach. We were ninety-nine percent sure that she'd been a victim of Le'Sinestre. I'm pretty goddamn convinced it was him based on what you just told me. We still need to figure out how the dead couple plays into all of this. But I'll tell you something, just between me and you." Barrett's face turned into a scowl of utmost seriousness. "If you hadn't been all tied up, my boys would have gunned you down in cold blood. You're one lucky man, Mister Marsh."

With that, Inspector Barrett left. As he slipped out the door, the taller of the two nurses returned with some paperwork to be signed. She still had that vacant, terrified expression on her face.

"Miss, are you okay? You look worse than I do." Erik tried to smile at her, but the pain in his head and the shock of hearing what transpired left him too stunned to muster a grin.

"Oh, do I? I'm sorry," the nurse said. Nora Pearson fumbled the papers clumsily in her hands. "I was the one who called the police. Whatever happened to you in that basement, it happened right next door to my home. I still can't believe my neighbors have been murdered."

Chapter 14

Abby Silverstein sat in the back of the white Econoline, staring down at the pretty European girl who now lay passed out on the van's bed. The stranger with the flowing locks and the long, crooked mustache was kneeling at the girl's head, gently caressing her scalp with bone-thin fingers and pointed fingernails. He'd called himself *Zee Doctor,* but Abby knew better. This was the Dark Lord sitting with her, the beast in the flesh. She'd communed with him back at the Mueller farm after stealing some of Warren's LSD, and then he came to her later on that night, hours after she'd returned to the Eastwyck, once Warren had that reporter guy who was trying to interview her bound and secured. She'd returned to her suite in a fit of anxiety after that whole fiasco went down, certain that Warren Pembroke had truly fucked up by allowing the reporter to live. While her fellow actors from *Death's Last Caress* were out canvassing the city on the eve of the film's premiere, Abby feigned illness, swore it was just nerves, begged James Roberts and the other cast mates to have a drink for her, and then went home. Instead of enjoying her big moment, she found herself gulping down sedatives and curling up in a fetal position in her bed, wondering just how badly she'd fucked up her life because of Warren.

"If he ever somehow gets free, he's going to be able to identify me," she'd told him. "He knows I spiked his drink and kidnapped him. Can we please just fucking kill him?"

Warren shook his head. "He won't get free. Don't you worry your pretty little head one moment about that. The ropes are way too tight, and nobody even knows he's here. We'll save him to be a witness of what's to come. And after he's seen and he truly believes, he'll wish he was dead anyhow. The Dark Lord has shown me all, my dear Abby. When we carry out our plans, Mister Marsh's son will be one of our disciples. After the Goat Parade, Erik Marsh will wish he'd never been born."

In her drug-induced dreams, the Dark Lord had come to her. "We must move quickly," *Zee Doctor* had told her. "If you still vant the *Omniscient Eye,* you need to find me in Portland tomorrow morning. If you can find your way into the heart of the city, I vill find *you* and help you acquire *Azezel's Eye.*"

Abby woke with a start from her dream. The digital clock on the dresser read 5:17 a.m. Abby quickly dressed in the dark and flew out to her Mazda Miata down in the hotel's massive underground garage.

The car was too small for her needs.

Warren would be dragging Caroline out for another dry run of following the school bus come first light. If she could borrow the Econoline long enough to carry out her plan and get it back into the darkened recesses of the barn before Warren and Caroline returned, everything would be fine. It would be a very claustrophobic window of opportunity, and if things went bad, she could perhaps lead Warren to believe that she needed the van for other purposes, and that would require a hell of a convincing story. Warren wasn't stupid, so she had to play her cards exactly.

Abby had no difficulty swiping the van once Warren and Caroline disappeared in the Mueller's station wagon. She already had a spare key to the van, and within seconds of Warren's departure, she drove her Mazda up to the barn, swapped out the van, and then drove her own car inside the barn and closed the door. The sun was just coming up over the eastern horizon when she closed the Econoline's door and zipped off back down to Portland.

A part of her had thought for sure that all of this had been insanity, that the man she'd pictured in her hallucination did not exist, but it turned out that she had no problem finding the mysterious figure from her dream. Once she parked the van—behind the same train trestle where they'd taken that old geezer hostage—and started walking up Congress Street, he fell out of the shadows and accosted her from behind.

"Ah! I've been vaiting for you."

To Abby, he sounded more like Bela Lugosi in *Dracula* than how she imagined the Prince of Darkness would sound. Her reaction was that he looked like Vlad Tepes, the Romanian count who had inspired Dracula, so at least the voice part was right. Part of her felt as if the hallucination had picked up right where it had left off. After all, nobody seemed to be paying the slightest bit of attention to this stranger in gold and burgundy frocks walking behind her, with his long hair and mustache and those piercing green eyes. For all she knew, her new associate was invisible to the whole world, except for her.

"Is this going to hurt?" she asked the Dark Lord as he stroked the pretty European girl's hair in the back of the van. It had occurred to her somewhere in her subconscious that the girl was lovely enough to fuck if she'd been given the chance.

"The pain will be fleeting," the Dark Lord said, his lips pulled into a dreadful smile. "And afterward, you will have the gift of sight. It is everything you wanted of me, yes?"

Abby nodded meekly. "What do I have to do?"

Zee Doctor reached inside his burgundy robe and withdrew a long, thin dagger. "You need to be the one to cut open her forehead. I vill extract zee eye." *Zee Doctor* smiled a lascivious grin and turned toward Abby. "Once I have it, I vill have to cut into *your* forehead. I vill placed zee eye inside you, and I vill reseal your flesh. You von't even have a scar when I'm finished."

"And then I'll be able to see?" Abby looked down at the unconscious girl on the floor of the Econoline. Was all of this part of some terrible nightmare? How was it that this beautiful girl could possess such a wicked gift?

"Yes, my dear," *Zee Doctor* rubbed his hands with glee. "You vill be able to see into the souls of whomever you touch. You vill know truth from lies. You vill know secrets and schemes and the darkness in men's hearts. There shall be nothing concealed to you once I give you this gift." His wicked smile grew, stretching the corners of his lips into impossible angles of gaiety. "Will you use this gift wisely?"

Abby nodded.

"Good. Take the dagger and make your incision."

Abby leaned forward and took the blade from *Zee Doctor*.

As she did, Svetlana's eyes flew open, and her hand reached up and grasped Abby's. "Please, I beg you. Don't do dis. You have no idea vat you are selling yourself into."

Svetlana's hand clenched down onto Abby's. When she did, the *Omniscient Eye* opened one last time, and Svetlana Barnyk saw into the soul of

Abby Silverstein. The things she saw made her groan in terror.

Abby lifted the scalpel and sliced it along Svetlana's forehead.

Azezel's Eye rolled forward into the pocket of the slit and stared back at her; its gray iris and dull, black puddle of a pupil gazed upon its new owner. As it did, Abby Silverstein heard a choir of demons chanting their terrible praise in an unending hiss of screams.

Abby was certain every soul in Hell was looking into her mind. The thought caused something in her brain to snap. She even heard it, the unmistakable and permanent sound of eternal damnation as it stared into her very soul.

Zee Doctor snatched the scalpel from her hand, grabbed her head with his free hand—*his hoof,* she thought. *It's just like Warren's. It's a fucking goat hoof!*—and guided her down beside the European girl. There was a flash of light as the scalpel's reflection filled the back of the van, and then the immediate sear of pain as the blade cut into her own forehead.

And then *Zee Doctor* was pushing *Azezel's Eye* into her brain, where it took root with an explosion of blood vessels and muscle fibers that dug and wove their way into Abby Silverstein's gray matter.

Warren Pembroke let Caroline drive the late Herb Mueller's station wagon as they followed the school bus yet again. Caroline still had the twitch in her eye, but at least she was sober and alert. Her long, red hair was wild with knots and snarls, proof positive that it had been ages since she'd showered and managed to drag a brush through those long, lovely locks. When he'd found her, Caroline had been life-toughened and street smart. There had been some level of sexual abuse from her previous exist-ence, but that really hadn't mattered much. She seemed to like sexual gratification and an endless supply of free drugs, and Warren was prepared to feed her both until her mind caved in and left her a broken mess of humanity. It occurred to him as she slowly pursued the yellow number 10 school bus that her fate would not be that far off from Charlene Tibbets, that she was going to die as the shell of the human she'd once been, but the thought seemed to not trouble him in the least. He'd never really thought of her as human. She was as much a pawn to the Dark Lord's plans as he was, and Warren had already accepted that his own life was going to end just as prematurely as Caroline's. Or Charlene's. Or Abby's, for that matter.

Abby.

Here was the truth about Abby Silverstein: everything was some big goddamn secret that she chose not to share with him. Abby's dad was a fucking billionaire, had built an empire in real estate and Wall Street investments, and knew all the trappings and pitfalls of capitalism. Abby couldn't give a shit about any of it. She had her allowances, a trust fund that would leave her the sole beneficiary to his worldly legacy, but it didn't matter to her. She'd already told him she had no intention of running any of his business dealings once he died—and she'd been perfectly clear about that during their last telephone conversation, the one where she'd congratulated him on being the wealthiest and most successful child molester on the planet. In fact, she'd also told him that he should burn in Hell for all the things his money let him get away with.—and after the lawyers settled all his worldly dealings, she'd take her tidy little inheritance and just disappear.

And that was why Warren didn't trust her. Because if that ever happened, if old man Silverstein upped and died, she'd slip through Warren's fingers and he'd never see so much as two fucking nickels to rub together and keep his fingers warm. And the bitch of it was, even if she had no billionaire daddy to keep her life blanketed in luxury, she'd have slithered her way upon it anyway. She was beautiful, talented, knew how to present herself in public with grace and dignity, and had the savvy to make things happen to her persuasion. Even if Abby Silverstein was penniless and insignificant, she knew how to turn fate around to her advantage. And she wasn't afraid to do it. At least not as afraid as Warren had been when he'd murdered his own father. Chances were better than average that if Abby had been in his shoes, she'd have slain her own father in cold blood without hesitation if she set her mind to it. In his own mind, Warren could see her slinking into her Daddy's bedroom as a child, the kitchen knife behind her back, and gutting him perfectly as he dreamed of sucking off little boys' cocks until they ejaculated. And the truth was that he deserved it.

"We've still got at least ten more stops," Caroline said, glancing down at her notebook after the school bus stopped to pick up the Chinese sisters on Main Street. Caroline watched as the younger sister climbed aboard first, waving goodbye to her Mommy as their mother watched from their doorway. The older sister climbed on afterward, oblivious to the world around them. Their parents had warned both of them against the notion of "stranger danger," but there they were in the post-school year lethargy, so numbed by routine that neither was going to give one flying fuck if the bus driver had been substituted for their last day of school. The younger sister once again made her way to the back of the bus, and once again raised a friendly wave to the car behind them—not even realizing that it was the same people from the previous day waving back—and took her seat. The older sister parked herself somewhere in the middle of the bus, undoubtedly with a close friend and confidant, and was already planning playdates over summer vacation.

Abby has *to go,* a voice in Warren's head suddenly whispered, and it was as if he was under the trance of the LSD and communing with the Dark Lord. *Abby is onto you and knows about your true plans.*

Warren Pembroke sat upright in his seat. He looked at the school bus ahead of the station wagon and watched as the brake lights once again came on, along with the flashing red indicators that meant other cars needed to "stop" and let the next child board safely. Warren watched as the little boy walked down the steps of what looked like a gingerbread house and climbed aboard the yellow metal beast that would deliver him to the Hetfield Community School, at least for today. Caroline smiled a cold, dead grin as she watched the little boy shimmy off the concrete sidewalk and onto the bus. Owen Marsh—not that she knew his name—looked so handsome in his plaid shorts and Polo shirt, with his L.L. Bean backpack strapped around his shoulders and dragging halfway down his ass as he marched down his front steps and climbed aboard the number 10 bus. Caroline Stork was never going to be a mother, that much she knew for a fact about herself. Never, ever was she going to produce an offspring that could be exploited and damaged by her terrible family, especially by her own self because she knew she could no longer be trusted. Whatever deviance and humiliation that had happened within her own family, along with the dreadful things Grandpa Del did to *her,* were going to end with her. Whatever plans Warren had for this kid was strictly up to Warren, and she would not interfere.

Warren Pembroke watched Owen Marsh climb aboard the school bus and take his seat. He, too, did not know the child by name, but there was already the seed of recognition there, already the feeling that all of this had happened before. The fact that there was a grown man tied to a chair in a basement somewhere in Portland who looked just like the kid was just beneath the surface. Perhaps, with a little time, it would dig its way out.

Déjà vu.

The little boy made his way down the middle aisle of the bus and found a seat with one of his chums. Come tomorrow, the boy would be his prisoner; he would be corralled in one of the pet cages that the late Charlene Tibbets had purchased from the Hetfield Hardware and Agriculture Supply store, and he would have his little mind erased.

That's a good little goat, Warren thought with contentment. *If you're lucky enough, you will lead my* Goat Parade.

And as far as Abby Silverstein was concerned, Warren had all the information he needed that her coup was coming. When the time was right, Warren Pembroke would be ready for her.

All the proof Warren needed of Abby Silverstein's betrayal was waiting for him back on the Mueller farm, where the Ford Econoline van had been swapped out with her daddy-purchased Mazda Miata in the old, red barn. He didn't even care to hear her explanation. No matter what, it was all going to be a lie. Warren wanted the van off the road for a reason. Her taking it out put the whole operation in jeopardy.

Abby felt the *Omniscient Eye* open moments after *Zee Doctor* pushed it into the gaping incision in her forehead. Once it was inside her, *Zee Doctor* licked the tip of his thumb and slid it across the wound, and white, searing pain gushed deep into Abby's body and soul. She bit down hard on her thumb, hard enough to draw slivers of blood from the indentures in her flesh, and waited for the pain to release. When it did, Abby felt her herself getting dizzy; swirls of new, forbidden colors swirled inside her mind as the orb sprouted roots that gouged and implanted themselves within the folds of gray matter in her brain. She saw phantom visions of the past, a gallery of snapshots from the millennia of humanity depicting abject horror that made her gasp and shiver in fear. Ghostly faces from biblical times to the crucifixion of Christ, to the Crusades, to the Black Plague, to the Holocaust. The last owner's visions, the girl now unconscious and bleeding on the floor of the van, came abruptly, and it was as if all those visions of ugliness had melted away. This woman had not used *Azezel's Eye* to gain power or fortune. She'd used it to help others rather than for her own self-interests. The visions now were snapshots of finding lost family members and ending rifts between friends and lovers.

This girl had no business ever owning the eye to begin with. Seeing these visions now made Abby Silverstein furious with her. It made her feel that much more wicked for having to take the *Omniscient Eye* from her. As the colors and the visions cleared inside her head, Abby sat up and looked down at Svetlana Barnyk. "You stupid fucking bitch! You have no idea what a gift you had, how much power you held because of The Eye. The world could have been yours, but *you* chose to ignore it. And now it's *mine*!" Abby leaned forward and slapped Svetlana hard across her cheek. The impact turned her delicate flesh pink. Svetlana moaned, and her eyes opened. Tears rolled down her cheeks as she spoke.

"It's not a gift. It's a curse. And on your deathbed, Satan vill come back to you and take it away, and he'll give it to someone else. In time, you'll vish you never had it." Svetlana closed her eyes. "I promise you. You vill be damned because of it."

Abby turned toward *Zee Doctor* to see if he would rebuke these claims, but *Zee Doctor* was already gone. Disappeared without a trace. There had been no quiet shuffling as he made his escape, no sound of the van's door slamming behind him as he departed. He was there one minute and gone the next. Like a magician. Like a ghost.

He didn't want me to touch him, Abby thought in horror. *He left before I could use* The Eye *against him.*

Abby looked down at Svetlana. There was so much blood streaming out of the gash in her forehead. If the bleeding didn't cease, she was going to die right there in the back of the van. And the last thing she needed was another body to dispose of. Or worse, to bring back to Warren and try to explain to him what had happened in the back of the vehicle he wanted off the road permanently.

What time was it?

Abby looked at her wristwatch. 1:45 in the afternoon.

Holy shit! Warren will be back at the farmhouse by now, and he's going to know I took the van.

Abby looked down at Svetlana Barnyck. "I can't take you with me," she said, watching Svetlana slowly writhe and clutch at her head with both hands as if she were in the throes of the most dreadful migraine ever. "You'll probably be dead soon anyway."

Abby leaned toward the back of the van and opened the doors. Fresh salt air from the nearby waterfront rolled in, along with the unbearable afternoon heat and the smell of burning diesel from the train approaching the trestle above the van. She could hear the sound of the engine humming and the *clickety-clack* of the cars following along the rails. It would be enough noise and distraction to dump Svetlana's body. Abby climbed over the writhing girl and began rolling her toward the rear doors until Svetlana rolled off the ledge, smacked into the rear bumper, and fell flat on the ground. The European girl hit the earth with a solid thud and dull *"Oof"* of pain, and then she continued writhing amid the dirt and gravel and broken glass bottles.

Abby pulled the doors shut, climbed behind the steering wheel, and drove off, pulling directly onto the on-ramp for Route 295 North. Back to the Mueller farm, where its two dead owners were being picked apart by coyotes somewhere in the woods behind the sheep pastures, where Warren Pembroke would be waiting for her, ready to sentence her to the same fate.

The sky was growing dark with storm clouds. At some point in the morning, the clouds formed and rolled in from off the coastline, had slowly canvased the sky in spite of the burning summer sun, and formed a cool gray blanket that filled the air with moisture. Joe could feel the impending thunderstorm in his old bones and found himself wondering where he was going to find shelter. Was there even a place here in the city where he could just blend in and not be recognized, not be sought out by the police after everything that happened back at the guitar shop?

Not likely.

Joe had stayed in Deering Park all morning trying to come up with a plan to steal back his guitar without getting caught, but every plan he came up with felt too risky and less than satisfactory to him, to the point where he wished he'd never laid his eyes on it in the first place. Around him, the rumor of mommies was saying their goodbyes to each other and gathering up their toddlers, anxious to move them along to the line of minivans parked along Forest Avenue and whisk them back home again. The same went for the duo of tennis players on the court at the far side of the park. The joggers and rollerbladers and bicyclists were all finishing their circuits and moving along as the clouds darkened above.

Go back to the railroad tracks, a voice in his head told him. *The train you were on went on the overpass just up the road. You can wait the storm out under the bridge. And maybe you can just start thinking about some food soon, 'cause your belly is empty again.*

Joe Walton stood up and felt his stomach growl; actually, he heard it through the layers of his filthy suit, cursing him out in guttural rumbles for not finding sustenance sooner. He sniffed hard, put his left hand on his belly, and tried to rub the grumbles away. In the distance, as if to answer, the sky resounded with a rumble of its own.

"Oh, Lord," he said. "Oh Lord, my God, I'm sorry for having offended thee."

The rain came just as he cleared the park and started walking up Congress Street toward the train trestle.

Joe saw the body lying face-down deep in the shelter of the stone pilings of the trestle. Huge raindrops pelted through the iron beams and wooden ties above, their spatter echoing hard off the walls. From a distance, he thought it might be some homeless person stretched out from a bad bender with cheap whiskey. Or worse, that said homeless person had lost the fight completely and was now as cold as the driving rain falling all around him. A flash of lightning struck to the west, and then the sky opened with the roar of thunder in response. Joe looked up at the steel beams and struts forming the bridge above and shuddered.

This was a mistake. This bridge looks like it was made to draw lightning.

Back in Luttrell, Joe saw the black-and-white film *Frankenstein*, which ran on the old reel-to-reel projector the warden kept hidden in the closet of his fastidious little office. It was rumored that he'd also kept his two-bit porn reels in there as well, the kind you had to special-order from New York City, but after his departure in the late 80s, the new warden made the transfer to VHS, and then to a DVD projection unit. He'd seen it on one of the movie nights during the summer. He remembered watching Colin Clive hoisting the prostrate body of Boris Karloff up a chain-pulled gantry until the body disappeared through a hole in the roof, the cadaver offered to a thunderstorm just like this one. He wondered as he approached the body if perhaps he, himself, could raise the dead.

As he moved closer, he realized it was a woman. He could tell by her muddy summer dress, and how it crept up her long, white thighs in the position she laid in. But it wasn't until he put his hand on her shoulder and turned her over that he understood who he was looking at.

It was *her*. That girl from outside the guitar shop, the one who tried to help him up and then screamed "Murderer!" at him while the crowd of onlookers watched and snapped pictures with their cellphones. The girl was barely breathing, and she was bleeding badly from the laceration across her forehead.

Joe pulled his hands off of her and watched her plop back down into the wet dirt and stones. The rain continued to fall from above, pelting her face and making the blood on her forehead turn her pretty hair crimson and wash down the front of her body.

If anybody sees me, they gonna think I did this. I gotta get away from here.

You can't leave her like this. If she dies, she's on your conscience as much as the things you did in the past. You can save this one. You can make this your last chance at redemption.

Joe looked up into the iron-gray sky and wept. "Why y'all fucking with me, Lord? I need help, and you just let that ol' Devil keep on riding me."

Joe took off his hat and wiped his sleeve across his face, trying to get the rain and the tears out of his eyes. He put the hat back on and knelt down next to the stranger who had accused him.

"Miss? Miss, you got to wake up now. We got to get you to the hospital. You've been injured, and you need help."

Svetlana opened her eyes and stared into the black man's pupils. "I remember you," she whispered. "You're dat man I saw arguing with da storekeeper. Please don't hurt me."

"Lady, I ain't gonna hurt you. Somebody else did this to you. You're bleeding pretty bad right now, and I got no idea how much blood you've already lost. I need to get you to someone who can help you. Are you from around here? Do you know this city well?"

Svetlana tried to nod, but the pain in her head sent a shower of stars over her closed eyelids, a meteor shower accompanied by the rolls of thunder all around her. She tried to recall what had happened, and the wave of terror in remembering made her sit bolt upright.

Zee Doctor had come for her! He had come for *Azezel's Eye* and had ripped it right out of her head. "He gave *The Eye* to…" she stammered. "He gave *The Eye* to dat girl that was with him. I touched her just before they cut me. I saw everytink. I saw the farmhouse they are living in."

"You just be quiet about that for now," Joe said, standing up and wrapping his arms around her shoulders. In one quick pull, he had Svetlana on her feet again. She swooned like she was going to fall back down, but he slipped her arm over his shoulder and squared himself to brace her.

"You don't understand," Svetlana said. "Dose people she's with are about to carry out the Devil's plans. Dey are going to—"

"Enough!" Joe Walton moved forward slowly, allowing the girl to usurp his weight and balance. She staggered at first, but as they continued out of the shelter of the trestle and onto the rain-driven sidewalk, she found her footing.

"Do you know if there's a hospital nearby?" Joe's free hand was now clamping down on his bowler to keep it from blowing off in the wind.

"Maine Medical Center is right up da hill. We just have to go up Saint John Street and get back onto Congress." Svetlana stopped walking. "Why are you helping me? I could have gotten you into much trouble vith all my screaming. If the police had been there a little sooner, they'd have arrested you and taken you away."

Joe looked down at his shoes for a moment, now soaking wet from the downpour. His feet were damp and cold to the bone inside his filthy socks. It had never rained *this* cold in Tennessee, had it? What difference did the truth matter now? "I'm helping ya because it's the last good deed I get to do before I die. You was right about me. I don't know how you knew those things about me, but you was right. The Devil used me, and he played me for a fool. Not I got to pay my dues. But that can wait until after you get that cut on yo forehead taken care of. Now, c'mon."

The two walked slowly up the hill, their bodies huddled tight against each other as the thunder and lightning crashed all around them. Cars passed by on the street, forming a never-ending serpent of headlights and taillights on the rainy avenues. Nobody took notice of them, nor seemed to care that they even existed. From a distance, they might have been lost lovers reunited by fate, or brother and sister consoling one another after dropping roses in a funeral plot.

This was, after all, how Serendipity moves the world.

Chapter 15

When Erik opened his eyes, he thought he was still dreaming. Reality felt fluid, as if his mind was swimming underwater, and the things coming into focus in his tired, bloodshot eyes took a bit too long to do so.

After Detective Barrett had come, filled him in on what had happened to him, and gone, he somehow managed to fall back asleep. There had been a small degree of trepidation about it at first, and he wrestled with the idea that putting himself back into the dream world would inadvertently toss him back into that basement on Ocean Avenue, where God only knew what details would bubble up to the murky surface of his subconscious. He'd also pondered the idea of checking out of the hospital—against doctor's orders, naturally—but he knew his body wasn't up for that. Even the proposition of trying to stand up on his own made him dizzy and queasy with nausea. They'd given him a blood transfusion, but that didn't necessarily eradicate every last trace of whatever drug they spiked him with from his system. Did it?

Not likely.

For all he knew, Devil's Breath was still clinging to neurons and delicate tissues inside him somewhere up in his gray matter, boring holes in his brain like parasites.

Seeing Owen's face peeking through the doorway wiped all these thoughts away, and the swimming sensation melted off instantaneously.

"Daddy!"

Erik Marsh's only son was all blond hair and freckles and wide, toothy grin. When he saw that his father was awake, Owen darted through the doorway and sent himself sprawling toward the hospital bed with arms stretched out into a comically wide bear hug. Before he could object, the boy was on top of him, wrapping his short arms around Erik's shoulders and squeezing him as hard as he could. Erik closed his eyes, and when he felt his son's lips press against his cheek to kiss him, he couldn't help but smile.

"Okay, Champ, okay. Please be careful. Daddy still has a needle poking in his arm."

Erik nodded toward his left forearm, where the intravenous needle continued to feed him the steady drip of fluid from the clear plastic bladder on the cold, metal pole.

"C'mon, Owen, give your daddy a break. He's had a bad day." Kelly was in the doorway now, the look on her face a mixture of fear and disapproval. When her eyes met his, she quickly lowered her face to her shoes. "The state police called me at work. I guess I'm still legally your next of kin, somehow. I was going to call your mother, but I didn't want to frighten her or get her all worked up when I didn't even know if you were okay or not."

"You're okay, aren't you, Dad?" Owen managed to relinquish the bear hug he was administering on his father and climb back down off him.

"Yes, I'm fine. Scout's honor." Erik lifted his pinky to his lips and kissed it, and then held it in the air to verify his oath. Owen smiled and grabbed his hand with both of his own. He pulled the pinky down to his own lips and kissed it as well.

Kelly made her way into the pod and grabbed the vacant chair, wheeling it over so that she was next to Erik's bedside.

"Do I even want to hear what happened to you?" she asked, and the tone in her voice was already making him feel rankled. He supposed he couldn't help himself for that. The fact that she even showed up filled him with mixed emotions. Obviously, she was here because she was concerned for him. But if Owen hadn't been in the picture—if their son had been Allen's son rather than his own, would she have troubled herself in the slightest to be there with him? Her inflections made him feel like the ordeal he'd been through was just some major inconvenience for her, and if that was the case, Erik was ready for her to get the hell out.

"Probably not," he answered. "You're probably better off not hearing any of it. Everything you ever worried about with me doing my job would somehow be justified, and the last thing I need right now is for you to sit there and tell me 'I told you so!'"

"I'm not trying to start an argument with you. You don't need to get all defensive." Kelly sat with her knees pressed together, her navy blue skirt spilling smartly over her pantyhose. They'd called her at her job, and that had to be as embarrassing and inconvenient as it was frightening, but Erik found himself not really caring too much about it. So what if the Princess of Propriety suddenly had to lower her guard and deal with a dose of reality? Her reality was still a thousand times better than his any day of the week.

Owen found the remote control unit on the hospital bed and started pushing buttons at random. Erik found himself being pushed into an upright position and then lowered back down again until he was flat on his back. And then his feet were elevating.

"Dad, look! I can make you sit up or lay down with this."

Erik put his hand on his son's and pulled the boy's bony fingers off the control. "Please don't play with that, Owen. You're making me dizzy."

"Sorry, Dad. It's just that it's kinda boring in here."

Boring is good, Erik thought. *Boring is safe.*

Kelly sighed. "I was terrified when I got the call. I realize that I worry too much, but how else was I supposed to feel? They wouldn't give me any details over the phone, so I just assumed the worst. But just looking at you, you don't even seem to have a scratch on you. I guess I worried for nothing. Just like every other time you came home late from work because you were busy digging into some god-awful story that you never seemed to want to talk about as you ate the dinner I left for you—long after it had gone cold and I went to bed by myself."

"You don't even want to know what I've been through, Kelly. Especially not in front of our son."

She rubbed a tear from the corner of her eye, then made as if her hand was really supposed to be brushing a lock of long blonde hair out of her face. Owen's hair was that same fine shade of yellow, the kind that girls would, in a few years, find irresistibly cute on him. By now, Owen had moved on to finding the remote control for the television dangling from the ceiling's corner. He was currently channel surfing, looking for cartoons, but Erik was nearly certain he wasn't going to find anything better than PBS.

"Was it— Was it that creep that's been in the news lately? That Le'Sinestre guy? Is that who did this to you?"

Erik closed his eyes, and the image of the deformed man blossomed in his head like a movie projection—the dark, curly hair and razor sharp chin; the soulless, piercing gaze; the hideous right hand that looked more like an obscene animal limb than a human appendage. How had this guy NOT been found out already? How did you carry that deformity in plain view with nobody feeling the slightest bit suspicious?

Because people feel guilty for wanting to accuse a handicapped person of anything. He carries sympathy and anonymity because people feel bad about themselves for being suspicious of him.

Could that be true?

Of course, it could. Even the notion of thinking of him as handicapped in the land of the politically correct was verboten. He's *differently abled*, as even Kelly might have explained it to Owen had they happened upon him in public, with Owen pointing at him absentmindedly and gaping in revulsion.

Because that's what people did when they saw him. He's spent his whole life dealing with it.

Erik had told Inspector Barrett that the guy's hand was deformed, hadn't he? Told him that Le'Sinestre was left handed *because* of that deformity? How hard was it going to be to go through criminal files and uncover the guy with the fucking goat foot for a hand?

"Yeah, it was him," Erik said. He took a deep breath, looked up at the ceiling, and exhaled. "Kelly, look, it was really nice that you brought Owen down here to see me. I really appreciate it. But this guy knows who I am. And for all I know, he thinks I'm still tied up—um, still thinks I'm in the situation he left me in."

Fuck, I could have phrased that one better.

"I think it's probably a good idea to just get Owen home safe until the cops get this guy."

She looked at him, her clear blue eyes meeting his, and he could tell her inner lie-detector was set to full throttle. "How soon do you think it'll be before they catch him?"

"Based on what I've told them, it'll be fast. I was already able to name one of his accomplices, and if she wants any kind of leniency in court, she'll turn on him quicker than—"

"Hey, Dad! Look! You're on the news." Owen's channel surfing had led him to news coverage of the house on Ocean Avenue. The screen was filled with a snapshot of Erik's professional image, taken presumably from *The Beacon*'s staff webpage, a scholarly looking photo of himself with his notebook clutched tight against his chest in his cocked right arm. Owen pushed the volume-up button.

"…Marsh of *The Portland Beacon* was admitted to Maine Medical Center directly after he was released from captivity last night. Police sources tell us that Marsh can expect a full recovery and that they hope his testimony will able to help them capture Le'Sinestre as quickly as possible."

Well, so much for him assuming I'm still fucking tied up in the basement. It's like I have no luck at all.

"Turn it off." Kelly was now crying for real. Tears slipped out of the corners of each of her eyes and slid down her cheeks. It made her make-up smudge, and it shocked Erik to realize that she'd graduated to the land of concealers and highlights. Kelly's skin had always been lovely enough without makeup. How much aging and changing had she done over the years? How much of it was a direct result of being married to him?

The screen flipped to a shot of the house, with police officers and paramedics removing covered stretchers through the front door. Blue and red strobe lights flashed through the first rays of dawn—Erik guessed the footage had been shot around 6:00 a.m.—and lit up the white aluminum siding of the house. Then the screen changed to still shots of the home's previous—posthumous—tenants, William and Charlene Tibbets, who were now considered the sixth and seventh victims of Maine's most notorious serial killer since Frank Dodd terrorized Castle Rock.

Erik put his hand on Owen's, pulled the remote control easily from his grip, and switched off the television.

"I'm sorry you saw that," he said. "I know all of this is really scary. But you have to believe me when I tell you they're gonna get this guy. Fast. It's looking like I'll be stuck here in the hospital at least for tonight. I'm not going anywhere. So please, just take Owen home and don't let him get all worked up about anything."

Erik turned toward his son. "And you. You've got two days of school left. You just get yourself through them, and then you're on summer vacation. And maybe I can get some time off from work, and you and I will do something fun together. Does that sound okay to you?"

Owen looked at him suspiciously at first, as if he was waiting for a catch to be nailed to that proposition, and when none came, he smiled. "Yeah, maybe we can go camping or something. Tommy Wilcox says his dad takes him camping over by Runaround Pound, where they rent a boat and go fishing every summer. Maybe we could do that. If mom says it's okay."

Owen turned and looked at Kelly, and for the tiniest moment, his son's action rankled Erik all over again. Was that how *he'd* looked at her every time he wanted to do something but had to run it by her first? If he caught an invitation from Officer Anderson or one of the other troopers to a poker night, or if he wanted to spend a Saturday afternoon watching races at the speedway in Oxford rather than mowing the lawn or cleaning the garage of the gingerbread house for the umpteenth time? Yes, he, too, had to castigate himself to her look of reproach, and then wait for the sigh of disappointment before she would relent and give approval, all the while making notes in her mental book of records that *she* had once again been the bigger person and put up with disappointment to make him happy.

Kelly did not do this to her son.

Instead, she stood up, adjusted her skirt so that it billowed perfectly around her once-again slender legs—*she really* did *lose weight; she looks fantastic*—and kneeled down beside their child.

"I think that's a great idea." Kelly lifted her thumb up to her face and brushed the tears quickly off her cheeks. She leaned forward and kissed Owen's forehead. "I think it would be great if you and your dad spent more time together. We can talk about it later when we get home. Now, c'mon. Say goodbye to Dad so he can get his rest and feel better again."

Owen sidled up to his father, leaned over the bedrail, and planted a hot, wet smack on Erik's cheek. "Bye, Dad."

Kelly stood, offered a polite smile to her ex, and then kissed his cheek as well. Compared to the first kiss, this one felt cold and emotionless, the kind you'd get from an old acquaintance at a dinner party or a social engagement. Whatever bond they had between them once-upon-a-time had been completely severed. There wasn't even a feeling of guilt or blame at this point. Just a sense of hollow remorse.

Erik watched Owen's blond head float out the doorway and then shouted after him. "Hey, Owen? I love you, ya know."

Owen peeked back in and smiled that wonderful, toothy, childish grin at him. "I love you, too, Dad."

It would be the last words Erik would ever hear his son tell him.

Gail Silvers, a.k.a. Abby Silverstein, was an absolute mess when she reached the Eastwyck Hotel. She'd spent the drive from the trestle on Congress Street to the Eastwyck Hotel staring in the van's rearview mirror, watching and waiting for the blue strobe lights of the state police to suddenly flash on and pull her over. Every now and then she would glance up at her own reflection, looking for some telltale scar on her forehead that bore proof that *Zee Doctor* had performed his terrible surgery on her, had put *Azezel's Eye* into her brain and blessed her with the gift of omniscient sight. When she did, her forehead was still smooth, perfect, and movie-star glamorous.

I'm already missing the press junket, she thought. *Right now, Jim Roberts is all by himself, answering questions for* Entertainment Weekly *and* TMZ *and* Popsugar.com. *Right now he's telling them I've been under the weather and hopes I'll be at the premiere later on tonight.*

And she still *could* be at the premiere. She could just skip driving the van back up to Hetfield, back up to the Mueller farm to swap out with her own car, not even bothering to offer Warren an explanation as to what happened. But Warren was already going to be furicus. There was no way he couldn't have noticed that the van was gone. He was going to want answers.

Besides, it wasn't like he was going to murder that one piece of ass he was dying to put his cock into, was he? Especially when she was quickly approaching celebrity status, and if anything happened to her, it would be traced back to him.

The dread in her belly told her otherwise. He could murder her in a heartbeat and never feel the slightest pang of remorse. And for all she knew, stabbing the life right out of her could perhaps make that cock of his hard enough to have his way with her once her last breath whistled out her bleeding mouth and her soul departed to whatever plane of existence waited in the beyond. Warren Pembroke could keep her corpse as a fuck doll for a long, long time if he chose to.

I'll know what his plans for me are once I touch him. Once I use the Omniscient Eye *on him and see what he's really been thinking about all this time.*

And that was what was driving her at this point. She needed to know. Immediately. But first, she needed to get cleaned up and swap those bloodied clothes for the Phillip Lim cocktail dress she planned to wear to the premiere. At the very least, if she turned up at the Mueller farm and Warren saw her dressed for the event, he'd be too busy lusting after her to ask a lot of questions anyway. And if he was distracted, she could fake her way through whatever alibi she could scheme up during the half-hour trip up to Hetfield.

It also gave her time to stash a weapon in her Vera Wang purse. A butcher knife, a can of pepper spray, a straight razor…

I can't go unarmed. Because God only knows what Warren's plans are, and if they are too dangerous, too risky to be carried out, I need to be able to stop him. He's already killed Charlene, and even now I don't know for sure if Caroline is alive. Warren is fucking crazy, which means he can't be trusted.

Abby parked the van at the rear of the hotel and used her personalized mag-key card to slip unnoticed into one of the service entrances. When she saw the coast was clear, she caught a maintenance elevator up to her suite, checked cautiously to make sure the hallway was free of the Latino maids that patrolled the penthouse area, and scuttled into her suite.

I need to make this quick, she thought, the feeling of paranoid dread only intensifying as minutes passed by on her designer watch. She pulled her cell phone from her pocket, noticed the five missed calls from the late Charlene Tibbets's cellphone, and decided resolutely *not* to listen to any of the messages Warren had left for her. Instead, she stripped quickly, showered, dressed, and groomed herself for the premiere.

While she showered, the cell phone rang once again and went directly to voicemail.

As she steered the van onto Route 295 North, Abby reached out her right hand and switched on the radio. She pushed the am/fm switch, and the sound of alternative rock was replaced with the monotone thrum of talk radio. The Econoline filled with the idle conservative chat of the *Howie Carr Show*, where caller after caller professed to the Boston news columnist and radio syndication mogul that both Hillary Clinton and Bernie Sanders were no damn good for the country's future, and those hard-nosed Republicans needed to be united on which candidate to vote for come November. It was when the show was interrupted by the special news bulletin that her heart sank.

"The *Portland Beacon* columnist Erik Marsh has been upgraded from critical condition to stabilized and alert and is currently working with State Police to identify those responsible for his abduction and subsequent blood poisoning. It is believed that Marsh was the victim of an opioid-induced attack with a South American drug called 'scopolamine,' or as it's referred to by its street name, 'Devil's Breath.' The drug is known to both cause hallucinations and leave its victims in a state of suggestion that diminishes their own sense of free will. In small dosages, scopolamine is prescribed by doctors to treat nausea and symptoms of motion sickness, but the drug has also been used by predators to cause victims to willfully empty their bank accounts in ATM transactions and allow personal effects to be taken from them."

It's over, Abby thought, and the butterflies in her stomach now swarmed like angry hornets. *That guy Marsh* knows *who I am and what I did to him. He's probably named me already. This is ALL Warren's fault. I told that asshole to kill the newspaper writer, and he didn't fucking listen. I have to kill him. I have to kill Warren Pembroke while I still have a chance.*

No. No, you don't.

The voice in her head was calm, collected. It almost sounded like the voice of *Zee Doctor.*

If they think you were drugged with Devil's Breath, if they think Warren drugged you and used you like they drugged the newspaper reporter…

Abby smiled. *Yes. Yes! If they think the poor, lovely starlet trying to find fame and fortune just got mixed in with the wrong crowd…*

It all made sense. Every last bit of the tragic life she'd been leading. The life of the rebellious child of the global billionaire who had a penchant for diddling boys in Thailand while his neglected wife popped pills and slowly drank herself to death on vodka martinis. Warren had coaxed her into a false sense of security and then used the drug to bend her will and act like some kind of subservient slave. "And—he raped me," she could imagine herself telling *real* journalists like Leslie Stahl or Truth Carson long after that twisted, devil-worshipping freak was either gunned down or locked up. "He raped me, just like he did to those other girls—Charlene Tibbets and Caroline Stork!"

Her heart was pounding in her chest. The sense of dread and anxiety were quickly filtering into a sense of empowerment and survival. There was going to be life after Warren Pembroke, a long, successful life with an ugly chapter in it that she would just have to own and take responsibility for. And for all she knew, the negative publicity might actually help to promote *Death's Last Caress,* maybe turn the low-budget indie thriller into something monolithic. After all, hadn't somebody famous once decreed that there was no such thing as bad publicity?

Howie Carr, the talk-show host on the radio, answered her. The topic had been about the billionaire-turned-politician Donald Trump, who had just made another round of unapologetic digs at the illegal aliens sweeping into the country from Mexico, and at President Obama, who was seemingly doing nothing to stem the tide of illegal immigrants.

"Donald Trump can say whatever the hell he wants," Carr told his last caller. "Ya gotta understand, there's no such thing as bad publicity."

Gus Bickford sat through the evening news, an ice-cold brewski in one hand and a loosely wrapped joint in the other. In the kitchen, the smell of burned hot dogs and beans issued from the stovetop, but at least he'd remembered to turn off the burner and let his dinner char and bubble over in the frying pan on its own accord and as God had intended it. It may have been burned to charred lumps of beef, but after he finished the joint he was smoking, he was going to be hungry anyway and would have eaten a dog turd if it had been cooked long enough.

Maybe. If he had some Doritos to give it flavor, of course.

The thought made him giggle.

His day at the Hetfield Hardware and Agriculture had been another long, dull one. Christ, the most interesting thing that had happened on his shift all week had been Ms. Pretzel Stick, the doped-up chick with the leathery skin and the vacant eyes, who came in on… What day had it been? Monday? He couldn't remember. What he could remember was that she practically cleaned him out on kennel cages, said she was planning on raising goats somewhere, or some such bullshit.

Gus held the joint to his lips and inhaled deeply, pulling the smoke into the lower recesses of his lungs, and then breathed out a long trail of ganja smoke that would have made Bob Marley proud. As the reefer smoke floated up around the light bulb in the overhead fixture, Gus hoisted his beer can and guzzled it down.

When Ms. Pretzel Stick's face appeared on the evening news, and the reporter—*Truth Carson. That's actually Truth Carson giving this report!*—gave her full name and pronounced her dead: Charlene Tibbets, formerly of Ocean Avenue, found murdered in her own home and was possibly the victim of Le'Sinestre, Gus Bickford leaned toward the set and watched the scene unfold.

Ms. Pretzel Stick actually had a name, and as the camera panned across the late Charlene Tibbets's home, Gus found himself wondering about the animal cages he'd sold to her. She told him that she'd acquired some land nearby and had planned to raise— What was it? Goats? She and her husband—also apparently dead, murdered, actually—were going to start a farm. The news report flashed from the late Ms. Pretzel Stick's home back to Truth Carson, and there was a surreal, terrifying moment when Truth Carson's eyes looked crazy, as if his pupils suddenly flashed to a blood-red hue that made the cable anchorman look more like some kind of demon than the trusted journalist from Cable World Media.

Gus Bickford dropped his empty beer can onto the floor, picked up the remote control, and flipped the station to something less reality-based and less close to home.

The screen filled with Judge Judy, who was condemning some black woman for damaging the car of her former boyfriend.

I sold her those cages, Gus thought. *What the fuck was she planning on doing with them?*

Don't get involved, his brain whispered. *It ain't none of your goddamn business.*

Judge Judy banged her gavel on his television. "You're an imbecile," she lambasted the defendant mercilessly. "You should have taken the hint that if he was cheating on you, that it was time to move on. You should have just minded your own business and moved on with your own life. Find for the plaintiff, for the entire cost of damages." Judge Judy banged her gavel again, and the case was over.

Gus Bickford took another hit off his joint and laughed.

"Goddamn right, Judge Judy," he said as the smoke exited out his mouth and nose. "All we need to do is mind our own business."

The sun was still out when Abby Silverstein pulled the van into the driveway of the Mueller farm and rolled up to just outside the big, red barn. Inside the farmhouse, the lower floor's lights appeared to be all lit up. She could imagine both Warren and Caroline sitting in the living room, patiently watching the news and already knowing what she knew—that the journalist from the newspaper had somehow gotten away from captivity from the Tibbets's basement. Abby felt hope beyond hope that this newest development would eclipse the fact that she'd borrowed the van for her own purposes, and that Warren was going to dismiss this coup over the more pressing issue at hand.

She turned off the ignition and climbed out of the van, and walked over to the barn's sliding door.

It was padlocked shut.

Fuck!

Abby knew there was only one key to the padlock—and that it was now in Warren's possession. The thought had also already crossed her mind that she could perhaps just drive up, swap her Mazda back out for the van, and be on her way back to the premiere in Portland without even having to deal with Warren that night, but that plan burst like one more bubble floating up into the heavens of impossibility. Abby opened the van's door, grabbed her purse, and sauntered over to the house. Her father's straight-razor was tucked neatly inside, and she was ready to pull it out and use it if she needed to.

Warren was waiting for her.

"Where have you been?" he asked, his voice never exceeding a level of irritation or annoyance in either tone or decibel.

"I had some business I needed to deal with," Abby answered, glancing from Warren to Caroline, who was now lying on the couch. On the coffee table in front of her were the rubber tourniquet and empty needle—the snake and the scorpion, as junkies often referred to the accoutrements of heroin. The spoon and lighter were both on the floor, fallen victims to her flight among the heavens. Caroline's eyes were wide open somewhere under that cascade of long, dirty red hair. At least her twitch had subsided.

She's now every bit the junkie that Charlene was, Abby thought. *And after Warren's used her up, he'll kill her, too.*

"Is that so? Tell me, Abby, what business did you have? Because I told you right out straight that we couldn't afford to drive the van in public anymore."

Warren was off his chair now, had moved so fast that Abby almost didn't have time to register that he was standing. She'd still been staring at Caroline, with her long red hair frazzled and spilling across her face and down around her neck and shoulders. Abby hadn't even realized that her previous lover was sitting in only her bra and panties and that Caroline's left breast was positioned so that the bra cup was exposing most of her tit, her nipple visible and rock-hard in the light of the overhead lamp. The light also exposed the small trail of blood down her left arm where she had injected herself.

Abby struggled to find her inner-confidence, that sense of authority within her that constantly kept his advances at bay and made him feel more like some frisky teenager who didn't know how to act appropriately around women. If she could find that strength, if she could keep him from letting him take control of the situation, then she could work her magic on him.

Maybe give him a taste of what he's been dying for from her, maybe placate to that inner desire that kept him so desperate for her.

"You haven't even mentioned how nice I look," she said. "I've got to be back down to Portland in forty-five minutes for the premiere. Tonight's my big night. You know how important this is to me."

Abby moved forward cautiously, hoping Warren was taking in just how lovely she looked in her new dress.

I just need to touch him, only for a second, and then I'll see everything inside his mind and his soul.

Warren's eyes lit with a lascivious shine. He was definitely looking her over, and she could see the bulge forming in the crotch of his jeans. Had he been older, Abby wasn't sure that her act of seduction would work even half as well as it seemed to be doing right now.

"I needed to borrow the van because the press junket was moved from the hotel to the State Theater, which meant I needed to move all my wardrobe and accessories from my own private suite to some god-awful dressing room in the basement of the theater. I swear to God, it's about the size of a broom closet with no running water or toilet. It's ridiculous!"

"I see." Warren was inching closer still. "And you couldn't have just— I don't know—thrown a couple of dresses and an extra pair of shoes into the back of one of them fancy limousines they hauled you around in all week? You felt a need to just do things on your own rather than consult with your director and let *him* deal with that shit?"

"Calm down, Warren." Abby let her voice drop an octave or two to a more-commanding tone, a trick she'd learned in a theatrics class back at USM. "Shit needed to be done, so I took care of it. That's what I do. That's why you appreciate me so much." She closed the distance between them and let her left hand fall down on the growing bulge in his pants. "Admit it. I take care of a lot of things for you—although there's still one thing I haven't taken care of yet."

Her right hand reached out and touched his deformed left hand, slowly at first, and then her delicate fingers were wrapping around his grotesque digits. As she did, the *Omniscient Eye* opened wide within her mind, and she saw everything.

She saw the children in kennel cages up in the barn. Their eyes were rolled back into their skulls, their little mouths quivering and grunting goat-like bleats. As they did this, she saw Warren fulfilling his true fantasy; the man with the deformed hand fitted each of the children with sticks of dynamite and tiny digital clocks, turning his parade of goats into a hapless team of suicide bombers.

Warren wasn't just turning their minds; he was going to use them as weapons. Warren Pembroke pulled each child from their respective cage, fitted them with a backpack full of explosives, and whispered into their ears which building they were to visit. The Devil's Breath kept them all under his command, his silent army of beasts, his Goat Parade ready to do the Devil's work.

Abby yanked her hands away from him in disgust, her eyes wide with terror.

"What's wrong, Abby? Didn't you like what you saw? I already know what you've done, Abby. Father Lucifer warned me you would turn on me."

Abby inched backward, her heart racing in terror. Her mind flashed to the razor blade she was hiding in her purse. Only, what had she done with her purse? Did she set it down when she came in? How could she have been so stupid?

All at once, Caroline was standing right behind her, blood still dripping from where the needle injected the heroin near her elbow.

"You stupid bitch! You betrayed us!"

Caroline Stork swung the straight razor directly across Abby's throat. The laceration was clean, deep, and Abby felt the burning sting of pain as her trachea split apart and blood gushed down her windpipe. She slumped forward toward Warren in a daze, her eyes wide with revulsion, her mind reeling at the vision of her life passing before her eyes. It played out quickly, perfectly in her head—the visions of childhood birthdays and holidays and moments of discomfort when her father relished a bit too much in spanking her bare bottom when disciplining her, and how her mother seemed vacant and uncaring on those occasions when she sought protection from him. She saw her own fear and hatred of boys growing within her heart and mind, and how she found love and comfort and sex with other girls and this wide-eyed fascination with spiritualism and the occult where the notion of religion had failed her. And she saw Warren, with his terrible, toothy grin before her, and Abby gasped her last real living breath when *Zee Doctor* stepped into the room behind him, passing him the same dagger she'd used to free *Azezel's Eye* from that European girl. The girl she left for dead under the railroad tracks.

"Cut her now, before she dies," *Zee Doctor* whispered into Warren's ear, and then Warren Pembroke was slicing open Abby's forehead before she could even fall to the floor.

Abby Silverstein convulsed on the bare hardwood floor of the farm-house in an agonized death as Warren Pembroke became the new heir of the *Omniscient Eye*.

Svetlana could barely hold herself up by the time she and Joe turned onto Bramhall Road and trekked toward the Emergency Room entrance. The storm was finally passing the city and moving back over the harbor, allowing the pouring rain to taper off into a slow, steady drizzle. Even the thunder and lightning were finally abating, making their journey to the ER almost bearable. Svetlana's skin had gone pale, except for the flaps of bleeding tissue just above her eyelids, which were now bright crimson even in the dullness of the iron-gray afternoon. It looked like an infection was beginning to set in, making the slit look more like a set of withered lips in the center of her cranium. Joe remembered his grandma telling him tall tales about Bertha, the hoodoo woman from Somerville, whose lips re-sembled shed snakeskins, and how when she sang under the full moon, it sounded like serpents hissed from her vocal chords. One of the old Delta blues ladies, a woman named Memphis Minnie, sang a song about her called, "Hoodoo Lady Blues," and when she sang, Joe could picture the old crone perfectly.

She's probably dead and gone now, probably downstairs with Ol' Scratch, just dying to make my acquaintance.

Svetlana groaned, and her legs buckled. Joe slipped his arm tighter around her waist and hoisted her up again before she could spill onto the wet pavement.

"Y'all just keep moving, miss. We're almost there."

"You aren't going to leave me, are you?" Svetlana looked to her good Samaritan, her eyes fighting to stay open. There were now large, dark patches spreading out around her eye sockets, making her look as if she'd aged a few decades since they left the safety of the train trestle. "Please. Please, mister. I vant you to stay vith me. I don't vant to die alone. Can you please stay vith me?"

"You ain't gonna die, miss. I promise you. I'll get you inside and them doctors are gonna fix you up good as new. You mark my words."

"Please, Aldo! I've missed you so much since you sent me avay. The angels must have sent you back to me, and now that you're here I don't want to let you go."

She's hallucinating. This poor girl is at death's door, and she's looking right at me and seeing somebody else.

The Emergency Room doors parted as they stepped onto the rubber mat, and then an intern in a white lab coat and two nurses were barreling toward them to offer help. Seconds later, another attending doctor was thrusting a stretcher toward the young European girl, and together the team of responders loaded her onto the gurney.

"This lady was attacked down on Congress Street," Joe told the first doctor, who was already slipping a blood pressure cuff around Svetlana's arm. "I think she's lost a lot of blood."

"Do you know her blood type?" the second doctor asked, now shining a penlight into Svetlana's eyes.

"Aldo, please don't leave me." Svetlana's hand clenched down tighter onto the skin of Joe's fingers. For a little thing, the lady sure had a hell of a grip.

"No, man, I ain't never met this lady before. I happened upon her after she was jumped. I didn't know what else to do, so I brought her here. You gonna be able to help her, right?"

"We're going to do everything we can. She's in good hands here, sir. Our team is the best." This was Doctor Two again, and Joe was noticing he looked a lot like…

A lot like Leon Hickey. Holy shit, he's got Leon's wild brown hair and freckles and all.

"We're going to need you to stay and talk to the police," Doctor One grinned as he released the valve on the cuff and let the air out. The resemblance now to Rufus Hickey sent daggers of dread into the pit of Joe's belly. He tried to step backward, away from the gurney, but Svetlana's hand held on for dear life. He could see the flesh of his knuckles slowly turning bone-white. "They're going to want to know what you did. They're going to want to hear all about the knife marks. Aren't they, brother?"

The skin on Leon's face peeled off and fell onto the floor in one nauseating sheaf of flesh. It made a wet plop as it collided with the green floor tiles. The boy's face was once again a wall of bloody sinew and muscle tissue, barely keeping the boy's lower jaw attached to his head.

"Don't go anywhere, nigger. We got business with this pretty little thing, here, but when we're done, we'll come back for ya."

The skin on Rufus's face plopped off as well. It joined his brother's face in the puddle of blood on the floor.

"Aldo! Brother, don't leave me!"

One of the nurses pressed a plastic breathing cup over her mouth, but by then Joe couldn't be sure if she was giving her oxygen or some kind of anesthesia to dope her up. All he knew was that he had to get away, had to leave that place as soon as he could. He did everything he could to bring the poor white girl up there to the hospital, but now she was on her own.

Just like he was.

"Tobacco Joe" Walton yanked his hand out of hers, pushed past the critical response staff, and darted back out the parting glass Emergency Room doors, back out into the world of the living and the dead, where gods and devils fought over the details while humanity crept through existence.

Chapter 16

Priscilla Baines was running just a few minutes late on Friday morning. It had been her habit—as it always did throughout the school year—to be up by 5:00 a.m., have a cup of black tea and a slice of toast with cottage cheese for breakfast, and then read a chapter or two from her latest acquisition from Annie's Book Stop. Now, at the end of the school year, it was customary for the forty-seven-year-old divorcee and empty-nest mom to ditch the comfy chair in her sunroom for the patio table out on her deck. Out where she could hear the *coo* of the mourning doves that favored her rooftop or the pleasant chirps and twitters of the chickadees and sparrows in the trees beyond her garden. She thought she had plenty of time this morning, and since the rainclouds from the night before had finally given way to a clear, perfect sky by midnight, she also thought the dawn was going to be picture-perfect and warm as can be.

She dropped the paper plate with her toast crumbs into the trashcan, picked up the cup of tea and her novel, and plodded out to her deck. The first rays of morning sunshine were glowing just above the crest of her home, and sure enough, the mourning doves were warbling their melancholy *coos* in a sad little choir. A handful of robin redbreasts were hunting for worms on her dew-scattered lawn, which she noticed was getting quite long. She supposed a cutting was in order once she had the kids dropped off at the Hetfield Community School. Today would be their last day of school, a half-day actually, and the kiddies were going to be hyperactive and unruly. That was always a waste, as far as 'Cilla Baines was concerned, but hey, she got paid for a full day of driving, so it wasn't like she was about to complain. Besides, it was good enough for her own children, and she knew a lot of moms and dads who would gladly take that last half-day of a quiet house, even if it was only to grab one last uninterrupted quickie and a second cup of coffee before she brought their kids back to them on the Number 10 bus.

'Cilla went to sit down in her chair but stopped before her rear end could hit the seat. The Kia—her little blue shitbox, as she usually called it—had a flat tire.

She set the book on the patio table and wandered down the walkway to her driveway, wondering what the hell she ran over that would have punctured the Firestone so that every last ounce of air had spilled out of it overnight. 'Cilla bent down and examined the treads, trying to mentally retrace her route from the night before, after she dropped the school bus off at the depot over by the public works lot and called it a day.

She had stopped at the library to see if the latest Diana Gabaldon novel was available to check out. It wasn't, so she placed it on reserve and then spent a good half hour gossiping with Dottie Saunders about the kids on her bus route and the kinds of families they came from, and they commented on how the times had indeed changed since both of them were schoolgirls. By then, the thunderstorm was in full force, so she abandoned any hope of the Dairy Maid being open for an ice cream cone and instead drove out to the Tim Hortons on the edge of Lewiston for a latte and a pastry. She'd brought her book with her and had knocked out a few more chapters before deciding to head back home and fix some dinner. With both sons off to college—Max, the older boy, was down in Boston working toward a political science major; and since the apple never falls far from the tree, Josh, the younger and lazier of the two, was down in Portland schlepping for an art degree, which she'd assured him dozens of times would lead him nowhere in spite of his deadbeat father's encouragement—it would only be herself she was cooking for. 'Cilla thought about fixing a light salad and maybe a tuna sandwich for dinner, but as she passed by the Mickey D's at the plaza, she eschewed that plan for a Big Mac and fries.

It's the end of the year, girl; live it up. Besides, it's not like guys are lining up to date a middle-aged bus driver anyway.

It sounded like something her deadbeat husband, Larry, would have muttered under his breath before walking out on her for that hussy waitress at the hotel bar.

'Cilla switched angles so that she was peeking under the front of the tire rather than behind it and found the offending culprit sticking out from the tire's treads. She wrapped her fingernails around the nail's head and pulled it effortlessly out of the hole in the rubber; it was a good inch-long roofing nail that she must have rolled over just right so that its point drove nearly straight into the wheel.

Was that even possible?

Maybe. If the nail had been propped up so that its point was vertical just as the tire went over it, thus jamming it into the rubber and steel-belted radials. No, that seemed impossible. If the nail were flat on the ground, the tire would most likely have driven over it with no repercussion whatsoever. Besides, it wasn't as if the tire had blown out on her, which it also most likely would have done between the car's speed and the tire's pressure and all.

So, what? Somebody came along with a hammer and nail and just pounded it into your tire just to inconvenience you or let you know they think you're a jerk or something? Who would do that?

Larry Baines, perhaps?

Possibly, but so unlikely that it didn't even warrant mentioning his name to the police if she decided to call them. A vandal, then? Some local kid who hated his bus driver enough to sneak out and pop her tire? Again, not likely. She drove the bus for the elementary and middle school, and those kids were too young to be wandering around alone after dark, much less go roaming the neighborhood and stalking bus drivers. But the older kids…the high school kids…

You're being paranoid. Just swap the tire out for the donut in the trunk, and then you can swing by the Quality Service Mart and get the old tire patched and have them put it back on. That kid, Dustin, can have you fixed up and on your way in no time.

'Cilla looked down at her watch. 6:17 a.m. She had to be to the depot by 6:40 a.m. to pick up the school bus and then be ready to begin her route by 6:50 a.m., starting with all those brats on Main Street. They were all going to be anxious about getting through school today, which meant they were going to be noisy as hell, to say the least.

You can call the school superintendent and take an emergency day. You've got plenty of time saved up, and God knows, it wouldn't be the worst thing ever to start your vacation a bit early.

You can't afford that, so don't even think it. Unless you want to take on a summer job.

Priscilla Baines sighed, plucked the keys out of her jeans pocket, and opened the trunk. She knew her way around a jack and a lug wrench, so she was pretty sure she could get this bitch changed and still be to work on time. Her novel long forgotten, she set to work lining the jack under the flattened lift strip behind the car's front tire.

It took longer than she thought. Some of the lug nuts were rustier than she'd expected, so she called Doris Jones, the driver of bus 5, and told her to let the boss know she would be a couple minutes late, but she was still planning on driving the kids to school.

By the time she had switched the tire for the donut and rolled her blue shitbox into the depot's lot, all the other morning buses were gone. She threw the transmission stick to park, jumped out of the car, and began hauling ass for her bus. As she hustled, she noticed the gaunt redheaded woman leaning against the yellow metal tire-well of her bus, just next to the accordion door.

"Good morning," the redhead said politely, and 'Cilla noticed that the woman's denim jeans and pink halter top were absolutely filthy. And she smelled to high heaven. The woman's body odor suggested that the girl hadn't showered in days, if not weeks. And all of those tattoos… The woman looked like some kind of crazed junkie, and for all Priscilla knew, she was about to get mugged in broad daylight now that all the other buses were gone and on the road.

Was this a parent of one of the kids on my route? If she is, I'm going to have to call DHHS and file a report.

"Good morning, yourself," 'Cilla replied, pulling the bus's key out of her own pocket. "I'm really late this morning, so if there's something you need to discuss, you're going to have to wait until—"

The woman pulled the butcher knife out from behind her. There was no way of her knowing it was the same blade that had stabbed the Muellers to death a few short days ago. There was only a fleeting glimpse of horror in 'Cilla's eyes before Caroline Stork droved the blade into the soft part of her abdomen, just above her navel, and started jackhammering the cold steel in and out of her intestines. 'Cilla tried to scream out for help, but the pain agonized within her and rose up out of her mouth in a big, thick bubble of red. The bubble burst as it passed through her lips, and then Priscilla Baines, the ex-wife and mother of two, fell down and curled into a fetal position in the dirt parking lot. She screamed in agony as she tried to stuff her bleeding intestines back into the cavernous gape in her stomach, as clouds of dust floated lazily around her in the warm summer breeze.

Caroline bent down and snatched the bus's key off the ground where 'Cilla had dropped it and boarded the bus. The ignition turned over on the first turn, sending a burst of diesel smoke out of the tailpipe. The noise of the motor drowned out the dying woman's sobs, which was just fine by Caroline. She shifted the bus into reverse, backed up the vehicle toward the tree line behind her, and then shifted into drive. The bus took a massive lurch upward, almost spilling her out of the driver's seat as the bus's wheels rolled over Priscilla Baines, crushing the rest of her life out of her in a rupture of bones and organs and blood. She was dead even before the rear tires could roll over her and finish the job.

She looked at her reflection in the rearview mirror for a moment and smiled. Caroline's facial tic was completely gone now. All that was left was the shell of a young woman with a deadened soul floating in the limbo behind her eyes. What mattered now was that she keep Warren satisfied and give him no cause to spill any more of her blood.

"Thy will be done," she told herself in the mirror, then turned the bus out of the depot's lot and drove the same route she and Warren had rehearsed over the past few days.

None of the children seemed to care that the bus lady had been replaced by a substitute, and none of the parents bothered to wait at the bus stop and make sure their kids boarded safely. It was the last day of school, after all, and everybody knew the drill perfectly enough not to worry.

Nobody knew the bus was missing until nearly twenty minutes after the school day started. After all, the driver had called to let them know she was running late.

❧ ❧ ❧

Svetlana Barnyk at first thought she was dreaming, but when Aldo and Shimi appeared out of thin air and floated to her bedside, it occurred to her that this was how life on earth was ending for her. The room felt warm, comfortable, and all the doctors and nurses who had been working on her had managed to leave the room inconspicuously. Even the pain where the laceration on her forehead bled and ached had vanished, replaced with a feeling of wholeness and serenity. She lifted her hand to her forehead and traced her fingers just above her eyebrows.

The bandage was indeed there, and she could almost feel the delicate railroad pattern of sutures through the gauze and tape. Aldo smiled at her and lifted her hand off her head, guiding it down so that it rested at her side again.

"It's not time for you, *Sérdeńko*," he said, and Svetlana smiled back at hearing that old, familiar term of endearment her brother used to call her in her childhood. The word translated roughly to "dearest heart." It was what her mother called her before she died.

Shimi stepped forward and stroked Svetlana's long, fine hair out of her face. "Ve are so proud of you, little sister. That awful curse is now lifted from you. Papa should have never allowed you to have *Azezel's Eye*. In time, you vill come to forget everytink it allowed you to see. And then you vill find happiness and peace."

Svetlana tried to sit up, but her siblings pushed gently against her shoulders, and she slumped back down onto her hospital bed.

"No, you don't understand. I need to remember. I need to remember vat I saw in dat woman's head. I saw dat farmhouse where dey are staying when I touched her. I have to tell the police. I have to tell dem how to find dat awful man, Le'Sinestre."

"Be at peace, little sister," Aldo was still smiling. "When you wake up, you vill find dat young man from da newspaper. He's da person you need to tell. He's da one who is supposed to confront the man with the goat's hand."

"It has always been Erik," Shimi agreed. "Serendipity has brought you together because he cannot face such evil vithout you."

Confusion spread across Svetlana's face as she absorbed this prophecy. She noticed that pain was creeping slowly back into her forehead. It slithered in like a scuttling insect, with footsteps that felt like tiny, hot sparkles at first, and then grew to something more potent, more sinister. She closed her eyes as the pain suddenly blossomed into her brain in white-hot pinpricks. The scar itself burned like fire. Her laceration was definitely infected. She was probably spiking a fever already.

Svetlana opened her eyes in time to watch the phantoms of her brother and sister floating off toward a light that had suddenly filled the far corner of the hospital room, and a sense of deep, terrible heartache filled her body. Experiencing such sadness, such emptiness, filled her with panic.

"Don't leave me yet! I don't vant for you to go. I've missed you both so much. Stay vith me for another minute." Tears streamed down her face.

"Ve can't stay, *Sérdeñko*. Ve have to move on now." Aldo's flaxen hair was not in the ponytail he used to keep but rather spilled down his neck and shoulders in golden locks. He had the same hair as their mother. It occurred to her that Aldo had no visible traces of their father in his facial features whatsoever.

"And you need to hurry and vake up," Shimi added. "Dere's not much time left. Zee man with zee goat hand has already taken Erik's only son." Unlike Aldo, her hair and complexion were every bit as swarthy as papa's, perhaps betraying a Middle Eastern lineage in their bloodline that, until now, she'd never even considered.

"Don't go! Don't leave me!"

Svetlana's eyes opened, and the hospital room as she'd remembered it was once again in its rightful plane of existence. The bright light that had unfolded in the corner was now replaced with an X-ray lamp, which revealed a negative that looked to be her skull in black-and-white composition. The doctor examining the film turned around, and she noticed he was a Hindu fellow with a lab coat and a stethoscope dangling around his neck.

"Ah, you're awake finally." The doctor walked over to her bedside and smiled politely. The name on the plastic badge just above his coat's breast pocket read, "J. Abnacki, M.D." He slid the stethoscope's earpieces into his ears and placed the instrument's cold disk onto the fabric of her gown, just above her heart. The doctor listened for a moment and then removed the earpieces.

"How are you feeling, miss?" the doctor asked.

"My head feels like it's on fire. I tink I have an infection."

The doctor lifted his hand to her forehead and felt delicately around the bandage.

"Yes, you are definitely feeling warm. The cut you came in with is definitely infected. I can up your dosage of antibiotics, and I will have the nurse bring you a cool washcloth. In the meantime, can you tell me what happened to you? You were brought in yesterday by a man who claimed you'd been mugged down on Congress Street. Is this true?"

Svetlana considered this for a moment and then nodded. "Yes. Yes, that must be what happened to me. I really don't remember much, to be honest."

Dr. Abnacki picked up his clipboard and wrote something down.

"Tell me, Miz Barnyk, if they mugged you, what exactly did they take? Because you still had your wallet on you when you were brought in. Your money, driver's license, and credit card all remained safely inside it. If you were mugged, they didn't do a very good job of robbing you."

Svetlana closed her eyes. She had not been prepared for a trick question. The wallet had been stashed in a hidden pocket she'd sewn onto her dress, but the dress and her wallet were nowhere to be seen. The pain and heat in her head were making her nauseous.

"I'll tell you what I think," Dr. Abnacki was giving her a cold, hard stare. "I think this was more likely an instance of domestic assault. That man who brought you here. How, exactly, do you know him? Was he the one who did this to you?"

She struggled to remember and discovered surprisingly that she couldn't. *How exactly* did *I get here?* "I can't remember how I got here," she said, and closed her eyes once again. That last thing she *could* remember was being abducted by that terrible woman— and *Zee Doctor.* They had tranquilized her with some kind of injection and then threw her into the back of a white van, and then everything went hazy. *No, that's not exactly true. I touched her hand, and I saw with the* Omniscient Eye. *I saw who they were and where they were living and what they were planning on doing.*

"I was told he looked like a homeless man. He was African American and wore a dirty black suit and hat. Does that sound at all familiar?"

She opened her eyes. "Dat man found me and saved my life. As for what happened to me, I'm afraid I really don't remember just yet. Now could I please have some medicine?"

Abnacki frowned and turned to leave. Before he could, Svetlana thrust her hand out and clutched his, squeezing her fingers around his until the muscles in her wrist began to hurt. Svetlana waited for the *Omniscient Eye* to open up and see into his past, but of course, nothing came.

"Are you okay, Miz Barnyk?" Abnacki tried to wrest his hand free of her grip. She was hurting the hell out of his fingers.

"Just please hurry," she whispered, and let him go.

Having no money and nowhere else to sleep, Joe Walton returned to the trestle on Congress Street.

On his way back down the hill from the hospital, he had managed to sneak into a few unlocked vehicles and pilfer some items to help him get through the night. Foremost, he'd found a polar fleece blanket in the rear of a Honda CRV that had kept him warm through the cold, rainy night. The blanket was navy blue and covered with pink and purple stars in a swirl of celestial activity. It would be easily identifiable if anybody were to come looking for it, and that was just fine by him.

Let them come.

He'd also found a few dollar bills and some loose coins in another car, a green Ford Focus, and a half-empty bottle of water in the cup holder of a silver Dodge Ram pickup truck, which had a parking ticket jutting precariously from under its driver's side windshield wiper. For Joe, these things seemed like enough to get him by without tempting fate.

He stopped at a 7-11 and used the dollar bills to buy a bag of Utz potato chips and two hotdogs from the frank roller-cooker machine; they had looked like they'd been rolled for days rather than hours, but he didn't care. To him, they still smelled like the finest meal he could imagine, and that was good enough.

When the guy at the register rang up his food, Joe turned out to be ten cents short. Joe could feel the grip of fear and despair overcoming him; he tried to count out the money he dropped on the counter, but in the end, the clerk waved him off. There was a line growing behind him, people waiting to buy their beer and pay for gas, so the clerk reached into his own pants pocket and floated the missing dime.

"You're all set, pops," the guy said with a disgusted tone.

To Joe, it was evident that he was filthy enough to be smelling up the place and the clerk just wanted for him to put an egg in his shoe and beat it before customers could start complaining.

"Thank you, kindly," Joe smiled and tipped his hat. He picked up his items from the counter and turned to leave.

"Hey fellah," the clerk said all of a sudden. Joe's heart froze in terror. *Now comes the part where the guy behind the counter suddenly recognizes the fugitive ex-con and calls the police,* Joe thought. *I can't believe it all ends like* this.

Now all the people in line were also looking at him. There was no getting out of this one.

The clerk stared him up and down. "Has anybody ever told ya that you look exactly like 'Tobacco Joe' Walton?"

Joe had to fight from trembling as he pushed the door open and hurried out into the night air.

It was morning now, though, and Joe could hear the sound of the coming train rattling the steel rails above him. He stood up, dropped the blanket on the ground, and stretched his arms.

"Good morning, Joe," the voice called to him from somewhere across the street.

Joe turned and gazed over at the other side of the trestle's stone pilings, where the morning sun streamed in at its most radiant.

Ol' Scratch was leaning against the stones.

The Devil smiled as he suddenly stood upright and walked out into the street into the path of the oncoming cars. None of the drivers seemed to notice him, and their vehicles flew effortlessly by him as if he wasn't even there. "It's been a long trip for you, hasn't it, boy?"

It was the same old man that had confronted him way back as a child, out in his father's tobacco fields. He had the same wild hair and the burning eyes that reeked of brimstone.

"I told ya I ain't got no business with you anymore," Joe said, staring down the Devil.

"You came all this way for your guitar," Ol' Scratch folded his arms across his chest and smiled his fang and tombstone grin. "And I mean for you to have it. If you still want it."

"I decided that I don't need it no more. I ain't got no earthly business trying to sing the blues no more. Not if I'm only going to die and have you drag me down to Hell with you."

"It doesn't have to be that way, Joe. We both know it. There's one little thing I need you to do for me. Do it, and you can have your guitar back. You can have the rest of your life back, and I won't come calling on you no more. At least not while you live here in *this* world."

Joe dropped his eyes and looked at his shoes. His feet were still cold and damp after sleeping in those wet socks. And he still had no underwear on beneath his britches after what had happened to him on the train. Joe Walton had nothing. What was there possibly left worth living for anyway? Even if he got his guitar back, it wasn't like he was going to get very far with the law still after him. It wasn't as if all those wrongs he'd committed would just disappear; they wouldn't just float away in the notes and words to some old blues number he'd play to whatever crowd was still there to listen to him. "My race is run,' Joe spoke to his shoes. "And I'm all done running from you, anyhow. I could just step out in front of the next car and end it all and let you just take me with you rather than let you play games with my soul."

The Devil's grin never left his face. "I don't believe you will, 'Smokehouse Joe.' But I'm curious to find out if you're telling the truth. Go on.

Step out into the traffic and end it all. Don't let little old *ME* stop you." Ol' Scratch let one arm fall down from his chest and waved it toward the road, as if to say, "Be my guest."

Joe Walton stood quietly and did nothing.

"Ah, well, there you go." Ol' Scratch drew his arm back up and re-folded it at his chest. "A man is going to come looking for you in a little while. He's going to tell you that he needs your help. And that the European girl you saved last night. The one you brought to the hospital. He's going to tell you she sent him to find you. When he shows up, all you need to do is kill him. Kill him, and then I will give you back your guitar."

"I don't want my guitar. I already told you, I ain't got no use for it no more in this world."

Satan laughed. "You drive a hard bargain, Joe. I *love* that about you. But business is business, and my business at hand is far more important than dickering with you. So here's my final offer: kill the stranger and you can have your soul back. I'll erase your debt to me permanently. You can have a chance at true salvation for whatever is left with your pitiful little life."

"I don't want it. So just take your evil ass outta here and find some other pawn."

The Devil's hands flew out and grabbed Joe Walton by his collar. He shook Joe with the strength of timeless hatred until Joe's teeth rattled together in his mouth. His hat fell on the muddy ground with an insignificant plop and splash of wet earth against his pant leg. "You fool!" Satan cried. "Do you know what a bargain I'm offering you? I could save you from eternal pain and damnation. I can keep you from roasting in the deepest fires of Hell, where the rest of humanity wallows in agony and anguish." Smoke flew from his nostrils. His eyes pierced like fish-hooks and razor blades. The Devil stopped shaking him and let him go, and Joe dropped down on his ass into the same cold, muddy earth where his hat had fallen. He felt that dampness driving into the bare skin of his ass cheeks under the thin fabric of his pants.

"This man will be coming to find you shortly." Ol' Scratch backed away a few steps. "When he does, I strongly recommend you do as I've asked you. Do that, and I will honor the bargain I offered you. But the choice is entirely yours."

With that, Satan stretched himself into the shadows of the trestle with obscene movements until his body vanished into the stonework. All that remained was the smell of burning brimstone.

Joe watched in horror. When he was certain he was alone again, he bent down and examined the wet, muddied earth for the perfect weapon. When he found the right rock, one big enough to smash the life out of another human being, he picked it up and concealed it in his jacket pocket.

It had never been about finding his guitar. This was the salvation he'd been waiting for.

Chapter 17

Owen Marsh watched as his school bus coasted its way up Main Street. The bus appeared to be moving much slower than usual; the normal routine had been for Miss Cilla to gun the big, mustard-yellow vehicle up the hill toward his house and then slam on the brakes seconds before coming to a halt at the curb in front of the Gingerbread House's front steps. The red warning lights would come on, and the extendable "Stop" sign would unfold from the side of the vehicle to signal oncoming traffic that official school business was underway. The abrupt change in normal procedure hung over him like a shadow, and as the bus crawled to a stop and the door swung open, he found himself hesitant to climb onboard.

Sure enough, there was a new driver behind the wheel; some crazy-looking woman with long red hair and lots of tattoos up and down her arms and legs.

Owen glanced back at the front door of his house, but his mother had already shut and locked it and was somewhere inside trying to get Allen off to work on time as well as preparing herself for her own business day. Mom was stressed enough as it was, vying to make the appropriate changes to her own job so that she could be home with him when summer vacation started next week, which she kept reminding him over and over again as if it was *his* fault that she decided to become a parent in the first place. That, on top of the fact that his dad—his *real* father—was still in the hospital down in Portland.

The woman with the red hair and tattoos was waving for him to come aboard. "Hurry up, Sugar. I ain't got all day," she shouted from the driver's seat.

All the kids on board, all his schoolmates, were deathly silent behind her. That was the strangest part. Usually, the bus was filled with excited chatter with summer vacation about to start. The kids would normally be yelling and laughing and throwing spitballs and practicing the age-old tradition of end-of-year hijinks on their way to a half-day of classes where nothing would be learned and nothing would be important. The most activity to look forward to today would be the receipt of the final Report Card for the semester and maybe a movie or two to watch on DVD as the teachers perused Facebook on their smartphones and shot text messages back and forth about their plans for the summer. Today was a nothing day. No tests or quizzes, no homework to be collected. No splintering off into subgroups to work on spelling or math or reading comprehension. None of that. No, today was a babysitting day to fulfill the curriculum set by the school board and nothing more. And if his mom didn't have to fulfill her own curriculum at her job, he might have very well just stayed home for the day.

I could be with dad, if he weren't in the hospital—

"Let's go!" the redheaded woman demanded, and now cars were backing up behind the bus on Main Street as he plodded down the walkway and over the curb. Owen climbed up the first few steps of the bus and looked at the driver.

There were bloodstains on her clothing. Big, red blotches of clotted plasma that stood out in contrast to the colors of her outfit. The children sat in their seats in stone silence, each staring forward at the heads of the people in front of them. They looked like zombies from that show on cable—*The Walking Dead*, he thought it was called. Owen was constantly reminded that he was too young to watch it and that it would give him nightmares if he did.

Owen looked at the driver.

"Where's Miss 'Cilla?" he asked.

The redhead smiled. It was a terrible, toothy grin that made him think of the wolf in the story *Little Red Riding Hood*. "All the better to eat you with," it suggested.

The woman lifted something to her lips. It looked like a McDonald's straw, only it looked to be filled with something. Before he could ask any more questions, the redheaded woman blew on the end of the straw, and powder flew into his face. Owen coughed a few times as the powder filled his mouth and nostrils, and then his eyes were rolling up into the back of his skull.

"Go sit down, and don't say a word," the redhead whispered, and Owen Marsh obeyed, just as all the other children had.

I need a drink.

Erik Marsh had made it through a nearly sleepless night. On those moments when he had dozed off, nightmares came quickly and freely, moments of unexpected memory recovery, where he was back in the basement in the house on Ocean Avenue, only he was now cognizant of two dead bodies on the floor, which he'd tried to feast upon after being drugged by Le'Sinestre. Only, in the dream, there was no gag in his mouth to prevent him from doing so.

The clock on the wall above the door to his hospital room read 7:41 a.m. The morning shift nurses had already been in twice; the first one, older and a bit too heavyset to be of practical use in the more stringent tasks of providing healthcare, came in to remove the port line that ran fluids into his blood vessels and record his vital statistics. The second one, a chirpy young girl who looked to be fresh out of college, came in to bring him his breakfast and help him to the bathroom.

"I don't *need* help," he told her through gritted teeth. It occurred to him that it was no wonder old folks were always so grouchy when everybody was trying to help them do the things they had been doing successfully by themselves all their lives. It felt a tad condescending, to say the least. Erik threw back the blanket and sheet covering him and slid his feet out of bed.

The dizziness hit him like a tidal wave. It felt like his skull was suddenly full of helium and warm air. He hadn't anticipated it; he had been feeling just fine a few moments ago, or so he thought. Erik placed his hands on his temples and waited for the sensation to pass.

Could I still be feeling traces of whatever shit they drugged me with? How long can this go on for?

"Are you feeling okay, Mister Marsh?" The chirpy young nurse was trying to be polite, but he was certain he could hear the sarcasm beneath the kindness, that sting of cold vengeance after he chided her for offering to help him. "It's okay if you need to lie back down. Nobody is rushing you."

"I'll be fine. I just… I…"

Erik heard a voice coming from the room next to his. It was the sound of choppy English being delivered by the young woman from Monument Square. The street performer who called her act The Carpathian Great and Tiny Circus.

Svetlana!

We still don't know that we can trust her, do we? After all, she possesses black magic, that Azezel's Eye, *or whatever the hell she said it was called.*

"Tank you, but I'm not really all that hungry right now," Svetlana Barnyk said to whatever nurse who had brought in her tray. Erik glanced down at his own meal: two eggs over medium, a slice of toast with side cups of butter and grape jelly, a plastic container with mandarin orange slices, and a cardboard half-pint container of apple juice. Even if the dizziness in his head dissipated, he was still certain that he wasn't going to eat his breakfast. "Maybe you could just leave zee juice for now. Okay?"

"Miss, you really need to eat something. At least try the yogurt. With all the antibiotics you're on, your digestive system is going to take a beating. The yogurt will help."

Erik heard her sigh heavily and then concede to the nurse's orders.

You're being paranoid, he thought. *She's never given you cause to suspect her of anything. So get your ass up and go check on her.*

The momentary feeling of dizziness was beginning to abate, so Erik pushed himself to his feet. He immediately felt the cool air blowing down his backside and paused long enough to tie the rear of his johnnie so that he was covered.

"Oh, before you do your business, could you please give us a urine sample?" The young nurse pushed a specimen cup at him. "That way we can do an update on your toxicology before we discharge you."

"I'm not going to the bathroom right now," Erik said as he sidled past her, completely ignoring the specimen cup.

The name on the patient chart on the door next to his read, "Barnyk, S." He rapped a few times on the already-opened door and then plodded cautiously past the nurse. Her bulky frame took some effort to negotiate around—his head was still fuzzy but getting better fast—and then he was looking down at the Eastern European woman in the hospital bed. She'd just pushed a spoonful of strawberry Yoplait into her mouth when she recognized who was visiting her and nearly spit out a mouthful of pink mush all over herself.

Erik saw the bandage across her forehead and felt the color drain from his own face. Something awful had happened, that much was immediately evident, something that was going to change her, perhaps permanently and probably for the worse. And judging by how large her eyes grew when she recognized him, perhaps she saw something similar in him as well. Svetlana set down the cup of yogurt on the table and thrust her arms out at him.

"Oh, Erik. Vat has happened to you?" Her normally cheerful, serene face contorted into a grimace of shame and unease. "Please, come hold me and tell me you are okay."

Seeing her that way made his heart break. Svetlana looked like every rape victim he'd ever seen during his years working his crime beat column. She had that look that reflected something deeply personal and important had been taken from her soul, stripped away mercilessly with no concern for how she would recover and carry on with her life afterward. Before he could stop himself, his legs were moving forward, and he was crashing desperately into her embrace.

"Don't worry about me," he whispered into the warmth of her hair. He hadn't realized it, but tears were streaming down his face as well. "I'm fine. What happened to *you*?"

Erik pulled back and looked into her beautiful eyes, taking time to calmly brush her tears away with the back of his thumb.

"Dey took it from me," she said, and pointed a shaking finger up at the spot the bandage covered. "Dey took zee *Eye* from my head. I don't know how he found me, but zee man who gave it to me when I vas a child—*Zee Doctor*—he came for me, and he cut it back out of my head. And now somebody *else* is carrying *Azezel's Eye*."

Erik sat down slowly on her bed, taking in the news and trying to process it. His mind was jumping into journalist mode, and he found himself wishing he'd had his notebook and pen. If he could start taking notes, they could possibly lead him somewhere useful, perhaps explain rationally why *both* he and Svetlana were hospitalized and in rooms right next to each other, and why the mysterious power she'd had, the one he had come to fear, was now in someone else's possession. Of course, Svetlana Barnyk would sum it all up with one single word: Serendipity.

"You called him *Zee Doctor*, and you said he gave you the *Omniscient Eye* when you were young. So why *now*? Why come back after all these years and take it away, just to give it to someone else? Did you see who he gave it to?"

Svetlana nodded. "Yes, he gave it to a woman with long, dark hair. She vas the one who cut open my head to take it out. She vas smiling the whole time as she ripped my skin apart. She looked crazy. Dere vas something in her eyes that looked like a wild animal vas hiding somewhere inside her. I don't know if dat makes any sense. It wasn't like she just wanted zee *Eye*, but more like she vas hungry for it."

Erik closed his eyes, and the image of Gail Silvers, a.k.a Abby Silverstein, floated through the final touches of his dizziness.

"Was she beautiful? Like a movie star or a celebrity?"

Svetlana nodded again. "Yes. Yes, exactly. *Zee Doctor* must have told her I had the gift of sight, so she vanted it for herself. She vanted it bad enough that…" Svetlana closed her eyes. "This is going to sound crazy, but I tink she had to sell her soul to zee Devil for it." She looked up at Erik. "I tink *Zee Doctor* is actually zee Devil, Himself."

If he'd had his notebook, Erik would have scribbled all these things down. It might have sounded crazy on the surface, but now at least things were beginning to make sense. If Le'Sinestre was doing the Devil's work here on earth, wouldn't it make sense for the Devil to stack the cards in his favor? Wouldn't Le'Sinestre be blessed with such benefits as knowing who would have the gift of omniscient sight, or at least how to find it? And since *Abby Silverstein* was definitely in league with Le'Sinestre, it was no mere coincidence that she'd found Svetlana.

Only, why hadn't Le'Sinestre taken Azezel's Eye for himself? If he was the mastermind behind the killings and the vandalism, wouldn't he have wanted as much power as possible? Would he have chanced allowing one of his underlings to keep the Eye *rather than keep it himself? Or was he planning on taking the* Eye *from her when she least expected it?*

"Okay, listen," he said finally. "I don't want you to worry about it. I've already told the police who they need to look for. She's the same person that—" Erik thought his words over carefully before continuing. "—that put me in my own situation. Her name is Abby Silverstein, and the police should have her in custody very shortly. From there, they can figure out who Le'Sinestre really is."

Svetlana put her hands out and clasped Erik's shoulders. "I already *know* who he is. I know who *both* of them are. I touched her hands before she cut me open, and I saw everything in her soul."

Erik gasped. "You're serious? You know who Le'Sinestre is? Svetlana, that's fantastic. We can call Inspector Barrett, and you can tell him everything, and they can have him behind bars before—" He stopped and looked at the bandage on her forehead, and the excitement faded from his voice the way the dizziness had faded from his head. "They're not going to be-lieve any of it. Not about *Azezel's Eye* or how the Devil just magically showed up to help in Le'Sinestre's plans. And we still don't even know what his plans *are* yet." He looked into her eyes. "Do you?"

Svetlana nodded slowly. "It's bad. They're going to hijack a busload of children. I saw dem in animal cages. They vere drugged so that their minds were gone from der bodies. Dat much I did see, but I don't know what he plans to do with dem afterward. But Erik—" She leaned closer until her face was inches away from his. "I tink dey have already done that part. I tink the bus was hijacked already. And I tink your son was onboard ven it happened."

Erik shot up to his feet, the weight of dread pulling his heart down into his stomach. "You saw Owen? How can you be sure?"

"Because I have seen him ven I touched your hand. And I saw him ven I touched hers. She has never laid eyes on your son, herself, but she knows that he is one of Le'Sinestre's targets. Dat's why dey chose the Hetfield Community School."

Erik rubbed his hand against his forehead and was surprised to dis-cover he'd broken out into a cold sweat. "I have to call the police," he said. "I have to tell them what's happening."

"It won't help your boy," Svetlana said. Her patience was beginning to ebb, as she'd known this revelation would cause him to come undone. If he was going to defeat Le'Sinestre, he was going to have to keep his wits about him and not panic. "Le'Sinestre has kept one step ahead of da police all dis time. They're not going to catch him. It's always been up to *you* to stop him." She laid her head back down on her pillow. "I am certain of dis. I've known ever since you first saw me back at Monument Square. I knew back den dat you were marked for something, only I wasn't sure if it was for good or evil. And it appears dat you've been marked to do good."

"Why me? I don't even believe in God or religion or anything re-motely like that."

Svetlana smiled, and her face lit up with that inner beauty that he found irresistible. "You only need to believe in Serendipity."

Erik started pacing back and forth, closing the distance in the tiny hos-pital room quickly and then turning around again. "I don't even own a gun or anything. Even if you told me where they were, I couldn't do much more than show up and confront them empty-handed. I can't do this by myself."

"You won't have to." Svetlana picked up the carton of apple juice and took a good, long sip. "The man who brought me here to the hospital can help you. I've felt it on him as well. I thought at first he was a bad man, but I understand now dat he's in the process of redeeming his soul before he dies. He can help you. I tink you will find him waiting by zee train bridge down on Congress Street. He is an old black man with no place else to go. You tell him I sent you, and he vill help you save your boy."

Erik looked at the clock above the door. The hour hand was now almost on eight and the minute hand was quickly approaching twelve. "Are you sure about this? I mean, are you absolutely sure you know what you're talking about?"

Svetlana smiled again, and in that smile came a radiance that filled Erik's heart with hope, more than he'd ever felt in his lifetime. If he hadn't loved her before, he was certain he did now.

"You vill find them at an old sheep farm between Hetfield and Topsham. The farm's real owners are now dead, and I tink all the sheep are as well. Zat is vere Le'Sinestre will be hiding the children until he can carry out his plans. Now go and find dat man who rescued me, and den go help your son."

Erik walked over to her bedside, leaned down, and, as gently as he'd ever moved in his life, pulled her up into his arms and kissed her lips.

"Thank you," he said.

"You're welcome."

"Before I leave, tell me—can you see anything inside me right now, as I'm holding you. Do you have any trace left of the *Omniscient Eye*?"

Svetlana shook her head sadly. "It's gone."

"If I can figure out a way to get it back for you, do you—"

"No. I do not want it anymore. Zee only tink I want from now on is *you*."

Svetlana felt the tears trickling down her cheeks again as she watched Erik rush out the door and into his own room to get dressed. His kiss still lingered on her lips, and she decided that she liked it a lot.

"Tank you, Serendipity."

❦ ❦ ❦

Beads of sweat dripped down Warren Pembroke's forehead and from his armpits to run over his ribs. He had just finished unloading the last of the bundles of C4 explosive clay he'd stolen earlier that week from the construction site out on Route 125. The Donati Brothers were contracted to build a new bridge across the Androscoggin River—the one connecting Durham and Hetfield—and the explosives had been obtained for taking down the old, rusted bridge. Warren had followed the directions he'd printed off the internet to the best of his ability, with a looming dread that his deformed hand was going to cause him to fumble and send him directly to Kingdom Come without passing Go and collecting two-hundred dollars. Not that it mattered much anyway, as he was certain Kingdom Come held no vacancy for him, anyway.

It doesn't matter because I've been through all of this already.

The feeling of *déjà vu* crept up on him once again.

How could he be so certain he was reliving a previous lifetime? How could he know for sure he wasn't just crazy-fucked in the head from the start of all this? Yes, he hated society. But that was a response to all the unkindness he had suffered because of that hideous, useless appendage at the end of his right arm. The ugly looks, the taunts, the bitter divide between repulsion and idiot sympathy from all the whole, complete people who had no clue what it was like to be him. He had to watch the rise of the Politically Correct Nation stand up and tell the uneducated masses that he *wasn't* a freak after all, but a pitiable soul who was still somehow useful and could be a productive member of society. Stop feeling sorry for him, but at the same time, stop treating him like a victim of being handicapped. The kid is capable of holding a job and being just as productive as everyone else—but not *really*; without *two* hands with working, opposable thumbs, he was already ill-equipped for society. Even *he* knew that much. And those grotesque, bulbous digits he called fingers weren't as shameful and unattractive as society thought. Oh, *of course*, they were. Even as a child he knew people fought not to stare at him, and when they did, they tried to pretend they weren't sickened to the core by his deformity. Society, as the Politically Correct understood it, was a world of pretend and pretentiousness.

It was going to please him to unleash his Goat Parade and wipe them all out.

By count over the last few days of following the school bus, Warren estimated that there would be twenty-seven children in all by the time Caroline returned to the farm. They'd been ill-equipped to give each child an individual cage with the number of animal pens Charlene purchased. She'd visited two additional pet shops after Hetfield Hardware and Agriculture and bought them out as well and there still weren't enough, so they would make due, doubling up here and there, keeping the smaller children tied with ropes or shackled with handcuffs. God only knew if Caroline was going to be able to remember to make all the stops she was supposed to, anyway. Now that she was shooting heroin, she couldn't be trusted to remember her own name.

Déjà vu.

Why? Where the fuck was this feeling coming from? There was *no* previous life to this one, was there? Was there really a chance that Warren Lee Pembroke had been born, lived a whole different lifetime, and died somewhere in the past? Was there a chance that the experiences he was going through had already happened before and he was just going through the motions all over again?

No. No, no, no!

This is MY lifetime. I've lived my own life, and I made MY choices, and there ain't a damn soul, living or dead, who can prove otherwise. I am Warren Pembroke, and I planned all of this out on my own, and nobody is going to stop me or change my will.

Warren looked at the backpacks he'd been preparing for the children: nylon school bags with Velcro straps, small bricks of C4 strapped where their spines would be, and small digital timers that would emit the right electrical sparks to set them off when *he* chose them to. The vision the Dark Lord showed him had his little goats parading down Congress Street in Portland, walking into churches and banks and businesses and restaurants; some would walk into City Hall while others walked into the Portland Library and the Children's Museum and Maine Medical Center. They would fill the public venues with the highest number of possible casualties; the bombs would go off and then there would be nothing but panic and terror and chaos.

You don't have *to do this.*

The voice came from nowhere and everywhere. It sounded exactly like his mother, like Janis Pembroke, and he could almost picture her standing behind him in her old blue Pillsbury apron, her aged face pulled into a tight grimace that suggested she was going to start crying any second. "*You don't have to do any of this, Warren. It's not too late to stop.*"

Warren glanced over at the rows of pet cages he and his Harpies had installed along the walls in the top floor of the barn; their metal bars gleamed from the overhead light. When he closed his eyes, he could almost picture the children penned up inside them, their eyes rolled back into their heads so that only their sclera was visible. They would all be drugged out of their little minds; all he had to do was suggest to their subconscious that they were goats, and they would start braying and bleating like the little animals they were. He opened his eyes and looked down at his deformed right hand, examining the grotesquery at the end of his arm.

Déjà vu. I don't know why, but I feel like I've been put through all of this once before.

"No, Mom, I really do *have* to do this. I made a deal with Satan, and now I have to honor my part of the bargain. Your boy is going to be remembered as the Harbinger of Hell on Earth." Warren smiled. "Doesn't that make you so fucking proud of your boy?"

He heard a noise coming from outside and turned toward the window. Caroline had turned the school bus off Route 196 and was pulling onto the dirt driveway of the Mueller farm. The bitch was ahead of schedule, which meant she had not made it through the full roster of bus stops as he'd rehearsed with her. It meant that he was going to have far fewer goats than he'd anticipated.

"Warren, honey, whatever your planning, please stop before it's too late," the phantom voice of his mother pleaded with him.

Warren remembered how he'd gotten the call from the State Police after her body had been discovered, telling him how her death had been "accidental" even though he knew better. The autopsy had revealed liver failure due to alcohol and pill consumption, and Warren quietly, stoically took the news while he celebrated his independence in his mind. Janis Pembroke's only son had been slowly poisoning her, had in fact started on the afternoon of his Daddy's funeral. While friends of the family stopped by at the luncheon they held in the basement of the First Methodist Church on Shiloh Road—they'd put out a deli platter from Hannaford's, and friends of the family had brought casseroles and potluck dishes in that old-fashioned, neighborly way—Warren began the slow, steady process of sprinkling ground-up acetaminophen into her food and beverages. As time went by, he upped her poisoning to quinidine and nicotinic acid, but by then Janis Pembroke was drinking heavily on her own and privately regretting ever falling in love or having a child. His mother had dropped dead at the local Wal-Mart, just keeled over and dropped onto the gray and tan linoleum tiles, clutching her belly and moaning and sobbing in one of the freezer aisles.

Warren hurried down the stairs at the back of the barn and threw open the sliding door. He'd already moved the van out behind the building—with the remains of Abby Silverstein decaying quickly in the rear—so Caroline could drive the bus right inside. The Dark Lord had led him perfectly to this place, which had appeared to suit his every need. It felt like Serendipity.

He watched as she piloted the bus into the garage; he closed his eyes in frustration as she managed to clip the mirror on the driver's side on the barn's door frame. With the mirror now shattered and crumpled, the bus would now stand out once they took it back out on the road again. Without the bus, there would be no way to get all his goats down to Portland to carry out his plan. Warren looked at the mirror dangling off the side of the bus and then down at his deformed hand. Then he reached up and closed the sliding door again.

He could feel his blood pressure rising as he herded the children upstairs and into their pens. He counted thirteen children as they climbed obediently up the stairs.

Joe watched as the Honda rolled down Congress Street and came to a stop by one of the parking meters across the road. The fellow driving it scooted out, dropped a couple coins in the meter, and then hustled down the block to the crosswalk. The guy was tall, stocky, with shaggy black hair that ruffled in the breeze coming off the ocean. He had a few days' growth of whiskers creeping down his cheeks and jaws, like dying ivy, that made him look much older than he probably was. He still moved with a young man's speed, which made Joe wonder if the smooth, cold stone in his jacket pocket would be enough to kill him.

Don't rush this. You don't even know what he wants yet. And you don't need to be seen by anybody while you're doing it. This is your ticket out of all this, so don't fuck it up.

Joe Walton put his hand in his jacket pocket and closed his eyes. The stone felt smooth, perfect, an easy tool that fit right into his curled fingers.

You don't know that for sure. Look where your life went last time you trusted Ol' Scratch.

"When it comes to His bad business, there's always a catch. Y'all just play it cool and see what this cat wants. And if the opportunity presents itself…"

The guy entered into the darkness of the trestle's stone alcove and approached him.

"You best get the fuck outta here. I ain't got no business with you."

The man stopped in front of him and put his right hand out to shake. "Please. My name is Erik Marsh. I think you're the guy who brought my friend to the hospital. She said you might be able to help me."

Joe eyed his hand suspiciously, sizing him up before deciding to return his handshake. All the while, feeling the coldness of the stone in his pocket, its primitive simplicity giving him quiet, complicit fortitude.

"Is the girl okay?" he asked, taking Erik's hand and squeezing it tight. "I didn't mean to run out on her, but it wasn't safe for me to stick around."

"She's fine. The cut on her head is infected, but they've got it sewn up, and they're treating her with antibiotics. She'll be good as new in no time. Except for the scar. I'm guessing even with plastic surgery that'll still be permanent. Look, I don't have a lot of time. I know how to find the people who hurt her. She said you might be willing to help me. She told me you might be worried about some things in your past, but I'm going to tell you right up front; whatever it is you did, I really don't give a shit. I think they have my son, and I need to get him back before they hurt him. So please, if you can help me at all, then come with me." Erik motioned with a nod toward the Honda parked across the street.

Joe lifted his hat and wiped his jacket sleeve along his forehead. The day was already getting hot. Mid-June and it already felt like a blistering July day. All the white folks would be lining up at the ice cream stands or taking that first summer dip in their swimming pools or sitting in their air-conditioned living rooms and bitching about how hot it was. And else-where the brothers would be working chain gangs and cleaning up trash by the side of the highways or selling drugs on filthy ghetto street corners. It seemed like there was nothing but bad business for the black man. It was no wonder Ol' Scratch had played him so easily. Joe had wanted talent, but what he suddenly realized in a blinding epiphany was that what he'd really wanted was to live with the blessings of the white man.

No, that's bullshit! All I ever wanted to do was play the guitar. I never gave a fuck about anything else. The Blues is suffering, and I chose my life of suffering so I could sing the Blues.

The stone in his pocket started singing to him. He could hear it as it slowly rose above the din of passing cars and construction work. It rose up like an angel's call, filling his head with sweet, sweet notes and words. "You don't have to sing the Blues anymore. You no longer have to suffer…"

Joe put his hat back on his head and placed his hand in his jacket pocket. He could feel the stone vibrating.

"Will you come with me? I really need to go now."

Joe smiled as his long, black fingers fondled the stone. "Yeah. I'm right behind you, chief. Let's go get your boy back."

Erik turned the car onto Route 295 North and stepped on the gas. On the opposite side of the highway, rush hour traffic coming into the city was crawling into the home stretch. In the northbound side, the flow of cars and trucks and the occasional Winnebago campers with out-of-state license plates was far more modest and negotiable. Even when the three lanes merged into two, he still had no problem maneuvering his Honda around slower vehicles and keeping the pedal pegged down to ten miles above the posted speed limit.

"I never caught your name," he said to the weary figure in the passenger seat. "What should I call you?"

He watched as the black man removed his hat for the umpteenth time and wiped the sweat from his brow with the sleeve of his suitjacket.

"If you're too hot, you could always take your coat off and toss it in the backseat. Here," Erik reached out and switched the car's air conditioner up to full blast. "This will help cool you down."

"If it's all the same to you, I'll just keep my coat on. And you can just call me Joe."

Speed limit signs, exit signs, and mile markers flew past.

"How come you ain't called the police to help you? What makes you think I can do anything that they couldn't do better?"

Erik reached down and dug into his pants pocket and pulled out his cellphone. "Goddamn thing is useless when you don't pay your overdue bills. I was told you can still dial 9-1-1 on a shut-off phone, but where we're going, I don't think the police are going to be able to help much."

"Y'all got a plan? What are we supposed to do? Just show up and grab your boy back? Do you even have a gun?"

Erik sighed and shook his head slowly. "I honestly don't know what I'm supposed to do. Svetlana told me where we have to go, but she was pretty vague about what happens when we get there."

Joe Walton sighed and buried his face in his large left hand. "Lord have mercy, ain't we both fucked."

"I'm sorry, what did you say?"

"Nothing. Listen, son. I don't know what you think is going on, but this ain't just some crazy kid we're dealing with. This is the Devil's business. For all we know, they're already hip to us showing up, and they're waiting for us. You dig? All of this is the doings of Ol' Scratch. We can't beat him."

"I have to try."

"You ain't listening to what I'm saying. Us two just showing up is a death sentence for both of us. We ain't going to make it out alive. And my soul is already damned. Tell me, boy. If you die today, where do you think your soul is going?"

"Are you asking me if I believe in Heaven and Hell?"

"Do you?"

It was Erik's turn to sigh. "I used to think I didn't until I met Svetlana. She was marked somehow by black magic. But someone, I think you called him Ol' Scratch, showed up and just… I think he showed up and took that magic away from her again. And I keep trying to convince myself that if one side is real, the other side kind of has to be real as well. Does that make sense?"

Joe grinned. "Boy, that's the first thing you've said so far that's made any sense at all. But tell me, when we get to where we're going, do you think God is actually going to be there waiting to help us?"

"I don't know. But I think Serendipity will be, and I think that will be all the luck we really need."

Joe Walton laughed. Slowly, quietly at first, and then he tilted his head back and howled with laughter. "Your plan is to show up and hope we get lucky? Seriously?"

Erik felt his face growing flush. "I suppose you have a better plan?"

Joe slipped his hand back down into the pocket of his coat and fondled the stone. Its magic had grown since the last time he touched it. Now the stone sent images to his brain of entering a set of pearly gates into a kingdom in the clouds. He saw angels around him, singing to him, and their music was unearthly and beautiful. He felt more calm and serene than he'd ever felt in his whole life, and the vision brought tears to the corners of his eyes until he let go of the stone and pulled his hand from his pocket. "We gonna need to distract 'em. One of us is going to have to get their attention so the other one can go find your boy and get him out safely."

"It ain't just my son." Erik looked at the old man in the passenger seat. "It's a busload of kids who were taken. I know it's going to sound terrible, but I only care about Owen. If we can stop Le'Sinestre and save them all, and that's a long shot, then fine. But if push comes to shove, we want Owen back, and we get the hell out of there. After that, the police can come and do their jobs." Erik stepped down on the gas and pushed to nearly twenty miles over the speed limit. They were well out of the city by now, and only ten short miles from the Topsham exit.

"If push comes to shove," Joe echoed. "Ol' Scratch is calling all the shots. We may be able to take out Le'Sinestre, but that won't mean the Devil is finished with us. I think both of us are gonna have dues to pay before this is over."

Chapter 18

Caroline Stork looked at the little blond-haired boy with the deepest disgust. The kid had pissed his shorts and the blue denim fabric had turned a deep navy hue. His bare legs were soaking wet as she pushed the little twerp through the bars of the dog kennel and pushed the door shut behind him. The boy fell on top of the girl that Caroline had pushed in before him, but she merely grunted and scooted out from under him without saying a word. She'd dosed every single child on bus number 10 with Devil's Breath, and the shit had made them entirely susceptible to her commands. Her last command had been to "keep quiet," and they were doing just that.

"You've done well," Warren Pembroke spoke from the doorway behind her. "You failed to get them all, but you got back here without being noticed." He walked toward her, and he sounded pleased. Caroline turned and smiled at him.

"I did exactly as you told me," she said. "I've done everything you wanted." Caroline took a few steps and closed the distance between them. When she reached him, she held her hand out and placed it against his crotch, examining the growing bulge of his erection. "I want to get high, now, and then I want to fuck the shit out of you." She traced her hand back and forth over his bulge. "Can we snort some coke, baby? Just a little bit so I can really enjoy what I'm doing to you."

Warren closed his good hand into a fist and punched her hard across her chin. The shot was so sudden, so unexpected that Caroline actually saw stars dance across her closed eyelids as she spun under the impact, stumbled, and fell to her knees.

"You numb, fucking idiot. Did you see what you did to the mirror on the bus? Did you notice that you totally demolished it, so now it will be immediately noticeable when we leave to carry out our plans? How the fuck are we supposed to drive the bus down to Portland when it's noticeably damaged? Don't you think the cops might get a little suspicious over it? Especially if they're looking for a bus full of children that was hijacked in broad daylight?"

Caroline clutched her mouth and wept. It felt like he had broken her jaw from the right side of her face. She tried to speak, but the lopsided feeling of her jaw caused her to sputter and lisp. "You fucking bafftard! What did you do to my fayshh?"

Warren went to punch her again, but he heard sounds coming from outside. He hurried toward the window and looked over at the Mueller house.

The house was on fire. Smoke was pouring out of the opened windows. "Oh, holy shit. Now what?"

Warren sped over to the cages where the drugged children sat, staring quietly out into space. "You're all zombies now. You are all zombies, and I want you to feast on living flesh."

One by one, Warren Pembroke unlocked the pens, and then he sped past Caroline, who had given in to the pain and was rolling around in agony on the floor. He paused at the stairs and looked back at her. "Goodbye, my love. I'm sorry it's had to come to this."

He waited until the children began to stir and creep from their cages before hurrying down the stairs and running for the door.

Before stepping outside, he stopped and listened for a minute as the children fell on Caroline Stork and started to feast. Her screams made him smile as he stepped from the barn and closed and locked the door. Then he turned and ran toward the burning farmhouse.

Erik Marsh had pulled his car over to the side of Route 196 around half a mile away from the Mueller farm. Based on what Svetlana had told him, he was almost certain he knew which farm she'd been talking about when she explained what the *Omniscient Eye* had shown her. Erik was familiar with this stretch of road, had driven it nearly every day for the last fifteen years on the jaunt to and from Portland. The only other farm along this road belonged to a dairy farmer, and that was still a few miles down the road.

He and Joe had spoken very little since turning off the highway. From time to time Erik noticed Joe's belly growling hungrily, and it had crossed his mind to stop briefly at the McDonald's just off of Exit 31, but his mind quickly snapped back to his son's plight. He wasn't about to risk Owen's life to feed this filthy, old man something off the dollar menu just to shut his belly up. Even now, Erik's mind filled with dread and panic.

"We'll park here," he told the old man. "We're far enough back that they'll never hear us coming.

"What did you say your friend's name was?"

"Who? Svetlana?"

"Yeah. Where did she say they was keeping your boy?"

"I think they're keeping all the kids inside the barn."

Both men got out of the car and looked toward the woodland that ran parallel to Route 196. Just around the bend, the tree line would turn into the backside of a sheep pasture, enclosed by wooden posts and electric fencing. At the far side of the pasture was the rear of the farmhouse, and beyond that the old, red barn. They could just see the barn's roof, its weathered iron rooster weathervane oscillating in the breeze.

"We should split up," Erik said. "I can follow the dirt road up to the barn. You can cut through the pasture and make it to the house. Once you get inside, figure out a way to cause a distraction. Something that'll be sure to draw their attention. When I know for sure the coast is clear, I'll get into the barn and find Owen."

He turned and stared at the farm again, and Joe found his hand slipping quickly into his jacket pocket, looking for the stone. As his fingers embraced it, he discovered that the music from the stone had grown louder still, at least in his mind. He wasn't sure how, exactly, that he could hear it so perfectly while Erik could not. It seemed to be radiating all around him, flowing in the purest harmony he'd ever heard. It sang with the voice of all the angels in Heaven, so melodious and beautiful that tears ran down his cheeks. It made him feel as if he was being baptized right there by the side of the road.

Do it! the voice in his head told him. *Crush his skull NOW while you have the chance. He'll never see it coming, and he won't feel a thing.*

Joe Walton took his fingers off the stone, and the song faded as swiftly as it had come. *I ain't your pawn, and I ain't doing your dirty work.* "We best get moving," he said. "If you want your son back, we got to get to work."

Erik turned and looked at the old man. "Thank you for this," he said. "It was a lot for you to trust me and put your own life on the line. I don't think I'll ever be able to repay you."

With that, the two men walked up the road, following it around the bend, and that's where they split up. Erik followed the dirt and gravel driveway, and Joe found a weak portion of fencing, climbed over, and made his way to the farmhouse.

Not all the sheep were dead.

Joe noticed quite a few carcasses rotting in the early summer sun, but a few stragglers still remained and watched in terrified suspicion as the old man pushed through the grass toward the house.

They was sacrificed, he thought. *These animals was killed for ritual. Not for food or sport but for the very act of spilling their lifeblood out of them.*

He thought of the Hickey brothers and how they'd bled all over the floor of his Daddy's barn. That had been a ritual as well, the only difference being that Joe's ritual had been an act of vengeance. These beasts had done nothing to offend anybody. *They'd been killed to offend God,* he thought as he passed the fifth or sixth carcass. *Just like Jesus had been put to death.*

The house ahead of him sat dead quiet in the June morning heat. It occurred to him that if he managed to let himself inside the house, he'd better find a weapon fast before anyone inside could discover his presence. There was no way of knowing how many people were helping Le'Sinestre, but they would most likely fight to the death to protect him and the covert plans he was preparing to carry out. He started to slip his hand into his pocket again but thought better of it.

It's not a weapon, he thought. *The stone is a great big lie. You haven't killed that white kid yet because you already know you can't be redeemed. Your redemption comes in helping him get his son back. You are helping him because you couldn't help your own Daddy.*

Joe spotted the bulkhead door leading into the basement. He bent down and lifted the door open, surprised that it wasn't locked from the inside.

It was dark as midnight down there, and for the first time since he'd gotten off the train, he was truly terrified of stepping inside. To do so meant there was no going back.

Joe Walton took a deep breath, lifted his foot, and placed it on the first concrete step.

The rest of the steps came easier.

Erik had broken into a run once his feet hit the dirt driveway. He moved quickly, silently, his eyes frantically scanning the farm to see if anybody was outside or at a window watching his approach. He closed the two-hundred yards between the road and the barn quickly and bolted around the building in a lumbering sprint. It was the biggest barn he'd ever seen. The thing was simply enormous, a monolith against the backdrop of pines and spruces behind it.

Erik turned the corner and nearly ran into the Ford Econoline. Its appearance hadn't been expected, and it startled him, but when he recognized the vehicle, his blood ran cold.

He noticed the scattering of maps and old newspapers and the nearly-gone roll of toilet tissue pressed between the windshield and the dashboard and found his mind returning to when he'd seen it back at Hillside Cemetery. He remembered clear as day the deranged woman who had appeared from behind the steering wheel. She had rummaged through the back of the van until she'd produced the bucket with the mysterious contents, which she'd hauled past the headstones and into the copse of trees flanking the cemetery grounds. She came back empty-handed and had driven past him as if he wasn't even there.

His heart pounded in his chest as he crept quietly, cautiously around the van. He had to draw in a deep breath before feeling brave enough to peek inside.

There was a corpse in the rear of the van.

Erik squinted against the darkness as he looked through the window of the Econoline. When he recognized Abby Silverstein's face, his knees buckled, and he collapsed onto the grassy ground.

Holy shit! Holy fucking shit! She's already dead!

From somewhere above him, on the upper floor of the barn, Erik heard another woman scream, and what sounded like an angry mob of people moaning and wailing. He heard the sound of large items being knocked over, and the clang and crash of metal against the walls and the floor.

The woman screamed and screamed until the voice choked right out her lungs and throat. Somebody else was dying somewhere up on the second floor of the barn.

Erik closed his eyes tight and prayed that Owen was safe.

When the panic subsided, he got unsteadily to his feet and staggered around to the front of the barn. He made it just in time to see the smoke pouring out from the farmhouse and the man with the deformed hand lurching out of the front of the barn and speeding toward the house.

"This is insane," he whispered to himself. He reached into his pants pocket and produced his cellphone. He held up the instrument, saw that he still had twenty percent of his battery left, and punched the numbers 9-1-1.

As if a miracle had occurred, a voice on the other end of the line piped through what had otherwise been a useless device, saying, "Emergency Services, how may I assist you?"

Erik Marsh dropped his phone in the grass, rounded the front of the barn, and made his way inside.

The top floor of the house was in full conflagration by the time Warren reached the front door of the farmhouse. His mind was full of panicked thoughts about his plans falling apart beyond his control and how the Goat Parade he'd so carefully schemed was quickly coming undone by outside forces. He was certain that Caroline had done something stupid to cause the fire, perhaps dropped a lit cigarette butt in the trashcan or something equally careless, but that seemed impossible. She hadn't been inside the house since he woke her up that morning and sent her on her way to kill that old bus driver lady and kidnap the children.

More importantly were the remaining bricks of C4 explosives on the dining room table, where he'd spent all of the previous night working on the backpacks. There still had to be somewhere between five and ten kilograms of the clay material that he hadn't used and had planned on planting somewhere in the city once his Goat Parade had begun. As long as the first floor was only filled with smoke, he still had a chance of rescuing the explosives.

The fire was going to be noticed for sure. Passersby on Route 196 were going to see it and report it. And very possibly, some good Samaritan or other was going to pull into the driveway, probably in some souped-up pickup truck, thinking they were going to rush into the burning house and try to rescue the Muellers, who were already dead by two days and turned to feces in the bellies of the coyotes.

Most infuriating was the fact that they were supposed to wait until the full moon on the following Thursday to carry out the Parade. They were going to hold their blood ritual there in the barn and then load up the bus with the kiddies and head down to Portland. In his visions, he'd imagined pulling the bus off Route 295 South and traveling through Munjoy Hill into the city. They would park the bus somewhere on the outer side of Franklin Arterial, get the kids strapped into their backpacks, and let them wander right down the middle of Congress Street. He was going to whisper to each of his goats, reminding them that they were Satan's beasts and tell them which buildings to go in. The Devil's Breath would keep them under his control, so there were no expectations of any failure, other than perhaps being noticed by a random policemen patrolling the area. Even then, with all those children bleating and braying as they ambled along, people would be frightened enough to keep their distance. They would see, and they would remember. They'd appear on the evening news. That asshole Truth Carson was still in town and would report the whole thing to the world like a good little soldier. He'd interview them, and they would tell the whole world how the city exploded all around them, how the gates of Hell had opened up on earth.

Warren threw open the door and ran into the dining room.

The table was empty.

"No! What the fuck? Where's my fucking dynamite?"

He reached out his good hand and his deformed hand, grabbed the dining room table, and sent it crashing into the china cabinet against the far wall. The glass doors smashed apart, and the ancient, delicate dishes that Herb and Karen Mueller had received on their wedding day toppled and splinter into thousands of brilliant white shards.

"I've gotta get out of here," he said, finally noticing the smoke burning his windpipe and filling his lungs. "I have to roll *right now* before everything falls apart."

Warren ran into the living room and opened the drawer on the table beside the davenport. He fished around inside for the moment, his bad hand now holding the cloth of his shirt over his mouth and nose until his good hand found the gun.

Obviously, somebody had intruded on *his* property and had set the fire as a distraction. Someone had come in and taken his dynamite and was probably up in the barn, trying to free the children. Whoever it was, it wasn't likely the person was going to survive the onslaught of little zombies waiting beyond the locked door. Whoever it *was* was going to meet the same fate as Caroline Stork, who by now should have been cannibalized to death.

Warren fled out of the burning house and ran back up to the barn.

Erik put his hands on the bolt that held the barn's upper door shut and threw it open. He wasted no time bolting for the stairs, taking them two at a time.

When he hit the landing and looked around, he found himself falling into a nightmare.

The first thing he noticed was the corpse in the middle of the floor. The body was curled into a fetal position as if the person had been trying to protect herself from the onslaught she'd endured. There was blood everywhere, spilling out of her very recently deceased body in arroyos that gushed and sprayed from the myriad bites and tears in her flesh. But more frightening was the cluster of children surrounding her, still feasting and clawing at her body. Some of them were so splattered with blood that they were almost unrecognizable.

It was when he saw the tuft of bright blond hair and the blue denim shorts that he realized Owen was among them, yanking on the woman's calf so that he could sink his teeth deeper into the meat of her leg.

"Oh, my God! Owen!"

Erik flung himself through the doorway and past the first few children. His arms were outstretched and reaching for his son, desperately trying to grab him and remove him from the mayhem inside the room. "Owen, please stop. Stop and come with me. You're safe now."

His heart pounded in his chest, hammered away inside him with the rush of adrenaline and the panic of confusion. The only thought that seemed to make any sense to him was that this dead body in the middle of the floor was one of Le'Sinestre's people and that the children must have risen up against her and attacked.

Owen still took no notice of him. His jaws were busy moving back and forth in a slow, grinding fashion, and Erik suddenly understood the depth of what was happening around him. *Le'Sinestre must have drugged them all with the same shit he used on me. They all think they're zombies.*

Erik closed the distance between himself and his son. When his hands clamped down on Owen's shoulders, he shook the boy with all his might.

"C'mon, son, you have to wake up now. We have to get out of here."

Owen's eyes looked dull, murky, and seemed to jiggle inside his eye sockets until Erik stopped shaking him. When his eyes settled again, Owen Marsh's lips pulled back into a terrible smile. His irises rolled upward into the back of his skull, and then the boy lunged forward. He opened his mouth wide, exposing bloodied incisors and bicuspids, and then he was clamping down into the soft patch of flesh around his father's Adam's Apple. Erik Marsh toppled backward onto the barn floor as his son ripped his throat apart. There was no time to scream and no way to make any sounds with his vocal cords exposed and flapping in the hot air of the barn.

Moments later, the other children turned and joined the boy in feasting.

Erik felt the hungry mouths digging into him, all over his body. They ripped and slashed and gnawed him apart, digging past his flesh and into the fibrous tissues of his organs.

The last thing he saw was the blanket of blinding light stretching open in the corner of the barn. He took one last look at his son before letting his consciousness float off into the light and allowing it to consume him.

The pain evaporated immediately as the light closed up behind him. There was only the growing tones and octaves of harmony, notes that carried Erik Marsh into his new home in this new plane of existence.

Warren Pembroke pushed into the room moments later, handgun clutched tightly in his good hand, and viewed the atrocity. There were now *two* dead bodies on the floor, with his tiny prisoners still feeding on both corpses. They noticed his presence immediately, stopped their feasting, and looked up at him. Their eyes looked glazed and lifeless, their little mouths covered with blood and humanly detritus. It nearly made him gag.

"Goats! You're all goats now. I want you all to crawl back into your pens. Do as I command!"

The tiny zombies stopped feasting immediately. There was a dreadful silence in the middle of the blood and carnage. Then the children toppled onto their hands and knees and began bleating and *baa*ing in dreadful cadence. Chunks of still-warm tissue spilled from their mouths and plopped onto the floor in messy crimson blobs. Slowly, each one crawled back into their pet kennels, found their way inside, and looked back up at their master in blind obedience.

Warren tiptoed his way around the growing, congealing puddle of blood on the floor and locked each cage. When the last of the children was penned and secure, Warren crept over to this new figure on the floor and turned him over.

It was the guy from the newspaper. Erik Marsh. The man who had continuously refused to print anything about Le'Sinestre, even after Warren had sent the personal invitation to him. Marsh's body was mauled nearly beyond recognition, with bite marks covering his face and his neck and his arms and chest. They had met once already in Charlene's basement, and Warren had left him there to die. How Marsh had escaped was a complete mystery, and yet Warren didn't feel surprised at all. When he'd left Marsh, the journalist was in a zombie state just like the children in the animal pens. Now, strands of flesh and ripped muscle tissue hung off his corpse like ribbons, still tacky with blood and catching the dust motes that floated through the barn. Flies with green bodies and red, bulging eyes swarmed around the carnage of Marsh's and Caroline's corpses, zipping in to feast and then moving on quickly.

"What did you do with my explosives?" Warren shouted at the corpse. "Where are they, motherfucker?"

Warren slipped the gun between the back of his jeans and the small of his back, bent down, and turned over Erik's body. The late reporter's corpse began to kick and spasm in a momentary release of neuron impulses, then fell still again. Warren patted down his torso and jeans but felt no indication that the explosive putty was hidden in his clothing.

Outside the barn window, the farmhouse was now entirely engulfed in flames. Pretty soon emergency response vehicles were going to come rolling up the dirt driveway to put out the fire and investigate what had happened. Warren Pembroke decided he needed to move quickly. If he could get the children loaded onto the bus and double back into town, he could pilot the vehicle down Route 125 South rather than jumping onto the highway, where the damaged school bus would be easily noticed. He was certain by now the missing bus would have been reported, but at least with the chaos of the burning house, there was the window of opportunity of slipping by unnoticed.

It wasn't too late to carry out his Goat Parade.

Warren hurried over to the row of backpacks and school bags and rushed them over to the workbench at the far end of the barn. His packages of explosives were neatly assembled and waiting to go. He merely had to stuff a bundle of explosives into each backpack and zip them up. He worked quickly, forcing his deformed hand to cooperate with his good hand to get the job done. In a manner of minutes, every backpack was loaded with an explosives unit. Warren merely had to open the animal pens and instruct his prisoners to find their backpacks, slip them on, and go downstairs to board the bus.

He never noticed when the stranger entered the room and locked the door behind him.

Joe Walton noticed the handgun tucked in the cracker's jeans almost immediately. He also noticed that Erik Marsh was lying stone dead in the middle of the barn's floor, along with some redheaded girl with tattoos sketched up and down her bare arms. Joe couldn't have cared less about the woman, but seeing his companion's body lifeless and ripped apart on the floor made him cringe. The corpse reminded him of Leon and Rufus Hickey and what he had done to them in his Daddy's barn all those years ago. Seeing the corpses felt a bit too much like history repeating itself, and Joe had to remind himself that Erik's boy was one of the children locked up in the pet kennels on either side of the barn. Owen Marsh had to be one of the kids with blood smeared across his face like a child that had buried his mouth into a heaping piece of strawberry pie. At the moment, most of the children in the cages were on their hands and knees, bleating like agitated farm animals.

What the fuck did this guy do to them?

Warren stuffed the last bundle of explosives into a blue nylon backpack and set it delicately onto the floor where the other school bags were already placed and waiting. He then turned to the row of cages on his right and hurried over to unlock the first one.

"When I open these cages, *all of you* are going to stand up, find your school bag, and go down the stairs and wait for me to let you board the school bus. You will all obey my command."

Warren Pembroke turned toward the staircase at the back of the barn and noticed the tall black man watching him.

"Who the fuck are you?" he asked.

Joe Walton took a few steps forward, his eyes never looking away from the man with the deformed right hand.

"It don't matter who I am," Joe replied. "But if y'all need to know, you can just think of me as the Good Shepherd. I've come here to bring my sheep home."

Warren Pembroke felt the wave of panic overcoming him. The Dark Lord had never mentioned any intruders, had never warned him that some mysterious entity was going to try and thwart his plans. As it was, everything was already falling apart all around him. Warren was chastising himself for killing Caroline, who was still vital to carrying out his plans even if she was strung out on drugs and had become unreliable. Had he not turned the children on her, she'd have been there beside him to help combat this new enemy, and then she could have helped him herd the children back onto the bus and get them on their way.

Warren made to reach behind his back and grab the handgun, but Joe was quicker. He pulled a wad of C4 explosive clay out of his suit's coat pocket and a cigarette lighter out of the other pocket.

"Stop right there, son," he said. "Or I'll blow us both to Kingdom Come."

"No, you won't," Warren smiled. "Not with all these kids around. You aren't going to harm the children if you really believe you're their shepherd."

Joe moved the lighter underneath the ball of explosive clay and flicked the spark wheel. A perfect cone of flame appeared, an orange-yellow spiral of burning gas that licked the bottom of the lump of explosive clay in his other hand.

"I'm already damned, boy. I sold my soul to Ol' Scratch long before you were born. If the kids die with me, they'll all go up to Heaven with God and Sonny Jesus. You won't. You'll burn in Hell right along with me."

Warren Pembroke could feel the panic flowing through him. This was *NOT* how his plans were supposed to go. With every second this interloper held him at bay, the plans for his Goat Parade fell apart before his very eyes. Everything that he'd worked for would fizzle and fray into a smoldering heap of failure. If he didn't act fast, he'd be just as dead as Caroline and the crime beat reporter who now lay rotting on the floor between him and the bastard who stole his explosives.

I have to get my gun. I have to distract him long enough to grab my gun and shoot him.

"Who sent you?" Warren asked.

"From the way my cards played out, the Devil, Himself sent me here. Only, I was supposed to kill that white-boy motherfucker that's laying on the floor between us. Satan wanted me to stop him so that you could carry out your little plans, but I suppose I didn't cooperate too well. I still got *free will*, and I choose to fuck up your plans and stop whatever it is you intend on doing."

Warren Pembroke felt absolute rage welling up inside him. He was losing control by the second, and if he didn't act quickly, all would be lost. He kept thinking, *Where is Father Satan? Why has He forgotten me?* All of this had been plotted and schemed by Lucifer, the Dark Lord, so why wasn't He appearing now to thwart the enemy before him so that he could finish what he'd started? All his visions of the Goat Parade depended on Satan's blessings and protections. Right now, Warren Pembroke had never felt more alone in his life. All those visions were coming undone, and it filled him with blind rage. It was the same rage he'd known all his life—at his parents, at those who picked on him, at the world for keeping him beaten down.

"You can't stop me," Warren sneered at his opponent. "You have no idea of the sacrifices I've made to get here. You have no idea of the lives I've had to claim to get this far. I don't believe you'll turn these children into victims. You won't sacrifice their lives just to stop me."

The children in the cages on both sides of the barn began bleating louder, their goat noises filling the top floor of the barn until the sound level was almost deafening. To Joe, they actually sounded like real goats, as if some component in their vocal cords suddenly turned animalistic. When he turned to look at them, the sight of them made him gasp in terror. Every child in every kennel had sprouted goat horns from their skulls. The horns on the girls raised in small, pointed nubs. The horns on the boys curled into long, ram-like spirals from the sides of their heads just above their ears. What terrified him the most was understanding completely that their little minds were no longer their own. Those places inside their brains that gave them identity and personality were, at that moment, totally gone. There were no thoughts about the last day of school or the families waiting for them back at home or all their hopes and dreams and plans for the summer that lay ahead. There was now only animal mentality. If Joe were to die, Le'Sinestre would prod them forward, and they would act out his deranged fantasies before their short lives came to a terrible, fiery end.

Joe Walton moved forward, the lump of explosives in his right hand and the cigarette lighter in his left. "I'm already damned," he repeated. "Nothing I can do is going to get me into the gates of Heaven. But I can stop *you*."

In the distance, both men heard the blare of sirens from the approaching fire trucks. Someone had reported the burning farmhouse to the proper authorities, although neither of them was aware that Erik Marsh had dialed 9-1-1 before entering the barn. Help was coming. Le'Sinestre was quickly running out of time and options.

"All right," Warren Pembroke sighed. "You win. There's no reason for us to die over this. Tell me what you want me to do."

Joe felt the relief flow through him. All of this was over. There was no more cause for bloodshed, no need to put the children in any more harm. The only thing left was for the white boy to remove the gun, set it on the floor, and then wait for the police to come take him away.

"I want you to walk over to me and turn around. I'll take your gun from you, and then I want you to lay down on the floor and wait for the police to cuff you. After that, all of this is done."

Warren Lee Pembroke smiled as he crossed the barn floor. He walked through the blood of the two dead bodies on the ground, making sure to tread hard on the dead fingers of Erik Marsh. He even chuckled when he heard the bones snapping beneath his feet.

In the distance, sirens were quickly approaching the Mueller farm from Route 196. There was now no possible way for Warren to load the children on the bus and carry out his plans.

Warren started to turn his back to Joe and then stopped. "You're gonna have to kill us all, motherfucker!" Warren's hand shot around his torso to his backside. He was reaching for his gun, meaning to shoot Joe Walton in cold blood.

Joe was faster. He dropped his cigarette lighter onto the floor and plunged his hand into his coat pocket. The stone was waiting for him, with all its magic and mysterious powers. He pulled the stone free of its concealment and swung it with all his might into Warren Pembroke's face. The stone connected with the area between Warren's nose and forehead, fracturing through bone and crushing the human symmetry right out of his cranium. Cartilage smashed into jagged, bloody fragments in an explosion that sent the villain to the floor, writhing in anguish that filled his eyes with tears and rendered him defenseless. Warren drew his hands to his face and rolled on the floor in agony, coating himself with the blood of the two bodies that lay lifeless in the heat of the early afternoon sun.

Joe Walton smiled as Le'Sinestre, broken and defeated, rolled around on the floor. He'd forfeited his chance at redemption by allowing Erik Marsh to live, but even that seemed minuscule in comparison to thwarting the plans of Ol' Scratch. The true author of evil had failed. Whatever plans Le'Sinestre had devised would now fall dead with the defeat of this cowardly sonofabitch on the floor before him. This whole journey he'd taken, leading him thousands of miles from his home, suddenly felt justified. Even if the police brought him into custody and dragged his black ass back to Mark H. Luttrell, he was okay with it. He'd go back willingly, and when the time came that old age caused him to succumb, he'd take that fate willingly as well. His soul belonged to Satan, but Ol' Scratch was always going to know that Joe Walton had thwarted his plans on earth. That was enough.

Joe never even noticed when Warren Pembroke pulled the gun out from behind him and pointed the barrel directly between his eyes. He only heard the blast of a gunshot after Le'Sinestre pulled the trigger.

There was only blinding heat passing through his forehead and into the recesses of his brain that gave him identity and purpose. And *free will*.

Joe Walton and Warren Lee Pembroke died seconds apart. The goats in their cages bleated away in fear and confusion as they witnessed the scene unfold. Their beastly cries continued long after the police burst into the room and freed them from captivity.

Chapter 19

Aftermath

Svetlana cried as Truth Carson filled her television set with his condescending, pretentious visage and announced to the nation of cables news followers that Le'Sinestre's body was recovered in Hetfield, Maine after a bloody standoff that left five people dead, including the local socialite who was about to make her big Hollywood debut after premiering the film in Portland. She wept with an open bitterness that left her feeling more drained than she'd ever felt in her life, even more than she felt after leaving her brother and sister behind and coming to America alone and afraid. Carson continued delivering his fodder, but she heard none of it. When the camera cut from Carson's anchor desk to the live footage from somewhere thirty miles north of her tiny living room—she'd been released from the hospital less than two hours ago and had returned home with her fever under control and a fresh gauze bandage taped to her forehead—her eyes became too blurry to discern Erik Marsh's image from the photograph the camera was displaying. Svetlana picked up the remote control, turned off the television, and wailed with all her body and soul.

Serendipity, the Goddess of Fate and Fortune, floated off out the door and through the windows, looking for other unfortunates to bestow her blessing and favors upon in the cold, lonely world. Happy endings, after all, always fall on people other than ourselves.

Others, like Owen Marsh, remembered nothing.

None of the children who'd been taken hostage remembered a thing of their time under Le'Sinestre's control. Their ordeal was nothing more than a long, deep slumber under the effect of the Devil's Breath. They were all hospitalized immediately after their liberation, and all had returned to their normal state of consciousness and normal personalities and routines long before the sun set over the western horizon and the moon floated up over the Atlantic Ocean to greet the night. Each child was questioned thoroughly by Inspector Barrett, but none of them could offer anything more than recalling that they were standing outside waiting for the school bus to pick them up. Everything else was a long, peaceful darkness where they felt neither fear nor pain.

Twelve of the thirteen children were returned to their parents, each family celebrating the miracle of their child's deliverance from the hands of evil. There were tears of joy and relief. There were hugs and kisses that seemed to last all night. There were prayers of sincerest gratitude and adoration offered to a higher power that none could produce any real proof of existence, and yet those words were nonetheless heartfelt, real, and true. No words were prayed to Serendipity, but she wouldn't have cared anyway.

Nearly a week had passed by before Kelly Marsh attempted to tell her son that his father was dead. She'd omitted his cause of death, for obvious reasons, as she still could not bear to comprehend it all, herself. She held her son on her lap as her fiancé washed the evening dishes alone, wrapped her arms around him, and told him as delicately as she could. Owen cried as well, but not as openly or bitterly as she'd expected him to. Owen remained quiet for the rest of the evening, quiet and contemplative as his mind began processing this new information about life in a world without his father in it.

When she put Owen to bed, he slept restlessly and had terrible dreams.

He dreamed that his Daddy was drowning in a roiling, turbulent sea of darkness. Owen was in a tiny rowboat that pitched and bobbed in the middle of the storm. Every now and then his father's head would crest the surface, and his long, bare arms would reach out to the boat, out to his little boy, trying to find purchase and rescue himself. When he did this, Owen dreamed that he leaned forward and sank his teeth into his father's flesh.

Those dreams would haunt him for years, mentally torturing him over and over again. And when he awoke from those dreams, he found himself swearing that he would give anything, *anything*, to make those dreams stop once and for all.

When he did this, Ol' Scratch laughed with glee.

What was left of the bodies of Herbert and Karen Mueller had been found out in the woods behind the barn. Bones that had been picked clean by wild animals were delivered to the State Medical Examiner for processing. There was no need for autopsies but pathological details were still recorded and delivered to the State's Attorney in accordance with Maine state law. Afterward, their bones were unceremoniously cremated and their ashes were returned to their children for proper burial. Abigail Silverstein received far more attention.

The story of the wicked double-life of the billionaire's daughter was sensational. Every news outlet from coast to coast carried the story for weeks, but none of them were able to get the facts completely correct. Everything was speculative, even after the FBI was called in to examine the evidence. They knew she'd been stabbed to death, but what they couldn't figure out was how the corpse of Abby Silverstein had somehow acquired the large gash across her forehead, or what it meant. Since the director of the Rowekamp Funeral Home in Portland was commissioned to cremate Abby's remains—her father had been mortified to learn of her involvement with Le'Sinestre and demanded that her remains be burnt to ashes—the mortician ignored the gash in the girl's forehead completely and followed the billionaire father's instructions.

By the end of the summer, Svetlana decided that she needed to get back to doing her street performances. Between the time she'd spent mourning Erik's death and longing deeply and profoundly for her beloved Aldo and Shimi, she felt that she needed to rediscover and reclaim her identity, and that meant reviving the Carpathian Great and Tiny Circus. So on a warm, sunny Saturday afternoon toward the end of August, she sat in front of her mirror and started braiding her long, lovely locks into rows of spiky fronds that she tied with rainbow-colored ribbons. She applied her makeup with pads and brushes, threw on her favorite blouse and tights, and her long, frilly skirt, and loaded her performance gear onto the pushcart. And then she was off to Monument Square.

With her radio blasting her CD of gypsy music and her old felt top hat set out on the bricks of the concourse, Svetlana slowly but surely slipped right back into her old routine. In her heart and her mind, she was the spry, quirky thirteen-year-old she remembered being once upon a time. People laughed and clapped for her as she juggled and performed her tricks and contorted her body through the hula hoops once again. And when her performance was over, they once again lined up to drop money in her hat and compliment her on her performance.

She could sense Erik's presence somewhere in the crowd and found her eyes darting back to the bench underneath the tree. Of course, Erik Marsh was not there, but she could still feel the gooseflesh rising up her arms and across the back of her neck. Her eyes scanned the remaining audience members, but his face was woefully absent. Svetlana felt her eyes well with wetness as she picked up her hat from the bricks, slipped the money into her purse, and placed the hat on her head.

She reached out with a trembling finger and shut off the music.

Even with the people dispersing back into their normal lives, all she heard was silence.

A few quick years later, Owen Marsh walked across the stage and accepted his high school diploma. His mom and stepdad—Allen offered to adopt him after his biological father was killed, but Owen Marsh had refused, had wanted to keep his Daddy's last name—clapped and whistled to him from the audience, cheering him on with all their hearts. As did a beautiful Eastern European woman who sat anonymously just a few rows behind them. Svetlana thought about approaching the boy after the ceremony but was concerned that doing so might ruin the happy occasion, and that was the last thing on earth that she wanted to do.

Svetlana watched the young man sit back down with his graduating class. The boy fixed the mortarboard on his head, loosened his necktie just beneath the fabric of his gown, and laughed with his friends. While he joked with the other boys around him, it was obvious that his glances were really floating over toward a beautiful young girl at the end of his row. And it was also obvious that she was throwing glances back at him. Owen Marsh was happy. It was enough.

Svetlana stood, folded the pamphlet the young woman at the door handed to her when she came in and stuffed it in her purse. As the school's principal read off the next few names of graduates, she promptly stood up and walked out of the gymnasium and into the hallway that led to the school's cafeteria, where she waited for him. She had a feeling that he would pass through this way before circling back to find his family and move on to the party that was most assuredly waiting for him. Her wait didn't last very long.

The graduating class sauntered through the pair of gymnasium doors, pushing back toward the cafeteria. Svetlana saw Owen with his friends and could not help but smile. Many of them were patting him on the back and wishing him well as the last true shackles of childhood fell off with the reception of his diploma. She was sure he'd had to work extra hard to pull his life back together after Erik died and work through a great deal of pain and sadness. When he was about to pass by her, she called out to him.

"Owen? Owen Marsh?"

The boy's focus dropped from his pals and from the cute girl, who had exited the gym just before he did, and he dropped out of the line to speak to her.

"Yeah, I'm Owen. Who are you?"

"I knew you're father, Erik Marsh. He vas a dear friend of mine. He vould have been very proud of you today. I just vanted to tell you that because he couldn't be here to do it himself. You meant the whole world to him. I just vanted to congratulate you on his behalf."

The boy's grin widened. He held out his hand for her to shake. She reached out politely and let his hand grasp hers.

"That's very kind of you, Svetlana," Owen Marsh said. "It sure means a lot to me that you could be here."

Svetlana Barnyk felt the wave of nausea sweep over her. It had been like being kicked in the stomach unexpectedly and having the air sucked right out of her lungs. "I didn't tell you my name, did I?" she asked, feeling the dread creep into the pit of her stomach.

Owen's grin widened into something dark and sinister. "I guess you must have. How could I have possibly known your name? We just met, after all."

Svetlana pulled her hand away, and in her mind, she could picture the *Omniscient Eye* staring at her from somewhere inside his head, still gathering up all the tidbits of memory and information she'd stored through her twenty-five years of existence. She'd gone through it once before with that dark-haired woman, back when *Zee Doctor* had returned to take the eye away. The feeling of having her identity and her privacy being invaded so easily had been akin to being raped. And now Erik Marsh's son was making her feel that way again.

"I have to go now," she whispered, then turned to leave.

"Thank you for stopping by, Svetlana. It was very nice meeting you."

Owen Marsh turned and raced back into formation with the other graduating students. The smile never left his face.

Epilogue

It wasn't a dream. It wasn't some bizarre fantasy or induced hypnosis. When "Tobacco Joe" Walton opened his eyes, he knew he was in Hell.

He was on the path to the crossroads once again, only the heat of the crimson sky now singed his black skin until it blistered and peeled across his face and his hands. Smoke rose in obscene tendrils from the cloth of his hat and his suit. Burning ash and brimstone filled the air, and when his soul tried to inhale breath in non-existent lungs, it still burned inside him. All around him, he could hear the wails and screams of the damned, and the fear welled up inside him just as understanding dawned that he was about to join their eternal chorus.

On either side of the path, the bent, spindly limbs of the trees whipped and lashed at him. He felt the sting of their fronds all over his body, a punishment worse than any switching his Daddy had ever given him during his childhood. He wondered if perhaps his father was somewhere in Hell, suffering right now and waiting to turn his suffering onto his only begotten son.

This was fear and loathing like he'd never felt before. Every step he tried to take made his feet feel like unfathomably heavy burdens. He moved slower and slower until he was almost at a crawl by the time he noticed the junction of the crossroads ahead of him.

Ol' Scratch was waiting at its center where the roads crossed each other.

"I thought you'd never get here," the Evil One announced, the smile spread across His terrible face. "You may think you've beaten me, but you haven't. It was never a test, nor a chance for you to redeem yourself. And though you may have acted admirably—and I give you credit, not many people would have had the fortitude to finish your life as you did—things still panned out as I'd wanted them to. And now your soul is mine."

Joe lifted his hat from his head and tried to swab the beads of sweat off his scalp with the sleeve of his coat. When he did, the skin on his forehead melted off onto his arm, exposing blood and muscle and white patches of skull. The pain was monumental, and he had to bite his lip to keep from screaming.

"Of course, I have to say that you would be a very valuable asset to me. I have the power to send you back to earth, Joe Walton. I could send you back, but you'd be a servant to my every whim and desire. I could save you the tortures of Hell for at least one more lifetime, but the price would be that you would lose that concept of *free will* that you so desperately love. What do you think? Could you live under those terms?"

Somewhere in the distance, Joe heard a bloodcurdling scream, as if being delivered on cue. In it, he heard his mother's voice, his Mom as a young woman, being forced to watch her husband being gunned down and then having two young men force themselves upon her and rape her. He also heard the sounds of Rufus and Leon Hickey laughing and calling to him.

"We've been waiting for you, Nigger!"

"We're gonna get you next!"

"We're going to spend eternity raping you and beating you and punishing you for what you did to us!"

The Devil smiled, and in it, Joe could see the wisdom of ages turned to unholy delight. Joe hung his head and wept. He was not ready to begin his eternity within this web of unending misery.

"Please send me back."

Ol' Scratch nodded as if he'd expected this decision long before it had been made. "Follow the path to the left and do not deviate from it. It will lead you back to the plane of existence you just came from. Only, beware—you'll find yourself fading away the closer you get. Oh, and one more thing. Before you leave, I'll need to mark you as my own, so the world will know that you belong to me."

The pain was immediate, devastating.

Joe held up his right hand and watched his fingers shrivel before him. They twisted and puffed out into loathsome caricatures of his mortal hand.

When the transformation settled, he wept bitter tears as he beheld the goat hoof at the end of his arm.

Joe's feet broke free of their paralysis, and he started sprinting down the path on the left. As he moved, he felt his head growing lighter and lighter. The pain subsided, and the noise of suffering and the burning heat evaporated. Eventually, Joe's eyes grew heavy, and he fell asleep.

Somewhere in the real world, the world of the living as we know it, a newborn baby wept as the doctor delivered him from his mother's womb. The mother was still gasping and panting from the difficult labor, and when she saw her child being swaddled in warm, clean towels, she wept in misery.

Her only son was deformed, and when the mother examined him later as he suckled at her breast, she would discover the numbers 666 tattooed hideously beneath the fingernails of his bulbous, misshapen fingers. To her, the babe's hand resembled the hoof of a goat.

ABOUT THE AUTHOR

Peter N. Dudar was born and raised in Albany, NY. A graduate of Christian Brothers Academy and an alumnus of the University at Albany, he moved to Maine in 1995 and began his writing career shortly after. His first novel, *A Requiem for Dead Flies*, was a finalist for the Bram Stoker Award in 2013. His other books, *The Angel of Death, Dolly and Other Stories, Where Spiders Fear to Spin, and Blood Cult of the Booby Farmers,* continue to draw critical appraise and adoration from genre fans everywhere. His short fiction can be found in numerous horror anthologies and literary websites. Dudar is a proud member of the New England Horror Writers and is a founding member of the writers group, The Tuesday Mayhem Society. He currently lives in Lisbon Falls, Maine with his wife and daughters.

Press
Presents

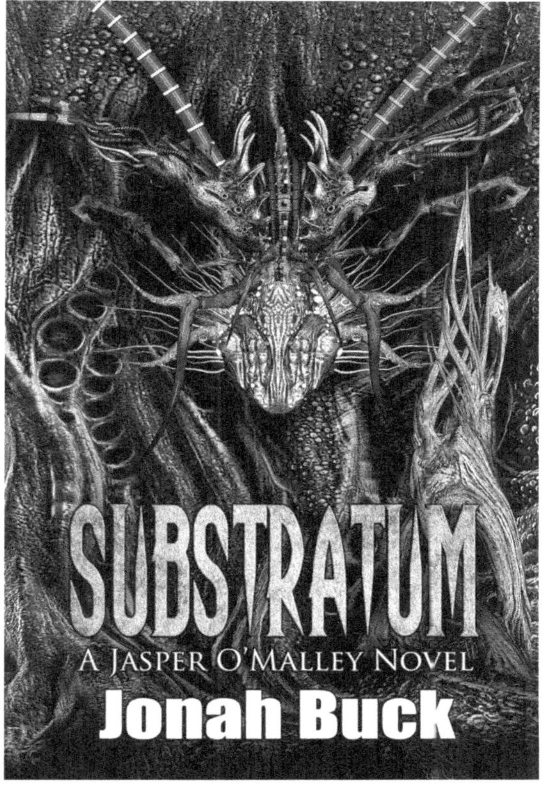

Deep beneath the streets of Detroit, someone—or something—is picking off the miners working the Detroit Salt Combine's salt mine. The company refuses to do anything, so the miners turn to the Attican Detective Agency's Jasper O'Malley to get to the bottom of things. Teamed with Sadie Dupree, a geologist, and Amelia Rio, a get-away driver for the local mob boss, Jasper delves into the secrets of the mine. Will they be able to unearth the truth, or will they suffer the same unfortunate fate of the Detroit Salt Combine's workers?

Something lurks beneath the surface of Cooper Lake. Something hungry. Something intelligent. Something that preys on those who venture too close to its domain. The native Indians had a name for it. ONIARE In 1939, its victim was a young drifter. Dave Longo fought and killed it then, but it won't stay dead. It returned in 1956 to claim the lives of two young men. For Dave, its return was a reunion in Hell. It's now 2014 and the creature has returned again, but Dave Longo is not around to face it a third time. The task becomes the responsibility of Ryan Lowell, a child the oniare had terrorized back in '56, but can he overcome his childhood fears to vanquish the oniare once and for all.

There's something in Troughton's Moss that speaks to the people of Ellsford;
it whispers in their ears, burrows into their minds, like a Brainworm, and tells
them what to do.

THE MADONNA
Twenty years ago it spoke to Paul Cunningham and set the wheels in motion.
He brutally murdered, then raped a young woman.
A short while later, within the narrow confines of her grave, she gave birth to
...

THE CHILD
Grown to young adulthood, it moves undetected among the people of Ellsford
with only one purpose.

THE END TIMES
The time has come. The Moss is beginning to give up its dead,
sacrifices made in its name throughout the ages.

THE CHOSEN ONE
Dobson Heather, a child of the Moss himself, has been marked. But is he
Ellsford's salvation, or their damnation?

The Caribbean Sea, 1708 AD. In Port Royal many have heard the legend of the Black Brig, a ship of the damned bringing a fate worse than death to the isolated colonies of the Caribbean Sea. But few know the true story behind the tavern tales. As the war between the Northern Alliance and the League of the Antilles looms on the horizon, an old captain is ready to embark on a venture to cease the blight of the Black Brig once for all and have his revenge. Set in an alternate historical setting, where a supernatural plague caused the fall of the European powers and where what was left of humanity struggles to survive in the New World, *Dead Men Tell No Tales* narrates the ghastly voyage pirate captain Daniel Drake Davies underwent in 1676, and the events that will force him to confront those same horrors thirty years later. For the dead do not rest peacefully in the Devil's Sea. Pirates, voodoo, and seagoing undead await you in this fantastic journey in a land that never was.